HELL ON WHEELS

BLACK KNIGHTS INC.

JULIE ANN WALKER

sourcebooks casablanca

Cover illustration by Craig White, Motorcycle (Fantasma de Lago) photograph courtesy of Freakshow Choppers

Published by Sourcebooks Casablanca, an imprint of Sourcebooks, Inc.
P.O. Box 4410, Naperville, Illinois 60567-4410
(630) 961-3900
Fax: (630) 961-2168
www.sourcebooks.com

Printed and bound in Canada.
WC 10 9 8 7 6 5 4 3

To my wonderful husband,
who didn't bat a lash when the staid
mathematician he married suddenly took it
into her fool head to drop everything and
write stories. Thank you, sweetheart,
for supporting me as I chased my dreams…

In war, there are no unwounded soldiers.

—Jose Narosky

Prologue

Jacksonville, North Carolina
Outside the Morgan Household

THOSE SCREAMS...

Man, he'd been witness to some bad shit in his life. A great deal of which he'd personally perpetrated but very little of which stuck with him the way those screams were going to stick with him. Those soul-tearing, gut-wrenching bursts of inconsolable grief.

As Nate Weller, known to most in the spec-ops community simply as "Ghost," gingerly lowered himself into the Jeep that General Fuller had arranged for him to pick up upon returning CONUS—continental U.S.—he figured it was somehow appropriate. Each vicious shriek was an exclamation point marking the end of a mission that'd gone from bad to the worst possible scenario imaginable, and a fitting cry of heartbreak to herald the end of his best friend's remarkable life.

Grigg...

Sweet Jesus, had it really been just two weeks since they were drinking raki in Istanbul? Two weeks since they'd crossed the border into Syria to complete a deletion?

And that was another thing. Deletion. *Christ*, what a word. A ridiculously euphemistic way of saying you put a hot ball of lead that exploded with a muzzle velocity of 2,550 feet per second into the brainpan of some unsuspecting SOB who had the appallingly bad luck of finding himself on ol' Uncle Sam's shit list.

Yep, two lines you never want to cross, horizontal and vertical.

"Get me out of here," Alisa Morgan choked as she wrenched open the passenger door and jumped inside the Jeep, bringing the smell of sunshine and honeysuckle with her.

Ridiculously pleasant scents considering Nate's day had begun in the seventh circle of hell and was quickly getting worse. Shouldn't that be the rotten-egg aroma of sulfur burning his nose?

He glanced over at the petite woman sitting beside him, stick straight and trembling with the effort to contain her grief, and his stupid heart sprouted legs and jumped into his throat. It'd been that way since the first time he'd met Ali, Grigg's baby sister.

Baby, *right*.

She hadn't been a baby even then. At seventeen she'd been a budding young woman. And now? Over twelve years later? Man, now she was *all* woman. All sunny blond hair and fiercely alive, amber-colored eyes in a face guaran-damn-teed to totally destroy him. Oh buddy, that face was a real gut check, one of those sweet Disney princess-type deals. Not to mention her body. Jesus.

He wanted her now just like he'd wanted her then. Maybe more. Okay, definitely more. And the inner battle he constantly waged with his unrepentant libido whenever she got within ten feet of him coupled with his newly acquired, mountainous pile of regret, guilt, and anguish to make him so tired. So unbearably tired of…everything.

"What about your folks?" he murmured, afraid to talk too loudly lest he shatter the tenuous hold she seemed to have on herself. "Don't you wanna be with them?"

He glanced past the pristine, green expanse of the manicured, postage-stamp sized lawn to the little, white, clapboard house with its cranberry trim and matching shutters. Geez, the place was homey. So clean, simple, and welcoming. Who would ever guess those inside were slowly bleeding out in the emotional aftershock of the bomb he'd just delivered?

She shook her head, staring straight ahead through the windshield, her nostrils flaring as she tried to keep the ocean of tears pooling in her eyes from falling. "They don't...want or...n-need me right now. I'm a...a reminder that...that..." she trailed off, and Nate had to squash the urge to reach over and pull her into his arms.

Better keep a wrinkle in it, boyo. You touch my baby sister and you die. Grigg had whispered that the day he'd introduced Nate to his family and seen the predatory heat in Nate's eyes when they'd alighted on Ali.

Yeah, well, *keeping a wrinkle in it* was impossible whenever Ali was in the same room with him, but he hadn't touched...and he hadn't died. Grigg was the one who'd done that...

Christ.

"They want you, Ali," he assured her now. "They need you."

"No." She shook her head, still refusing to look at him, as if making eye contact would be the final crushing blow to the crumbling dam behind which she held all her rage and misery. "They've always been a pair, totally attuned to one another, living within their own little two-person sphere. Not that they don't love me and Grigg," she hastened to add as she dashed at her tears with the backs of her hands, still refusing to let them fall. "They're *great* parents; it's just...I don't know what I'm trying to say. But how they are together, always caught up in one another? That's why Grigg and I are so close..." Her left eyelid twitched ever so slightly. "*Were* so close...*God!*" Her voice broke and sympathetic grief pricked behind Nate's eyes and burned up the back of his throat until every breath felt as if it was scoured through a cheese grater.

It was too much. He couldn't stand to watch her fight any longer. The weight of her struggle compounded with the already crushing burden of his own rage and sorrow until all he could do was screw his peepers closed and press his clammy forehead to the backs of his tense hands. He gripped the steering wheel with fingers that were as numb and cold as the block of ice encasing his heart. The one that'd formed nearly a week before when he'd been forced to do the unthinkable.

A barrage of bloody images flashed behind his lids before he could push them away. He couldn't think of that now. He wouldn't think of that now...

"Nate?" He jumped like he'd been shot when the coolness of her fingers on his arm pulled him from his brutal thoughts. "Get me out of here, okay? Dad...he shooed me away. I don't think he wanted me witnessing Mother's breakdown and I think I can still hear her..." She choked.

Uh-huh. And Nate knew right then and there those awful sounds torn from Carla Morgan's throat weren't going to stick with just him. Anyone who'd been within earshot would be haunted forever after.

And, god*damn*it, he liked Paul Morgan, considered him a good and honest man, but *screw* the bastard for not seeing that his only daughter needed comfort, too. Just because Ali put on a brave front, refusing to break down like her mother had, didn't mean she wasn't completely ripped apart on the inside. And damn the man for putting Nate in this untenable situation—to be the only one to offer Ali comfort when he was the dead-last person on Earth who should.

He hesitated only a second before turning the key and pulling from the curb. The Jeep grumbled along, eating up the asphalt, sending jarring pain through his injured leg with each little bump in the road. Military transports weren't built to be smooth rides. Hell no. They were built to keep chugging and plugging along no matter what was sliding under the wheels. Unfortunately, what they gained in automotive meanness, they lost in comfort, but that was the least of his current problems. *His* pain he could deal with—brush it aside like an annoying gnat. He was accustomed to that, after all. Had trained for it and lived it over and over again for almost fifteen years.

Ali's pain was something else entirely.

Chancing a glance in her direction, he felt someone had shoved a hot, iron fist straight into his gut.

She was crying.

Finally.

Now that she didn't have to be strong in front of her parents, she let the tears fall. They coursed, unchecked, down her soft cheeks in silvery streams. Her chest shook with the enormity of her grief, but no sound escaped her peach-colored lips save for a few ragged moans that she quickly cut off, as if she could allow herself to show only so much outward emotion. As if she still had to be careful, be tough, be resilient.

She didn't. Not with him. But he couldn't speak past the hot knot in his own throat to tell her.

He wanted to scream at that uncaring bitch, Fate. Rail and cry and rant. But what possible good would that do them? None. So he gulped down the hard tangle of sorrow and rage and asked, "Anywhere in particular y'wanna go?"

She turned toward him, her big, tawny eyes haunted, lost. "Yeah, okay." He nodded. "I know a place."

After twenty minutes of pure hell, forced to watch her struggle to keep herself together, struggle to keep from bursting into a thousand bloody pieces that would surely cut him as deeply as they cut her, he nosed the Jeep along a narrow coast road, through the waving, brown heads of sea oats, until he stopped at a wooden fence. It was gray and brittle from years spent battling the sun and weathering the salt spray.

He figured he and that fence were kindred spirits. They'd both been worn down by the lives they'd led until they were so battered and scarred they no longer resembled anything like what they'd started out being—and yet they were still standing.

Right. He'd give anything to be the one reduced to an urn full of fine, gray ash. Between the two of them, Grigg had been the better man. But on top of being uncaring, Fate was a *stupid* bitch. That's the only explanation he could figure for why he'd made it out of that stinking, sandy hut when Grigg hadn't.

A flash of Grigg's eyes in that last moment nearly

had him doubling over. Those familiar brown eyes... they'd been hurting, begging, resigned...

No. He shook away the savage image and focused his gaze out the windshield.

Beyond the fence's ragged, ghostly length, gentle dunes rolled and eventually merged with the flat stretch of a shell-covered beach. The gray Atlantic's vast expanse flirted in the distance with the clear blue of the sky, and the boisterous wind whipped up whitecaps that giggled and hissed as they skipped toward shore.

It just didn't seem right. A day like that. So sunny, so bright. Didn't the world know it'd lost one of its greatest men? Didn't its molten heart bleed?

He switched off the Jeep and sucked in the familiar scents of sea air and sun-baked sand. He couldn't find his usual comfort in the smells. Not today. And, maybe, never again. Hesitantly he searched for the right words.

Yeah, right. Like there *were* any right words in this God-awful situation.

"I won't offer y'platitudes, Ali," he finally managed to spit out. "He was the best man I've ever known. I loved 'im like a brother."

Talk about understatement of the century. Losing Grigg was akin to losing an arm. Nate felt all off-balance. Disoriented. More than once during the past week, he'd turned to tell Grigg something only to remember too late his best friend wasn't there.

He figured he wasn't suffering from phantom-limb syndrome, but phantom-*friend* syndrome.

"Then as a brother, tell me what happened...what *really* happened," she implored.

She'd always been too damned smart for her own good.

"He died in an accident. He was cleanin' an old gas tank on one of the bikes; there was a spark; some fuel on his rag ignited; he fell into a tray of oil and burned to death before anyone could get to him." The lie came out succinctly because he'd practiced it so friggin' often, but the last word still stuck in his throat like a burr.

Unfortunately, it was the only explanation he could give her about the last minutes of her brother's life. Because the truth fell directly under the heading *National Security Secret*. He thought it very likely Ali suspected Grigg hadn't spent the last three-plus years partnering with a few ex-military, spec-ops guys, living and working in Chicago as a custom motorcycle builder, but it wasn't *his* place to give her the truth. The truth that Grigg Morgan had still been working for Uncle.

When he and Grigg bid their final farewells to the Marine Corps, it was only in order to join a highly secretive "consulting" group. The kind of group that took on only the most clandestine of operations. The kind of group whose missions never made the news or crossed the desk of some pencil-pushing aide at the DOD in a tidy little dossier. They put the *black* in black ops, their true identities known only to a select few, and those select few were *very* high up in government. *High*. Like, all the way at the friggin' top.

So no. He couldn't tell her what *really* happened to Grigg. And he hoped to God she never found out.

She searched his determinedly blank expression, and he watched helplessly as the impotent rage rose inside her—an emotional volcano threatening to explode. Before he could stop her, she slammed out of the vehicle, hurdled the fence, and raced toward the dunes, long hair flying behind her, slim bare legs churning up great puffs of sand that caught in the briny wind and swirled away.

Shit.

He wrenched open his door and bounded after her, his left leg screaming in agony, not to mention the goddamned broken ribs that threatened to punch a hole right through his lung. *Blam!* Wheeze. That quick and he'd be spending another day or two in the hospital. Fan-friggin'-tastic. Just what he didn't need right now.

"Ali!" he bellowed, grinding his teeth against the pain, running with an uneven, awkward limp made even more so by the shifting sand beneath his boots.

She turned on him then in grief and frustration, slamming a tiny balled-up fist into the center of his chest. *Sweet Christ…*

Agony exploded like a frag grenade. He took a knee. It was either that or just keel over dead.

"Nate?" Her anger turned to shock as she knelt beside him in the sand. "What—" Before he knew what she was about, she lifted the hem of his T-shirt, gaping at the ragged appearance of his torso. His ribs were taped, but the rest of him looked like it'd gone ten rounds with a meat grinder and lost.

"Holy shit, Nate!" He almost smiled despite the blistering pain that held him in its teeth, savage and unyielding as a junkyard dog. Ali never cursed. Either it was written somewhere in her DNA or in that contract she'd signed after becoming a kindergarten teacher. "What happened to you?"

He shook his head because, honestly, it was all he

could manage. If he so much as opened his mouth, he was afraid he'd scream like a girl.

"Nate!" She threw her arms around his neck. God, that felt right…and so, so wrong. "Tell me! Tell me what happened to you. Tell me what really happened to Grigg." The last was breathed in his ear. A request. A heartrending plea.

"Y'know I can't, Ali." He could feel the salty hotness of her tears where she'd tucked her face into his neck. Smell, in the sweet humidity of her breath, the lemon tea she'd been drinking before he knocked on her parents' door and told her the news that instantly blew her safe, sheltered world apart.

This was his greatest fantasy and worst nightmare all rolled into one. Ali, sweet, lovely Ali. She was here. Now. Pressed against his heart.

He reluctantly raised arms gone heavy with fatigue and sorrow. If Grigg could see him now, he'd take his favorite 1911-A1 and drill a .45 straight in his sorry ass. But the whole point of this Charlie Foxtrot was that Grigg wasn't here. No one was here to offer Ali comfort but him. So he gathered her close—geez, her hair smelled good—and soothed her when the grief shuddered through her in violent, endless waves like the tide crashing to shore behind them.

And then she kissed him…

Chapter One

Three months later…

SHE HAD THAT FEELING AGAIN.

That creepy, crawly sensation prickling along the back of her neck. The one that made her shoulder blades instinctively hitch together in defense.

She was being watched.

Ali Morgan hastened her steps. Her black, patent leather, ballet flats slapped against the hot pavement as she darted a quick glance across the street.

Nothing.

Not that that was unusual. She rarely saw him, the man she'd begun to think of as her elusive shadow. But somehow she sensed he was there…somewhere…

Snapping a fast look over her shoulder, she rapidly scanned the faces of the pedestrians behind her. Nope. He wasn't back there, either. Not that she'd ever seen him full-on, but she'd caught enough glimpses of him to know her elusive shadow wasn't the middle-aged man caring the brown-bagged loaf of French bread, nor was he the black-and-yellow-rugby-jersey-wearing guy who—

Yikes, who let him out of the house this morning? He looked like a giant bumblebee, and the fact that he was gazing through the front window of the flower shop momentarily overcame her mounting fear. She snorted a giggle. Then the baby-fine hairs on the back of her neck twanged a loud warning, freezing the laughter in her throat like it'd been hit with a harsh blast of dry ice.

Crapola. Maybe she really was going crazy.

She'd had that thought more than a time or two in the past three months, because it wasn't like Jacksonville was a huge place. It wasn't necessarily abnormal to see the same faces over and over again.

"But that's the whole problem now, isn't it?" she muttered to herself.

She'd never actually *seen* her elusive shadow's face. Maybe if she had, maybe if she'd gotten the chance to look into the guy's eyes, she wouldn't be feeling this alarming sense of…pursuit.

A sudden chill snaked down her rigid spine as her palms began to sweat. Her tight grip on the handles of the plastic grocery bags started slipping, and she adjusted her hold, hoisting her purse higher on her shoulder in process.

Two more blocks…

"Just two more blocks and then I'm home free," she murmured, realizing by the quizzical look of the couple passing on her right that she was talking to herself again. That was another little eccentricity she'd picked up since Grigg's death. The whole going-crazy thing was starting to look more and more likely.

She trained her eyes on the bright pink flowers of the potted begonia bushes positioned in front of her condo building—the ones the amiable Mrs. Alexander from 3C had planted just last week.

Just one more block. Just one more block and then she could throw on her front door's chain lock, twist the dead bolt and finally take a normal breath.

She was so focused on those potted plants and the sanctuary they promised, she didn't see the hulking shadow lunge out at her from the deep, murky alley.

It wasn't until the first brutal, bruising jerk of her purse strap against her shoulder that she realized she might be in serious trouble. The second hard yank had her spinning around like a top, sending her shopping bags flying out of her hands, their contents scattering in the busy street like edible confetti.

A maroon sedan mowed over her sack of pecans, the shells exploding in a series of loud *rat-a-tat-tats* frighteningly similar to the sound of automatic gunfire.

"Hey!" someone yelled. "He's trying to mug her!"

That was enough to snap her out of her momentary shock, and she grabbed hold of her purse's inch-wide leather strap, pulling with everything she had. According to every self-defense guru on the planet, she should just let go. A purse wasn't worth her life. But this particular Coach satchel had been a gift from Grigg…

The guy clutching her purse in his meaty fist was built like a German Panzer, all brutal, bulging muscles and non-existent neck supporting a ski mask-covered face. He easily could've ripped her little Coach from her desperate grasp if he hadn't been simultaneously trying to fend off the strangely heroic man beating him about the head and shoulders with a hard loaf of French bread.

"Call the police!" Mr. French Bread bellowed, landing blow after blow until the loaf began to disintegrate and the smell of fresh-baked bread filled the humid air.

That was just the impetus needed to yank the frozen, slack-jawed onlookers into action. As Ali and Mr. French Bread wrestled with her mugger, people started pulling cell phones from various pockets and running in their direction.

The guy in the rugby jersey was the first on the scene, and he jumped on her assailant's broad back, wrapping an arm around the guy's meaty throat and squeezing until the mugger's eyes—the only things visible inside that frightening mask—bugged out like a Saturday morning cartoon. Ali was suddenly sorry she ever compared Rugby Jersey guy to a giant bumblebee.

"Get his legs!" Rugby Jersey yelled, and Mr. French Bread dove at the mugger's knees, tackling him and sending the three of them sprawling onto the sidewalk in a tangle of thrashing arms and legs.

Somehow her assailant managed to disentangle himself from the pile. He pushed his substantial bulk up off the concrete only to dart across the street, dodging traffic and nearly getting hit by a speeding UPS truck in the process. For such a *large* man, he was surprisingly agile. The UPS driver slammed on his brakes with a squeal of melting rubber and leaned from his doorless truck in order to shake a fist at the fleeing man's back.

Ali dragged in a ragged breath and tried to keep sight of her assailant as he zigzagged around people and parked cars. Then she stopped breathing entirely, more stunned than if she'd been hit by lightning, when her elusive shadow suddenly emerged from Swanson's Deli across the street.

At least she *thought* it was him. She could never tell for sure because he always wore a baseball cap that effectively shielded his face. Still…this man had the same solid build, the same square jaw…

Okay, it was getting too weird.

"Hey!" she yelled at the guy as both Mr. French Bread and Rugby Jersey picked themselves up off the pavement.

The man in the baseball cap gave no indication he heard her.

"Hey, you!" she called again, stepping off the curb. She was gosh-darned sick and tired of every day feeling this sense of...*paranoia*. If she could just get a look at him, she might—

The mysterious man took off like a shot.

What? Was he really running away from her?

When he hopped into a big, tough-looking SUV, quickly gunning the engine, she had her answer.

He *was* running away from her.

What the h-e-double-hockey-sticks?

Just when she would've taken off after him, she was jerked back onto the sidewalk by Mr. French Bread. "Whoa, there," the guy said, still trying to catch his breath. "The dude's long gone. Don't go getting yourself run over trying to catch him."

Mr. French Bread gave up attempting to appear collected and bent at the waist to put his hands on his knees and drop his head between his shoulders, panting like a dog in the summer heat.

He thought she was going after her attacker, of course, which yeah, probably made a lot more sense than running after some elusive man whom she was sure had been shadowing her every move for the past three months.

Laying a comforting hand on her savior's sweaty shoulder, she reached into her purse—the mugger had *not* succeeded; score one for Alisa Morgan and her two unlikely heroes—and pulled out her BlackBerry.

Zooming in, she snapped a quick photo of the SUV's license plate right before it careened around the corner. Then she bent to peek into Mr. French Bread's red, perspiring face.

"I don't know how to thank you," she said, glancing up to include Rugby Jersey. The guy was also blowing like a winded racehorse, leaning limply against the front window of the hardware store. Obviously neither of them was accustomed to much physical activity, which only made their actions all the more heroic. "You both risked an awful lot—"

Rugby waved a hand, cutting her off. "Damsel in distress and all that," he chuckled, wincing and grabbing his side.

Great. Just what she'd always dreamed of being. Not.

"Are you hurt?" she asked, dismayed by the thought of him getting injured while trying to save something as insignificant as a purse.

"Nah. I think I just bruised a rib."

She opened her mouth to thank him again when the piercing cry of a siren interrupted her.

"Looks like the cavalry's almost here," Mr. French Bread observed.

Black Knights Inc. Headquarters on Goose Island
Chicago, Illinois
The next day…

"Yeah, right. This is a chopper shop. Just a little ol' custom motorcycle business…and I'm the queen of England," Ali muttered beneath her breath, as she glanced through her front windshield at the expanse of the...*compound* was the only word to describe it.

No wonder Grigg had always insisted she stay at a hotel whenever she managed to make it to Chicago to visit him. He'd claimed the loft he lived in atop the "shop"—which would heretofore be referred to as Fort frickin' Knox—was too small to sleep a guest comfortably, but she'd suspected he was feeding her a line of bull even then. And now?

Now, she *knew* it was bull.

Most folks would look through the huge iron gates at the multitude of small brick structures tucked around an immense factory building and dismiss it for simply what it claimed to be on its website, a top-notch custom motorcycle shop. Most folks would disregard the ten-foot-high brick wall topped by huge rolls of razor wire and the 360-degree pivoting cameras as the necessary precautions taken by savvy businessmen who had a small fortune in tools, bikes, and equipment, and who knew this wasn't Chicago's nicest neighborhood.

Yes, that's what *most* folks would do.

She wasn't most folks.

She'd had a Marine for an older brother who'd taught her a thing or two about security, and Black Knights Incorporated had it out the wazoo.

Unwelcome tears suddenly pooled in her eyes, because here was the proof that Grigg hadn't trusted her. He'd died and she'd never really gotten the chance to—

"You'll have to leave your vehicle at the gate, ma'am," instructed the redheaded giant manning the gatehouse. He had a thick Chicago accent, turning the word *the* into the more percussive sounding *da*. "We don't allow unsecured vehicles on the premises," he went on to explain. "Someone will be down to escort you to the main shop momentarily."

"Uh...oh-*kay*," she said as she pulled her lime-green Prius to the side and parked, shaking her head. She glanced in the rearview mirror and dabbed at the tears still clinging to her lashes before pocketing her keys and slinging her beloved purse over her shoulder. Exiting the vehicle, she strolled back toward the gatehouse and the behemoth inside.

"So," she said as she leaned an elbow on the sill of the window and eyed Big Red, "have you worked for the Black Knights long?"

"Long enough," he grunted, never taking his gaze from the series of TV screens showing different angles of the grounds around the compound.

Ah, a talkative one. Wouldn't it figure?

God, what was she doing here?

Nate Weller certainly wouldn't welcome her. For Pete's sake, he didn't even *like* her. Always eyeing her with such cold calculation. Those fathomless black eyes of his following her like she was some strange bug, and he was the dispassionate scientist charting her activities.

Sheesh.

Okay, so maybe she had the tendency to talk too much. But that was partly his fault because he *never* talked, instead remaining constantly and aggravatingly aloof, which was a state so totally foreign to her that she, in turn, started jabbering like her mouth was attached to a motor.

Which was lovely, just lovely.

So fine. He didn't like her. As far as she was

concerned, he could just take his opinion of her and stuff it where the sun never shined. He didn't have to like her in order to help her.

And why she was even mentally chewing over the state of his rather glaring lack of regard was beyond her. Because to tell the truth, she didn't particularly like *him* either.

He was too solemn, too remote, too...*something*.

She could never determine just exactly what that something was—which was extremely irksome. But she'd have to deal with it, or ignore it, because she'd made her decision. She was here.

And speaking of here, where the heck was her escort? She tapped her fingers and glanced around impatiently. "Do you own one of their custom bikes?" she asked, just to have something to talk about because, yeah, waiting to see Nate was driving her crazy.

Big Red made a noise vaguely reminiscent of the bellow a mildly annoyed grizzly bear might make, and she didn't know whether to take that as a *yes* or a *no*.

Great. Just great. This is turning out even worse than I imagined.

"So we got our very own helo. Guess now we need our very own helo pilot." Frank "Boss" Knight, boss of Black Knights Inc., said as he glanced across the scarred expanse of his desk at Nate "Ghost" Weller.

He couldn't help but search the guy's impassive face for any signs of PTSD. Frank had been doing that a lot in the past three months, but no matter how hard he looked...

Nada.

No fidgeting hands or darting eyes or tapping toes.

But he knew, just because the guy didn't show any of the more obvious outward signs of the disorder didn't necessarily mean he didn't have it. Nate had been tagged Ghost because he was so damned stealthy in the field. But ever since Grigg Morgan, Nate's all-time best friend and ace spotter, died—especially considering the *way* Grigg died—and wasn't *that* just one more happy thought Frank would rather not have today? Nate'd given new meaning to the nickname. Now he was Ghost because he was a walking dead man. No emotion. It wasn't like the guy had been a big bowl of jolly to begin with, but now? *Damn…*

"What about Colby Ventura?" Ghost said. "He's not with the Army anymore."

"Really?" Frank lifted a brow, jotting down a quick note on his legal pad, excited by the prospect. "Yeah, man, Ace would be a *great* replacement."

And as soon as he said the words, he winced and glanced at Ghost. Gone was the detachment. Now the man's eyes were bright and his jaw so hard Frank wondered if, when he finally opened his mouth, there would be anything left but nubs and stumps where his teeth had been.

Grigg had been licensed to fly helos, and this was just one more tough reminder that Grigg was gone. He wished like hell they hadn't lost him, but they had. Because despite all the precautions they took against it, the possibility of violent death came part and parcel of the job.

Still, that knowledge didn't make the loss any easier. Not for any of them. But especially not for Ghost. Those two had been connected at the hip since graduating together from Marine Scout Sniper School in Quantico. The dynamic duo or, in certain circles, the *deadly* duo.

Ghost had barely given himself time to heal from the wounds he'd sustained during his torture by those Lebanese militants before he'd gone back and tried to hunt down every last man who'd dared to lay a hand on him and Grigg—and hadn't that been a pretty mess for Frank to clean up?

He shuddered, remembering all the fast talking he'd had to do.

Kissing ass certainly wasn't his forte and it always left a decidedly foul taste in his mouth, but he'd done it for Ghost—the best damned sniper on the planet.

Fortunately, Ghost's search was for naught, because someone had beaten him to the punch. Those Hezbollah boys had been dead to a man—not surprising, really, considering the Syrians didn't take too kindly to Lebanese militants operating on their soil. And the fact that the fuckers met messy ends didn't break Frank's hardened heart one little bit, and not just because they'd deserved it for what they'd done to Grigg and Ghost, but because it'd saved Ghost from perhaps making one of the greatest mistakes of his life.

The Knights broke, bent, and flagrantly ignored most rules, with the exception of one. Pure and simple, revenge had no place in their operating procedures. Should they ever kill outside a sanctioned mission, they'd be no better than the men they hunted. "We should also probably start the search for a communications specialist," he added quickly, hoping to wipe that killing look off Ghost's face. As frightening as his stony detachment could be, this was even worse. "That last job in Brazil would've gone a whole helluva lot smoother had any of us spoken Portuguese."

"What about the ex-Mossad agent?" Ghost managed.

The Mossad agent…Great. One more thing for Frank to worry about today. Usually when General Fuller asked him and his boys to do something, they hopped-to with a salute and a resounding *Hoo-ah*! But hiding this Israeli had required a few negotiations. And, all in all, it wasn't such a bad deal. Because now they found themselves the proud owners of a slightly less-than-new UH-60 Black Hawk.

Okay, perhaps that was putting it a touch mildly.

In truth, the chopper was a mess. It took a sound beating back in '89 when the U.S. invaded Panama and sat in a warehouse collecting dust ever since. But if anyone could get the twenty-something-year-old beast up and running again, it was Rebecca "The Rebel" Reichert—their resident wunderkind mechanic and *his* personal weakness.

Of course, he wouldn't allow himself the perverse pleasure of thinking of her now…

"No-go on the language skills for the new guy," he said as he surreptitiously glanced at his titanium wristwatch, remembering what he really brought Ghost in to talk about. "You seen that psychologist I told you about?"

He leaned forward. The body language equivalent of, *I'm concerned about you, buddy*.

Not that he was necessarily a proponent of the touchy-feely psychoanalysis thing, being of the school of thought that sometimes a man just needed to work through his own shit in his own time, but after what Nate had to do?

Fuck. The guy surely needed to talk to someone.

"We should ask Dan Man and Ozzie who they'd choose for the CS position," Ghost said, and the small hope Frank had that Ghost might've gone to see the good doctor was flushed straight down the crapper.

Ho-kay, talk of psychologists was clearly off the table.

"Well, let's go find them," he capitulated, promising himself he'd come back to the question of Ghost's mental state at a later date.

He pushed up from his desk when Patti, Dan's wife and Black Knights Inc.'s office manager, walked into his office.

"Sorry to interrupt, gentlemen," she said. "But Geralt says we've got a visitor at the gate. Alisa Morgan. She's asking to see Ghost."

And all the black fire that'd been burning in Ghost's eyes after Frank made that asshole statement about Ace being a *great replacement* banked in an instant. The guy's face once more fell into its usual mask of rigid impassivity.

Well, now, isn't that interesting?

"What'r'ya doin' here, Ali?"

Ali jumped as she was cut off from her pointless questioning—if Big Red hadn't told her where to park her car, she might've assumed he was mute—by the sound of Nate's deep voice.

Sheesh! No doubt Nate'd inherited his stealthiness from his Cherokee grandfather along with that blade of a nose, those jet-black eyes, and that raven hair. The man had the most exasperating habit of just suddenly...materializing.

"Nate, I…I'm sorry to b-barge in on you like this." Her heart and mouth simultaneously proceeded to s-s-stutter just as they always did when he caught her off guard. Somehow he managed to change her from a prepossessed, confident woman into a stammering, hesitant moron. *Great way to start, Ali.* "Maybe I should've called…"

But she'd been afraid calling and hearing his voice would change her mind. And she was certain, really certain this time, she needed his help.

His only response was a resonant grunt that sounded like it came up from the soles of his feet. He and Big Red had obviously taken lessons and been star pupils at the School of Non-Answers and Uncommunicativeness.

Typical. Just the reception she expected.

She had to rein in the urge to roll her eyes. Instead, she decided to indulge herself and let them roam over Nate as he stood filling the space between the two halves of the wrought iron gate.

He put on some weight since last she saw him. Not that that was a bad thing. He'd been too thin then. Now all six-plus feet of him was hard, honed muscle and deeply tanned skin. His thick black hair was a bit longer, brushing his collar and curling around his ears invitingly. Well…what some *naïve* woman might consider invitingly. Give that woman ten minutes in his presence and she'd soon realize there was absolutely nothing inviting about Nathan Weller except for his ridiculously handsome face.

And it *was* ridiculously handsome.

Too bad he had all the manners and personality of a skunk.

"Are you going to invite me in?" she asked grudgingly when it became clear he was perfectly happy to simply stand there in the sweltering summer sun and eye her like she was something smelly that'd stuck to the bottom of his shoe.

He cocked his head and crossed his arms over his chest, causing his impressive biceps to bunch into hard balls, straining the sleeves of his gray T-shirt. She shivered despite the heat when she remembered what it was like to be held in those desperately strong arms…

Sheesh, Ali, just forget it.

Trouble was, she'd been unable to forget it for even one night. In the last three months, she'd been plagued by dreams that—

"What'r'ya doin' here?" he asked again. The man had the strangest way of making contractions out of multiple words. As if he couldn't be bothered with those pesky, extra syllables.

"I need to talk to you."

He shrugged. "S'talk."

"Not here," she gave him her patented, *what are you, an eeediot?* look. "Somewhere private. You live here on this property, don't you? Just like Grigg did? Why don't you take me back to your place, maybe offer me a drink?"

He narrowed his eyes and waited.

Lifting her chin, she firmed her shoulders and her resolve. "I thought you might feel that way." Another reason why she hadn't called and alerted him to her imminent arrival. She hadn't wanted to give him time to come up with an excuse not to see her.

She spun on her heel and marched back to her car.

Popping the trunk, she mentally called him every dirty name she could think of and cursed both him and the relentless blast of the sun beating down on her shoulders as she hauled out a suitcase. Setting the wheeled carrier on the ground, she popped up the telescoping handle, hoisted her purse higher on her shoulder and marched back toward him as a trickle of sweat slid between her shoulder blades.

She wasn't sure if it was the sweltering temperatures or the discomfort she always experienced from being around Nate that made her so grouchy. Probably both. Or maybe she was just pissed at having to make this trip in the first place.

Grigg had managed to get her into one too many scrapes when he was alive—granted he'd always been the one to get her out of them, too—but it was beyond tolerable that her big, lovable, idiotic brother was still involving her in his dubious affairs even from the grave.

Problem was, now there was no way he could come to her rescue.

Which was why she was there, melting in the heat waves oozing up off the Chicago pavement, nerves stretched taut in the resounding silence that surrounded her as she waited for Nate to say something...*anything*.

Of course that hope was about as constructive as peeing into the wind since he just continued to stand there, staring at her, not moving so much as a muscle to help her with her luggage—the inimitably rude sonofagun.

"So where do you want me?" she finally asked in order to fill the stifling silence.

Something blazed in his eyes for a second, a quick flash that brightened the ebony of his impassive gaze.

Then whatever it was disappeared so fast she was left wondering if she'd really seen anything at all.

Nah, she decided, surely not, because that would mean she fired some emotion in him, and as far as she knew, the man was a complete cyborg.

"Well?" she demanded impatiently when the big idiot just continued to stand there. Nate had a kind of predatory silence to him that always disconcerted her. And yes, Big Red was able to pull his eyes away from the television screens to watch the little drama playing out in front of him.

Great.

"You're gonna stay here? With me?"

Why did he make it sound like she was taking her life in her own hands?

"Yes, I am. I've just spent nearly twenty hours in the car, and I don't have the patience to spend another twenty on a return trip. Greasy roadside café food has left me bloated. Too much caffeine has my eyes rolling around inside my skull like pinballs. I'm tired. I'm thirsty. I'm definitely not staying in a hotel, for reasons I'll explain once you let me in, and I'd greatly appreciate it if you'd proceed so I can get out of this blistering sun. I thought Chicago was supposed to have temperate summers. It's a gosh-darn oven out here. In fact, I think my deodorant is starting to fail, and that super-sized slushy I bought over the border in Indiana means I'm pretty sure I'm going to need to use the facilities PDQ. So yes, I've a mind to stay here with you."

...And she'd done it again. That telltale tick beat away in his jaw, informing her he thought she blasted him with a big ol' load of verbal diarrhea.

But, she told herself, at least she got past the first hurdle—she stated her intentions—even if the delivery was a little long-winded and laughably heavy on the TMI.

"How long?" he asked grudgingly.

"As long as it takes." She lifted her chin, giving him the facial equivalent of *Come on, I dare you.*

Silence.

So what else was new?

"Look, it's the least you can do for the little sister of your best friend," she added. Yes, she knew that was a low blow, but sheesh, he forced her to pull out the big guns.

"Fine," he capitulated, though his face was wall-papered with I-*so*-don't-want-to-do-this. "But we'll be going to the main shop…for now." He turned and headed back through the gates.

"Fine," she hoisted her purse higher and her gaze snagged on the delicious bulge of his male butt hugged so lovingly in a pair of khaki cargo shorts. Wow. Talk about a gluteus maximus that defied gravity. Even though he was a complete jackass, she couldn't help but drool.

It was a total waste, in her opinion, that the guy was so surly. Or maybe it was an incredible stroke of luck. Because if he'd had even one ounce of charm, she'd have been a goner from day one.

At seventeen she'd been bursting with hormones and curiosity and the need to fall in mad, passionate love with a boy who'd worship the very ground she walked on. At the time she'd been certain this hypothetical boy would be handsome and funny, with the most amazing, heart-melting smile.

Nate had certainly filled her criteria for handsome. *Whew!* The first sight of him had fairly knocked her back on her booty.

She remembered it like it was yesterday…

It was the second-to-last day of high school. She wore her favorite pair of cutoff shorts and the T-shirt she'd gotten at the Bon Jovi concert the weekend before. She was preoccupied with the AP Calculus final she was taking during first period—she hadn't studied as much as she should have—when she skipped into her parents' kitchen and *bam!*

It was love at first sight.

That love lasted all of five minutes.

Because it quickly became clear, PFC Nathan Weller lacked any sort of sense of humor and she soon suspected the man didn't even know *how* to smile. On top of those woeful failings, he got a pained expression on his face every time she tried to engage him in conversation, which pretty much blew the whole worshipping-the ground-she-walked-on thing right out of the water.

So yeah, it was probably a good thing Nate was surly, or else she'd have lost her heart to him years ago.

He turned around and caught her staring. "You comin'?" he asked laconically, as if he couldn't care less if her answer was *no*.

"Of course," she lifted her nose in the air, doggedly following him into Fort frickin' Knox.

When they finally reached the huge steel doors of the factory, he pulled some sort of strange-looking key thing from his pocket and slid it into an even stranger looking hole in the door—one she hadn't noticed because it was concealed behind a rivet. A series of clicks and beeps sounded, followed by a mighty clang.

The huge metal door swung open with a whispered groan.

Yeah, just a chopper shop. *Right*.

Chapter Two

Washington, DC

Sitting in his long black sedan, parked in the grease-stained lot of a 7-Eleven, Senator Alan Aldus watched a young black man in a holey wife-beater flick a cigarette butt over his scrawny shoulder before sauntering toward a silver Mercedes parked by the hose-strewn air machines. The guy's sagging jeans showed a laughable amount of underwear, and his shoes probably cost the dumbass more than he made in a month.

Kicks was the term the kids were using nowadays. Morons.

Aldus watched the window of the Mercedes lower, saw the quick exchange and the gold cufflink on the wrist of the other car's driver. That little bit of jewelry all but screamed wealth and affluence, and Aldus figured he was witnessing one of America's great government officials out buying his daily ration of self-prescribed anesthesia.

It didn't surprise him. Nope, not here in Washing-*sin* DC. There were more secrets and more secret obsessions in the U.S.'s great capital than anywhere else in the world. And it was the possibility of having one of *his* secrets revealed that had him flipping open his ringing cell phone. "What?"

"She's stopped in Chicago."

"Hmm," he ran a hand over his face, then hastily

checked his reflection in the rearview mirror to make sure he hadn't disheveled his hair.

Good. Not a single follicle out of place. The twin gray streaks at his temples were pristine as always. He dyed them, of course. At fifty-five, most men would crow over still having a thick head of sable brown hair, but in his position, the silver added a reassuring touch of maturity. It led people to think he harbored some secret wisdom beyond the norm.

He liked to believe they were right.

He *did* have an uncanny ability to see what needed to be done and then do it, no hesitation, no wavering. He considered himself a man of action, leaving the doubting Thomases of the world to stew and hash out every little thing. Whole countries could rise to power and fall before some of the world's leaders ever finished spell-checking their dossiers.

He'd come to realize nothing would ever change the snail-like pace of the U.S. government, so he'd decided his only course of action was to work around it.

The irony of that stance given his position wasn't lost on him. But they could debate and harangue and review and debate some more. While those sluggish wheels turned, he took it upon himself to implement solutions.

Of course, there were those who wouldn't understand that and many who certainly wouldn't condone it. But who were they to judge him? Complacent fools living safe and sound inside their pretty little homes, cocooned from the rank evil that hung like a slimy, black cloud over so much of the world.

They were all idiots.

But powerful idiots, capable of toppling the pristine

image he'd so carefully and scrupulously built over the years. An image he fancied would eventually have him sitting pretty at 1600 Pennsylvania Avenue.

He shot his cuffs with their ivory-and-platinum links and tapped an impatient finger on the steering wheel.

Alisa Morgan was proving to be problematic. She had the files, whether she knew she had them or not. Grigg Morgan had mailed them to her; *that* much they'd been able to determine soon after Morgan's death. But all the searches of Ms. Morgan's home and work had come up empty—which could mean only one of two things. She was either carrying the files on her person, or she'd squirreled them away somewhere. The solution to either scenario was simple, a quick snatch and grab. Kidnap the woman, shake her down, and obtain the files. Easy as one, two, three.

Or at least it should've been. Unfortunately, his man in the field had a little problem with that scenario.

Aldus could *not* abide a strictly moral man, and ex-CIA agent Dagan Zoelner was turning out to be just that. Unfortunately, Zoelner was also the absolute best at what he did. So Aldus had gone along with Zoelner's plan to simply watch Ms. Morgan until Zoelner could determine a way to obtain the information from her without resorting to strong-arm tactics.

At least he'd gone along with Zoelner's plan for a little while. Then, he'd become impatient…

Now he regretted his eagerness to end this thing once and for all.

The botched mugging had caused her to flee to Chicago, which was a goddamn pain in the ass.

Not that he thought Nathan Weller knew anything.

If he did, Weller certainly would've cracked under the hellish torture of those Hezbollah militants, because nobody knew how to wring the truth out of a man better than the bloody Lebanese.

Of course, he thought with gnawing unease, those Hezbollah boys hadn't been able obtain the whereabouts of the files from Grigg Morgan, and they'd had him in their clutches for three whole days, so perhaps they weren't as proficient at extracting information as they claimed.

That thought was more than a bit disconcerting. The only reason he'd allowed Weller to live after he escaped the hard death Aldus had planned for him, was Aldus's certainty that Weller knew nothing.

Could he have been wrong?

But, no. If Weller had been in on it, he would have already gone to the authorities with his information.

No one knows about the deal, he assured himself and heaved a calming breath. The people who had known were all dead…which brought him back to his current predicament. Namely, getting those pain-in-the-ass files from Alisa Morgan.

"I'm tired of waiting for you to befriend the woman, Z. Now we're going to do this *my* way," he instructed firmly. "Wait until she leaves and then take her. Find those files."

Christ, this was turning into a bigger mess day by day, and he was quickly becoming sick and tired of dealing with it.

It would probably be easier and certainly more expedient to just get rid of her, he thought as he rolled up his window to block out the fumes from the gas pumps.

Instead of hiring Johnny and his boys, those three ham-handed guys out of Las Vegas he liked to employ to take care of his more…violent needs, to mug Ms. Morgan, he could have them contrive a fatal car crash like the one that'd befallen that FBI agent who'd gotten too curious.

It was certainly tempting…

But in situations like this, it never paid to be hasty. And killing American citizens on American soil could be tricky, particularly when he wasn't sure her death would result in the destruction of the files.

So…he'd just keep that contingency in his back pocket.

For now.

"Sir," Zoelner sounded restless, "I've got a question."

"What is it?" he growled, growing more and more impatient with Dagan Zoelner each passing day.

"Did you authorize yesterday's mugging?"

"What?" he sputtered, feigning incredulity. "I can't believe you'd accuse me of such a thing. I never condone violence. You know that."

"Then what do you call your idea to kidnap Ms. Morgan?"

"I call it necessary, Z. Plus, I trust you to handle her with kid gloves."

The silence coming through the receiver was telling. Zoelner wasn't comfortable with the plan, the aggravatingly high-minded bastard.

Well, tough. He was finished waiting for Zoelner to come around to his way of thinking.

"Look, Z" he spat into the phone, blood rushing to his face to make his ears and cheeks tingle with rage. "I pay you quite an exorbitant amount to do this fucking job. I would think that much money would buy me the benefit of having you choke down your misgivings. Am

I wrong? Shall I find someone else who shows a little more gumption, a little more intestinal fortitude?"

"No, sir."

Zoelner's response was immediate, but the tone coming through the receiver didn't sound particularly conciliatory, and that had Aldus's already frayed nerves screaming. He was one of the most powerful men in the whole goddamned country, and no one took that tone with him. He wanted very badly to reach through the phone and strangle the impertinent little prick.

Perhaps when this was all over, when he was president, he could have the fool deleted. The thought was gratifying enough to decrease his blood pressure from a rapid boil to a slow simmer.

"Good," he sniffed and adjusted his silk Brioni necktie. "Keep me informed."

"...But I know the neighborhooooood, and talk is cheap when the story is goooood..."

The place was a madhouse.

There was just no other way to describe the scene playing out around Ali as she stood by the railing on the second story of the warehouse with its cacophony of sights, sounds, and smells.

She'd learned from the handsome man currently going through her luggage with some strange, black wand thing—while singing along to the pounding beats of REO Speedwagon—that the place used to be a Spud Menthol Cigarette Factory. Which accounted for the slightly minty, alcohol aroma still lingering in the air despite the more overpowering smells of oil, grease, and coffee strong enough to burn all the hair from one's nostrils.

She could account for this last observation personally, having been immediately given a cup of said coffee by a cute, slightly matronly shaped woman named Patti.

In his correspondence, Grigg described Patti as Black Knights Inc.'s receptionist/secretary extraordinaire. The woman certainly showed superwoman promptness with the beverage cart, appearing from out of nowhere before Ali even had the opportunity to set down her purse. Unfortunately, what Patti gained in hostessing prowess, she obviously lacked in the culinary arts, because after one sip of the toxic waste that passed as coffee at Black Knights Inc., Ali was forced to set her cup aside in order to concentrate on keeping her eyes from tearing up.

Luckily, before Patti could witness her struggle, someone yelled, "Patti! We're out of alpha whiskey in the head," and Patti disappeared down the hall, presumably to replace the bathroom's alpha whiskey—otherwise known as ass wipe or the much-less-colorful toilet paper in the civilian world.

The things Ali learned having Grigg as an older brother...

"Take it on the run, baby!" The man going through her things—he'd introduced himself as Ethan Sykes, but Grigg had always referred to him as Ozzie—belted out in a surprisingly clear tenor. "If that's the way you want it, baby, then I don't want you around!"

The guy was wearing a T-shirt with a picture of Mr. Spock's favorite hand gesture and the slogan 100% TREKKIE, which was slightly incongruous when compared to the shoulder holster and the mean-looking, matte-black gun secured to his side. He looked like some strange combination of geek and warrior. The man you'd call if you needed to invade a small country or translate a message written in Klingon.

Unaware of her observation, he continued to methodically go through her clothes, stopping only occasionally to play some air guitar or air drums.

The whole scene was insane, surreal, she felt sure Ashton Kutcher was going to pop out from behind that sweeping bank of computers and yell, "You've been punk'd!"

And that was another thing…those computers. The place looked like it was retrofitted to operate as a tertiary NORAD base if Cheyenne Mountain and Peterson Air Force Base ever simultaneously disappeared from the map.

Totally surreal.

But then Ethan prepared to open the separate little case she kept her delicates in, and the reality of the situation suddenly clicked into Technicolor focus. Oh, yes. She figured now would be the perfect time to excuse herself from this little exercise.

"Cripes," she muttered.

"What?" Nate asked. He was watching the entire process, strong arms crossed, big-booted feet planted shoulder width apart, taking in every minute detail and cataloging it away in that inscrutable brain of his.

"Nothing," she said, forcing what she hoped was a nonchalant smile. She was already nervous enough after the way she apparently set off some alarm when she first entered the building, which resulted in Nate turning and scowling at her. Of course that had made her start to blabber uncontrollably about the lack of governmental restrictions on off-shore drilling.

Yeah, *what?*

Off-shore drilling? Had she really gone there?

She nearly groaned while recollecting the inane, one-sided conversation—not that that was atypical when it came to the two of them. One-sided conversations, that is. What was typical was the way her ability to instantly contract the linguistic version of the trots made his face blank, his eyes glaze over, and that little tick start to work in his jaw.

Of course in about two seconds, when Ozzie/Ethan dumped out her panty case, she figured Nate's eyes would be anything but glazed.

Crapola.

If she hadn't already begun to regret her decision to make this trip, the forthcoming episode of abject mortification would no doubt do the trick. To use one of Grigg's favorite sayings, *it's either shit or go blind.*

Since neither of those was a particularly pleasant sounding option, it was best just to turn her back on the entire scene, walk a few yards down the way, and try her best to disappear into the floor.

"You're an adult. They're both adults. It's certainly not the first time they've come into contact with women's underwear. Just act like it's no big deal," she coached herself as she started to inch along the railing.

"What didja say?" Nate asked, and she spun around to find him eyeing her like maybe she was growing a second head.

She *really* needed to get the talking to herself thing under control.

"Nothing," she assured him again and realized from the hard look he sent her that response wasn't going fly a second time. "Okay, you're about to dig into my panty case and, *sheesh*, having a stranger paw through my underwear is a bit disconcerting. So I'm just gonna take myself over there." She hooked a thumb over her shoulder to indicate the far corner where the second story railing connected with the wall.

Nate's expression got even harder—if that was possible—as he asked Ethan/Ozzie, "Is this really necessary?"

The guy waved the black wand-thing over her panty case and it buzzed, sounding like a giant, angry bee.

Nate sighed resignedly and swung back to her. "Sorry. It's gotta be done."

"Yeah," she said, trying a smile that must've looked kinda sick because Nate's hard expression morphed into one of apprehension. "I mean it. It's fine. I'm just going to stand over there and check on the goings-on down below."

Before he could say anything else—because, really, what more could he say about rooting around in her delicates?—she made good on her decision to excuse herself from their company.

"Jesus, the woman's got quite a collection," the kid murmured while using his knife to snip the tiniest stitch in order to pull out the filament-thin tracking device secured in the hem of yet another pair of Ali's panties.

Correction. Another one of Ali's *thongs*.

"Mmph," Nate grunted, not knowing whether to laugh or cry. It appeared the woman was the proud owner of the entire Victoria's Secret catalog.

Plus, he detected the slightest aroma of honeysuckle emanating from the pile.

Sure, it was probably just fabric softener or lotion or something, but his wayward dick started to stiffen in response to the smell combined with the feel of the satin and silk he clutched in his fist. It brought back memories of that day on the beach. A deep, visceral recollection of soft panties brushing against his searching fingers and the even softer sensation of the warm, wet flesh beneath—

No, goddamnit! He wouldn't think of that now. *Couldn't* think of that now. Not with her standing so close. He didn't trust himself not to go all caveman and—

No!

Somehow he managed to wrangle some superhuman effort to pry open his reluctant fingers and throw the entire mess back down on the table.

"Did you know Grigg's sister was so hot?" Ozzie pressed.

Uh, *yeah*.

Ali'd been the feature starlet in his personal spanktrovision for the last dozen years, and after that day on the beach? After first-hand knowledge of what it was like to have her lithe arms tight around his neck, her soft breasts pressed firm and snug against his chest, her agile tongue personally introducing itself to his tonsils?

Uh-huh, he could certainly vouch for the woman's hotness.

She was smokin'.

"I mean like *hot*," Ozzie stressed unnecessarily. "Like she seriously gets my blood pumping, if you know what I mean. Of course, skimpy women's lingerie has been giving me wood since I discovered my best friend's older sister's Frederick's of Hollywood catalog when I was twelve, so maybe that accounts for my semi. Not to mention I've always been a fan of red lace." The kid held up a red lace bra and wiggled his eyebrows.

Geez. More information than Nate ever wanted to know about the guy.

Plus, the sight of Ali's underwear in another man's hands, especially knowing it was turning the little shit on, made him want to chew nails.

Since there were no nails around to chew, he found himself saying something he never in his entire sad life thought he'd say, "Dude, just shut the hell up and sing."

What were they talking about?

Ali flicked a glance in the direction of the two men mangling her underwear and—

Bad move.

Ozzie/Ethan was holding up her red bra and wiggling his eyebrows.

Great. Just…great. This day was going from bad to worse in pretty quick order.

To distract herself, she leaned over the heavy rail and surveyed the wide expanse below.

The distance to the first floor was dizzying, made even more so by the overwhelming fifteen-foot-tall caricatures painted all over the brick walls in colors so vibrant and saturated it would take a mind much more creative than hers to try and put a name to them all. The murals gave the huge space the appearance of some strange cross between a funhouse and workshop. Each of the cartoonishly exaggerated figures was obviously one of Black Knights Inc.'s employees. They looked like something that belonged in a graphic novel, all bulging muscles and straining tendons.

The concrete floor was a fascinating landscape of stains from old and recent oil spills—a giant Rorschach test on speed. The brightly painted brick walls were lined with mammoth, rolling toolboxes, and the main floor was dotted with highly technical-looking machines of various shapes and sizes. She wouldn't have been able to identify one of them if her life depended on it.

What she *could* recognize was the line of gleaming custom choppers along one wall, their paint jobs varying in color from dark to vibrant, their designs alternately fierce and whimsical. They were a visual barrage of glinting chrome and sparkling paint, testament to the fact that at least *some* actual custom motorcycle work went on here.

And she might've been fooled into thinking perhaps Black Knights Inc. was exactly as it was purported to be had one entire section of the "shop" not currently housed a…yes, that was a helicopter.

A helicopter with a tiny blond woman straddling the rotor while a guy stood below, yelling up instructions over the din of REO Speedwagon. "You loosen that bolt and the whole goddamned thing's gonna fall off!"

Ali assumed the woman must be Black Knight Inc.'s brilliant resident mechanic, but for the life of her she couldn't recall the woman's name.

Renegade, maybe? It was something like that.

"That's the whole point!" Renegade, aka Helo Girl,

or whatever her name was, called back with a healthy dose of *well, duh.*

Of course, what put the cherry on top of Ali's incredulity sundae was the undeniable fact that that black behemoth down there was not your typical civilian helicopter. Nuh-uh, not with those menacing machine guns mounted on both sides. Although, she had to admit the thing didn't look very scary right now considering major portions of it were pieced out and scattered around on various drop cloths.

It was obvious the bird wasn't going to take to the air any time soon.

Still, if Ozzie/Ethan's sidearm and the room behind her—which would make the attendees of DEF CON swoon in the computer geek equivalent of orgasmic bliss—hadn't already convinced her that her instincts about Black Knights Inc. were spot-on, the sight of that deadly military chopper certainly would have.

There was a certain satisfaction in finally knowing, without a shadow of a doubt, she'd been right all along. Grigg had been up to much more than playing grease monkey in a motorcycle shop. Unfortunately, along with that piece of gratifying knowledge returned the hard wedge of sadness she first experienced when she'd pulled up to Black Knights Inc.'s front gates. The frustration and remorse because Grigg hadn't felt he could tell her the truth.

What gives, Grigg?

She should've asked that question when he was still alive. She should've made him share that portion of his life with her. She should've insisted she actually get to *know* him instead of constantly biting her tongue, waiting for the day when he'd finally trust her enough to come clean.

It was too late.

The boulder of remorse, lodged in her throat since Nate walked into her parents' home and told them they'd never again lay eyes on Grigg's handsome face, grew until it threatened to choke her. She blinked rapidly and tried to swallow it down.

Which never worked.

Crap.

Don't cry. Don't cry.

She'd never been the stoic type. Far from it. She'd once bawled so hard on a flight to London while watching the movie *Marley and Me,* the man beside her got up twice to go to the bathroom and come back with a handful of toilet-paper to try and help her mop up the mess. But this bursting-into-spontaneous-tears-without-the-slightest-warning thing had become a recent talent of hers. One she hoped to lose PDQ, but she wasn't sure that was gonna happen. Not when the loss of Grigg was still so fresh…so unbearable…

"Heard it from a friend whooo…heard it from a friend whooo…heard it from another you been messin' arounnnddd," Ozzie/Ethan finished with dramatic vibrato.

The sudden silence caused by the end of the song was shattered when the opening bars to Rick Springfield's "Jessie's Girl" blasted through the speakers. Obviously Ethan/Ozzie was a big '80s music fan, although the guy didn't look old enough to have lived through much of that decade.

"Meerreow!" Ali nearly jumped out of her skin when something warm and furry brushed against her calves—which didn't do a thing to steady her jittery nerves or assuage the feeling of having suddenly fallen down the rabbit's hole. But it did succeed in keeping her stupid tears at bay.

"Well, hello," she murmured to the biggest, ugliest cat on the planet.

She crouched down to stroke patchy, ash-colored fur. The tom was the size of a small horse, with enough scars around his face and notches in his ears to earn him the look of a battered warrior. When his big, yellow eyes blinked up at her in weary, feline sympathy, as if to say, *I understand. I've seen the ugly side of life, too,* the tears hovering behind her eyes threatened to spill all over again.

Oh, double crap.

To comfort herself, she pulled the mammoth cat into her arms and stood.

Or tried to...

It was a bit difficult given he seemed to weigh as much as a St. Bernard. Finally, she was able to pull herself up by the railing, only to have to spread her feet in order to balance under her furry load.

She heard a deep rumble and thought someone started up one of the Harleys down below. She chuckled when she realized it was the deeply contented, terribly unattractive gray bundle in her arms causing the racket.

"Now you've done it! Peanut will expect everyone to carry him around, and I, for one, don't have the strength for it," Frank Knight, a giant of a man who, contrary to his words, looked strong enough to bench press a Volkswagen, yelled over the booming music as he appeared from one of the side doors to come and lean on the rail beside her.

"Peanut?" She pulled her chin back and glanced down into a furry, gray face only a mother could love. The cat's golden eyes were half-closed in satisfaction, and she was blessed with the rather dubious honor of his kneading nails pricking through the thin cotton of her T-shirt. "He looks more like a Goliath, or Brutus. Peanut? Really?"

"Yeah," Frank laughed as he ran a hand through his curling mop of brown hair and watched the progress down on the shop floor. His smile quickly faded as his eyes zeroed in on the woman doing a pretty fair version of a bronco rider—only her steed was made of steel instead of flesh and blood.

Ali thought she heard him mutter "sonofabitch," before he physically forced himself to look away. "When we moved into this building, it was home to rats and this guy here," he reached out a giant mitt of a hand and scratched under the cat's chin, eliciting a resurgence of purring that vibrated through Ali's chest like a lawnmower, "who'd made his bed on a pile of old peanut bags—hence the name. We managed to get rid of all the rats, and we shipped Peanut off to live with a sweet local lady who takes in strays, but within two days he'd found his way back to us. I'm Frank Knight, by the way. I'd shake your hand except both of them appear to be full." He winked and a delightful web of wrinkles gathered at the corner of his eye.

"I know who you are. Grigg spoke very highly of you. He had a great deal of respect for you."

The big man's face contorted. "The respect thing

went both ways. Grigg was…well," he ran that giant paw back through his hair again and grimaced slightly, flexing his shoulder as if the motion hurt, "…there's just no words. He was the best. I'm terribly sorry for your loss. We were all devastated."

And…triple crap. The tears were threatening again.

Just when she thought she'd have to turn away or lose it right on the spot—she'd turned into the Queen of Blubberingtown today—all hell broke loose in the madhouse.

Chapter Three

"GOT IT!" BECKY REICHERT CROWED AS THE LAST BOLT finally twisted loose and the bent rotor fell to the floor with a resounding *Boom!* The sound bounced and echoed around the warehouse like a cannon explosion.

Deafening silence ensued, sufficiently informing her the earsplitting ruckus had resulted in the switching off of ol' Ricky Springfield—which was fine by her. Ozzie had deplorable taste in music. She'd tried to enlighten the man to the salient fact that quite a lot of really fantastic stuff had been written in the last twenty years, but he seemed immune to her attempts at musical edification. That he *occasionally* allowed her to pipe in The Killers was about the only victory she'd ever won, which meant she usually had her iPod earbuds screwed in tight, blasting her own music into her brain to drown out Ozzie's less than discerning taste.

However, last night she forgot to charge the sucker, so she was tortured with '80s rock ballads all morning. Of course, not having her earbuds in allowed her to hear the horrified screech immediately following the cacophonous clang of the fallen rotor blade.

She glanced up to see a woman standing at the rail wearing a gray cat-hat. Only it appeared, by her flailing arms and Peanut's hissing, the fashion choice was unintentional.

Wait for it. Wait for it…

"Rebecca! Damnit!"

Ah, there it was.

Frank "Boss" Knight had a way of furiously screaming her name followed by that familiar epithet. It made her wince and grin at the same time.

Grin because the Knights liked to joke with her and say Frank might actually be under the mistaken impression her last name *was* Damnit. And wince because, other than her father, Frank was the only one to ever call her Rebecca—which made her feel about six years old, and she'd wondered more than once if Frank did it intentionally, just to drive home the difference in their ages.

That one word virtually screamed, *Yes, I've seen the way you look at me, but I'm old enough to be your father*.

Which wasn't really true unless he started his sexual adventures at thirteen—although, since she thought about it, that seemed completely possible. She'd seen pictures. Even at thirteen it'd been beyond obvious Frank would grow into a beautiful man.

Of course he would never admit to being beautiful. On the contrary, she'd heard him mention on more than one occasion, "It's a standoff who has more battle wounds, me or Peanut."

And Becky supposed that was true. The slashing scar bisecting Frank's left eyebrow gave him the look of perpetual skepticism, while the little white line snaking up from the corner of his mouth made his full lips quirk up just a bit. Taken together, it created an incongruent combination.

Okay, so maybe beautiful wasn't quite the right word to describe him. His face had far too much character to be put in such vapid terms. Unfortunately, it was a face she'd learned to admire from afar, because that was as close as he ever let her. Not surprising considering she seemed to annoy the ever-lovin' shit out of the man.

"Yes, Frank?" she innocently replied to his having bellowed her name at the top of his lungs.

Frank. Everyone else called him Boss, but not her. Oh no. Not when calling him by his given name made his eyelids twitch.

"Are you trying to get yourself killed," he roared down at her, "or just give me a flippin' heart attack?"

Heart attack. Yeah, right. The man had a resting pulse of sixty beats per minute and a cholesterol count that would make a triathlete weep with envy. He was more likely to get hit by a freak bolt of lightning from the clear blue sky than die of a heart attack.

And since she reckoned his last question was rhetorical, she didn't bother to answer it. But when he yelled, "Get your ass down from there ASAP," she did as she was told with only a minimal amount of eye rolling.

"I saw that," he growled once her feet were safely on the ground.

"No way could you've seen that all the way up there," she called back, hands on hips, incredulously chewing the cherry Dum Dum she'd shoved into her mouth before tackling that last bolt. She'd taken to eating the stupid things three years ago in order to help herself quit smoking. Unfortunately, she'd simply exchanged one addiction for another.

"You're right. I couldn't. But you just proved my little theory." The implied *gotcha* basically flew off the second story to land on her head.

She cursed and called him a colorful name beneath her breath.

"I heard that, too," he barked, and she clamped her mouth shut, just in case he was telling the truth this time.

When the explosion ricocheted around the warehouse, Nate instinctively lunged toward Ali while simultaneously reaching for the Para Ordinance CCW .45 he kept concealed in the waistband of his shorts. Luckily, before he could take her to the ground and cover her with his body, he realized what'd happened—namely, Rebecca "The Rebel" Reichert doing what she did best. Making an unholy ruckus.

He managed, just barely, to halt his flying lunge.

It was a good thing, because Peanut was now stuck to Ali's head like some weird feline version of the Daniel Boon raccoon hat.

"Oh my God, get him off me," she whispered as a trickle of blood oozed from her left temple where Peanut secured himself to his precarious perch with one sharp claw.

The sight of that crimson drop sliding down her pale, flawless cheek made Nate want to kill someone. At the moment, he figured he'd start with Peanut and work his way over to Becky and then up to Boss, who wasn't helping to calm the stupid cat by yelling at Becky.

Go figure. The guy was always yelling at Becky.

Man, the list of friends he was ready to murder was mounting at an astonishing rate since Ali minced her sweet ass into the shop. Just before the uproar, he'd been ready to cap Ozzie for his unnecessary interest in her lingerie.

"Be still," he whispered as he reached for the cat. The animal was foolish enough to lay back his ears and hiss a warning.

"Um, yes," she said as she tightened her hold on the rail. "Being still is certainly the plan since movement might cause one of two outcomes. One, it'll unset the hefty Peanut here and break my neck. Or two, it'll result in a scalping. And though I've been thinking for a while now about cutting my hair, I'm seriously considering keeping the roots."

"Be quiet, too," he instructed as he made another attempt to reach for Peanut. It was impossible to concentrate when he was this close to her, especially with her jabbering in that adorable way she had.

He spared a glance at her distressed face and knew it to be a mistake instantly.

He was momentarily arrested because…man, six feet away she was pretty.

Up close like this? Total gut-shot.

Of course, having just seen all of her unmentionables didn't help matters. *Unmentionables?*

Whoever came up with *that* ridiculous term? Underwear that fantastic deserved to be mentioned on a regular basis.

Shit, he wasn't going to think about her underwear. Which, of course, only made him wonder what color she had on under those tight, distressed jeans and that thin T-shirt. Pink? Her shirt was pink. Women often matched their underwear to their outfits. At least that'd been his experience. So…probably pink.

Holy shit! He was *not* going to think about her underwear!

"Being quiet might be too tall an order." She nervously licked her lips and he couldn't help but eye the movement. "Y-you see, when I'm nervous or in pain I tend to talk. It helps me not dwell on the fact that I'm... well, n-nervous or in pain. Like right now? I'm both. So it's best if I just keep talking. So I'm gonna keep talking, okay?"

He watched her slightly frantic eyes swing toward the table where it looked like a panty-bomb had gone off. Ozzie was standing wide-eyed with a bra in one hand and his pocket knife in the other. "I take it there actually was something in my clothes. Either that or Ethan, er, Ozzie has an aversion to purple satin."

"Yeah," he told her as he gently reached toward Peanut, determined not to think about pink silk or purple satin. "You're bugged. Devices in all your underwear."

"My underwear? My gosh, that's so sick—"

"No, not sick," he interrupted and managed to snake an arm around Peanut's substantial middle. "It's smart. You always wear underwear, therefore, you're always bugged. Whoever tagged you knew what they were doin', not to mention they were able to get their hands on some pretty hard-to-come-by, high-tech gadgetry."

She shot him a look.

"What?" he asked.

"Where's my journal? I want to jot this down for posterity."

Huh?

He lifted a confused brow and she smirked, ornery light glinting in her amber eyes.

"You just spoke, like, what? A whole four sentences? Not to mention there were a few adjectives thrown in there. That must be some sort of record. It should be memorialized accordingly, don't you think?" She batted her lashes.

Jesus, the woman was too much.

She rolled her eyes at his fierce frown. That is until he tightened his hold on the damned cat.

"Oh, aahhhh!" She shrieked as he swiftly lifted Peanut from her head and unceremoniously dropped the hairy ton of fun to the ground.

Wow, somebody needed to talk to Becky about what she was feeding the beast. Nate was pretty sure the floor actually shook.

"Here," he reached into his back pocket and handed her the bandana he always kept there. "You've got a drop of blood," he pointed to his own cheek.

"Thanks," she said as she pressed the cloth to her temple.

"We, uh, need you to give us the underwear you're wearing," he muttered and tried not to glance at the multi-colored mountain of lingerie heaped on the conference table. It only made him imagine just what she'd look like in each and every piece and that certainly didn't do a thing for the semi-wood he was sporting—semi-wood which threatened to turn into a Louisville Slugger with the slightest encouragement.

Was there a particular name for the kind of reaction this woman engendered in him? Compulsive fixation might begin to cover it. Unreasonable horniness certainly did.

Just the thought of her handing him a pair of panties still warm from the heat of her body—and the recollection it invoked—had a shaft of red-hot lust zinging down his spine.

That was immediately followed by a harsh flash of memory…his hand shaking on the handle of the bloody KA-BAR and Grigg's mutilated, lifeless body going cold in his arms.

He was hit by a crashing wave of guilt.

Uh-huh, yeah, and that pretty much summed it up when it came to his relationship—or *non*-relationship—with Ali Morgan. Lust and guilt. The two were so intertwined it was a wonder he'd ever felt one without the other.

What a goatfuck.

And now here she was, standing not a foot from him, probably wearing silky pink underwear, looking half-frightened, half-amused, with almond shaped eyes that titled up at the corners and sparkled like gold bullion.

Shit. Eyes that sparkle like gold bullion? She turned him into a friggin' poet—and not a very good one at that.

"Right. I'll uh, just go take care of that underwear issue." She gathered herself, squaring her thin shoulders, trying somewhat successfully to throw off the weight of her fatigue. She'd been without sleep for over twenty-four hours. He knew as soon as her adrenaline dropped—which, by the slightly glazed look in her eyes was gonna happen pretty soon—she'd hit the proverbial wall and then he'd have to wait for answers until she'd gotten twenty winks.

He didn't want to do that.

The sooner he figured out just what the hell was going on, the sooner he could fix whatever it was, and the sooner Ali would be on her way back home.

Halfway across the country.

Which sometimes still felt too close. Particularly when he remembered that day at the beach when they—

"Point me to the bathroom," she said.

He hooked a thumb over his shoulder. "Down the hall. Second door on the right." When she headed in that direction, he added, "Hey, Ali?"

She glanced back at him.

"You're a kindergarten teacher." It came out of his mouth before he had a chance to think about it.

"Yes," she tilted her head and frowned. "So?"

He simply looked at her. Yeah, so? So what? Geez, he was a complete moron. "So what'd'ya need that stuff for?" In for a penny, in for a pound.

Despite the assurances to himself only minutes ago that he wouldn't think about her underwear, all that sexy silk and see-through lace was really bugging the hell out of him.

Was there a man in her life? Some lucky sonofabitch she wore those titillating scraps of material for? Some unworthy bastard who had the honor of touching all that warm, smooth flesh? Of kissing all those sweet, sensitive spots? Of eliciting that sexy little whimper of longing in the back of her throat?

The thought made him want to shoot someone. The faceless prick she'd purchased all that junk for would be an excellent place to start. And then he could move on to his friends.

Damn, having her around made him undeniably bloodthirsty.

"What stuff?"

He lowered his chin until he was scowling at her from under his brows. She knew exactly what he was talking about.

Her lips quirked and he was reminded how soft they were, how sweet the inside of her mouth—

No.

He squashed the thought as effectively as Grigg had squashed all those orange-spotted roaches that'd been happy to cohabitate with them that time in Colombia.

"Are you actually saying there's no need for a kindergarten teacher to have sexy underwear?" she asked, shooting a wary glance toward Ozzie. The kid was doing a fairly good impression of a deaf-mute.

Nate crossed his arms. Watching. Waiting. He just had to give her time. Soon, with no more encouragement than drawn out silence, every thought in her pretty head would tumble from her succulent, peach-colored mouth. A mouth that was—

Fuckin'-A, there went his mind again. It was a problem under normal circumstances. With her standing arms' length away? Man, it was a goddamned obsession.

He almost smiled when she started in, her tone defiant.

"Look, I spend all day long with five-year-olds. I sing silly songs. I color with crayons and make barnyard animals out of clay. I glue and glitter. I play Duck Duck Goose and Red Rover. I wipe bottoms and noses. I wear shirts with embroidered ABC's and skirts that can stand up to three dozen grubby little hands. So," she made a face that dared him to comment, "it helps to know underneath all that is the heart and body of a woman."

"Hmm," was all he could manage, rendered nearly comatose with lust by the challenging gleam in her eyes.

"Hmm?" she repeated disbelievingly. Thrusting out her chin, she rolled in her lips. "Okay, lookie here, bucko. Considering the amount of electronics I was unknowingly carrying on my person when I walked in here, it's pretty obvious we're going to have to suffer each others' company. At least for a couple of days. And if we have any hope of getting along, you're going to have to learn how to use actual words. For Pete's sake, my kindergarteners have larger vocabularies than you."

"Autoschediastic."

"Huh?" She blinked up at him suspiciously.

"Juxtaposition."

"What?"

"Verisimilitude."

"What in the world are you doing?" she demanded.

He shrugged, loving the play of emotions over her animated face. "Proving I know more words than a kindergartener."

Ali blinked.

Did Nate Weller just make a joke?

Nah. Couldn't be. That would mean he had a sense of humor, which she was absolutely certain he did *not*.

"Then why don't you ever *use* those words?" she demanded, hands on hips, glaring at him and trying to ignore the breadth of his shoulders beneath his T-shirt. "I swear, sometimes talking to you is like trying to converse with a tree." A very big, very solid, very *male* tree.

He made the facial equivalent of a shrug. "The fewer I use, the more you use."

"Sheesh," she rolled her eyes at the man's obliviousness, "that's the whole problem. You clam up, which, *poof*," she snapped her fingers, "just makes me talk all the more. It's like I can't help but spew forth words."

Nate grinned and Ali's heart stopped.

God, the man was beautiful. His smile transformed his face the way dawn transforms the night.

It was a good thing he didn't whip that puppy out very often. The thing was a lethal weapon. Far more dangerous to a girl's fragile heart than the rifle he'd used as his tool of trade while sniping for the Marine Corps.

"I like the way you talk," he said simply, with a little shrug.

Uh, Billy Bob Thorton in *Slingblade* anyone? She stifled a chuckle. *Mmm, hmm. I reckon.*

Then the import of what he said sunk in and she gaped at him. "You do?"

"Yeah." He nodded, a shiny lock of black hair curling over his forehead. For some inexplicable reason, she wanted to stroke it between her fingers. See if it was as cool and silky as she remembered. Which was odd in the extreme since she didn't like him. Preferred to stay as far from him as possible.

Well…save for that time on the beach…

Grief. Grief. That'd been guided by grief…hadn't it?

Yes, it most certainly had. Anything else was just too bizarre to consider.

She shook her head. "But…but whenever I start to chatter, you always eyeball me like I'm some sort of bizarre bug that's just crawled over your shoe."

Ethan/Ozzie turned a chuckle into a cough and she was reminded they had an audience. Glancing over, she saw the guy try to appear industrious as he waved that black wand-thing over her empty suitcase.

Well whatever. This conversation was far too

compelling to worry about something as insignificant as another set of ears listening in.

When she swung her gaze back to Nate, his black eyes were shrewd. "There, you see?" she pointed at his face. "You're doing it again."

He sighed heavily and began a thorough examination of his boots. "I don't mean to. I don't think you're a bug at all. I think you're..." he shook his head and slanted a look at Ethan/Ozzie, who was no longer even trying to pretend he wasn't listening. The guy was gawking in slack-jawed fascination.

Nate grimaced before he shrugged, seeming to search for the right words. "When you talk, you always sound so happy, so sunny."

Ali was rooted to the spot, her heart beating a mile a minute while her brains scrambled like breakfast eggs.

Things were definitely getting weird. As if the whole day, nay, the whole past three months, weren't already redlining her personal bizarre-o-meter, now Nathan "Ghost" Weller was actually being...nice. "I think...I think that might be the sweetest thing anyone's ever said to me," she admitted slowly.

He shrugged again and she thought maybe there was a slight flush staining his cheeks.

Nate blushing? Forming whole sentences? Actually smiling? Had she missed the warning signs somewhere and been sucked into a parallel dimension? A parallel dimension where Nathan Weller acted like a human being?

"Grigg once told me you rarely spoke, but when you did it was usually something erudite," she confessed while warily watching to see just what strangeness he might attempt next. "I didn't believe him then. Now maybe I do."

His face instantly darkened.

Startled by the swift change, she lifted her brows. "You don't like to talk about him?"

"Can't."

She huffed out a peeved breath. He'd forced the word through a hard set of sawing teeth. "So we're back to monosyllabic answers?"

He only grunted and she realized they'd gone one step further, back to mere guttural responses.

"Perfect. That's just perfect," she hissed through her own set of grinding teeth. She'd thought they were making some sort of progress…

Yeah, what a joke.

She spun around, stomping toward the bathroom to remove her underwear. She wasn't even going to *think* about the upcoming humiliation of handing over her *dirty* panties.

Crapola.

Chapter Four

"Why don't you start by telling us what brought you here, Ali," Frank said as the three Knights in residence settled themselves around the conference table. The group was mighty thin, what with Steady in California at some fancy-dancy medical conference while Rock and Wild Bill were away covertly keeping an eye on a bigwig politician during his ill-advised trip to the Sandbox. He wasn't even going to *think* about Christian and Mac and that goddamned Mossad agent.

Man, he absolutely *hated* having so many of his men out at once, especially when he wasn't with them. It gave him a severe case of nut-shrivel every time because he was used to being in the thick of things, neck deep in reconnaissance or bad guys, not sitting all snuggly warm at a conference table.

But that was the price he paid, he supposed, for running his own crew. And it was a small price indeed when he considered the fact that it was in exchange for choosing which assignments they'd take and more importantly, having the green light to gather Intel and carry out those assignments as they damned well pleased without any input from some desk-surfing, thumb-up-his-butt, pencil pusher in Washington.

Of course, it also meant he had to deal with visitors who strolled into his shop at the most inconvenient times.

And speaking of that inconvenient visitor, Ali

Morgan stared at the cup of coffee Patti placed in front of her like it was an unstable nuclear warhead.

Uh-huh. He and the rest of the guys preferred their caffeine able to stand up without benefit of a cup, but it obviously wasn't for everyone.

Standing, he made his way over to the refrigerator where he removed a can of Coke, popped the top, and set it on the table in front of Ali before claiming her cup of coffee for his own and retaking his seat.

She shot him an oh-god-you're-my-hero smile right before she chugged down a healthy slug of soda. Wiping the back of her hand over her mouth, she took a deep breath, gathered herself, and blurted, "Someone's after me."

Ghost twitched.

That was the only way to describe the subtle tightening of every single one of the man's muscles.

Well, now, isn't that interesting?

Frank recognized Ghost's intensely neutral expression. It was obvious the man was rigidly controlling his responses because he was scared shitless he might give something away. Anything away. Frank could certainly identify with that unfortunate predicament. He found himself in the same situation every goddamned time Becky walked into the room.

And speak of the devil…

"Someone's after you? Cool." Becky flopped down in a chair, bringing with her the weirdly appealing combination of smells that were acrylic paint, motor oil, and the softly clean scent that was all Becky.

She unwrapped a Dum Dum. This one was green. Sour apple. He knew every Dum Dum flavor on sight because, pervert that he was, each time Becky popped a new sucker in her mouth, he fantasized about kissing her and tasting how that particular flavor would combine with her own personal essence to create—in his mind, anyway—ambrosia.

"Are you insane?" Ali gave Becky the stink-eye. "You wouldn't think it was so cool if whoever was after you had broken into your home, planted bugs in all your underwear, and tried to mug you."

"You're bugged, too? Sweet." Becky pulled a root beer Dum Dum—Frank's favorite—from her hip pocket and slid it in his direction.

He stopped the sucker from skimming off the table with a slap of his palm. It was warm from her body heat. That warmth made a barrage of wildly erotic images flash across his frizzled brain.

Her, naked. Him, trailing the sucker over the skin of her hip and then licking away the stickiness with the flat of his tongue.

Fuck!

He'd like to say he could ignore the candy, but he knew if he stuck it in his shirt pocket, it'd only burn a damn hole through to his chest until he couldn't concentrate on anything save for shoving it in his pie hole.

Disgusted by his lack of self-control where root beer-flavored Dum Dums and Becky Reichert were concerned, he angrily ripped off the wrapper and crammed the sucker in his mouth, managing to frown around it at her. "If you're just going to offer up inane observations, why don't you go back to whatever it was you were doing?"

"Because, *Frank*," she emphasized his name and

his eyelids twitched, "at the moment this is much more interesting."

Ali glanced back and forth between them, one eyebrow raised. Everyone else at the table was so accustomed to their constant bickering they didn't bat a single lash, which only served to exacerbate Frank's frustration. He was supposed to be the shining example of how they should all conduct themselves, lead by example and all that bullshit, but he couldn't seem to wrangle his temper—not to mention his libido—whenever Becky was around. It was a problem. One he'd yet to find a solution to.

"Fine," he growled, unaccountably mad at her, and even more pissed at himself for his lack of self-control. "But if you're determined to stay, zip it, unless you have something constructive to add."

Becky pantomimed zipping her lips, while simultaneously managing to give him her patented, you're-such-an-asshole look.

If she only knew…

He swung his attention back to Ali because continuing to scowl at Becky wouldn't do a damn bit of good to further this conversation, nor would it do a damn bit of good for his redlining hormones. "Okay, let's start at the beginning. You say someone broke into your home?"

"Sort of."

"How can someone *sort of* break into your home?" he asked, pretending he didn't see Becky's exaggerated eye roll.

"Okay, look, what I'm about to tell you is going to sound crazy and maybe a little paranoid." Ali rubbed her temples as she sat up straighter. From what Ghost said, the woman was closing in on the twenty-five-hours-of-continual-consciousness mark, and he could tell she was starting that inevitable slide into mental oblivion. That place where the body was still moving, the mouth was still able to string a few largely coherent words together, but the brain was checking out. *Good-bye, see you in, oh, say four hours.*

He'd been there more than a time or two himself. She needed to get some sleep and soon. But first they needed some answers, because she'd come into their shop so wired he was surprised her underwear wasn't picking up signals from the Hubble Space Telescope.

"Why don't you give us a try," he told her. "We specialize in paranoid and crazy."

She tried to laugh, but the strain she'd been under, combined with her lack of sleep, made the effort fall flat. Rolling in her lips, she looked around the table as if she'd suddenly lost her nerve, then, "It all started about a week after we found out about Grigg."

Everyone at the table, including him, shifted uncomfortably.

She continued, unconsciously flicking at the tab on her soda with her thumbnail. The hollow metallic pinging was particularly loud in the strained silence of the conference room. "I came home from work one day and just *knew* someone had been in my condo."

"Was anything missing? Moved?" Ozzie asked, leaning back in his chair and running a hand though his mad scientist hair. The kid might have terrible taste in music and T-shirts, but he had an IQ off the fucking charts.

"No, everything was just how I'd left it, but there was this...this feeling. It sounds dumb, I know—"

"Not as dumb as you'd think," Frank assured her.

"Intuition is a powerful tool. One each of us sitting around this table has learned to credit. Plus, given the level of technology you've been wearing beneath your clothes, I'd say your paranoia was on the money."

Ali flashed him a grateful smile.

I'm just racking up the hero points with you today, aren't I, sweetheart? Right, if she knew of the wild fantasies he was entertaining about Becky, she would surely be wearing a totally different expression. The kind someone might don after catching the neighborhood weirdo garbed in nothing but a trench coat in the middle of July while walking by a playground full of kids—which was exactly how he felt when it came to Rebecca Reichert. Like a dirty old man.

Shit.

"Thanks," Ali said, dragging his attention back to the subject at hand. "That makes me feel better. I really thought I was going nutso there for a while. And this is probably going to sound strange, but I'm kinda glad you guys found all those bugs on me. Now I know I'm not losing my mind."

"So you get home from work and you know someone's been in your place," Ozzie prodded. Like usual, the kid's brain was flying about ten steps ahead, gathering information and cataloging it into recognizable patterns. "What happened next?"

"Nothing," Ali lifted a shoulder and unconsciously slid a little farther down in her seat. The woman was on the short path to going horizontal. "For a few days, that is. I thought maybe I was just being paranoid, thought maybe my personal radar was going haywire because of Grigg's passing."

Passing.

Frank hated the euphemisms people used while talking about death. What was so wrong with that word? Death. Dead. Die. It was direct, simple, so much more succinct than, say, giving up the ghost or kicking the bucket, or, his personal favorite, pushing up daisies. Though technically more accurate than the previous two, that last one sounded far too happy and sunny in his opinion. Maybe it was because he'd dealt in and with death for most of his adult life, but he preferred to call a spade a spade.

Grigg was dead. It was as simple and as complicated as that.

"But about a week later," Ali continued, "I walked into my classroom early one morning and...same thing. That feeling like someone had been there. But this time I had proof. When I went back through the history on my computer, I saw someone had logged on to my machine around midnight the night before."

"Could you see what they were looking for? What files they accessed?" Ozzie asked.

"No...I, uh, I'm not that tech-savvy. And I guess, looking back, perhaps I should've called in one of those companies...the Geek Squad or whatever, to see if they could figure out what'd been done to my PC, but then school let out for summer break and I started to see him and I completely forgot about my computer."

"*See him*?" Dan "The Man" Currington asked the question they were all thinking.

"Yes," she made a helpless gesture, "sort of."

"Any way to clarify that?" Dan pressed.

Ali took another deep breath and slipped a little

farther down in her seat. She rested her head on the back and blinked rapidly at the ceiling, then she suddenly pulled herself upright again.

That-a-girl, just keep it together a little while longer.

"Okay, again, you have to understand I thought I was going crazy, but I kept seeing this guy out of the corner of my eye. Never full on. Just a glimpse here or there. In the parking lot at the grocery store, a few cars behind me at a red light, walking into the ice cream shop across from the place I always get coffee. It's like I'd catch a glimpse…then he'd be gone. But yesterday, right after some big brute of a guy tried to mug me," she waved everyone off when they started making noises of concern. "Don't worry. I wasn't hurt, and the big jerk didn't get my purse, thanks to the help of a giant bumblebee and a loaf of French bread." Again, she sliced her hand through the air. "Long story for another time. *Anyway*, so right after my mugger ran off, I see the guy who's been following me for months come out of the deli across the street.

"Now, my adrenaline was pretty high because of the mugging, so I call to him and guess what he does?"

"What?" Becky asked, eyes bright with excitement. The damned woman loved trouble, lived for it and, much to Frank's chagrin, too often found it.

"He took off!" Ali exclaimed. "Just jumped in his SUV and burned rubber. Headed in the same direction as my mugger, mind you. I started after him—"

There was a collective gasp heard around the table.

"Yes, yes," she rolled her eyes and pressed forward before anyone could throw in their two cents about what a colossally dumbass move that had been. "I know.

Stupid, right? But I was so sick of feeling like I was going crazy. Don't worry, though. One of the guys who helped me fight off the mugger kept me from following."

Ozzie whipped open a paper-thin laptop, tense fingers poised above the keys like a snake getting ready to strike. "Vehicle make, color, model?"

Young Einstein had dropped his charmingly affable facade. Now he was all business. This was *his* specialty. Give the kid a few scant bits of information, and he could use his crazy-mad computer skills to find you the remaining pieces of the puzzle because, according to Ozzie, *everything* could be accessed through the World Wide Web and the lightning-fast fingers of a clever hacker. And Ozzie was as clever as they came.

"Sorry," Ali shook her head. "I'm about as good with cars as I am with computers. It was black, I can tell you that much. Black and big. Like a Ford Explorer or a Chevy Tahoe."

"So it was a domestically made SUV?" Ozzie asked, already typing away on the keyboard while his eyes remained glued to Ali's face.

Mad skills.

Frank congratulated himself for about the thousandth time over his decision to recruit Ethan Sykes away from the Navy.

Again Ali shook her head. "I'm not sure. But I did get a picture of the license plate."

Ozzie instantly stopped typing. In the resounding silence of the room, you could've heard the proverbial pin drop.

Becky was the one to break it. *Of course*.

"Kick *ass*, sista. Way to keep your head about you."

Ali blushed prettily and bit her lip. Out of the corner of Frank's eye, he thought he saw Ghost's jaw twitch.

"Thanks." Ali smiled. "But before you congratulate me too much, I'm not sure it'll be that much help. It's fuzzy." She pulled her BlackBerry from the back pocket of her jeans and punched a few buttons. "By the time I grabbed my phone, the vehicle was pretty far away, and I had to zoom way in..."

"Did you give the photo to the Jacksonville Police?" Frank asked, wondering what the local PD had to say about the incident.

"I did." She made a sound of disgust. "And when I laid out my theory linking the guy who's been following me and the mugger, they paid me some pretty nice lip service. Secretly, I think they went in the other room and swirled their fingers around their temples. Look, I know the story is crazy, but I'm convinced I'm right. Those two men are linked. Everything that's been happening is linked."

She handed her phone to Ozzie who glanced at the screen before his fingers started flying over the keyboard again.

"It's North Carolina plates. That last digit there," she tapped her phone with one fingernail, "it looks like either a B or an R...or maybe a 3."

"Doesn't matter," the kid said. "I can work with it."

"You can?" Ali's eyes brightened. "The Jacksonville police said it was too blurry to do anything with."

"The Jacksonville police don't have my image enhancement software," Ozzie boasted, the excitement on his face making him look about twelve years old, which made Frank's trick shoulder start to ache.

Thirty-nine certainly wasn't headed for the rocking chair, but with the kind of life he'd led, closing out his fourth decade meant that there were aches…and pops…and shit that just didn't work right anymore. His trick shoulder being the most annoying of all his current ailments.

He reached for the bottle of ibuprofen he kept in his hip pocket and quickly swallowed a couple of tablets without benefit of water before shoving the Dum Dum back in his mouth.

"Good job, by the way, " Ozzie added.

"Thanks," Ali accepted his offhand compliment and watched him jump up from the conference table with the same energy a child jumps out of bed on Christmas morning. The kid snagged his laptop along with her phone and scurried over to his domain. Pulling a long cord from a drawer, he attached it to the phone before jacking it into one of the main computers.

"Anyway," Ali turned her attention back to the group at the conference table, "the whole incident spooked me, especially when the police didn't believe me. And since I didn't want to end up strapped to a wheelchair with my eyelids taped open, pumped full of drugs and falling down a staircase while screaming, "He's flying!," I immediately hopped in my car and drove straight here."

"Be still my heart," Ozzie swiveled in his desk chair, clutching his chest. "Marry me, Ali. Marry me right now."

"What am I missing?" Dan asked.

"Come on, man. Mel Gibson? *Conspiracy Theory*? Do you *ever* go to the movies?"

"Ha!" Dan laughed, cocking his head and smoothing his tightly trimmed goatee. "Unlike some people I know, I haven't spent the last ten years with my head buried in electronics. I've been busting my hump doing man's work and—"

"Spare me one of your speeches," Ozzie waved a dismissive hand. "I've heard them all before. And I don't know why you're always trying to shut me down, anyway. 'Nobody puts baby in the corner.'"

Ozzie waited a beat and when Dan only raised a skeptical brow, he threw his hands in the air. "You've got to be kidding me! *Dirty Dancing*? How can you never have seen *Dirty Dancing*? It's a classic!"

"Yeah," Dan snorted, "a classic piece of shit."

"Them's fightin' words, mister!" Ozzie howled, jumping up to dance from side to side like a boxer.

Dan snorted so loudly, Frank thought the guy might've swallowed his tongue which, considering Dan's propensity toward slinging bullshit and provoking Ozzie, might not be such a bad thing.

The ex-SEALs on the team, Ozzie and Dan Man included, considered themselves to be the best of the best—which made them all cocky as hell. Of course, truth be told, each member of Black Knights Inc., ex-SEAL or not, was on the team because they were at the very tip-tipity top of their game.

Black Knights Inc. had nine guys—soon to be twelve, with the addition of the Mossad agent and the prospective helo pilot and communications specialist—who could go in, finish the job, and make tracks without a whiff of Uncle's involvement.

The powers-that-be in the monster otherwise known as the U.S. government absolutely *loved* all those intricate little layers of plausible deniability. Didn't matter that each man on the Black Knights' payroll ultimately reported back to the Grand-Poobah himself, *El Jefe*, the good ol' commander in chief. What mattered was that, should any of their missions be discovered, there was no way to trace that mission's origination to anyone in the U.S. government—which was just fine by Frank. After the clusterfuck that prompted his decision to part ways with the Navy SEALs, he preferred to run his own show.

Then again, by running his own show without the benefit of military hierarchy and the inherent discipline therein, it meant he very often had to put up with these kinds of antics.

And not to be all Danny Glover cliché, but he was getting too old for this shit.

"Cut it out you two," he growled and Ozzie flashed him a wink before retaking his seat.

"I wasn't kidding about that proposal." The kid wiggled his blond eyebrows at Ali.

"I'll take it under consideration," she said, smiling sweetly, and Frank noticed Ghost's fists clench. "So anyway, like I said before the conversation took a crazy turn, I drove straight here. I only stopped to fill up on gas and caffeine. But I uh, God this is so crazy…I think maybe I saw the guy at a Phillips 66 along the way. Not my mugger. The other one. The shadowy one."

"So for the question of the hour," he said, "just what have you gotten yourself involved in?"

Chapter Five

"THAT'S JUST IT," ALI THREW HER HANDS IN THE AIR, exhaustion and frustration making her voice crack. "I haven't done anything. I'm a kindergarten teacher, for Pete's sake. The most exciting thing to happen to me in recent months—apart from the stalking and mugging, that is—are the hardwood floors my landlord finally got around to installing. So, the more appropriate question is, what are *you* guys involved in, or perhaps more precisely, what was *Grigg* involved in that somebody thinks maybe I have something they want?"

There was a sudden oh-God-nobody-move tension in the air. A real deer-in-the-headlights moment.

Sheesh, they must think her completely blind or a total moron.

From the moment she'd set the bug-detector they had mounted out in the front hall screaming, she'd known without a shadow of a doubt they were *not* simply motorcycle mechanics.

Fed up with all of it, particularly with men who refused to believe she could keep a secret, she slammed her hands down on the conference table and stood. Her chair slid backward with a satisfying screech.

"Look, goddamnit!" Six pairs of eyes flew wide. They probably thought there was some national law against kindergarten teachers swearing. "I know this isn't just some custom motorcycle shop. How stupid do you think I am?" She waved a hand to indicate the bank of state-of-the-art computers and shot them all a look of disgust. "Did you suppose I'd think it was routine for a bunch of motorcycle mechanics to equip their shop with bug-detection devices? Not to mention the fact that it's obvious you're all loaded for bear."

Dan shifted in his chair, "Ali—"

"You're wearing a knife in the top of your right boot and a handgun in the waistband of your jeans," she cut him off. It was clear, given all the raised eyebrows around the table, she'd managed to surprise them again, this time with the accuracy of her observation. Somewhat vindicated, she continued, "Nate's got the same setup, only he keeps his knife under his shirt in a clip by his right-front pants pocket." She turned on Frank. "*You* aren't carrying a firearm, but you've got at least two knives, one in your waistband and another strapped to your calf. I'm assuming there might be more in the careful way you arrange yourself when you take a seat, but I'm not totally sure."

"Damn, give the girl a gold star," Becky laughed and winked at her in approval. "Big brother obviously taught baby sister a thing or two."

"You don't even know the half of it," she told Becky, feeling a smidge of camaraderie with the young woman. At least *someone* in the room seemed to be taking her seriously. "At least Ethan, er, Ozzie over there," she hooked a thumb over her shoulder to indicate the man, "doesn't attempt to conceal his weapons."

"Call me Ozzie, doll," he called back. He hunched over the keyboard like a starving man hunches over a plate of food. "And there's no need to conceal my weapons. I figure everyone should see what's in store for them should they attempt to fuck with me."

"Oh man." Dan groaned and rolled his eyes. "Next thing you know he'll be coming to work shirtless with bandoliers strapped across his chest and a red bandana tied around his head."

"Ah, so you *have* seen a movie or two." Ozzie swiveled in his chair, his eyes sparkling with devilish glee. "*Rambo*, huh? I can give you Rambo." He lowered his voice. "'They drew first blood. Not me…'"

"What a crock of bullsh—uh, crap." Dan scoffed.

"Are you sitting there dissing Stallone?" Ozzie demanded, making like he was about to stand in defense of the Italian Stallion.

"No. I'm sitting here dissing *you*, you stu—"

Were they really going to banter back and forth like this and completely ignore the fact that she was mere moments away from a meltdown of nuclear proportions?

"Look," she jammed her finger into the table for emphasis. "Somebody better start coughing up some answers pretty darned quick, or…or I'm gonna scream!"

She was nearly shaking with fear and frustration and weariness.

It wasn't every day she got mugged, nearly confronted her stalker, drove halfway across the country, discovered her brother really *had* been keeping secrets from her for years and, as a result, she'd somehow been targeted and bugged. She felt like her life had taken on the relative dimensions and kinetic energy of a tsunami, and she had nothing but her own two hands as protection against the coming onslaught. The kicker being that human palms had no hope of halting a monster wave.

It'd just slam into her without stopping to notice the insignificance of her puny body.

And now, on top of all that, she was stuck in a room with Grigg's closest friends and they seemed more intent on one-upping each other than helping her figure out just what the h-e-double-hockey-sticks was going on.

And crap!

She was on the verge of tears again.

"We are a very small shop of government defense contractors," Frank said evenly, ignoring Dan and Ozzie's continued bickering.

Say what, now? The threatening tears dried up like a desert mirage as she turned to gape at Frank.

Well…that'd been…remarkably easy.

The slightly amused tilt to Frank's storm-cloud gray eyes assured her he'd had every intention of giving her the answers to her questions from the very beginning.

Okay, so double crap. She'd indulged in a petulant outburst for no apparent reason, which was perfect. As if watching two men rifle through her underwear and being forced to hand over her dirty panties wasn't humiliation enough for one day.

"All right…" she reached behind her for the chair, mentally shifting gears and shakily retaking her seat. The rush of adrenaline drained from her body, and she suddenly felt like a wet rag, limp and lifeless. So this was it. Finally…the truth—at least more of it than Grigg had been willing to share. Oh, triple crap! Now she *really* felt like crying. "You guys are like…what?" she sniffed and refused to give in to the need for a good ol' fashioned bawl-a-thon. "*The Expendables*?"

Ozzie barked with laughter, concluding his verbal

sparring with Dan and rejoining the conversation. "I'm in love with you, woman. I swear I'll make you the best husband ever. And yeah, we're the Expendables. Just younger, better looking, with cooler bikes and *real* bullets."

All righty then. So comparisons with *The Expendables* were not appreciated. Message received. Loud and clear.

"I'm out of the loop again," Dan groused.

"Dude, of course you are," Ozzie said. "The movie is less than twenty years old—"

"So then you're...spies?" she interrupted Ozzie before he and Dan could start going at it again.

Dan rolled his eyes and blew out a disgusted breath. "What is everyone's fascination with spies? Of all our assignments, those including espionage are usually eye-crossingly dull. Lots of sitting around waiting for that perfect piece of information to land in your lap. No, thank you. Give me a rescue mission or target demolition any day."

Sheesh, she obviously wasn't making any friends by trying to categorize them. Thankfully, Frank came to her rescue.

"On occasion we do infiltrations to gather information—what you'd consider your typical espionage. Mostly, however, what we do is the stuff the U.S. government needs done but can't afford to overtly do itself."

So okay, he didn't need to spell it out for her. She'd lived with Grigg working for the Marine Corps long enough to read between the not-so-subtle lines.

"O-*kay*," she murmured, lifting her Coke toward her mouth, only to stop halfway and set it back down. "Okay," she said again, a little louder, still having trouble grasping the fact that she'd been given the answer so easily. After years of speculation and waiting for Grigg to come clean, suddenly here she was, with the truth tossed out so matter-of-factly.

Why hadn't Grigg just told her? Why hadn't he trusted her to—

No.

Those types of questions weren't going to get her anywhere. Particularly since the only person who could answer them was gone forever. She swallowed past the hurt and asked a question that *did* matter. "So what sort of assignments was Grigg working on? And what does it have to do with me?"

"Anyone?" Frank looked around the table.

"We disrupted that arms deal out of Brazil right before Grigg and Nate were slated to go to Syria," Dan offered.

"Yeah," Ozzie said, while back to rapidly typing on his keyboard, "but that was a clean job. No way anybody could've found out who was involved. It's gotta be something else."

"Ghost?" Frank asked. "Any way Grigg might've given up information that…I don't know…that could've in some way given someone the idea Ali might be in possession of something of value?"

Ali watched Nate's face harden until it was a wonder it didn't just split right open.

"Never," he ground out.

"Yeah," Dan huffed, "but you weren't actually in the room with him and, from your report, it must've been pretty fucking sick—"

Dan abruptly stopped talking, glancing up at her with a face that'd turned slightly green.

Ali was no dummy.

"What? What room weren't you in with him?" She swung her attention to Nate. Now *he* was the one who looked ready to cry and, *oh God*, she was *really* getting scared.

"Nate?" her voice broke. "Dear God, what happened?"

He flicked a cold glance toward Dan, clearly telegraphing his intention to rip off the guy's head.

This was bad. This was very, very—

Frank called her name, his deep voice firm.

Hesitating, searching Nate's hard, impassive face, she finally dragged her eyes to the man at the head of the table.

"I'm the one who should answer that," he informed her. "And it goes without saying, what I'm about to tell you can never go beyond this room. Never. Do you understand what that means?" His eyes were frighteningly intense.

If I tell you, I might have to kill you. That was a joke, wasn't it? Or maybe not.

She gulped before nodding, aware that this was the turning point.

"Don't, Boss." Nate spat.

Frank turned to him, his expression darkly resigned and fiercely uncompromising. "She deserves to know, Ghost."

Nate swore violently beneath his breath, then glued his eyes to the table.

Ali suddenly felt the need to throw up. A sick foreboding settled at the bottom of her stomach like a disease-encrusted rock.

"Nate and Grigg were on a mission to Syria." Frank began. "Before they could complete their assignment, they were captured by tangos, uh, terrorists, and tortured for three days. Nate was able to make it out. Grigg wasn't so lucky."

He stopped there. Just stopped.

She frantically searched around for a trash can. No lie, she was going to hurl.

Becky must have recognized the look on her face, because the woman jumped up and before Ali could begin to heave, a plastic-lined waste basket was shoved under her nose.

The first wretch brought up the Coke she'd been drinking. The second one was all blue slushy.

As she looked down at the regurgitated Coke and slushy covered smattering of papers and discarded Post-its, she realized, despite her less than gracious response to the news, Frank had no doubt given her the short, clean version. If tales of torture could ever be short and clean.

Holy crap.

Saliva pooled hot and acrid in her mouth, but nothing else came up. Thank goodness. As if she hadn't humiliated herself enough today, now she had to go and lose her lunch in front of these iron-willed, no doubt iron-stomached, men and women. They probably thought her a total wimp. They probably thought, *no wonder Grigg never told her the truth. She's got the backbone of a jellyfish.*

Wonderful. Just...wonderful.

And maybe they were right. Maybe Grigg hadn't trusted that she could handle the truth.

The urge to cry returned in earnest, but someone offered her a distraction when they handed her a bandana. Choking back her disgrace and horror, she wiped her lips before lowering the trash can.

Hesitantly, she returned her attention to the group and was simultaneously gratified and humbled to note there was no censure, no disappointment or disillusionment on any of their faces. In fact, most of them looked as torn-to-pieces as she felt and that just made the tears gather faster. She blinked rapidly and fervently wished for a moment of privacy. Unfortunately, privacy wouldn't help her figure out what was going on. Sticking it out, hearing the rest of the story—no matter how awful—was the only thing that would help with that.

Dragging in a trembling breath, she folded the bandana into a neat square and asked the only question there was, "Why?"

"Why were they captured and tortured?" Frank replied calmly, as if he hadn't spent the last couple of minutes watching her completely lose it.

She nodded, though part of her wanted to plug her fingers in her ears, shake her head, and sing *la-la-la*. Sometimes ignorance really was bliss, but she'd come too far to back out now. She wanted to know it all. She *needed* to know it all.

Frank dropped his reluctant gaze to his big hands, carefully folding them around his cup of coffee as he shook his head. "We don't know. Wrong place at the wrong time, as far as we can tell. The terrorists who took them weren't supposed to be operating in that region, considering Syria and Lebanon aren't exactly cozy neighbors. All our sources indicate it was happenstance. Piss poor luck. Grigg and Nate were in transit to their target when their vehicle was ambushed by Hezbollah militants."

She shivered and swung her teary gaze back to Nate. His square jaw was working hard enough to crush granite. Then she remembered. "Oh, my God, I *hit* you that day. You'd been tortured and I *hit* you. I…I'm so sorry, Nate. P-please forgive me."

She hiccupped and one mutinous tear escaped. Her chest was so tight she wondered how her heart continued to beat through the constriction. She'd hit a man, a patriot who'd sacrificed so much, who'd been recently tortured.

"Nothin' to forgive," he managed to grind out. "I'm the one who should be sorry."

Huh?

She dashed away that single tear with shaking fingers. "For what? What have you possibly got to be sorry about? It wasn't your fault you made it out and Grigg didn't."

Becky made a strange strangled sound, and Ali's eyes darted over to the young woman. She was using the frayed hem of her grease-and-paint-stained T-shirt to wipe at the fat tears running down her reddened cheeks.

What in the world was going on?

The horror on the men's faces, the anguish on the women's was about more than Grigg's death and her ill-timed venture into physical violence.

"So," Dan said softly as he put an arm around his wife, who was also fighting a flood of tears. "If it wasn't Brazil and it wasn't the capture by the Lebanese, what else could it be? Grigg hadn't been tapped for anything previous to those assignments in about two months."

He was changing the subject. Ali knew a blatant evasion when she heard it. She opened her mouth to ask just exactly what it was they weren't telling her, but Becky beat her to the punch.

"No," the young woman announced firmly, every eye in the room settling on her tear soaked face. "He did have one other mission in there. A brief, personal security job he did for some senator."

"Say what?" Ozzie turned away from the computers. "I don't remember getting any authorization for that."

"It didn't come through the usual channel. It was on his personal computer. He was only gone for one evening. Came home early in the morning. I just figured he was doing some off-the-books work."

"The hell you say," Nate barked and Ali jumped. She totally forgot about trying to ascertain what dark secrets they were still keeping from her, what chilling knowledge had caused them all such immediate anguish, when she turned to see Nate's livid expression. "He never told me anything about that."

"You were away doing that Colombian job with Mac and Christian," Becky supplied, wiping the last of her tears away with the back of her hands.

"How do you just happen to know what's in Grigg's personal correspondence, Rebecca?" Frank growled.

"Uh," Becky nervously glanced toward Ozzie. The young man's face was totally covered in oh-you've-done-it-this-time.

Frank glanced back and forth between the two. "What? What have you two been up to?"

"Okay," Becky said, chewing on the soggy stick of her last sucker. "See, the thing is, me and Ozzie have an equitable little exchange going. I teach him how to disassemble, clean, and reinstall a carburetor, and he teaches me how to code. I teach him how to fabricate an oil tank, and he teaches me how to hack."

"And that hacking includes personal email accounts?" Frank asked, his expression like a thundercloud. "Rebecca! Damnit!"

"Hey," she yelled back in defense, "I thought he might've been in trouble! We were supposed to order pizza and watch a movie that night. But after he checked his email, he suddenly said he had to bail on me. He grabbed up his go-bag and a fistful of extra magazines and made tracks like the hounds of hell were baying at his heels. I got worried, so I," she shrugged, protectively wrapping her arms around herself, "I peeked."

"You *peeked?* At *personal* files? That's *not* okay, Rebecca. Sticking your nose in the wrong place could very well get you killed one of these days. Do you understand me? Say you understand me," Frank pressed and Becky dutifully nodded her head, but then she opened her mouth. Before she got a chance to say whatever it was she was about to say, Frank angrily waved her off. "No. Absolutely not. That's the end of the discussion."

Becky snapped her mouth closed and settled back in her chair, her face a mixture of defiance and misery, and Ali couldn't help but feel a twinge of sympathy. She understood the need to keep close tabs on those she loved and knew from first-hand experience how frustrating it could be when she couldn't do that. She also knew that, like Becky, if she'd had a way to inconspicuously dig around in Grigg's business, she'd have used it and not thought twice.

Maybe it had something to do with that extra X chromosome. Something about having a uterus and set of ovaries just made a person intrinsically more curious and infinitely more nosy. Whatever it was, she did her sisterly duty and flashed Becky a brief look of alliance. Becky smiled shakily in response.

"He never mentioned the job to you?" Frank asked Nate.

"Never."

"Huh." The big man rubbed his stubbled chin, shooting one last disgusted look at Becky, before turning toward the wall of computers. "Ozzie? You mind accessing Nate's account to see just what Rebecca's talking about?"

"Already on it, Boss." Ozzie said.

Something was obviously…off about this entire scenario.

Ali's stomach—never a reliable organ—turned over again. She grabbed her Coke and took a hasty sip.

"Is it unusual for one of you to take an off-the-books assignment?" she asked, some sixth sense telling her she wasn't going to like the answer.

"*Yeah,*" Frank emphasized. She gulped more soda. "Unusual in that it's just not done. Ever. And even if we *did* agree to take on independent work, we'd never accept a job without letting at least one member of the team know about it. You know, in case backup's needed."

Crapola.

"See," Becky grumbled. "Now you know why I was so worried and why I…"

Frank flung her a look so ferocious the young woman's shoulders hitched up around her ears as she trailed off, dutifully fixing her eyes on the table in front of her.

"Huh," Ozzie interrupted, and Ali decided she was beginning to hate that word. "Simple and concise. Someone from the FBI, a Special Agent Jordan Delaney, asked Grigg to perform a private security detail for a party Senator Aldus threw for the Pakistani Ambassador to the Vatican. Dude," Ozzie groused, "there's a goddamned official for everything." Shaking his shaggy blond head, he continued. "Anyway, according to this, more specific information was supposed to be forthcoming upon Grigg's arrival in DC."

"Get Special Agent Delaney on the phone," Frank commanded. "Let's figure out just what the hell is going on here."

Ali couldn't help but wholeheartedly agree.

"Uh-oh," Ozzie murmured, and she decided that was another phrase she could do without. "No go on talking to Delaney. The man's dead."

"*Dead*?" Frank bellowed. "How? When?"

"Car crash. According to this," Ozzie indicated his glowing computer screen, "police assume he fell asleep at the wheel. His car ran off an overpass on Highway 1 and ended up in the Potomac on the..." He leaned in closer to his monitor. "Shit. The crash happened the very night—or early morning more precisely—of Grigg's supposed security detail for the senator."

Oh boy, this was *so* not good. Even Ali, naturally cock-eyed optimist that she was, didn't believe in coincidences of this magnitude.

Apparently neither did Frank.

"So Grigg takes a job for the FBI without telling any of us," he said, "and that very night his FBI contact is dead and Grigg is less than twenty-four hours away from being snatched out of the middle of the Syrian desert and tortured by a group of terrorists who were never supposed to be in that region? Something stinks."

"Yeah," Ozzie said. "And this time it isn't your socks, Dan Man."

No one was in the mood to appreciate Ozzie's attempt at levity.

"Okay," Frank slapped his wide palm on the table, taking charge. "I'm going to get on the horn to General Fuller. Let him contact those fucks...uh, 'scuse my language, ladies, at the FBI. Hopefully, he can convince their director to look into whatever this Agent Delaney was investing. "

"Dude," Dan snorted, "good luck with that. Those folks are tighter than a virgin's pu...er," he glanced sheepishly at Ali then winced when Patti slapped him on the back of the head. "Sorry," he mumbled, kissing his wife's hand and looking genuinely apologetic before returning his attention to Frank. "Let's just say they're never happy to share their secrets."

"Well, they better *get* happy or we're going to have to start rattling their fucking cages." Frank winced. "Uh, 'scuse the language again, ladies—"

"Oh for fuck's sake, Frank," Becky grumped, "we're not gonna pass out because you've got a goddamned, shitty, little sonofabitchin' potty mouth."

Ali couldn't help it, one corner of her mouth twitched.

Patti giggled behind her hand and Dan snorted.

Everyone in the room felt the release of pent-up tension, like a stretched rubber band had suddenly been turned loose. Nothing better than laughter through tears. Thank you, *Steel Magnolias*.

Frank, it seemed, was the only one who didn't find Becky's little speech entertaining. He glowered so fiercely, Ali wondered how Becky's hair didn't spontaneously combust. She had to give the young woman definite props for being able to flash the Black

Knights' boss a very convincing so-whatcha-gonna-do-about-it grin.

Ozzie piped up. "Oh, and FYI, that license plate Ali snapped a photo of belongs to a midnight blue Lincoln Navigator owned by a Mr. John Robert Godfrey. He's a sixty-five-year old middle school principal who's been working for the Wilmington School District for over twenty-two years."

"No." She was already shaking her head before he could finish. "I know the difference between black and blue. This vehicle was black, jet black. And the guy behind the wheel was closer to thirty-five than sixty-five."

"Yeah," Dan intoned. "It couldn't be that easy."

"What?" she asked.

"The first thing any professional operator would do while on a stake-out or doing reconnaissance is switch out license plates."

"Oh," her shoulders hunched. She'd been so proud of getting that picture. And it was all for nothing. "So that's that then."

"Not necessarily," Frank assured her. "We've got a couple of strings we can pull and see what unravels. Now, I know you're tired, but I need you to concentrate."

She dragged herself upright and nodded, using every bit of self-discipline she possessed to keep functioning even though her stomach ached, her sleep-deprived brain operated through a sticky film of tar, and she really, really needed a little privacy to indulge in a good cry. Not to mention the fact that all the Coke made her need to pee like a Russian racehorse.

"Did Grigg send you anything out of the ordinary? A file, a letter? Perhaps even a package?"

She chewed on her bottom lip, wracking her sluggish brain. “No,” she finally shook her head. “Nothing.”

Chapter Six

"I've had no opportunity, sir."

The impertinent tone coming through the phone made Senator Aldus's blood pressure threaten to shoot through the roof like Old Faithful.

His doctor warned him to cut his stress levels. How the hell he was supposed to do that when he was surrounded by imbeciles was anyone's guess. If he looked in the mirror right now, his face would probably be the same burgundy color as the dress his wife decided—after much hand-twisting and hem-hawing—to wear to tonight's charity ball.

His wife…

He'd married her almost twenty years ago for her political connections and bourgeois status. And he'd grown to hate her more and more each day since.

Just thinking of her made the thick vein in his forehead pulse in time to the beat of his heart.

"What the fuck do you mean you've had no opportunity? She's been there nearly twelve hours!" The plastic casing of his cellular phone crackled in warning, and he took a deep breath in order to make himself release the death-grip he had on the device before he crushed it in his hand.

"Miss Morgan hasn't left Black Knights Inc.'s premises."

"So?" Aldus couldn't help it; he once more tightened his grip on the phone and wished like hell it was the stupid shit's neck. What good did it do to hire an ex-spook when the sonofabitch couldn't do something as simple as a little snatch and grab? Obviously the CIA was losing its touch if this was the caliber of agent it was churning out nowadays.

"Pardon my saying so, sir, but you're not paying me enough to break into Black Knights Inc. It might look like nothing more than a high-tech, highly secured custom motorcycle shop from the outside, but I've studied the schematics of the place, and it's a goddamned fort. If all they're doing is building bikes in there, I'll eat my jockey shorts for dinner."

Aldus's wife poked her head into his home office, her ice-blond hair arranged to perfection, the diamond clusters he'd bought her for their tenth wedding anniversary—because he had to keep up appearances, even with the missus—glinting in her ears.

Christ! What now?

"Sweetheart," she said in her nasally, upper-crust Boston accent. It screeched down his spine like fingernails on a chalkboard. "Hurry or we're going to be late."

"Just another minute, dear." He pasted on a smile when he really wanted to throw his lead paperweight at her pretty, insipid face. Just thinking of the snap of those delicate bones and the bright burst of blood had his inauthentic smile turning genuine.

She nodded regally and backed out of his office. He listened until he heard the delicate click of her Prada slingback pumps echoing down the tiled hallway before he hissed into the phone, "I don't give a fuck how you do it. Find a way to grab her. And do it now. Tonight. I want those missing files on my desk by tomorrow morning."

He punched the end button on the cell phone so hard he chipped the manicure he'd received just this morning.

Fuck!

What am I doing here?

It was the second time in less than twenty-four hours Ali had the thought. Only *here* happened to be Red Delilah's.

Not necessarily a quintessential biker bar name, but this was certainly a quintessential biker bar. Peanuts littered the floor, Metallica blasted from the jukebox but still couldn't drown out the loud continuous click of a cue ball making contact with its target at the felt-covered table in the back, and the musty smell of spilled draft beer and old cigarette smoke lingered in the air.

Yes, this was certainly a quintessential biker bar. One that just happened to be run by *the* most intimidating, stereotypical, '50s pin-up girl on the planet.

As if her day could've gotten any worse.

But wait. It had. Because she was here. In this god-awful place, wearing these god-awful clothes, finishing up her last bite of this...well, in truth the dinner was far from god-awful.

She'd woken up from her nap—if you could call eight hours of near comatose sleep after a good solid hour of crying herself sick, something as simple as a nap—totally ravenous.

Becky'd spotted her as she'd stumbled down the stairs, rubbing the sleep from her eyes. Without preamble or prudence, Becky demanded, "Get changed. We're all headed over to Delilah's. We'll order dogs from the joint next door."

Uh, what? "Dogs?"

"Yeah," Becky eyed her with a sly grin. "You *have* had a traditional Chicago-style hotdog before, haven't you?"

"Ugh. Processed mystery meat. No thanks," she said, even though her stomach was busy gnawing a hole through to her backbone. She'd take a pass.

"Oh!" Becky grabbed her chest as if shot. "Bite your tongue." She hooked a friendly arm around Ali's shoulders and herded her back upstairs. "A traditional Chicago hotdog is an all-beef frankfurter with a boat load of toppings. We say it's a dog that's been dragged through the garden. You'll love it. I promise."

Ali had her doubts, but they were totally assuaged as she licked the last bit of celery salt from her fingers. No joke, there was only one word to describe the concoction she'd just wolfed down. Delicious.

Her outfit was another matter entirely. She warily glanced down at her bare midriff for about the thousandth time.

If the faculty and students of Ridgeline Elementary could see her now…

They'd probably run screaming in the other direction. Sheesh.

A ragged AC/DC tank top that did humiliatingly little to hide the lacy straps of her red bra combined with a skintight pair of Becky's low-riding Guess jeans—which had more holes than material—to have her tugging once more at the cropped hem of her shirt in a vain attempt to conceal her belly button ring. Obviously Becky approved of that little item of jewelry because it was the one thing of her own the woman allowed her keep.

Pfft. Really, *Ali* was the one who needed advice on fashion?

Glancing around at the other patrons, she scowled. No. Absolutely not. Not unless it was fashionable for a guy who closely resembled Santa Claus to squeeze himself into leather pants and a holey white T-shirt with a slogan that read FREE MUSTACHE RIDES.

Ugh. Her hotdog started to reverse direction at the thought as the constant rumble of motorcycles coming and going echoed through the building over the sound of the jukebox. A group of businessmen, whom Becky described as "weekend warriors," looked completely out of place in the rough-and-tumble joint, especially since they were bellied up to the bar beside a handful of burly looking guys wearing leather jackets with patches depicting a fearsome-looking angel holding a cigar in one hand and a handgun in the other and the words DARK ANGELS stitched across the top.

This place was surreal. Scratch that. Ever since Grigg's death, her entire *life* was surreal.

And it didn't lessen her foul mood in the slightest when the sky-high, red patent leather pumps that'd been foisted on her began killing her toes, even while sitting down.

How was that even possible?

Obviously the shoes were designed by some sadistic man who liked to cripple women…probably so they'd be unable to scamper away while he tried to give them free mustache rides.

"Stop fidgeting. You look great," Becky assured her

while absently scanning the bar. Patti had gone to use the ladies' room, and the men of Black Knights Inc. were huddled around the jukebox in the corner, presumably to pick out more music.

Anything besides Metallica would work, Ali thought.

Or not.

Pantera started screaming from the speakers, and she supposed next time she needed to be more specific when asking for small miracles.

Funny how the Knights were supposed to be plugging in new tunes, but not one of them was digging in his jeans for change. Neither were any of them actually *looking* at the jukebox.

They must consider her to be a real moron if they thought they were fooling her for a second.

They weren't over there for the music. Oh no. They were over there discussing what options they had concerning her "situation."

Over dinner, Frank told her General Fuller was unable to contact the director of the FBI. The Director was supposedly in closed-door meetings all day and wouldn't be able to return Frank's inquiry into what Agent Delaney was investigating until tomorrow.

Frank tried to give Ali the impression he intended to leave it at that, at least for the night. But one look at his frustrated expression and she quickly surmised he wasn't the kind of man to simply wait around for answers to fall in his lap.

"I feel like a fool," she groused as she toed out of Becky's ridiculous shoes.

Becky shot her a sharp look. "What? You look fantastic. Very mysterious. Smoldering. So stop fidgeting."

Ali snorted.

"You do," Becky insisted. "Didn't you see the look on Ghost's face when you stepped into the shop?"

Yes, she saw it. And again she thought perhaps something hot flashed behind his eyes. But then when they'd all fired up the engines on their Harleys—which was a sound and sensation Ali would never forget for the rest of her natural life—she moved to hop up behind Nate, but he waved her off with a muttered, "You're ridin' with Ozzie."

Okay, she thought. *I don't even* know *Ozzie but... whatever*.

She supposed she really shouldn't have been so surprised. Nate always went out of his way to avoid touching her. Not everyone. Just her.

"Stop pulling at that shirt," Becky demanded now, giving her the evil eye. Not hard to do with a quarter inch of jet black eyeliner smeared around her lids. Alice Cooper was somewhere applauding and biting the head off a chicken. "You're going to stretch it out and then I'll have to trim the hem again."

Trim the hem? If Becky trimmed the hem any more, it'd be nothing but a cotton collar attached to a couple of arm holes.

"I should've just worn my own clothes," Ali sighed in resignation as it became apparent no amount of maneuvering would lengthen the hem of the tank top.

"Yeah, 'cause a pink, sparkly bebe T-shirt would've fit in so well here," Becky stated dryly.

Okay, the woman had a point.

Red Delilah's sported more leather than a herd of Texas cattle. All black, all shot through with silver studded detailing. All very intimidating—and that was before one started to read the T-shirt slogans.

And then there was Delilah. The bar's proprietress.

She made the patrons look shockingly under-leathered. Ali couldn't begin to guess the woman's age. She had a sort of timeless quality about her. Like an old film star. And like those old film stars, her figure would make an hourglass weep with envy. Of course, it helped when all those curves were on display beneath a black leather cat-suit whose top must've come from a Victoria's Cleavage catalog.

Sometimes God giveth and then he just keeps on giveth-ing.

Ali glanced in the woman's direction as she sashayed—there was really no other way to describe the dramatic sway of those dangerous, leather-clad hips—out from behind the bar and over to the group of men by the jukebox.

If the Knights were dogs, they'd be panting.

She decided right then she didn't particularly like Delilah—if that was really the woman's name. Not because she was gorgeous. No, no. Ali objected to her existence because she managed to do the impossible.

Looping long arms around Nate's neck, Delilah kissed him full on the mouth and leaned in to whisper something in his ear.

That's when it happened. The impossible, that is.

Because that's when Nathan Weller, former sergeant of the Marine Corps, current government defense contractor, and all-time Ice Man—as in cold as ice, heart like ice—laughed.

And not your regular ol' tehehe-that-was-funny laugh.

Oh, no.

A big booming roar rose above the pounding rock 'n' roll. His whole body was overcome by it. His head thrown back, thick throat working, big shoulders shaking.

It was the most amazingly...*bizarre* thing Ali'd ever seen.

Which was saying something given the clientele inside Red Delilah's.

And for some reason she absolutely refused to think about, it...well...it rankled. She'd known the man for twelve years, and she'd never seen him laugh like that, which just proved she didn't really know him at all. Case in point: she'd always considered him to be a little limited in the vocabulary department and then he goes and whips out a word like autoschediastic. What in the h-e-double-hockey-sticks did autoschediastic mean?

It was disconcerting to think she could've been so wrong about—

"Got room for one more?" a deep, scratchy voice ripped her attention away from the couple by the jukebox.

Oh, good heavens.

She wasn't sure if the guy who slid into the booth across from her and Becky was a welcome distraction or not. He had more hair than a mountain man and a belly that looked entirely capable of holding a whole keg of beer.

He winked at her and flashed his gold-toothed smile.

Really, no joke.

Like, all his front teeth were sparkly, solid gold.

Cripes. At least his shirt had no slogan. She supposed that was a saving grace...and would you look at how her standards had dropped since entering Red Delilah's?

The guy had chewing tobacco stains in his beard, and she was ready to give him intelligence points simply because he'd chosen to leave the personal advertisements at home.

Wow, the day had truly reached a new low.

"Buzz off, Buzzard," Becky made a shooing motion with her hands. "No one's interested."

"Now Rebel, darlin'. Let the lady speak for herself." Again the man…Buzzard? Really? fixed his troublingly licentious gaze on Ali. "Come home with me tonight, darlin'. I'll give you a ride so good you'll never hanker for the seat of a Harley again."

Jesus, Mary, and Jos—

"*Whatever!*" Becky rolled her eyes. "Shirley told me your thing's as crooked as those insurance scams you tried to get us all to invest in."

"But crooked in the right direction." Buzzard winked again, not in the least bit concerned to discover there were women sharing his bedroom secrets, nor was he denying the fact that he was involved in criminal activity. He leaned forward and his breath smelled like cheep beer and strong cigars. "Gotta a little upward tilt to it that hits *just* the right spot."

Oh God.

What was she doing here?

Scotch.

That's what he needed. A nice single-malt. Lagavulin if he had his choice. And while he was taking his little trip through fantasyland, he might as well throw in a quick slap and tickle with that brunette in the corner.

The one who'd tossed him a couple of shy smiles. The one whose leather skirt and V-neck Motley Crüe T-shirt were doing a fairly fantastic job of enhancing what were already quite a few blessings from God.

Right. Like either of those were even a slight possibility.

Not that ex-CIA agent Dagan Zoelner didn't think he had the sexual chops to seduce the brunette. He figured he could have her naked and sweaty in no time at all. A few compliments, some sensual music, a nice glass of wine...

Which just served to remind him of the scotch that was also *so* not gonna happen. Two things he didn't mix on a job: booze and women. And wasn't that just a crying shame?

Damn! The day had gone from bad to worse.

Because he was no longer sure he was working for the "good guys."

Well...to be completely truthful, he'd been having doubts for weeks, ever since Aldus instructed him to snatch Alisa Morgan and bring her in.

Dagan was confident that there wasn't cause for such drastic measures.

After following the woman around for nearly three months, after monitoring her every move and all her correspondence, he'd come to the conclusion she was just what she appeared to be—a kindergarten teacher who led a normal, if somewhat dull, life. She was less likely to be involved in a scheme to sell government secrets to the highest bidder than he was likely to be involved in an abstinence lecture.

"Can I getcha something else?" the middle-aged cocktail waitress asked as she sidled up to his table, her stick-thin legs protruding from the top of a pair of loose, calf-high boots until it looked like she was standing in buckets. From the weary lines around her eyes and lips and the way she unconsciously wielded a tray full of drinks, Dagan could tell the woman had been slinging beer for a couple of decades.

He glanced down at his tonic water before smiling up at her. That had its usual effect. The woman's eyes widened and the wrinkles around her mouth softened as she grinned in response. "Thanks," he told her, "but I'm fine for now."

"Okay, sugar," she purred, laying a thin hand, tipped with long, pink, fiberglass nails, on his shoulder. "But when you change your mind, my name's Shirley. Just holler."

"I sure will." Dagan winked at her, and she giggled like a woman half her age before turning to deliver the contents of her tray to a group of rambunctious college kids at the back of the bar.

Dagan took a sip of tonic and glanced at the booth where Alisa Morgan was sitting.

He'd convinced Aldus to let him handle the situation. As opposed to the senator's plan to kidnap her, he'd contemplated seducing the woman. He'd figured he could oh-so-innocently inquire about the missing files while she was hot and heavy. In his experience, a little pillow talk went a long way. But she was just so damned...*sweet*, and in the last three months she hadn't had any men in her life, which proved she wasn't the type to casually hop into bed with a handsome stranger. So even if he could somehow seduce her—okay, he knew he could—the question quickly became: did he want to? Did he want that on his conscience?

No. He most certainly did not.

Changing tactics, he'd been in the process of devising a way to casually bump into her, to befriend her and then…she'd been mugged.

He was pretty sure Aldus was behind the attack on Alisa Morgan despite the senator's protestations of innocence. And that just didn't sit well with him…at all.

He was absolutely convinced that, whether or not Ms. Morgan had the files, she was an innocent pawn simply caught in the middle of…whatever the hell this was turning out to be.

He hadn't been too surprised when she'd taken off after the mugging. Nor had he been surprised when she'd stopped at her dead brother's former place of employment. After all, what could make a woman feel safer than to surround herself with a bunch of ex-spec ops types?

Oh, he knew all about Grigg Morgan and his friends and their custom motorcycle shop. At least he thought he did…

One look at the blueprints of the compound that was Black Knights Inc. had convinced him he didn't know dick.

Earlier this afternoon, when Dagan tried his contact within the CIA—he still had one even after that horrible little incident in Iraq, saints be praised—in order to get more information, he'd run into the proverbial brick wall. Which fell directly into the downright spooky category, because the CIA was supposed to know *everything*.

Well, it appeared *they* didn't know dick about the guys at Black Knights Inc. According to his source, the

Knights were just what they seemed. A group of ex-military men who'd traded in their knives and guns for wrenches and grinders.

Um. No.

The whole motorcycle thing was only their cover. Anyone with any sort of military training could tell you those bad boys absolutely reeked of government affiliation.

Which meant that Grigg Morgan had been affiliated with the government. And that didn't lend much credence to Senator Aldus's claim that Morgan had become tired of living on a grease monkey's salary, had taken the skills he'd learned from Uncle, and employed them in order to steal highly classified and potentially threatening government documents. According to Aldus, Morgan had planned to sell those documents on the black market.

Sure. And Dagan was the bloomin' tooth fairy.

He was beginning to suspect the good senator was completely full of shit. Which meant the intelligent thing to do would be to quit this sketchier-by-the-minute job, haul ass back to DC, and forget he ever heard the name Senator Alan Aldus.

But something held him in his seat in the corner table, deep in the dusky shadows of Red Delilah's. And it wasn't the brunette who'd become disheartened with his lack of follow-through and decided to take her gin and tonic and her very nice ass—*Sweet Lord! It's heart-shaped!*—into the next room.

He almost groaned at the lost opportunity, but he didn't give chase as his always-intrepid cock begged him to do.

Because like it or not—which he most certainly did

not—he'd allowed himself to be dropped center-stage in the middle of what was promising to turn into a shit-storm of near epic proportions.

So he'd do what he did best.

Watch. And wait.

And then former sergeant Nathan Weller turned dead black eyes on him and Dagan's entire plan for the evening did a one-eighty.

His CIA contacts *had* been able to give him the military files on the employees of Black Knights Inc., and despite all the black ink hiding about fifty percent of what the documents held, the damned things *still* read like a catalog of Great American Heroes.

Shit! It was a rare thing when an ex-spook was genuinely rattled.

But there you had it. He'd spent the entirety of his adult life weighing the risks, playing the odds, and right now, looking into Ghost's eyes, he suspected both were stacked up against him.

Like any smart man, Dagan Zoelner knew when to cut his losses and get the hell out of Dodge.

Chapter Seven

"I COULD BE WRONG, BUT I'M THINKIN' ALI AND GHOST are sittin' in a tree," Ozzie whispered in Nate's ear as Delilah returned to her position behind the bar. Nate snatched a surreptitious glance back at the table where the ladies sat.

"D'you have a death wish?" he asked the kid in all earnestness, even though he was only giving Ozzie about half of his attention because Buzzard—that dick—was reaching across the table to grab Ali's hand.

"K-I-S-S-I-N-G." Ozzie singsonged. "I'm right, aren't I? You *like* her." He didn't wait for Nate's reply before he announced gleefully to the others, "Nate 'Ghost' Weller, aka Mr. Emotionless, has *feelings*."

Sweet. Christ.

What *was* it with everyone today? First Delilah and now Ozzie. Did he have some sort of flashing neon sign on his forehead?

"Y'better get away from me," he advised Ozzie, skating another quick glance toward the booth. Now Buzzard—that dick—was levered halfway across the tabletop, whispering in Ali's ear, and the woman was just crazy enough to laugh at whatever the licentious old fart was saying.

"But dude, that's so sweet, so roman—"

Nate grabbed the kid's arm none-too-gently and jerked him into the corner behind the jukebox. Boss lifted a brow at the two of them but continued his conversation with Dan.

"—tic," Ozzie finished, rubbing his upper arm where Nate'd manacled him. "Easy on the goods, man. The ladies love these guns." The kid flexed his biceps and bent his head to give each of his "guns" a kiss.

"I don't know what you think," Nate growled, "but there's nothin' doing between me and Ali. She's just the little sister of my best friend. End of story."

He really, really wished that was the end of the story.

"But her voice is so happy, so sunny," Ozzie reminded Nate of the one rather humiliating moment of his day. Was he...? Yep, the kid actually had the audacity to flutter his eyelashes and make exaggerated googly-eyes.

Death wish. There was just no other answer.

He stared at the kid, hoping Ozzie would realize how close he was to getting plugged.

He didn't.

"I think you should ask her out," Ozzie declared, wiggling his brows.

"I don't give a rat's ass what you think I should—"

He stopped right there because the hairs at the back of his neck suddenly twitched with life. Carefully setting his beer atop the jukebox, he scanned the bar.

There. In the far corner. He allowed his vision to adjust to the shadows, and his eyes clashed with a cold, gray stare.

Uh-huh. He experienced a moment of...well, not recognition, because he'd never seen the man before. But it was certainly an instance of like-meeting-like.

Ol' Mystery Man in the Corner was an operator, for

what or for whom he couldn't begin to guess. But the guy was an operator. He had a certain deadness about the eyes that said he'd been stripped of all his idealism and left with only one thing: the mission.

Lifting his chin in a gesture that succinctly conveyed *come on over and introduce yourself,* pendejo, Nate was momentarily stunned when Mystery Man simply slipped a hand into his jacket pocket and shook his head. Once. One quick jerk of the chin from left to right.

Just Nate's luck. A man with balls bigger than brains. Did the guy really think he could get out of the bar?

Not likely.

Not with four of the Black Knights in residence.

"What?" Ozzie asked, instantly alert. The kid may be a nuisance of legendary status, but he was as much a warrior as any of them. He instinctively knew when the customary shit was about to hit the proverbial fan.

"Guy in the corner," Nate said. "He's gonna try'n' make a break for it. We're not gonna let 'im."

Ozzie turned just in time to see Mystery Man slowly lift himself from his shadowy seat. Upon standing, Mr. Mystery faced the trio in the booth. Ali, Becky, and Buzzard—that dick—were completely unaware of the little war of calculated movements and cold, intense eye contact that was waging around them, which was just as well. Then Nate noticed the unmistakable hollow outline pressing into the fabric of the front pocket of the guy's jacket, and his head nearly exploded. That distinct circle was pointing straight at Ali.

The fucker dared?

Rage poured through him, hot as iron through a smelting furnace, but there was nothing for him to do about it. One wrong move and Ali could take a bullet. And that just wasn't going to happen.

Not on his watch.

Not ever.

He stood stock-still and silently seethed. Had anyone been paying attention, he felt sure they'd see him pulling a teapot routine, steam pouring from his nostrils and ears.

The instant Mystery Man slid out the back door, both he and Ozzie bolted, grabbing for weapons as they went. The cold steel of his 13RTK Recon Tanto blade felt truly satisfying as he palmed it with one hand while reaching into his waistband for his .45 with the other. Just in case that wasn't enough, he had two extra seven-round clips in his jacket pockets.

He just never felt quite dressed without enough firepower to start a small war, which probably said something rather unpleasant about his psyche, but who cared?

Not him.

He could hear the heavy footfalls of Dan and Boss behind them as both men sprang into action. Years of instinctual readiness made them react in less than a split second.

He smiled at the taletell *shnick* of Dan chambering a round into his baby—the Ruger P90 he'd inherited from his father.

The Knights liked to tease Dan about spending more time caressing that gun than he did his wife.

My wife isn't likely to have to save my life anytime soon, was Dan's stock reply.

Well Nate, for once, was mighty glad to know the little .45 was in good working order. Because they were likely going to have to shoot someone.

Mystery Man had had the extremely bad sense to point a gun at Ali. Chances were fairly good—unless he had one hell of an explanation—the dude wasn't going to walk away from the encounter without a couple of extra holes in him.

The four of them burst through the back door into the alley. The overflowing dumpster across the way had gone from ripe to emanating what Nate could only assume must be poisonous fumes, but Mystery Man was nowhere in sight.

Damnit!

With a hand signal, he motioned for Boss and Dan to head left while he and Ozzie searched right.

Geez. This whole thing with Ali was steeped in un-fucking-believable. To recap, she'd been mugged, bugged, and threatened with a bullet. And all of that in less than thirty-six hours.

Grigg, my brother, what the hell did you get us all involved in?

"The part of hovercraft doesn't suit you, Frank," Becky snarled as she tried to keep up with Ozzie and the program they were simultaneously trying to hack. "Breathing down my neck doesn't make this process go any faster, it just makes me nervous."

So back the hell off, you big, dumb, blind, exasperating oaf! She couldn't say that last part. Not if she valued her job—which she did. Unfortunately. There was something about eating three times a day that appealed to her. Then, of course, there was her lollipop habit. Not cheap.

"Didn't you tell me just this morning that you were

learning all of this in order to take on a more lucrative position within our organization? Well, stress comes with the job, Rebecca. Get used to it."

Rebecca, Rebecca, Rebecca. Grrreat. God, he made her want to get a name change.

And yes, she'd told him this morning after she'd confessed how she'd broken into Grigg's personal email account that she was learning these rather, er, dubious computer skills from Ozzie in order to better serve the team. Frank'd been ape-shit pissed enough about that little revelation, she figured it was probably prudent he not know Ghost was teaching her to shoot, Billy was giving her private lessons on explosives, and Steady was schooling her on rudimentary field medicine.

Yepper. It was best to just keep all that to herself. Ease him into the idea of her joining the team, really joining the team, a little at a time.

But first, she had to handle him looming over her, casting that monster shadow with his unbelievably wide shoulders, heating her back with the insidious warmth of his hard thighs, smelling like hot leather and cold beer and…Frank—which she could totally do. Yessiree, she could handle it. No problem.

Her fingers typed in the wrong command, and she cursed.

"I'm in," Ozzie announced, and she threw her hands in the air.

In consolation, she unwrapped a grape Dum Dum and angrily plugged it into her frowning mouth. She nearly cracked a tooth, but seconds later the explosion of sugary flavor helped her focus on the task at hand instead of Frank's distracting nearness.

Oh, and the teensy tiny minor fact that he was a total dill-hole where she was concerned.

Exiting her machine, she rolled her chair toward Ozzie's monitor and watched code zip across the screen. They were plugged into the City of Chicago's surveillance system. Not a totally difficult hack job, but the resident computer virtuoso had beaten her again.

Whatever.

She'd continue to practice. At everything.

Because maybe then Frank would take her seriously, instead of viewing her as the necessary nuisance that kept all their covers intact. Maybe then he'd see her as a grown woman instead of the grease-covered, lollipop-sucking little sister of one of his men. Maybe then—

"Now we just need to upload the partial picture we got of Mystery Man from Delilah's security camera into my program and compare it to possible matches in the city's system. If we can get a better picture of the guy's face, we can run it through the facial recognition software and determine just who in the world we're dealing with," Ozzie explained while his fingers continued to blur above the keyboard.

"Did you get a chance to see this guy?" Dan asked Ali. "Is he the one following you?"

Ali leaned in closer to the upper right hand corner of Ozzie's monitor where the grainy photo of Mystery Man flickered rapidly as it was compared to the city's surveillance footage.

"Looks like him," she murmured, concentrating on the picture. "The hair's right. The build's right. He's certainly not my mugger. That guy was huge. More the size of Frank, but..." she frowned at the photo, "I can't positively tell if that's my elusive shadow or not," she finished with frustration.

Yes well, they were all frustrated. But the fact that the guy had simply disappeared after supposedly pointing a gun at Ali's head wasn't what was putting a hard kink in Becky's mood.

Nope. Her kink had everything to do with a certain man whose *nom de guerre* was Boss.

Why did he have to be such a hardass? Why couldn't he just admit—

Suddenly the flickering stopped, and two photos appeared side-by-side on Ozzie's computer screen.

"Damn, the boy's good," Dan whistled when the two snapshots pulled from the city's site revealed less than the one taken from Delilah's. They were clearly of the same man, but in both photos the guy's face was averted. "Seems to know just where the cameras are and is careful to avoid them."

"Told ya," Ghost muttered. "The guy had spook written all over 'im."

"CIA?" Frank asked, thankfully turning away and taking his heat, smell, and omnipresence with him. She could finally draw in a full breath.

"If I had t' hazard a guess," Ghost replied.

She noticed how Ali's eyes widened at that particularly disturbing news and wondered if the woman consciously realized she'd just taken a step closer to Ghost, or if Ghost realized he'd unhesitatingly placed a reassuring hand on her shoulder.

Those two are fighting a losing battle, she thought. *They should just do it already and get it over with*.

Yeah, right. Who was she trying to kid? Like she had

any expertise when it came to the vagaries of romance, considering the only things keeping her warm at night were flannel sheets and Mr. Blue.

She was *such* a loser. Here she was, twenty-five years old, not too sore on the ol' eyes—at least that's what most of her friends of the male persuasion assured her—and all her action came from a seven-inch piece of sculpted bright blue rubber that required D batteries.

"Fuck!" Frank raked a hand through his hair and winced when he realized he'd let his potty mouth run away with him again in front of the ladies. She wondered if he was careful to act like a gentleman when he headed up north.

Oh yes, Becky knew all about his visits to Lincoln Park. She just didn't know who he was visiting. And short of following him—she still had *some* pride left where he was concerned, thank God—she'd exhausted all other avenues of discovering who his secret trysting partner, or partners, ugh, were.

"First, it's the FBI; now maybe we can add the lovely CIA to this unholy alphabet soup mix," Frank growled. Shaking his head, he glanced at his timepiece. "It's oh-one-hundred. Let's hit our racks for the night. Maybe tomorrow will shed some light on this…this," he shook his head again, "whatever the hell this is."

Yeah, and maybe tomorrow Becky would finally get up the nerve to tell him how she really felt.

And also maybe tomorrow pigs would fly.

Ali couldn't sleep.

It had nothing to do with her eight-hour nap or her

strange surroundings, because even though the guest loft at Black Knights Inc. was more the size of a hotel room, just big enough for a little kitchenette and a white-tiled bathroom with a shower stall—at least Grigg had been telling her the truth about *something*—it was still beautifully appointed and completely welcoming.

The warm brick walls added texture and ambiance to the silver ductwork and exposed pipes overhead. Whoever did the murals out in the shop had obviously put their hand to different work, evidenced by the abstract diptych painting above the bed. The technique was totally different, but the barrage of color was unmistakably signature. It tied in beautifully with the turquoise-and-green coverlet on the bed and the area rug partially covering the lacquered, original-wood flooring.

So the room and the to-die-for feather mattress weren't the problem. Neither was her insomnia due to Peanut curling his substantial self against her side with his motor running full tilt.

Well…maybe that had a little bit to do with it. It was sort of like lying next to a jet engine.

But no, her real problem? She was scared.

She thought she was scared when she hopped in her car back in North Carolina with the intent to make it to Chicago without stopping to sleep. Now, she understood she'd only been spooked. Because at the time she'd expected to show up here, present her problem, pass it off to Nate, let him handle it, and head back home after maybe a minor excursion to the shops on the Magnificent Mile.

Oh ho! Boy, had she been naïve. Not only did that *not* happen, but she also learned she was bugged, her brother had gone off the reservation, his FBI contact was dead, and she was likely being followed and threatened at gunpoint by the CIA.

Now she was well and truly scared.

Whose life was she living?

Not hers, that's for sure. Things like this didn't happen to kindergarten teachers. Unless of course those kindergarten teachers had older brothers specializing in covert operations for the government. Which, unfortunately for her, she did.

Dang it, Grigg! What in the world were you thinking getting me involved in this?

As soon as she had the thought, she felt disloyal. Grigg would never knowingly put her in danger. There was something else going on here, something niggling at the back of her mind like a worm. But when she tried to focus on it, it just slipped farther and farther into the dark depths of her subconscious.

Okay, so it was time to think of something else. That's what her mom always advised when her belabored brain was flitting around an answer like a butterfly flits around a flower.

Taking a deep breath, she cleared her head. And what do you know? The first thing that leapt to mind was that wonderfully horrible day on the beach with Nate. The way the hot sun had warmed her bare shoulders. The way the cool waves had crashed to shore with foam and fury. The way the seagulls had cried in seeming sympathy with the breaking of her heart. And the way Nate had instinctively understood the strange longing inside her. The unlikely need to reaffirm beautiful, vibrant life after facing the dark specter of death.

Oh, yes, it wasn't a new story or a novel reaction to loss. Probably as old as time. The cavemen no doubt mounted their mates in heated urgency after one of the clan passed on to that great unknown. But the commonness of her reaction hadn't registered at the time.

She'd been dying inside and she'd needed...something. Something real and raw. Something to keep her from falling into an abyss of black sorrow so deep she'd never return.

And somehow Nate had known. He'd understood. Dark, scowling, brooding Nathan Weller had seen inside her, past all the pain and despair. He'd given her a rare and wonderful gift that day.

Tender.

That's what he'd been when she'd pulled her desperate mouth from his surprised one to whisper recklessly, "Make love to me."

She remembered now how his Adam's apple bobbed as he searched her face as only he could. With that savage alertness, that probing intensity. Black eyes searing into her very soul. He'd reclaimed her mouth in a kiss that still brought flaming heat to her cheeks.

It was passionate, but, oh so carefully and tenderly thorough. He'd made love to her mouth. There was just no other way to describe it. Possessive, fierce, compassionate love. And when his big hand with its warrior's collection of calluses and scars softly cupped her left breast, she'd sighed. With a gentle pass of one large thumb, he'd brought her nipple to aching attention.

The result had been instantaneous.

Instantaneous lust.

Cripes.

She shivered now. The memory making her squirm until Peanut raised his scarred, furry face and slanted her a disgruntled look.

"There are other beds you could be sleeping in, you know," she told him.

His response was to lift one hind leg behind his head and begin meticulously cleaning his balls.

"Well, that's a succinct answer if ever there was one," she grumbled, flopping onto her back and throwing one arm over her eyes.

She'd tried, oh, *lordy*, how she'd tried over the past three months to forget about that day. To forget the expertise of his mouth and hands. To forget the way she'd responded, with such abandon, giving herself over to him.

And for the most part, during the daylight hours, she was successful.

The nights were another matter.

At night, she couldn't push the memories away. Often awoke with her fingers between her legs trying to ease the ache her dreams built. And now, lying in bed with Nate only two doors down, her usual powers over the past were lost, and it all played out again. Her mind's eye supplying vivid, graphic detail.

Hot.

His broad palm had been so hot when he'd brushed it along her cool thigh, under the short skirt she'd been wearing, never hesitating as he pushed aside the lace and elastic of her thong. His rough thumb had been unerring when it landed on the hot knot of nerves at the top of her sex to circle slowly.

Big.

His calloused fingers had been so big when he'd gently pressed one, and then another, inside her.

What had followed was more a visceral recollection than an actual memory. Because her brain had ceased to work at that point. She'd become strictly physical. A thing of liquid bones and racing blood. An entity made solely of desire, of *want*.

Her mouth remembered the taste of him as his tongue plunged and retreated. Her breasts tingled with the memory of his broad chest and the friction he'd created while moving against her. Her fingers itched in recollection of the tense and release of the lean tendons and heavy muscles of his forearm, the one that'd been angled down between their bodies.

At the time, she didn't know when she grabbed him whether she wanted it to stop or go on forever, so she simply clung.

She remembered the explosion of her release, of screaming his name and then crumpling into a boneless heap in his arms. And she remembered her astonishment when he simply held her for long moments, murmuring nonsensically and rubbing his hand up and down her back before bundling her up and carrying her back to the Jeep.

She shivered again, and Peanut stopped licking himself just long enough to direct an annoyed *mrrreow* directly toward her face before returning to his mission of impeccable nuts.

"You keep that up and you won't have any hair left," she advised him before throwing back the covers and padding to the bathroom. She looked at herself in the mirror over the pedestal sink and grimaced.

Crapola.

She wanted Nate Weller.

There was no more denying it.

At a distance of a thousand miles, it was easy to blame her behavior that day three months ago on soul-tearing grief. But being here and seeing him? It made it impossible to continue to deceive herself.

That itchy feeling, the tightening of her scalp whenever he came within ten feet of her, her inability to stop jabbering like one of her kindergarteners? They were all the result of her impossible physical reaction to him.

And that *something* about him that always irritated her to no end? Well, *that* was simply the hurt and frustration she felt knowing he didn't suffer any similar difficulties.

She'd been a fool not to understand it before, or maybe she'd just been afraid. Afraid of everything he made her feel. Afraid of everything he made her want. Afraid of…rejection.

Double crapola.

She huffed out a breath and splashed her hot face with tepid water. It was all too much. Too complicated.

Turning off the tap, she patted her face dry with a fluffy turquoise towel. She was never going to get any sleep tonight, so she might as well head downstairs and see if anyone else was up. Maybe Becky was in the mood to share a glass of wine—a *big* glass of wine—and commiserate with her about the unceasing frustrations of men.

Tying the satin belt of her robe, she peeked out into the quiet hallway. All the lights were off, including the ones downstairs. A faint glow of yellow pooled below only one door.

Nate's.

Wouldn't it figure?

The one person she *didn't* want to share of glass of wine with, especially a *big* glass of wine. Sufficiently lubricated, she didn't trust herself not to attack him, tie him to the bed, and sit on his face.

Of course, there *was* something she'd like for him to clear up…

Chapter Eight

"C'min," Nate murmured, looking up from the screen of his laptop where Ozzie had dumped—er, the kid preferred the term *transferred*—all Grigg's email correspondence from the last three years. He'd volunteered for the onerous task of finding out just how often his partner, his best friend, his sole confidant, had flat out lied to him and rest of the team and done jobs for the FBI.

As if that wasn't enough to put the shit-icing on top of this crap cake of a day, now Boss was back at his door.

What more could the man possibly have to ask him?

After everyone had gone to bed, the two of them hashed out, or should he say *re*hashed out, every sickening, macabre detail Nate could remember from his oh-so-happy time in Syria in order to see if maybe there was some connection between that and what was happening now.

Oh boy, and hadn't that been a real barrel of monkeys?

Because even after months had passed and he'd told the story enough times to recite it verbatim, he couldn't stop the flash of memory that suddenly stabbed in front of his grainy eyes anytime he let his mind travel down that path. That's all it took, just the mere thought of it, and instantly he was back there, back in that dingy little house out in the middle of bumfuck Syria.

The guards, a group of three guys too cruel to be

called men and too inventive in their cruelty to be called animals, had gone somewhere to get drunk—as per their usual schedule—and he'd finally managed to chew through the cheap ropes binding his hands. Getting through the door had taken some ingenuity and more than a little brute force, but he'd eventually managed, and it'd only cost him three broken ribs.

He'd been dizzy with pain and hunger while dragging himself across the hallway, finally succeeding in accessing the room next door.

He saw it all so well, in stark, Blu-ray definition.

Grigg, lying on that rough table. Blood everywhere. Too much blood. And viscera. And that smell…*Sweet Christ*, he'd instantly recognized that smell. It was the scent of a dead man who didn't yet know he was dead.

"Nate?"

The sight of Ali standing in his open doorway instantly snapped him back to the present.

Thank God.

Too much more of that and he'd have to go see that shrink Boss kept harping about. Although, if he was really honest with himself, he probably *should* go. Back when he'd been with the Marines, he'd known a lot of guys who'd been forced by their commanding officers to go through some form of therapy. And even though most of them had gone in kicking and screaming, they'd come out the other side more balanced, more accepting of the horrors of war. So yeah, it could be a good thing, but the thought of telling a perfect stranger what he'd done made him break out in a cold sweat.

Wiping a clammy hand across his forehead, he vaulted from his chair to pad barefoot across the small room. Once he got to the door, he realized he'd just left behind his worst nightmare to stand directly in front of his wildest fantasy.

Well, almost.

Minus that flimsy, cream, thigh-length robe, it would be his wildest fantasy. Because he could just make out the faint hue of…was that blue?…bra and panties so lovingly covering everything he'd ever dreamed of putting his lips on. Her Disney princess face looked even more innocent scrubbed clean of makeup, and her hair was damp in front, wet little tendrils sticking to her cheeks and jaw.

Geez, just kill him now and get it over with.

"Ali? What's wrong?" he managed to ask through a mouth that wanted to drool like a dog. For some reason, the temperature in the room jumped ten degrees.

"Can I talk to you for a minute?" she peered up at him, all sweetness and light.

"Sure," he made to step out into the hall, but she halted him with a hand on his forearm.

He would not think about how she'd dug her nails into that same arm as she'd reached her climax that day on the beach. Oh hell no. He would most definitely *not* think of that.

Shit. Now that's all he could think about.

"In private?" She glanced furtively down the hall to Becky's closed door.

No, no, no, *no*. Supremely bad idea. "Uh, sure."

He backed up and held the door wide, surreptitiously glancing around his bedroom to make sure nothing untoward was left lying about, like the candid photo of her he usually kept hidden in his nightstand. The one

Grigg snapped the summer before he died. The one where Ali's golden hair was caught in the soft breeze coming in off the ocean and her head was thrown back in laughter. The one Nate looked at so often the edges were starting to bend.

Luckily, it was still buried in the top drawer of his bedside table under some cough drops, tissues, and a dog-eared John Grisham novel.

Shooting one last glance down the hall, he quietly closed the door.

And closed Ali into his bedroom.

Just the thought had his crotch tightening. Not good. Not good at all.

It was super strange how his pulse could stay metronome steady while he was inches away from a drug lord, jihadist, or enemy combatant but raced out of control the minute he was alone with one little wisp of a woman.

"What's wrong, Ali?" Hopefully this time he'd get an answer. Preferably something he could quickly solve so he could shoo her out, double-time, because right at that moment his gaze snagged on her clasped hands.

And somehow, despite the fact that he'd never really considered fingers sexy before, he wanted to get his lips on them. They were just so darned cute. So petite and slender—just like her—and perfectly polished a seashell pink. They virtually screamed *female!* And Lord knew that was something he'd gone without for a long while now. Too damned long…

"What did Delilah say to you tonight?" she asked, her brow puckering adorably.

Well, wasn't that just a kick in the nuts? It was also the dead last thing he expected to hear.

"Uh…"

"We've known each other for a dozen years, and I think that was the first time I've ever heard you laugh like that." She took a step closer.

Whoa. Not good. And getting not gooder by the minute.

Not gooder? His brain was ceasing to function.

"Uh…"

Now she was standing in front of him, so close he could sense the soft feminine heat rolling off her body in gentle waves, and smell the sweet aroma of her honeysuckle shampoo mixed with the scent of Ivory soap on her skin.

Where was that humming coming from? Was all his blood rushing to his head?

"Uh…" And what was the question? He swallowed and tried to drag in a much needed lungful of O_2. Was it just him, or were the walls closing in?

"It's a bit strange, don't you think?" she asked.

Yeah, it was all very, very strange. Strange that she was here in Chicago. Strange that she was being chased by some spook. Strange that Grigg had put her in the position to be chased by some spook. Strange that she was standing half dressed in his bedroom. His. Bedroom.

Strange that she was looking up at him imploringly instead of watching him like a mouse might watch a hungry hawk. Not to mention the fact that he *felt* very, very strange. Like maybe he was about to pass out. *Bam!* Down for the count. And wouldn't that impress upon her what a macho man he really was?

"Ali—"

"What?"

Yeah, what? What was he about to say? *Get out*, maybe? *Get naked?* That was much more likely.

He simply shook his head. "Nothin'."

"Back to playing the strong, handsome, silent type?" she asked, her head tipped teasingly to the side.

"Handsome?" She though he was handsome? Not that he should be *too* surprised, he supposed. He was no Brad Pitt, but he wasn't necessarily Quasimodo either.

She shrugged. "Of course. You do know you're, like…sorta drop-dead hot, right?"

Did he? Maybe once, years ago when he'd been young and carefree. Innocent of the world. But not now. Not with the years spent battling the elements. Not after having carried around the weight of what he'd been forced to do three months ago. He felt like an old man.

"Wow," she shook her head, clearly surprised. "You really don't get it, do you?"

"Get what?"

"That you're beautiful."

"*Beautiful*?" Okay, now he *knew* she was blowing smoke up his ass.

Because handsome he figured he could maybe understand. Women were strangely wonderful in that they liked a little character in a man's face.

Drop-dead hot was probably pushing things a bit. But beautiful? Huh-uh, no way.

"Yes," she slid her tongue into her cheek, her eyes bright with amusement as she leaned toward him. "Men can be beautiful."

He laughed even as his spine snapped ruler-straight.

He clasped his hands behind his back, gritting his teeth with the effort not to reach out and touch her. She muddled his thinking on a good day. And now, standing so close, especially when she lifted a hand toward his face? Well, that caused all conscious thought to stop dead in its tracks. Every single cell inside his body focused with a capital F on the feel of her sweet, pink-tipped fingers.

"Nate?"

When she said his name like that, he wanted to take on the world. "Hmm?"

"You just laughed."

"I do that on occasion." He used to do it all the time when Grigg was alive. The exasperating sonofabitch had done his level best to keep Nate in stitches. Of course, Ali wouldn't know that. Anytime she was around him, he was usually concentrating so hard on not springing a boner that any attempt at appreciating humor was out of the question. Since Grigg's death though, all the laughter had left him, flown away with Grigg's last breath. But something about having Ali there made him feel…lighter. Dare he admit it? Maybe even a teensy bit happy?

"Nate?"

Scratch that. He didn't just want to take on the world when she said his name like that, he wanted to take on the whole friggin' galaxy. "Yeah?"

"I'm touching you."

No doubt about that. The baseball bat he was trying to conceal behind his zipper was testimony enough. "I noticed."

"You're not jerking away. Acting like I'm carrying around a double whammy of hepatitis and bubonic plague."

Double whammy of…he could only shake his head

and fight a grin. She was simply adorable. No bones about it. And, yeah, that warm feeling slowly seeping through his veins could only be happiness. He remembered the sensation…vaguely. "What are you jabbering on about now, woman?"

"That fact that you don't like for me to touch you."

Was she insane?

"You *don't* like it when I touch you, do you?" she asked.

"I never said that," he muttered through clenched teeth because she was in the process of running her hands over his shoulders. Was it possible to feel happiness while in the midst of being killed?

"Then why have you always gone out of your way to avoid any physical contact with me? We've known each other for…well, sometimes it seems like forever. You're like a second son to my parents. You grab up my mom and hug her until she's giggling and ruffling your hair. Even that awkward male combination handshake-hug thing you do with my dad proves you're not allergic to human touch. And you and Grigg had your arms thrown around each other's shoulders so often mom sometimes called you the USMC's only set of Siamese twins—attached at the armpit. But all I ever got was a tip of the chin, if that. So what gives? Why do you turn sideways when we pass each other in the hallway?"

For a brief instant, he considered lying. But there were so many bitter truths he couldn't tell her, so many questions she'd asked that he absolutely could not answer. This wasn't one of them. So…the truth it was. "I like it too much."

"Huh?" There went her nose again, all wrinkly and wonderful.

"Your touch. I like it *too* much." Hell, now it'd be *her* going out of her way to avoid physical contact. Which was just as well. He was only a man after all, and with her within arm's reach—not to mention actually touching him—his hold on his usually stalwart restraint was tenuous at best.

Downright threadbare at worst.

Her delicately arched brows snapped toward her nose. "Like it too much. What does that mean?"

Geez. The woman wasn't usually slow, but she was pulling the ol' bag of hammers routine with this one. Instead of explaining it, he simply reeled her in until she brushed against the irrefutable evidence centered directly behind his fly.

Sweet lovin' Lord, it was hell. Or heaven. He wasn't sure. If his dick had a voice of its own, it'd start shouting a rousing chorus of hallelujahs.

Her beautiful eyes shot wide. "Oh!"

Oh was right.

Lightbulb moment, Miss Morgan. "Yeah, does that clear things up for ya?"

Any second now. Any second she was going to jump back and give him that look she'd perfected over the years. The narrowed eyes and pursed lips, the canted head, the one that said she thought he'd just climbed out from under the nearest slimy rock.

Any second now…

"You *want* me?" she asked incredulously.

"I'd say that's undeniably apparent."

"But you don't *like* me." Inexplicably, she was still pressed against his pulsing, aching-like-a-month-of-Mondays erection.

Not like her? Was she crazy? "Of course I like you, Ali."

He silently counted to ten and recited the team roster of the 1998 St. Louis Cardinals. Over the years, he'd learned it was the mental equivalent of a cold shower.

"No, you don't," she adamantly shook her head.

"Ali," he knew he must be wearing the expression of a tormented man, "all evidence points to the contrary."

Okay, so the ol' Cardinals trick wasn't working tonight.

And uh-oh, he knew the look she was wearing now. It was the one Grigg so often complained about, all calculating and wily. This was *so* not going to be good.

"So *that's* why you've been acting so…so surly and disagreeable all these years?" she asked in disbelief. "Because you *want* me?"

Surly and disagreeable? He hadn't been surly and disagreeable. He'd been noble and honorable. *Jesus.* Couldn't she tell the friggin' difference?

Deciding she wasn't going to budge unless he prodded her, he tried to push her away. With lightning reflexes, she locked her thin arms around his neck and clung like a barnacle on the hull of an aircraft carrier.

"Ali," he warned, grinding his teeth together against the pleasure/pain throbbing inside his pants. This was getting worse by the minute. Or better, maybe? Christ, he wasn't sure anymore. His brain was only half working—which he figured was still pretty good considering it was likely being deprived of most of its blood supply. "Back off."

"Not until you answer me," she declared with that pointy little chin of hers lifted defiantly.

His patience snapped along with his control. "Yes,

damn you! Yes, that's why I always keep you at arm's length. Because anytime I get near you, all I wanna do is peel away your clothes, lay y'down on the nearest horizontal surface, and plunge balls-deep inside you until your squirmin' beneath me like a worm on a hook and beggin' me to never stop. There! Y'happy now?"

Nate expected a number of things from Ali after that rather insensitive and vulgar outburst. The mind-blowing sensation of her lips opening over his was certainly not one of them.

Oh buddy.

Her tongue.

It was sweet and supple and darting in and out, and licking and laving and making him lose his mind.

His wickedest fantasies had nothing on reality. For all their crude, raw carnality, he generally didn't spend a lot of time kissing Ali in his dreams. Usually choosing to skip ahead to the really steamy parts.

Which he now understood had been a huge mistake. Gargantuan.

Because the hard suction of Ali's mouth was the steamiest thing he'd ever known—which was saying something considering he'd lost count of the number of lovers he'd had over the years. And some of those gals had had more than one novelty packed away in their big bag of bedroom tricks.

The feel of her skin…

It was hot and satiny smooth beneath his rough hands. Her robe split wide when she shimmied up him like a logger climbs a pine and wrapped her slim legs around his waist. Instinctively, he caught her hips.

Good! Lord!

Hips that were undulating against him in a most infuriating and satisfying way.

"Ali," he wrenched his mouth away. His lungs were going to burst. "Stop this."

"No," she trailed a string of wet kisses across his jaw and down to his earlobe, pausing to suck it into the moist heat of her mouth. His eyes literally crossed. "I want this. You want this. We're both adults, and there's been this…this overwhelming chemistry between us from the very beginning. So there's nothing to stop us."

For a moment, every reason why she shouldn't be in his arms sprouted feathers and flew right out of his mind. For one delicious instant, he knew only the sensation of her body moving against him. Her arms around his shoulders, her fingers tunneling through the hair at his nape until goose bumps erupted along his skin.

Before he realized what was happening, he was kissing her back with all the passion and hunger that had been building inside him since that time he walked into the Morgans' kitchen on a cool May morning and watched her swing a Pearl Jam backpack over her shoulder.

He remembered it like it was yesterday…

Because beyond all reason—she'd been just a girl, a senior in high school and he'd been a twenty-one-year-old man of the world by that point—he'd wanted her. With a force that had knocked him senseless. So much so he'd only been able to stare in narrow-eyed wonder and blink at her when he was introduced.

Then she'd bestowed on him her bright smile and laughed her sunny laugh, and he'd fallen in...*lust*. He didn't believe in love at first sight, but something had certainly happened right then and there.

Grigg had instantly recognized the hot hunger gleaming in his eyes and had leaned in to whisper a phrase he'd repeated too many times to count over the long years to follow. *Lay a finger on my baby sister and die, asshole*.

And that was just the bucket of ice water Nate needed...memories of Grigg.

Shit! What am I doing?

"This can't happen again," he told her as he unwrapped her legs and set her feet on the floor before pulling away. Was that his voice sounding like gravel rolling around in a dump truck?

"What? Why?" She blinked up at him.

He had to turn away. He couldn't look at her kiss-swollen lips or the color riding high in her cheeks and know he was responsible for both. "It just can't."

"That's not an answer!"

"There are things you don't know about me, Ali." Things she'd hopefully never know...

"Okay," she walked to the leather La-Z-Boy he kept in the corner and plopped down. Good Lord, they were baby blue. Baby blue panties. He got just a glimpse before she closed the edges of her robe and crossed her legs. "So, are you gay?"

He coughed. "Uh, what d'you think?"

She eyed the bulge behind his zipper and shook her head.

Yeah, that's a big negative, little lady.

"Do you have some incurable STD?" she asked, head canted just so, like she was a loan officer interviewing a potential borrower.

This was getting out of hand. "*No*. Ali I—"

"Do you have a girlfriend or wife I'm unaware of?"

"Course not. If you'll just—"

"Then there's absolutely no reason why we can't continue doing exactly what we were just doing." She stood up to make good on her word, and he nearly stumbled backward when his heel caught on the rug.

He held up a hand to ward her off like she was some hungry jungle cat instead of one small woman.

One small, *determined* woman. Oh, yes, he recognized *that* look, as well.

He was losing the battle here. Time to quit jacking off and lay it all on the line. "I've done horrible things, Ali. Unforgivable things. You don't want anything to do with me."

"No," she shook her head, her face softening. Christ, he was going to bust out crying if she continued to look at him with those softly sincere eyes. "I don't know exactly what you've done, and I probably never will. But one thing I do know is there's no shame in answering the call of duty and doing what must be done to protect the freedom and the way of life of all the people you love. You'll never convince me otherwise. I'll never see you as anything other than what you are, Nate, a hero."

And that did it. Because, *Jesus*, she had no idea. Not one friggin' clue.

Just how heroic would she think him if she knew he'd been the one to end Grigg's life?

Chapter Nine

THE FIRST, SOFT PINK RAYS OF DAWN SPILLED BETWEEN the wooden slats of the blinds, and Frank tossed aside the covers. It was barely past oh-five-hundred, but it was beyond obvious he'd get no more sleep.

Too much to worry about. Starting with the fact that one of his men had involved them all in a situation absolutely reeking of foul play, and ending with the fact that Becky was under the hugely mistaken impression he'd let her join the team if she could prove herself Ozzie's equal.

To put it mildly, no fucking way. Over his dead body.

He rotated his trick shoulder and grimaced when it clicked into place and set up a steady throb like a bad toothache.

Getting old not only sucked, it suckety-suck-suck-sucked. Grabbing the bottle of ibuprofen from the nightstand, he threw two tablets to the back of his throat and swallowed.

Come on, you little chemical wonders, work your magic.

Twenty minutes later he was showered, shaved, and down in his office with a glazed donut in one hand, his telephone in the other.

Nearly oh-six-thirty DC time, which meant General Fuller was due for a little wake-up call. One the ol' hard-ass would probably rather not take, but life's a bitch and then you die.

Interrupting the General's beauty sleep rated real low on Frank's list of things not to do today, way under *don't kiss Becky* and *don't start a war with the FBI or the CIA*. And getting General Fuller up and cranking away on his end of this rank-ass deal would go a long way to allowing Frank to put big red checkmarks next to some items on his list of things to do today. Hopefully, right beside *find out just what the hell Agent Delaney was investigating* and *find out why the hell there's a spook on Grigg's little sister's tail*.

"Frank?"

He ended his call before it got a chance to go through and glanced at his open office door.

He wasn't the only one who'd gone without sleep last night. Alisa Morgan had dark bruises under her eyes. It also—*kee-rist*—looked like she'd been crying.

From fear? Because of her brother? Man, either reason made him want to wrap her in cotton and keep her safe on a shelf. Women, those adorably soft creatures, should never wear that particular expression. He felt partly responsible, because he should've known one of his men had gone off reservation. Should've sensed something in Grigg to warn him.

He hadn't, and now Alisa Morgan was paying the price.

She held Peanut in her arms, her pert nose sunk deep into the cat's patchy fur, looking like a little girl seeking comfort.

"Come on in, Ali," he said and then realized she might not hear him over the loud purring of Sir Eats-a-Lot. He motioned to the set of chairs in front of his desk.

She hurriedly took a seat and arranged a contented Peanut on her lap. "I thought of something. I don't know if it's anything, but it might be…"

He motioned for her to continue.

"The memory box."

Was that a new band? Man, he really *must* be getting old. "Pardon me?"

"Growing up, our parents were always so wrapped up in—" she shook her head. "Forget it. None of that matters. Crap. My brain feels all spongy…full of holes, you know?"

"I'd offer you a cup of coffee…" She made the facial equivalent of *I'd rather be tarred and feathered*.

"Yeah," he chuckled, "I didn't think so."

"That stuff is motor oil," she declared, her tone full of disgust.

"Mmm hmm, but it works wonders for mental acuity." And for helping a guy resist the lollipops some tiny temptress insisted on shoving into his shirt pockets. It was hard to enjoy the taste of root beer when your tongue was wearing a caffeine sweater.

"I'll pass," Ali replied dryly. "I value my stomach lining too much to—Ouch!"

She gingerly pulled Peanut's kneading nails from the denim of her jeans. "They say love hurts. I never knew they meant it literally until I met Peanut."

Funny. The woman was funny. Add that up with cute as a button, smart as a tack, and surprisingly tough underneath that cupcake exterior, and Frank understood why Ghost went all Cro-Magnon around her.

"Anyway, back to the memory box," she said, scratching Peanut under his scarred chin until his yellow eyes rolled back in abject feline ecstasy. "It's something Grigg and I started when we were kids. Putting little keepsakes inside. You know the kind of stuff I mean, his little league baseball glove, my first Barbie, our good report cards, things like that."

Yes, Frank had a memory box himself. Filled with childhood memorabilia and stored in his sister's attic. But what did that have to do with Grigg's work for the FBI or the fact that Ali herself was now being ghosted by some man oozing CIA training in every calculated move like a snail oozes a slime trail?

"As we got older," she continued and once more grimaced as she gently withdrew Peanut's painfully loving claws, "we started keeping copies of more important documents in there. Wills, employment contracts, that kind of thing."

Now they were getting somewhere. Frank sat forward.

"About once a year, Grigg would send me a zip drive filled with all the pictures he wanted to keep copies of, and I'd add it to the memory box," she explained. "Usually, they were photos of him and Nate. Sometimes there were shots of the rest of you guys and the bikes you were working on."

A little niggle of excitement stirred in the bottom of his stomach.

"So," she made a motion with her hand and Peanut meowed his displeasure at the interrupted chin scratching. Ali dutifully resumed her task. "I guess it was about a week before we found out about Grigg, I received a zip drive from him in the mail. I opened it up, found a set of pictures just like always, so I put it in the memory box and forgot about it. When you asked if I'd received anything from Grigg that was out of the ordinary, I didn't even think twice about the zip drive. Especially since I'd opened it and glanced through the pictures.

But there was something else on the drive besides the pictures: a file I couldn't access. It was secured with a password. Knowing Grigg, I figured it might be racy photos of him and some woman, or women," she rolled her eyes. "But maybe it was secret files or something?"

Or something…hot damn! This could be the break they were all waiting for.

"It might be nothing, but the timing is awfully coincidental, don't you think?" she asked hopefully.

He certainly *did* think. "Yes. Have you told Gho—ah, Nate about this?"

Her face fell, and she grabbed up Peanut to once more burry her nose in the cat's patchy fur. In response, the stupid feline ratcheted his motor into overdrive.

Hello.

So something had obviously happened between Ali and Ghost last night. Something to make her eyes all wounded and wary.

Frank never thought he'd say it, but Nathan Weller was a goddamned moron. Couldn't the man see this woman adored him? Didn't he notice the catch in her breath every time he entered the room, the way she instinctively gravitated toward his side even though he was about as welcoming as a prickly pear cactus?

Probably. Ghost was nothing if not observant. So, yeah, he no doubt saw all of it. Which was probably exactly why the guy was always careful to keep her at arm's length.

Ghost had some serious issues. No doubt starting and ending with Grigg and what happened in that filthy, stinking hut in Syria. It didn't take a genius of

Ozzie's caliber to figure out Ghost's feelings for his dead friend's kid sister must fall directly into a category appropriately titled It's Complicated.

"No," she shook her head. "I didn't tell Nate. I wanted to run it by you first. I didn't want to look like a fool if you thought it was nothing."

Ah yes, not wanting to look like a fool in front of the one person you wanted more than you wanted your next breath? Frank could relate.

And speaking of fools...Dan poked his head into the office followed by his much prettier, much better half.

"Whadup, kiddies?" he asked as Patti pushed by him to glare at the donut in Frank's hand.

Busted.

"I thought you said you were gonna start cutting sugar from your diet," she harrumphed, hands on hips.

Ho-kay, he'd made that grandiose statement in front of the Knights in the hopes Becky would leave off stuffing those ridiculous suckers in his pockets.

The ruse hadn't worked. Either Becky was determined to undermine his alleged new diet, or she simply reveled in the fact that he was a total wuss when it came to resisting root beer-flavored suckers.

If he had to lay down money, he'd bet on the latter.

Now, looking at Patti's perturbed face, he figured maybe it was better to actually *go* on the sugar-free diet.

But, shit, he really loved his morning donuts.

Sometimes the best defense, especially in the face of an agitated woman, was evasion and diversion. "Ali just remembered something that might help us figure out just what in the world is going on here," he replied, neatly sidestepping Patti's looming lecture.

"She has?" Ozzie asked, appearing in the doorway dressed in his pajama bottoms. Did they…? Yes, they did. They had tiny Starship Enterprises all over them.

The kid absently scratched his smooth, bare chest while simultaneously trying to pat down his hair—which was wild on a good day. This morning it was out of control. Frank never knew hair could actually stand on end. He'd always thought that was just an idiom.

"Yes," he replied, for once happy for Ozzie's interruption. "She has, and we need to—"

"We need to what?" Ghost shouldered Ozzie aside and cast a wary glance over Ali.

The poor woman tried to disappear behind Peanut. That it was actually kind of working spoke to the salient fact that Becky needed to put the damned cat on a diet…yesterday.

"As I was saying," Frank's patience started to shred. "Ali received a zip drive from Grigg about a week before you gave them the news of his death. And she—"

"Jesus, woman! You're just now tellin' us this?" Ghost's face was enough to give small children nightmares.

"You misunderst—" Frank tried and was immediately cut off by Ali.

"I didn't remember until this morning, you big jerk!" she shouted and Peanut turned cold, warning eyes toward Ghost.

"How can you forget somethin' like that?" Ghost shot back, taking a step toward Ali. Peanut hissed menacingly. "I swear I'm gonna have to kill that cat," he spat, his fists clenched at his sides, his nostrils flaring.

"Ghost," Frank tried again, "if you'd just shut the hell up and give me a chance to expla—"

"Don't forget I know where you sleep, Ghost Man," Becky threatened, pushing into the office.

Oh, good. The gang's all here. Now if everyone would just stop interrupting him, maybe, just *maybe* they could come up with a game plan to retrieve that zip drive.

He opened his mouth, then snapped it closed and decided to see just how this little scene would play out when Becky stomped over to stand toe to toe with Ghost.

Funny, considering toe-to-toe put Becky's nose on level with Ghost's chest.

What? Did the woman think she could shin-kick the guy to death?

"You harm one hair on Peanut's head," she stuck a stiff finger in Ghost's flexing left pectoral muscle, "and I'll change you from a rooster to a hen one night when you least expect it."

Ho-kay. No shin-kicking for Rebel. When she plotted revenge, she knew to keep the timeline abstract *and* aim for a man's most prized possessions.

Duly noted.

"Is this really necessary? It's eighty degrees out there."

"Uh." Becky eyed Ali as the woman dubiously pinched at the butter soft leather chaps Becky'd loaned her. "Yeah, but only if you'd like to keep the top three layers of your skin should you guys get in a wreck."

"You think we'll get in a wreck?"

Lord, help me to not strangle this prissy little woman. "No," she sighed. "But in life there are no guarantees."

"Don't get philosophical with me while I'm wearing

leather." Ali complained as she slid her arms into the equally soft, summer-weight leather jacket.

"Ha! Like leather and philosophy are mutually exclusive? I bet Plato and Aristotle wore leather while pondering life's elemental questions. Leather sandals, for sure."

"Hmm." Ali bent to pick up Peanut who was busy winding his substantial self around and between her legs. When she managed to struggle to a stand and pull him to her chest, the traitorous animal—come on, Becky was the one to scoop his massive cat turds out of the litter box and keep him nose deep in Fancy Feast; was a little loyalty too much to ask?—started purring loud enough to drown out the sound of Pat Benatar wailing "Heartbreaker."

Thank God she'd remembered to charge her iPod last night. One more day of '80s music and she'd have to schedule a lobotomy.

"Well, I hate thinking about the poor animals that lost their lives so I could fashionably sit on the back of a motorcycle." Ali changed tactics.

"Excuse me, but are you the same woman who ate not one, but two all-*beef* hotdogs last night? So you're saying you have no issue with animals on your plate, but can't stand the idea of one strapped across your back?"

"Oh!" Ali dropped Peanut to the ground, and the stupid cat had enough nerve to start slithering around her legs again. Even mistreatment didn't seem to negate his misplaced adoration. That was the last straw. He was going to be on dry food from now on. No more pampering the furry little Judas. "Stop starting arguments with me I can't possibly win," Ali demanded, looking kinda kickass in all that leather with her hands fisted on her hips.

Becky shook her head and laughed. The poor woman would do anything to take her mind off the fact that she was going to be snuggled up to the back of Ghost for the next fifteen hours. Whatever had happened between the two of them last night, whatever had caused them to circle each other like wary lions this morning, would no doubt only be exacerbated by the close confines of a shared motorcycle seat.

"Sorry," Ali made a face. "I'm not usually so… so…" Her hand turned circles as she searched for the right word.

"Bitchy?" Becky offered helpfully.

"I was going to say irritable," Ali harrumphed.

Yeah, bitchy. Becky chuckled. She liked Ali. She really did. Even if the woman was a bit naïve and a little too prissy…of course, that probably wasn't really fair. Most women were a little too prissy when compared to herself. Maybe that's why she irritated Frank so much. Maybe he thought she was too manly. Maybe if she—

Dang.

Why did every thought have to wind up back on Frank? *Maybe* what she should do is seriously consider that lobotomy.

"It's going to be okay, you know," she told Ali, laying a kind hand on the woman's leather-clad shoulder.

"It is?" Ali asked hopefully. "How do you know?"

"Because you've got the Black Knights on your side, and they are the absolute best. Besides, Ghost would sooner die than let anything happen to you."

"Yeah." Ali took a deep breath and shuddered. "That's what I'm afraid of."

Wow. Those two sure had it bad.

Ghost practically lifted a leg and pissed on Ali anytime she walked in the room, and Ali got all doe-eyed and flushed the minute Ghost looked at her.

Perhaps this trip would do them some good. Some forced togetherness might be just the thing they needed to finally compel them to break down and admit they were totally white-doves-and-orange-blossoms *in love* with each other. Of course, it might do just the opposite. Fifteen hours was a long, *long* time to be sitting on a bike. Becky was usually wiped out after just four or five. Thinking of riding bitch on the back of Phantom for fifteen hours was…well, it was pretty crazy in her book.

Yepper, Ali certainly didn't know what she'd signed herself up for when she'd insisted on accompanying Ghost on this little errand, but it wouldn't take the woman long to figure it out. About three hours, Becky guessed. Then muscles Ali didn't even know she had would start complaining—loudly.

Of course, thanks to her and Steady Soto, there really wasn't another option. Nate didn't trust commercial flights because, quote, "They let anyone and *everyone* on those." There wasn't a military transport leaving Great Lakes Naval Base for the east coast within the next twenty-four hours. Taking Ali's little Prius was dismissed by everyone with a snort and a laugh because, really, the thing was basically a go-cart with power-steering and AC, and, unfortunately, the only two vehicles of the four-wheeled variety in the Knights' employ were the Hummer and Christian's souped-up silver Porsche—living in the city, with parking such a challenge, the Knights usually relied on public transportation or taxicabs when the weather was not conducive to riding the bikes.

And regrettably, the Hummer was currently sitting idle in the back of the shop without a transmission thanks to Steady's rather unusual driving style—unusual in that the guy seemed to have a strange aversion to the clutch. And the Porsche was up on the lift with its engine in pieces, which was where Becky's culpability came into the matter. She'd decided since the ex-SAS agent was away, it was the opportune time to get her "grubby little hands"—Christian's words, not hers—on his baby and overhaul that gleaming eight cylinder. Because, come on, every engine could use a little tweaking. Unfortunately, the helo had arrived, and she'd gotten sidetracked.

Which reminded her, she better get going on reinstalling that turbo-charged sucker, or Christian was going to kill her very slowly and very painfully when he finally got home.

So…that left them with only one option for retrieving the thumb drive in a timely fashion. Namely, fifteen hours on the back of a rumbling, roaring piece of two-wheeled steel.

Oh, man, Ali was *so* in for it.

"Let me introduce you to Phantom," she said, hoping to reassure the fidgeting woman a bit, because who wouldn't be reassured with such a badass piece of machinery grumbling along between her legs? "Along with Ghost, this bad boy's gonna take good care of you."

She herded a reluctant Ali toward the bank of cycles parked against the east wall. They were as much her works of art as the murals on the walls or the paintings in the lofts upstairs. She was proud of each and every one of them. Not because they were über-sweet bikes, but because they represented each of the men she'd grown to love and respect over the years.

Each one was as different as the Black Knight who rode it. Each one was as tough as the man who'd helped her design it.

"Okay," she motioned to the fourth bike in the row. "This beauty here is Phantom. He's an El Diablo Sturgis Special with a six-inch stretch, a Baker six-speed transmission, S&S 124ci engine with LBC pipes that sound like hell on wheels. I replaced the single seat with a king and queen this morning, so you guys are good to go."

Ali smoothed a reverent hand over the black leather king and queen seat. "Are you speaking English?"

"To put it simply, Phantom is one kickass bike," Becky boasted, taking a shammy from her front pocket and polishing the already sparkling forks on the front end.

"It's very pretty," Ali enthused.

Pretty? *Pretty?*

The sucker was a wicked mofo raised to the nth degree. It was a mean machine with enough...Okay, Becky had to admit. It was pretty.

"Do you do all the work yourself?" Ali queried, touching a tentative finger to the chrome gas cap.

"Nah, each Knight helped in the design and the building of his individual bike. It's as much their creation as it is mine. They provide the inspiration; I provide the technical expertise, and together we supply the blood and sweat."

Except for Frank's bike. Building Boss Hog had been

an exercise in blood, sweat, *and* tears. At least, Becky had cried herself silly a time or two during the process. Particularly those days when Frank worked side by side with her for eight long hours only to pat her on the head like a kid sister and make an evening trip to Lincoln Park.

The big, stupid dill-hole.

"Is the artwork yours? I noticed paint on your T-shirt yesterday." Ali used her finger to follow a swirl of glittering ghostly gray paint on Phantom's custom-made gas tank.

"Yeah. It's my release." Her escape from the fact that she was crazy about a man who—

No. She had to stop thinking of him. She had to get on with her life and stop clinging to childish dreams—like winning the love of a knight in shining armor who'd whisk her away on his glowing white steed.

Yepper, and it didn't escape her attention that Frank's last name was Knight or that Boss Hog just happened to be painted a shimmering pearly white.

Talk about life's little ironies.

"You're very talented," Ali said, tracing the face of the phantom barely discernable in the middle of the gas tank. "It's amazing how you made that ghostly face appear out of the mist like that."

"Thanks, I—

"Everything ready?" Ghost suddenly materialized beside them.

Phantom appearing out of the mist? Ghost materializing out of nowhere? Wow, perfect timing.

Becky glanced down at the thick-soled biker boots on Ghost's big feet and shook her head. His stealth never ceased to amaze her.

"You sure you don't need some more firepower?" she inquired innocently while watching Ghost stow three gun cases in Phantom's saddlebags.

One of those cases contained his M-40 A5 sniper rifle, nicknamed Sierra. Sierra came with a detachable PBS 27 night optic and 10-round detachable magazine that fired 7.62 X 51 NATO rounds. At a thousand yards, that beast still had more kinetic energy than a .357 fired at point-blank range. Two words: stopping power.

She hoped someday Ghost would teach her how to shoot it, but he'd told her she had to learn to crawl before she could learn to walk, so he'd been practicing with her on a Remington Model Seven.

But someday. Someday he'd let her lay her hands on ol' Sierra.

Ghost shot her an amused look before leaning in to hook a heavy arm around her neck and knuckle her head. That was her, everyone's kid sister.

"We'll be back by tomorrow night," he told her. "Try not t'give Boss a heart attack between now 'n' then."

"Whatever," she cuffed him on the arm. "And you try not to shoot anyone between now and then."

They both glanced to the bulging saddlebags.

"How much you wanna bet I hold up my end of that bargain better than you hold up yours?"

"Smartass," he growled with fondness, then swung one long leg over the bike.

"It's now or never, sista," Becky turned to Ali as Ghost started Phantom.

"Can I choose never?" Ali yelled above the motorcycle's guttural roar.

Becky just smiled and plopped a helmet into Ali's

trembling hands. "Excuse me if I'm wrong, but didn't you demand this assignment? Wasn't it you who refused to give up the location of that zip drive unless you were allowed to go along?"

Becky had to give the woman snaps for tenacity. Had Nate focused that black-laser gaze on her, she'd have probably folded like a poker player with a bad hand, but Ali had simply thrust up her chin and dared everyone in the room to nay-say her.

Now the poor woman wasn't looking so sure of herself. Her next words confirmed it. "Is it too late to change my mind?"

It was a good thing Ghost hadn't heard that above Phantom's loud rumble, or he'd jump at the chance to leave Ali behind. Becky, however, thought this little journey was going to be good for the both of them.

"Just hang on," she told Ali, giving the worried woman a quick, sisterly hug. "That's the only advice I'll give you."

Ali made a face before slipping the helmet over her head and gingerly mounting up behind Nate. She adjusted herself, then adjusted herself again.

Uh-huh. Now Ali was beginning to get the picture. Riding backseat on a bike like Phantom was better than Mr. Blue any day. Not to mention the highly erotic act of wrapping one's legs around the man you loved.

Becky secretly grinned at the thought of the very *long* ride Ali had ahead of her.

Ghost gave a thumbs-up, and Becky whistled. Dan Man, Ozzie, and Patti jogged down the metal stairs to the shop floor at the shrill sound of her summons.

Wow. Becky had to admit, Patti looked pretty

frickin' hot in her long, blond wig. And by the way Dan kept shooting steamy glances over his shoulder at his wife, she assumed the guy wholeheartedly agreed with her assessment.

She watched Dan and Patti mount up before shoving her helmet into place and swinging up behind Ozzie.

As the motorcycle rumbled to life beneath her, through her visor she watched Frank step off the stairway and amble toward the big, red button beside the ten-drawer rolling Craftsman tool cabinet. Smashing it with his wide palm, the red warning light blinked, and she turned to see one whole section of the shop wall slide back and to the left until there was nothing but a gaping black hole. It was the beginning of a tunnel dug down under the north branch of the Chicago River that would terminate in a parking garage two blocks west.

The smell of damp concrete and stale air drifted inside her helmet as she watched Ali lean past Ghost's broad back to get a better look. She smiled when she imagined the woman's surprise.

Holy secret tunnels, Batman!

Yepper, sometimes working for a group of clandestine government operators had its perks.

They'd decided to play the classic shell game. If whoever was watching—namely Ali's mystery man—managed to somehow catch them even after they'd exited through their secret tunnel, he'd still only have a one in three chance of being able to follow the correct couple. Their plan was to take three bikes, three men, and three blond women covered head to toe in identical black leather out on the highway. Once there, each couple would quickly veer off in a different direction.

Their tail, if they even had one, would have to choose. It wasn't a foolproof plan, but it was better than nothing.

"Rebecca!"

What had she said about working for a group of clandestine government operators having its perks? Well, it had its drawbacks, too.

"Damnit!" Frank's voice vibrated with frustration, loud enough to be heard over the three roaring bikes.

She winced as she glanced over her shoulder and saw him holding two fistfuls of suckers. Okay, so she could totally explain why she'd filled his jacket pockets with root beer Dum Dums this morning, and it had nothing to do with getting a little revenge for the hissy fit he'd thrown yesterday when she'd been forced to come clean about Ozzie's techie lessons.

Okay, maybe it had a little bit to do with that... Okay, so it had *everything* to do with that, but the dillhole deserved it.

She felt devilish delight knowing that big Frank Knight, the man with unshakable will, couldn't resist those little suckers.

Just went to show, even *he* had a weakness.

Unfortunately, his weakness wasn't her.

Chapter Ten

Whoa. What the hell?

Dagan threw some folded George Washingtons on the counter, grabbed his double-shot espresso from the startled barista, and scrambled out the door of the little coffee shop on the corner of Noble and West Division just in time to see three of the Black Knights' monster bikes fly past.

The three leather-clad figures clinging to the men's backs were all petite, all blond. And, unfortunately, any one of them could've been Alisa Morgan.

Damn.

He fished inside his pocket and pulled out a small device. Jumping into his newly rented SUV, he started the engine and swerved into traffic amidst the blaring horns of pissed-off Chicago cabbies. Glancing down at the device in his hand, he frowned at the glowing green light.

So…

They hadn't exited the Knights' compound by the front gate.

He'd planted a sensor there last night to alert him whenever the gates were opened, and his reconnaissance revealed no other way in or out of the grounds, which left only one thing…

Black Knights Inc. came equipped with a bolt-hole.

He'd figured they might have one, because those

guys would never allow themselves to be put in a situation where there was only one avenue of escape.

Battle Strategy 101.

And, honestly, didn't he understand that life? Never relaxing your guard, always having a contingency plan for every minor thing, and most importantly, always having a way out if discretion was the order of the day or if, more importantly, things went from sugar to shit, as they so often had the tendency to do?

And that only proved you could take an operator out of the field, but you could never un-program a man who'd been programmed.

Dagan himself was a bitter, shining example of that unsavory fact.

The CIA didn't want him anymore after the unhappy little goatfuck in the Sandbox, but he hadn't been good for anything besides this…this *work*. This skulking about in shadows, gathering Intelligence, abstaining from the women and the scotch he so loved because there was always a national security secret to be uncovered and he was the goddamned best at making sure no one uncovered them.

Case in point: he chose that particular coffee shop because it was across from the only highway access for fifteen blocks in any direction and he determined it was his best bet for catching them if and when they emerged from their compound via any route other than the front gate and, like usual, following his instincts had paid off.

Now the question became, where the hell were they all going?

As he tailed the trio up the onramp onto southbound

I-94, he figured he had a pretty good idea. They were going to retrieve the files.

If the damn things even existed. He was really beginning to wonder…

"*Sonofa—*"

He blinked in disbelief as two bikes peeled off. One took the nearest off-ramp, a big loop that would swing them back north. The other motorcycle veered onto westbound I-290, while the third continued heading south.

He had a split second to make his decision.

Swiveling in his seat, he cursed and squinted a look at the bike on the off-ramp. Nope. That wasn't the ghostly gray beast he'd seen Nate Weller mount last night outside Red Delilah's, and he would lay odds there wouldn't be anyone but Grigg's best friend tasked with this particular mission. Craning his head to the right, he got a quick glimpse of the bike heading west. Another negative.

So that left the southbound chopper.

Back to Jacksonville?

"What the fuck do you mean you're out, Zoelner?" Senator Aldus shouted into his cell phone as he pulled his government issue black sedan into the parking lot of a rest stop off I-95.

He couldn't believe what he was hearing. Could not *fucking* believe it. He was going to have that insubordinate cretin deleted. That's all there was to it.

"Like I said, you aren't paying me enough to go head to head with former sergeant Weller. And I've been made, sir. Weller is onto me. So I'm out."

Dagan Zoelner's voice didn't sound the least bit contrite, nor the least bit frightened. And that wouldn't do. It simply would not do.

Aldus felt his head threaten to explode. It was going to burst through his skull and discharge gray matter all over the cream leather interior of his car, because he was SOL if Zoelner quit. There was no one else who could do the job. No one else he trusted to quietly snatch Alisa Morgan and shake the location of those files out of her.

"What about the money, Z? You need that money. Or have you forgotten about your brother and that spot of trouble he's in?"

Christ, families were nothing but weakness and misery.

Lucky for him, he'd learned long ago how to prey on that weakness in others and had worked damned hard not to allow himself the same Achilles heel. His wife thought they were childless because he'd had a bad case of the mumps as a young boy. The real truth was he'd known right from the start he never wanted to have someone who could be taken from him, held for ransom, or used as blackmail. So he'd gotten a vasectomy two weeks before he'd said his "I dos," and he hadn't regretted that decision in all the years since.

He was untouchable, his reputation unblemished, a man destined for great things. That is, if he could ever get out from under the dark shadow of Grigg Morgan and those fucking missing files.

Things were getting complicated. He absolutely hated when things got complicated. Of all the loose ends on this deal, he had only one left to tie up, and it was proving to be so much harder than it should've been.

She was one small woman, for Christ's sake. She

should've been taken care of months ago along with everything else.

It'd been easy to drop a bug in the ear of those bloodthirsty Hezbollah quacks, giving them the whereabouts of the covert operatives who'd killed their esteemed leader, Hassan Kassim, in exchange for them torturing the whereabouts of a certain set of files out of the pair. It'd been just as easy for him to alert the local Syrian militia to the Hezbollah operatives working in their backyard once those same operatives were of no more use to him. And, likewise, it'd been a piece of cake to make sure that nosy-ass Delaney and that shithead Morgan were crucified after they'd had the audacity to break into his secret computer files…or at least they'd tried to.

It was a bit of tragic irony who'd done the *actual* crucifying in Morgan's case. Christ, when he'd read that report detailing Grigg Morgan's death, even *his* hardened stomach had shriveled at the horror of it.

So…he'd managed all of that, but somehow he couldn't manage to get his hands on one untrained, uninformed woman?

It was absolutely beyond the pale, and he'd reached the limit of his patience, especially when Zoelner quietly informed him, "There are other ways for me to get the money."

Aldus ground his jaw so hard his eye sockets ached. "Is that so? Who's going to hire you, Z? Who wants a washed up ex-CIA agent who managed to get his whole team and two civilians killed? No one, that's who. No military, no government body, not even one of those contractor outfits. Because they're not going to trust you, Z. No one's going to trust you. So your best bet to get that cash to poor, misguided Avan is to stick with me."

There was a long pause, and Aldus held his breath. He *needed* Dagan Zoelner and, *goddamnit,* he hated needing anyone.

"I don't think you've been playing straight with me, sir," Zoelner finally said. "I think you orchestrated that mugging, and I know for a fact there's more going on here than you've led me to believe. Both of those things make me decidedly uncomfortable. So, thank you for the opportunity, but I'm out."

"Where are you?" Aldus demanded, maybe he could talk the idiot into—

"On I-90, heading south."

"You're coming back to DC?"

"Maybe, but I doubt it."

"What the hell is that supposed to mean?"

"That's no longer any of your business…sir."

Aldus heard the faint roar of a motorcycle in the background, and the top of his head felt like it was lifting away. "You're following them, aren't you, you asshole? Where are they going?"

"Good-bye, senator."

Fuck!

He smashed the cheap, plastic pre-paid cell phone against the dashboard twice, but even when the device splintered into pieces in his hand, his rage wasn't satisfied. The only thing that kept him from jumping from the car and stomping the remaining bits of the phone to hell and back was the young mother who carried a toddler on her hip. She was eyeing him with blatant apprehension as she scurried up to the restrooms.

Not good. She might recognize him. Because of his position, his face wasn't a stranger to national television.

Okay, okay. Get a handle on yourself, Aldus. He took a couple of deep breaths and forced himself back under control.

This wasn't the end of the world. He had another option.

An option he hadn't wanted to employ, but now he was left with no choice. His back was to the wall. So just like always, and despite his personal feelings on the matter, he'd make the tough decision.

Looking at the broken pieces of plastic in his hand and littering the gray pinstripe of his suit pants, he silently cursed his earlier burst of temper.

He needed that goddamned phone.

His personal cell phone wasn't useful in this particular situation, because the call he was about to make could never be traced back to him.

She'd finally fallen asleep.

Leaning heavily along his back, Ali's slim, leather-clad thighs rested softly against the outside of Nate's legs, and he could detect the heavy rise and fall of every breath she took.

For the first three hours of their trip, she'd been studiously careful to keep a handful of inches between their bodies, her knees angled *way* out.

Wouldn't want to get too personal now, would we? Wouldn't want to touch him anymore than was *absolutely* necessary.

Geez, he'd handled last night all wrong, literally tossing her out of his bedroom when he couldn't stand having her look at him with such sweet compassion and desperate longing. So he had no one but himself to blame for the hurt look on her face today, for those dark smudges of exhaustion beneath her eyes.

Someone should kick his ass.

Unfortunately, as he looked in his side mirror and again caught a glimpse of that silver Escalade way back there, he was starting to think someone just might try.

If he had to guess, it was Ali's Mystery Man on their six. Their shell game obviously hadn't worked. Which left them with two options.

One: Given Mystery Man had tailed Ali for months, knew where she lived and worked, the dude had to surmise from their current trajectory that they were headed back to Jacksonville. So what was the point of trying to shake him?

Or...Nate could go with option numero dos. Namely, lose the fucker.

Given he didn't particularly care to have an unknown at his back for the next six hundred miles, there was really no question which option he'd choose.

"Wake up, Ali," he said into his helmet mic. He hated having to do this. Riding on the back of a bike was exhausting for those not accustomed to it and, man, she needed the z's. Unfortunately, there was no other way.

"Uh." He felt her move against his back. "Wh-what?"

Even through the tinny-sounding communications system, he could hear the huskiness of her sleepy voice. His gut tightened in response.

"Y'needa wake up, sugar." Crap. That little endearment just slipped out. He'd always thought of her as such, considering she was about the sweetest person he'd ever known, but he'd never dared say it her face. He comforted himself with the fact that he hadn't really done so now, either. She was at his back, after all. "I'm gonna need you to hold on tight."

She stiffened against him and pulled her thighs wide.

Yeah, she was fully awake now.

"What? Why?" she asked.

"We got company, and I'm gonna need t'employ a few escape and evasion tactics. It may get fairly hairy for a few klicks."

"What kind of company?" Her arms tightened on his waist as her thighs snapped securely around his.

Hey now, how about that?

Had he known that's all it would take to get her to stop twisting herself into a pretzel, he'd have played the whole *escape and evasion* card a long time ago.

"I'll give you two guesses and the first one doesn't count," he replied dryly.

"The CIA agent?" she asked, her hand crawling up to lay over his heart, as if the rock-steady beat somehow comforted her.

"If that's indeed who Mystery Man is workin' for." He covered her small hand with his gloved palm, giving her fingers a reassuring squeeze.

Shit, he should've insisted she stay back at headquarters. The woman was a kindergarten teacher, for Christ's sake. She wasn't cut out for escape and evasion tactics employed from the back of a tricked-out Harley. Of course, there wasn't a damned thing he could do about it now. She was here, and it was his job to make sure nary a hair on her pretty little head sustained so much as a split end.

"I need to call headquarters," he told her. "See if Ozzie can't do us a huge favor and find us a nice little hidey hole."

"Uh, okay…"

He pulled his secure, encrypted cell phone from his jacket pocket and thumbed two on the speed dial. There were a series of clicks. He stated his password.

"Go ahead, Ghost," the voice came clear as a bell through his headset. Ozzie rigged all their helmets with Bluetooth technology. Kid was an asset; no bones about it. Only that wasn't Ozzie on the other end of the line.

"Rebel?" he asked.

"The one and only," she answered proudly. "Ozzie's in the can. What can I do ya for?"

"I've got company," he told her, quickly glancing into his rearview mirror only to find the silver SUV nowhere in sight.

He took no comfort in the fact.

"Can you access our location—we're on I-65 just past Lexington, Kentucky—and find me a place to lie low for the next few hours?"

"No luck with the shell game, huh? That sucks."

Yep, and then some.

"Okay, I'm mapping your location via Phantom's tracking device," Becky said, all business, "but in order to view your company I'm gonna need…." Nate heard the rapid clicking of a keyboard. "Yepper," Rebel came back. "Hold please while I access Eyes in the Sky."

Eyes in the Sky, huh? Ozzie had obviously schooled Rebel on temporarily hijacking a few key military surveillance satellites.

Handy.

Not to mention *very* difficult.

"Okay, Ghost, I've got you on my screen," Becky quickly related. "Looking for viable escape routes and cover."

Wow, that was fast.

He couldn't help but think, *way to go,* chica. The girl was obviously gettin' good and not just at the techie stuff. She could also handle a bolt-action rifle better than most seasoned soldiers.

Boss was going to blow a gasket when he realized just how hard baby girl was trying to turn herself into a full-blown operator. Nate could only hope he was out on assignment when the shit hit the fan…

"Our tail is drivin' a silver Escalade," he told her. "I can't see him now, but at last visual he was 'bout half a klick back."

"Got him on my screen, too," Becky quickly confirmed. "He's still trailing, back farther now, a little over a klick. All right, Ghost, local real estate listing has an empty house in Winchester. Old one. Been on the market a long time, so no real danger of some enthusiastic realtor barging in on you. Its detached garage doesn't have a garage door opener, so you won't have any trouble accessing. In two klicks, you're gonna see your exit."

Nate didn't slow as he zoomed down the exit ramp. Ali squeaked and he wished to God he didn't have to do this. She'd been frightened enough recently without entertaining the very repulsive thought of acquiring a terminal case of road rash.

"First right." Becky's voice was steady in his headset. "End of the block, head left until you hit Magnolia Street."

The little wood-sided houses flying past them had

basketball hoops in their driveways. There was a forgotten blue tricycle in the yard on the corner, and across the street a red Radio Flyer was abandoned with its cargo of stuffed animals.

Thank goodness it was lunchtime and most of the kiddies in the neighborhood were inside eating bologna sandwiches, or this little maneuver would've been much trickier.

"Silver Escalade just exited. He's slowing," Becky informed him.

"Yep, probably trying to listen for us," Nate said through clenched teeth. One of Phantom's little drawbacks.

"Turn left on Magnolia. Tenth house down on the right. Off-white siding, crimson front porch railing—"

"I see it."

"Garage is in the back. If there's a lock—"

"I got my bolt cutters," he interrupted her.

But when he cut his engine and coasted up to the old, rickety, one-car garage, he quickly noted its lack of even an attempt at security.

Small towns. Geez, you just gotta love 'em.

"Hop off, sugar, and..." Shit. He winced. There he went with the whole *sugar* thing again, "lift that door for us, would ya?"

"Well I would, *honey*," Becky drawled through his headset, "but I'm a little busy right now. Not to mention three hundred miles away."

Nate ignored Rebel as he watched Ali stagger toward the garage door. Uh-huh, over four hours on the back of a bike tended to bowleg anyone not used to it. She bent to grab the bottom of the door and—

Jesus. No one should look that good in worn jeans

and a pair of leather chaps. A brief image of her wearing nothing but those leather chaps flashed hotly through his degenerate mind.

Oh…great. Talk about one piss-poor time to spring an erection. Here they were, hundreds of miles from the nearest trustworthy help, with a mysterious operator on their trail and God-only-knew-what waiting for them in Jacksonville, and what do you suppose he was doing? He was reaching down to inconspicuously rearrange himself because his pecker had decided now was a dandy time to snap to attention.

Obviously, he was in need of some serious psychological analysis, because the possibility of imminent death coupled with the sight of Ali in those jeans and chaps shouldn't cause this intense physical reaction. That it did only solidified the fact that there was something really wrong with him. Of course, if growing wood in the middle of battle was any indication of mental deficiencies, then every guy he knew needed to go in for some head-shrinking. Something about the punch of adrenaline tended to work on the male anatomy the same way a Playboy centerfold usually did—and that was one strange evolutionary phenomenon he would never understand.

Once the door slid up with a cranky screech, he quickly walked Phantom into the cool, dusty interior of the garage. Old paint cans rusted on the back shelves, and the place smelled like mildew and mothballs. Dust motes hung heavy in the stale air.

It certainly wasn't the local Hilton, but it'd do in a pinch.

"Close 'er up," he instructed Ali, and she reached up to pull the garage door down. Her shirt lifted above her navel, and that goddamned red jewel in her belly button ring caught the light and taunted him.

Super, now his balls ached in time with his dick. Could this day get any more perfect?

"Silver Escalade is searching the neighborhood," Becky informed him.

Yep, and there you had it. He should know better by now than to ask rhetorical questions.

"Let him search," he replied as he swung himself off the bike and performed the typical squat and shuffle every guy on the planet perfected in order to better situate dangly bits that were no longer so dangly. "He won't like what he finds. Switching to handset," he informed Rebel as he pulled off his helmet and attached a Bluetooth device to his ear. "Mic check. Mic check."

"You're coming through loud and clear, Ghost Man," Rebel chirped happily. This was her first time to man command central, and the position obviously suited her just fine.

Boss was gonna have a conniption.

"Good." Nate lifted a case from his saddlebags and quickly began assembling his long-range weapon. "I need you to monitor the local police bands. We made an almighty ruckus the likes of which they're probably not used to around here. I wouldn't want the local five-oh getting nosy. They'd give away our position in a heartbeat."

"Will do," Becky replied, and he heard more keyboard rattling.

"Ali," he turned to find her standing beside him, golden eyes getting wider and wider by the minute, growing right along with the assembly of his sniper rifle. "I'm going into the house to observe and secure our position. I need you to stay here and keep quiet, okay? No matter what you hear, you do not come out of this garage."

She swallowed and nodded. He could see her rapid pulse hammering away in her neck, and she looked like she wanted to faint.

Once again, he acknowledged the ball-twisting truth that she just wasn't cut out for this shit.

"I'll need a weapon," she said, her voice steadier than he would've guessed.

Whoa. Or maybe she *was* cut out for this shit. Nothing she could've said would've surprised him more.

"Way to go, sista," Becky barked her approval of Ali in his ear.

He hesitated only a second before bending to pull his reserve from the top of his left boot. He handed her the Colt .45 and watched in growing admiration as she press-checked the chamber to make sure the first round was loaded.

So, Becky was right. Grigg *had* taught baby sister a thing or two. Nate wasn't much for man-on-man action, but if Grigg had still been alive, he would've kissed the sonofabitch smack on the mouth right at that moment. Whatever Grigg had intentionally or unintentionally involved Ali in—and Nate would bet his left nut it was *un*intentional—at least Grigg'd tried to prepare her to handle it.

"Don't open that door for anyone," Nate told her as he shouldered his rifle. "I'll announce myself before comin' in."

He turned to head out the side door then stopped and swung back to face her. His conscience was eating away at him, and he cursed himself for the hundredth time for letting her come along, despite her obvious familiarity with a handgun. What had he been thinking? Oh yeah, he'd been thinking how wonderful and torturous it was going to be to have her pressed all along his back for fifteen straight hours.

He'd underestimated both.

It was far more wonderful than he could have guessed and far, *far* more torturous. "It could be awhile," he told her, searching her frightened face. "You gonna be all right in here?"

She nodded her head so bravely he just couldn't help himself. Sighing in defeat and resignation, he stomped back over to her, looped an arm around her slim waist, and dragged her toward him until she was crushed all along the length of him, and her eyes were flying wider than ever.

Then he kissed the bejeezus out of her.

Kissed her until he could no longer ignore what is was he was supposed to be doing. He stormed out of the garage's little side door, trying not to think about the way her eyes had gone all dreamy and glassy, or the way she'd lifted a hand to her chest as if to hold her heart in check.

The woman was going to be the death of him.

"About time you did that," Becky chimed smugly in his ear.

"Can it," he told her.

"I'm just sayin'—"

"Don't just say anything!"

Geez, he was *so* losing it.

"Yo."

Senator Aldus grimaced at the salutation.

Johnny Vitiglioni had about as much class as a music festival Port-o-potty, but Aldus figured a guy whose specialty was Colombian Necktie executions didn't really spend much time polishing his social skills.

"I've got another job for you and the boys," he said without introducing himself. There was no need. Johnny knew exactly who he was talking to.

"I'm listening."

Of course the fool was listening. Aldus paid Johnny a ridiculous rate to make sure the guy was always ready to listen.

"Yes well, let's hope you do better with this one than the last one."

"Hey, dude, I told you Rocco—"

"I don't care," Aldus growled. "Besides, what's done is done. Hopefully, this next assignment is a little more to Rocco's taste."

"Wha' didja have in mind?"

What did he have in mind? Death, that's what. And an end to this pain-in-the-ass situation.

"There's a man traveling with the woman I hired you guys to mug." Thinking of Zoelner quitting when his target was out on a motorcycle—a statistically dangerous device—where it could've been so *easy* for the ex-CIA agent to simply wait for a barren strip of road to careen into the guy, made Aldus's blood pressure boil. Of course, clean-up would've been a problem, but that was a moot point. Zoelner was far too high-minded to engage in such nefarious tactics.

Thankfully, Johnny and his boys had no such hang-ups.

"And?" Johnny prodded when Aldus had been silent for too long.

"And they're on some big, loud Harley. Probably on the road between Chicago and Jacksonville. They need not to be."

"That's a pretty big swath of country, dude," Johnny drawled.

Good God.

Aldus abso-fucking-lutely hated being called "dude."

He wasn't a *dude*. He didn't ride a pony, wear a Stetson, or yell, "Git along li'l doggie!" Nor did he bum around some beach smoking pot and waiting lazily for the next big wave while drawing unemployment.

He was a goddamned senator of the United goddamned States of America, and if he ever made it to the big office, he planned to make it a little harder for the *dudes* of the nation to skate by so easily.

"That's why I'm sending two additional addresses to your secured email account," he told Johnny, trying to hold on to his patience. It was never an easy task, and this...*situation* only made his already volatile temper worse.

And the fact that he'd had to stop in to buy a brand new prepaid phone only illustrated that point. "One of those addresses is the man's residence in Chicago," he went on to explain. "The other one is the woman's parents' house. You still have her home and work addresses?"

"Yeah."

"Good. Now, they will most likely end up at one or the other of these locations within the next twenty-four hours. When they do, I want you to take them out."

"An accident like the last job?" Johnny asked.

Aldus wished it could be that easy, but he was finished taking chances. This had to end now.

"No. It's imperative their bodies are never discovered." He needed assurance that if Alisa was somehow carrying the files on her person, they'd never reach the light of day. "I mean *never*. Encasing them in lead and dropping them into the Mariana trench still isn't going to cut it."

"The what?"

Oh, for crying out loud. Johnny was a walking, talking, stupid Italian mobster cliché. Francis Ford Coppola would absolutely love the little prick. "Just make sure you dispose of the bodies in such a way that no trace of them will ever surface. Is that clear?"

"As fuckin' lead crystal, dude."

Aldus felt the vein in his forehead bulge.

"Hey," Johnny said, "I've got two pictures of dudes on my screen here. I thought you said it was a man and that Alisa woman we were taking out. Neither of these is her."

Wow, this just gets better and better. Someone sign Johnny up for Mensa. Sometimes it was so depressing to know the world was populated by idiots.

Lucky for Aldus, idiots were easily manipulated. Just look at his constituency...

"That second man," he said slowly so Johnny the Dimwit could follow, "means a bonus for you and the boys. I want you to make sure he receives your specialty."

"Ah," Johnny chuckled, and it sounded sort of sick, like the laughter of a little boy pulling wings off a butterfly. No doubt Johnny had done his share of wing-pulling as a child. "Dude must've pissed you off, huh?"

"Yes," he ground his back molars together, "the *dude* definitely pissed me off."

The sound of his wife talking to their housekeeper out in the hall caused him to glance down at his eighteen karat, yellow-gold Cellini Prince Rolex.

He was due in session in twenty minutes. Time to wrap it up.

"Call me when it's done," he told Johnny and didn't wait for a reply before ending the call.

Now, he'd go listen to his peers drone on and on and *on* about making emergency supplemental appropriations for border security.

What a *colossal* waste of time.

In his not-so-humble opinion, the Chinese had it right all those years ago. Build a wall, supply it with armed troops in guard towers, and kill anyone stupid enough to try and cross that big-assed line you just drew in the sand.

Chapter Eleven

AFTER HAULING HIS ASS INTO THE ATTIC OF THE EMPTY house—Christ, he needed to lose about fifteen pounds in order to make the fit through that narrow opening even slightly comfortable—Nate secured his camouflage M-40 A5 USMC issue sniper rifle on its bipod and hunkered down.

He used a string of detcord coiled in a spiral to blow a loophole in the attic wall beside the window and, as always, the feel of the weapon in his hands was like coming home. It simply became an extension of his arm.

Those armorers at Quantico sure knew how to put together one smooth-working machine…

Sierra was his rifle of choice when honing in on a target within a thousand yards.

The ol' girl could do a far sight better than that, evidenced by the time his mark had pulled a fast one and left via a warehouse a good two hundred yards farther away than he or Grigg had planned for. Still, that greasy al-Qaeda operative was leveled by 671 grains of diplomacy before his cache of bodyguards ever heard sweet Sierra's barking report.

As he lowered his eye to the scope and took a brief pass of the park across the way, he tried to forget those days in the field.

Talk about boring. Hours and hours of systematic

recon inevitably followed by about half a minute of insane, ball-shrinking activity.

Grigg had loved to quote other snipers. And one of his favorites had been, *Sniping is poetry in slow motion, up until the moment you pull the trigger*.

From the pull of Nate's trigger, it was twenty measly seconds to the time when their gear was stowed and hidden and they were hell and gone from their hide site. Twenty seconds of balls-to-the-wall, get-it-done-or-die activity. Toward the end, they were doing it in eighteen.

They were that damned good. That fast…

A man was walking in the park, he observed as he instinctively switched to tactical breathing. Three big breaths and then exhale.

The guy had on a University of Louisville baseball cap, a blue button-up shirt, and nondescript, white sneakers. His hands were shoved deep in the pockets of his jeans as he strolled along, head down between his shoulders, watching the sidewalk in front of him.

Perhaps the guy was simply out enjoying the balmy summer day, but then again, Nate hadn't lived to the ripe ol' age of thirty-three by taking chances. Saturday-in-the-Park Dude appeared to be about the same height and build as Mystery Man. *Can you dig it? Yes I can. And I've been waiting such a long time…*And, geez, he'd been spending far too much time around Ozzie—who broke into lyrics every other sentence. At least Nate could say he had better taste than the kid. In his not-so-humble opinion, Chicago beat out '80s glam rock any day of the week and twice on Sunday.

"Come on, look up. Let me get a peek at you," he whispered into the silent, sweltering attic.

Sweat beaded on his forehead and dripped down his temples. The dust and insulation particles floating in the air made his lungs itch. There was a decaying mouse carcass in the corner perfuming the space with the sickly sweet scent of death.

The guy in the park didn't cooperate with his whispered demand.

Go figure. No way was Nate getting *that* lucky.

Then an elderly woman passed by with her overweight wiener dog—the poor thing looked like it was about to split its skin—and Mr. Saturday-in-the-Park bent to give the little chubber a scratch behind the ears.

Nate saw his chance.

Pulling out the high-powered guidance laser from his jacket pocket, he kept his eye on the scope and, with a flick of his thumb, the red line of the laser streamed to life. Focusing on his target, he aimed the thin stream of light.

One thing was for sure: it would be enough to scare the shit out of Mr. Saturday-in-the-Park if he was anything other than a complacent civilian out for a little stroll. Because the mind of a complacent civilian didn't immediately associate a red laser dot as coming from a weapon. Oh no. That type of instinctual reaction was only earned through training and experience, through having lived in a heightened state of awareness where the first thing to come to mind in any situation was not the possibility but the *probability* of an unknown threat…

Automatically his heartbeat slowed.

The world around him faded to black, the discomfort

of the steamy attic forgotten as every cell in his body focused on only one thing. The five S's of the snipers' mantra: slow, smooth, straight, steady, squeeze.

Well, he'd forgo the squeeze part.

After all, if the guy was CIA, he was on a government-sanctioned mission. *So* even though Nate would've liked to add a nice, neat hole between the man's eyes for having the colossally bad taste to point that piece at Ali, he kept his finger poised outside the trigger guard.

Instead, he focused the laser on the scene in the park. And, sure enough, when he centered that evil red dot smack-dab on the back of the guy's extended hand, Mr. Saturday-in-the-Park's exposed jaw turned white as bleached sugar before he bolted into the nearby woods.

The woman holding the dog's leash jumped back, startled. Her fat pooch let loose a mournful bellow, floppy ears slipping down its swollen back as it lifted his head and cried its surprise.

The walls of the attic snapped into view as Nate lifted his head from the scope and cursed.

He ignored the urge to throw down his weapon and give chase; Mystery Man would be halfway to Texas by the time he even made the park.

So, yeah, the best thing for him to do would be to stay exactly where he was. Watching. Waiting. With five rounds of angry lead that could quickly affect an attitude adjustment in any unfriendly individuals.

Just like Grigg always said, *The quickest way to change a person's mind on a subject is a 138gr boat tail.*

Fuckin'-A and Hoo-ah!

As Ali sat on a five-gallon paint bucket in the filthy garage with the cool, disturbing length of Nate's reserve weapon resting against her thigh, she was having second thoughts about her decision to accompany him on this little errand.

It hadn't been a pretty sight that morning when she'd demanded to come along. All the Knights, except for Becky, had sided with Nate, demanding she tell them where the zip drive was located so Nate could go retrieve it.

"No way. This is as much my problem as it is any of yours. More so, come to think of it. I'm the one being followed, mugged, bugged and, oh yeah, I'm also the one who had a gun pointed at her head," she'd said, glaring at the group squeezed together in Frank Knight's small office.

"Which is exactly why you should stay here," Frank said, cool gray eyes watching her warily.

"Oh," she lifted her chin, "so it's perfectly fine for Nate to go out and risk his life, but there are different rules when it comes to me? I don't think so." Just the thought of sending Nate out alone made her want to scream, especially knowing he'd probably retrieve the drive, solve the mystery, and deign to keep her completely in the dark.

"He's trained, Ali," Ozzie spoke with soft authority, which was a little weird considering the guy was wearing nothing but sci-fi pajama bottoms to go along with his rioting hair. It looked like he'd hopped out of bed and in order to blow dry his hair. Backward. "And you, my dear, are not."

"I have more training than any of you likely know. Grigg wasn't a slouch when it came to—"

"Ali," Nate interrupted her, his voice gravelly, black

eyes hard as slate when she swung her attention toward him. "Please come with me."

Oh…perfect.

She cast a furtive glance around the gathered group and was met with impassive expressions.

Okay, so no help from the peanut gallery.

Except for Becky. Becky made a face and then gave her a reassuring wink. Ali appreciated the gesture, but it did nothing to calm her roiling stomach.

This was going to be bad, very bad. But it wasn't like she could refuse him. If she did, she had no doubt the Knights would just file out of the office, leaving her in the same predicament. Alone. With Nate.

She grimaced and blew out a breath before gathering the cat in her arms. She stood and followed Nate up the metal stairs and into his spartan bedroom.

The scene of last night's crime, she thought sourly and wanted to cry at the piercing memory of his callous rejection.

Instead, she mustered all her self-confidence and, lifting her chin, strode purposefully past him to sit on the edge of his bed. At least there he wouldn't notice her legs were wobbly as wet noodles, not to mention the fact that her arms were aching from Peanut's considerable weight.

"You're not going to change my mind," she told him, watching warily as he casually lowered himself into his leather recliner, pushing back and propping his big-booted feet on the footstool. He regarded her with diamond-hard eyes.

"*Why* d'you wanna come?"

"Because Grigg was my brother, and I'm sick to

death of secrets. If I let you get your hands on that zip drive, I'll never know what this has all been about."

He simply watched her.

"You don't deny it?" she asked incredulously.

He didn't move an inch, didn't speak; it didn't even look like he breathed.

So it began. The part where he simply sat and waited her out.

Well, it wasn't going to work this time. Nuh-uh. No way. No how.

The silence stretched on and on and *on*. She could actually hear the second hand ticking away on his wristwatch. Peanut's rotund belly gave a warning growl before he emitted a very un-feline fart.

"Cripes," she said, waving hand in front of her face, trying to waft away the fairly rancid aroma of partially digested Fancy Feast.

Nate blinked, unmoved by Peanut's gastrointestinal attempt to break the tension.

Dropping her hand to scratch Peanut's chin—the cat actually seemed to be smiling—she glared at Nate's frustratingly impassive face. This *wasn't* going to work. She could wait him out until their hair turned gray. She could just sit here and bide her time and—

"Oh!" she threw her hands in the air. It was either that or she was going to use them to strangle the man. "Speak, for the love of God! Speak!"

Peanut let loose with a soulful, drawn-out *mereeow*. His scarred black nose pointed toward the ceiling as his crooked tail flicked back and forth in agitation.

"Not you!" she admonished the cat in annoyance. "You!" she pointed a finger at Nate's muscled chest.

"What'd'ya want me to say?" he asked, sighing resignedly. "If I deem the information too delicate for civilian consumption then, yeah, I'll make sure it's only seen by authorized personal, which you're not."

"But he was my brother!" she screamed at him, furious and frustrated and scared she just might lose this battle and then she'd never know what any of it meant. "I deserve to know just what the devil he was involved with."

"No," he stated with ultra-cool conviction. The Ice Man was back in full force. "You don't. Besides, you already know too much."

"Sheesh," she pulled Peanut to her chest, comforted by his kitty warmth. "So what does that mean? Now you're going to have to kill me?"

Did government spies/covert defense contractors really snuff-out snoopy civilians, or was that just in the movies?

Although, come to think of it, fiction was usually built, at least in part, on fact.

Well, crapola.

"Never," Nate vowed, his already deep voice reduced to a guttural growl, almost savage. "I'll never let anyone or anything harm you, Ali."

Wow. She swallowed the knot of...*something* that'd sprouted furry legs and crawled up to sit in her throat. What did a girl say to something like that?

"Th-thank you?"

His jaw firmed, if that was possible considering it already looked like it was made of marble. "I promised Grigg."

"Oh," she said, and frowned.

What was that strange sensation in her chest? Disappointment?

"So given that," he pinned her with a pointed look, "you're stayin' here."

"Read my lips," she told him sweetly, more determined than ever. She was sick and tired of no one trusting her. It ended now. Today. "No effing way. You want that zip drive? Well, you're taking me with you to get it. I'm finished being left out in the dark. I *can* keep a secret, you know."

If only Grigg had trusted her, told her the truth years ago, perhaps they wouldn't be in this situation right now.

"Ali." It was a warning.

"Yes, Nate?" she smiled and batted her lashes.

"You're gonna give me the location of that zip drive if I hafta paddle your ass 'til it blisters."

The erotic imagery momentarily seared her weary brain as something hot fluttered low in her belly.

Huh. How about that? Did she *want* to have her bottom spanked? She'd never thought she was into that before, but with Nate?

Yeah, maybe…

Then the import of his words sank in or, more importantly, the infuriating male arrogance and lack of respect behind them.

"*What*?" she demanded, standing and ignoring Peanut's disgruntled growl when he slid off her lap and plopped to the ground with a heavy thud.

"Y'heard me," he answered, one brow raised tauntingly.

Oh, that did it. She could almost forgive him for not telling her the truth about Grigg's death. He might have sworn some sort of oath on the Bible, or the U.S. Constitution, or his mother's grave, or whatever it was they made spies/covert defense contractors, or whatever the h-e-double-hockey-sticks he was, swear oaths on.

But one thing she could not, would not, abide was this macho male attitude, this arrogant highhandedness.

Oh no, he di-int!

She did a mental z-snap and channeled her inner badass.

With as much aplomb as she could muster, given she thought she might explode in a blast of righteous fury any second, she marched over to where he reclined *oh so* nonchalantly.

Her smile was feigned and feral as a jungle cat when she stopped in front of him. “I may have come to you for help, but last time I checked I’m not a six-year-old girl and you’re certainly not my father.”

“Thank God for that,” he mumbled under his breath, eyeing her I’m-gonna-kill-you expression with enough mild indifference she was hard pressed not to punch him in the middle of his damnably attractive face.

What was it about the man that made her thirst for violence? She was mild mannered by nature, but something in Nate Weller brought out the tigress in her. She wanted to bite and scratch and hiss…

“So it stands to reason, bucko,” she fisted her hands on her hips and leaned down to put her face mere inches from his, “that you can take your misogynistic threats and shove them straight up your butt.”

Your really fine, really hard butt! The one she usually wanted to take a bite out of, but currently craved kicking straight into next week.

When his lips twitched, her right bicep bunched in readiness to take a swing.

He seemed to read the intent in her eyes, because he

democratically cleared his throat and managed to wipe the semi-smirk from his face. "Sounds painful. I'll just forgo that, if y'don't mind."

"Oooh, don't go getting a sense of humor now!" She was so irritated, she actually stomped her foot—and she was not the foot-stomping type.

"'Scuse me?" He actually seemed genuinely perplexed.

"Y'heard me," she mimicked his accent and mashed-up word usage. "I'm too furious to deal with the sudden appearance of your nascent wit. So you'd better just watch it."

When one black brow inched slowly up the broad expanse of his forehead, she slid him a murderous sidelong glance.

"Oh, yeah?" he taunted with a slow drawl. "Or you're gonna do what?"

Was it possible for blood to actually boil? Because there was a definite sizzling burning along her veins.

"I may be small, but I'm mean," she warned. Plus, Grigg had taught her a few very effective ways to outmaneuver a man twice her size. She itched for Nate to give her one good reason to put those skills to the test.

Just. One.

When his lips twitched again, that did it.

Before she even thought about her next move, she lifted her foot and stomped down on the recliner's footstool, propelling him jerkily into a sitting position. His big feet clunked on the floor as his hair whipped forward to momentarily cover his eyes. He slowly raised a broad palm and carefully raked it back into place.

She stood over him, her eyes shooting steel daggers as her nostrils flared like an angry bull's.

Yeah, give him a red flag and she'd certainly charge headlong.

"You're playing with fire, Ali," he warned, but she was too angry to heed it.

"Oh, I'm real scared."

Slowly, purposefully he uncurled his large frame from the deep seat and stood in a fluid series of bunching muscles and flexing tendons. She had to tilt her head far back in order to continue to glare into his impassive face, but she didn't so much as give an inch.

Nor did she intend to.

She needed to lash out, to bite and scratch and cry. To make someone feel as hopeless and powerless and wretched as she did.

And who better than Nate? The man who'd lied to her, rejected her, and was now attempting to threaten and bully her into giving up the only hope she really had of ever knowing what Grigg was involved in before his death.

"You'll *tell* me where you've hidden that zip drive," he rumbled as he grabbed her shoulders and gave her a gentle shake.

The sudden narrowing of her eyes should've warned him he'd succeeded in pushing her last button, but he did nothing to dodge her clenched fists as she swung them up in a two semi-circles, effectively knocking his trespassing hands away. Nor did he duck the fairly impressive right hook she aimed straight at his solid jaw.

She smiled with vicious glee when his teeth snapped together with a loud clack as his head jerked back on his neck.

Take that, you low-down, rejecting, brooding, cold-hearted, lying *sonofagun!*

She was startled at how quickly he shook off the blow, missing her opportunity to step out of his reach as he swiftly swooped in to secure her arms against her sides, pulling her into his wide chest until he acted as a flesh-and-bone straight jacket.

Uh-huh, pretty slick move, but it only managed to secure her upper body. Her legs were still free, and boy-howdy, she put them to good use.

Hastily swiveling his hips, he grunted and swallowed a low curse when her sharp knee landed just to the right of his family jewels. Somehow, he managed to pin her struggling legs between the steely power of his thighs until all she could do was hiss and wiggle ineffectually.

She called him every dirty name in the book and several more of her own personal construction. But to her utter dismay, her futile struggles soon turned to heart-wrenching sobs.

Why had Grigg felt he had to lie to her? What had he gotten her involved in? Why did he have to go and die and leave her alone? And why had she been foolish enough to fall for Nate Weller? How could she have let herself feel this way about him?

Was she in love with him? God, she didn't know, but she was afraid she just might be.

It was all so useless. She felt so helpless. She wanted to scream, but all the fight drained out of her, leaving only despair and grief and exhaustion in its place.

When she sagged bonelessly inside the manacle of his strong arms, he gently, oh so gently, resumed his seat in the recliner, taking her with him into his lap.

"Feel better?" he asked softly when a full sixty seconds passed after her last snotty sniffle.

"Y-yes," she hesitantly admitted, her head tucked beneath his hard chin, golden blond strands getting stuck in the black whiskers on his jaw. She raised the hem of her shirt and wiped her running nose. She didn't even care how gross it was. "But I shouldn't. It's not right to hit someone."

Even if she'd known the punch she'd thrown wouldn't really hurt him, not that unyielding wall of flesh and bone, it still didn't excuse her tendency toward violence whenever he was around.

"You just make me so...*mad* sometimes. You're the most infuriating man I've ever known, and that's saying something considering I grew up with Grigg."

"Y'needed t'vent a little steam or you were gonna explode."

She pushed back and pinned on him a watery, sidelong look. "Are you saying you intentionally provoked me?"

One big shoulder twitched. She took that to be a *yes*.

"But, why?"

"Like I said, y'needed to vent."

Well crapola. She felt just *horrible* about the whole thing.

"You are a complete dichotomy, you know that? Just when I've crowned you King of the Buttholes, you go and do something...*sweet*. Sweet but kinda weird in the same breath. I mean, who offers themselves up for abuse?"

"It's part of my charm," he said, one corner of his fabulously male mouth twitching.

She rolled her eyes. "You just keep telling yourself that."

Lifting a finger, she lightly touched alarmingly solid bone beneath the harsh bristle of his whiskers. “I’m sorry I hit you. Does your jaw hurt?”

“Yes.”

She winced in sympathy. “Sorry,” she said again.

“Don’t be. Y’did a fabulous job.”

“I did?”

“Yep,” he rubbed at the spot on his jaw and grinned like a loon. “You led with your shoulder. Just like Grigg taught you.”

“Don’t sound so pleased,” she scolded, still a little astonished she’d actually *hit* him… *again*. She’d never laid a hand on anyone in her entire life—the punches she and Grigg had thrown as kids didn’t count—but somehow she’d managed to hit Nate Weller twice. “Knowing how to throw a punch isn’t necessarily something I’m proud of.”

He made the facial equivalent of a shrug. “Next time aim for the nose. It’s a lot more difficult for a man to defend himself with a broken nose. Causes the eyes to water so much it makes it nearly impossible t’see. Not t’mention the blood chokin’ you as it runs down the back of your throat.”

“I didn’t want to hurt you. Not really,” she admitted.

“I know.”

“Nate?”

“Hmm?”

“I’m going with you.”

She watched as he searched her face and almost whooped with victory when he sighed and slowly nodded.

“Okay, but y’do exactly as I say when I say it. No questions. No hesitation. And you’re wearin’ Kevlar. It’s gonna be hot as hell, but that’s my condition.”

"Yes, sir," she snapped him a salty little salute.

He frowned before he growled, "Get up." Nearly dumping her on the floor as he suddenly stood.

"Whoa!" She stumbled but managed to catch herself before she face-planted. "What the heck was that abo—*Oh!*" Her cheeks heated as she saw the hard ridge outlined behind his denim-covered fly.

"Yep," he muttered, "*oh* is right."

"Well why can't we just—"

He cut her off, slashing his hand through the air like a karate chop. "Leave it alone, Ali. I *don't* want to have this reaction t'you, so if you really wanna come with me on this little mission, you'll just leave it alone. Y'got that?"

Yeah, she got it. Loud and painfully clear. And now here she was, somewhere in Kentucky, hiding out from a mysterious government agent who'd threatened her at gunpoint, sitting on an old paint bucket in the quickly warming garage and trying not to hyperventilate.

She hadn't really expected any trouble on the trip.

Crimeny, she really *was* naïve. No wonder Grigg had kept her in the dark for so long.

The sound of a footfall outside had her tightening her grip on the little Colt.

Silently standing, she took the shooting stance Grigg had drilled into her. Right arm extended, left hand supporting the edge of her right palm, head tilted ever so slightly so her right eye lined up with the gun's sights.

All that cloak and dagger stuff in the movies was obviously real, and somehow—because she'd been a complete idiot and insisted on coming along—she'd landed herself right in the middle of it.

Hopefully in real life the ditzy blonde wasn't the first one to bite the bullet.

She quivered when she realized that last bit didn't necessarily have to be a euphemism.

"Ali?"

At the sound of Nate's deep voice, she plopped down on the paint bucket and released her pent up breath in a loud whoosh.

Good heavens, she was so not cut out for this.

"I'm comin' in," he said softly. "Don't shoot me, 'kay?"

"I make no promises," she told him shakily, prying her finger away from the Colt's trigger guard.

She shook her head when she heard him chuckle. The man was too strange. Of all the times to break out that elusive laugh, now was not it.

He poked his head around the side door and gave her a sympathetic smile when he saw her wilted condition.

"It's gonna be all right, sugar," he told her, pushing the rest of the way into the garage. Walking over to his motorcycle, he began to breakdown his weapon with sure, concise movements.

Sugar. He'd taken to calling her that. She wasn't sure if she should be flattered or irritated. She certainly didn't feel like sugar, not today. Today, she felt far too… unmoored to be something as fine and delicate as sugar.

Syrup, maybe. All messy and sticky and slow moving.

Yeah, she could probably go along with being called syrup.

"What'r'ya thinkin' 'bout?" he asked her while precisely stowing the pieces of his vicious-looking sniper rifle into the foam cutouts of his gun case.

What was she thinking about?

She was thinking about her brother's death, about his lies not just to her but to the men of Black Knights Inc. She was thinking about the fact that someone was after her, had been after her for months. She was thinking since Grigg's death her world had turned upside down. She was thinking about what a fool she'd made of herself with Nate, how he'd rejected her despite his body's obvious clamoring to do just the opposite because he didn't *want* to have a physical reaction to her…

Of course, before he'd run off to do whatever it was he'd just done, he'd had the audacity to do an about-face and kiss the daylights out of her.

So what the h-e-double-hockey-sticks?

Either he wanted her or he didn't want her. The back and forth was making her insane.

She glanced up to find him watching her, his expression growing alarmed.

Uh, what was the question again?

Oh, yeah, what was she thinking about?

So much had happened in such a short period of time with so little sleep in between that her usually quick brain was reduced to a slow-moving, doughy mush—about the consistency of pancake batter. Pancake batter to go along with syrup.

How appropriate.

"Pancakes," she finally told him, figuring that was as close to the truth as anything else.

His face relaxed as he lifted one dark brow. "Hungry?"

"No. Not really. Although, now that I'm thinking about it, I'm starting to get a craving. Weird, huh?"

He lifted a shoulder. "Grigg always said you made the best pancakes."

A hard knot instantly formed in her stomach, nauseating her.

That'd been her special treat for Grigg whenever he'd come home on leave or during the few visits he'd made back to North Carolina after joining the Knights. Usually that special treat was also shared with whichever girl Grigg'd managed to bring home with him the night before.

That had been his M.O. Hook up with some woman he met in a bar and cart her back to Ali's spare bedroom for a night of headboard-pounding debauchery—because, of course, he couldn't take his newest conquest to their parent's house. He had *some* discretion, after all.

Come on Ali, he'd once said when she accused him of being a total hound dog, *a guy like me works hard and plays hard. If you'd move that damned bed away from the wall, you wouldn't even know I was there*.

Um, yeah right. 'Cause it was so easy to ignore *Oh, Grigg, yes! Oh, Grigg. Oh, Grigg. Yes, yes,* yes!

She smiled sadly, missing her big, stupid, lusty brother like crazy. What she wouldn't give to wake up tomorrow morning to make pancakes for him and whatever barfly he'd managed to lure home with his masculine wiles.

"Yeah," she told Nate now, "I do make good pancakes. At least, his lady friends always seemed to like them."

He cocked his head.

"You know Grigg. He was always with *someone*. Plus..." she frowned and glanced down at the menacing looking gun in her hand. She knew how to handle the weapon—Grigg had made sure of that—but the thing still looked foreign with her pink-tipped fingers curled around the handle. Whose life was she living? Certainly not hers. She was a kindergarten teacher, for Pete's sake.

"Plus," she shook her head and set the gun on the paint bucket beside her, wiping her sweaty palm on the fine leather of Becky's borrowed chaps. "After their… uh, *excursions*, they were always hungry. And I figured it was a better send-off than Grigg would give them. He usually just kissed them at the door and made some asinine noises about calling them when he was next in-country." She rolled her eyes. "For some reason, it made them feel better to hear it and Grigg knew that, so he said it. I gave him hell about it, the lying, but he said it wasn't a lie so much as an altruistic misrepresentation of the truth. Which, if you ask me, is just a bunch of hooey. Still, those women never complained, so I always figured they were as much to blame as my brother who seemed to have a perpetual pilot light going behind his zipper. Not that he was so different from other handsome, single men of his age, but a baby sister always expects more from her big brother. I'll be the first to admit I suffered a little hero worship where Grigg was concerned and I—"

"Ali," Nate interrupted softly, "it's gonna be all right."

Crapola.

She beat back the burn of tears.

There went her mouth again. Put her in a stressful situation, add a nice dollop of rejection and humiliation along with a big ol' spoonful of Nate Weller—stir until frothy—and she suddenly couldn't stop yammering.

It was a problem, but for the life of her, short of biting her tongue in half, she didn't know how to solve it.

Swallowing, she released her pent-up breath and met his steady gaze.

"How do you know it'll be all right?" she asked him, not even caring about the pleading edge to her voice.

"'Cause I won't let it turn out any other way."

God help her when he said things like that.

Chapter Twelve

"ETA ON CHRISTIAN, MAC, AND JAMIN IS FORTY-EIGHT hours," Becky reported as she stood leaning a slim shoulder against the metal doorjamb to Frank's office.

The sight of her there, so negligent and unknowingly sexy and so, so…*young* made Frank grit his teeth as he reached for the one thing that would keep him from jumping down her perfectly lovely throat just for being her. For being the one thing on the face of the planet he craved more than those damned root beer Dum Dums, or that new shipment of thermal imagery optics they'd all been waiting on for the last two weeks, or…or his next stinking breath, come to think of it.

"Jamin?"

"Yeah," she crossed one bare foot over the other. Her little toenails were painted a bright, do-me-big-boy red.

He'd always thought it crazily intriguing that a girl… woman…girl…*shit! Woman*, she was a *woman*, he told himself. A *young* woman. A young woman who was more often than not covered in thick grease. A young woman who was better than any man he knew at rebuilding an engine—any engine. A young woman who could fabricate sheet metal into anything her creative brain could conceive of with the help of a blowtorch and a mallet. And it was strange and enchanting and goddamned beguiling that a woman like that could be so girly as to insist on having a weekly mani and pedi.

"You know, our new…er, guest of the Israeli persuasion," she said and he yanked his attention away from those fascinating little toes. "That's the alias Christian picked out for the guy."

Ah, yes. That goddamned Mossad agent.

Great. That was just great. One more thing he didn't want to think about.

"He's not a guest. Supposedly, he's gonna be an asset to us."

Becky raised a skeptical brow, and he could only shrug in silent agreement. He was more than a bit leery himself.

"On a separate note," she continued, "Steady says he's staying an extra day at the conference, something about a historical lecture on wound excision and early reconstruction in the treatment of compound fractures during the first World War." She rolled her eyes. "Sounds über-boring if you ask me, but no one ever does."

She shot him a meaningful look that he responded to with an equally meaningful scowl.

"*Anywho*," she continued, "Rock and Billy checked in to say they'd be home at the end of the week, and all's quiet on the eastern front, as it were. Ghost and Ali are about an hour outside of Jacksonville, and Ghost says he'll contact us once he has the zip drive."

It suddenly occurred to Frank, all this should be coming from Ozzie. He narrowed his eyes. "Where's the kid?"

"He's elbow deep in the flight control systems of the Hawk," she said. "He closely resembled a guy with a terminal case of ants in his pants waiting for his turn at the helo. And seeing as how I successfully, and without detection I might add," she pantomimed doing a little curtsy, "hacked Eyes in the Sky this morning, Ozzie figured it was safe to leave me manning the control center so he—"

"Rebecca! Damnit!" he cursed as he reached into his pocket for the bottle of ibuprofen.

Just the thought of the danger she was courting by trying to involve herself in their work made every single aging bone in his body ache. "That's not your job. Your job is to do what you do best. Fix things. Maintain our cover, and keep your nose out of our goddamned business."

She uncrossed her ankles and took up a fighting stance, her slim legs shoulder width apart, her grease-and-paint-free hands—now *that* was a novelty—fisted and held loosely by her sides. "I can do a hell of a lot more than that, *Frank*."

His left eyelid twitched.

"That's not the point," he told her, careful to keep his voice calm. One of them needed to maintain some control, or they were going to tear into each other—and God help them then. "We pay you to do a certain job and—"

"And I do that job!" she yelled. "But I'm capable of more. If you'd only—"

"It's never gonna happen, Rebecca!" he yelled back. So much for control. He was never able to maintain it whenever she was around. "You're *never* going to be an operator."

"Oh, yeah?" Her cheeks were bright red, and it was a good thing eyes couldn't really shoot fire or he'd be nothing but a smoldering pile of ash. "Says who? You're not the only outfit out there, Frank. With the training I've received from the Knights, there are quite a few firms who'd gladly add me to their roster."

What? Training? Knights?

He was going to hurl.

Knowing the things his men could teach her made his bowels grumble, like he was suffering a serious case of Montezuma's Revenge.

"What…training?" he enunciated slowly, precisely. It was either that or he was going to start screaming his head off.

"Ghost is teaching me to snipe," she said smugly and suddenly all those times she and Ghost disappeared made a whole helluva lot more sense.

"Is *that* what you two were doing when you snuck away from the compound? I thought maybe Ghost was confiding in you and—"

"What*ever*," Becky rolled her eyes. "Have you met Ghost? He doesn't tell his troubles to anyone."

Okay, she had a point. He should've known better.

Damn, this was *not* good.

Crazily undaunted by the fact that his face was turning purple, she continued, "Billy is teaching me about explosives and demolition, and just the other day I—"

"*What?*" he interrupted. "How the hell can Wild Bill do that?"

Becky was the guy's kid sister, for crying out loud, and Frank didn't even want to begin to think about what she might've done just the other day. Fucking-A.

"Because I asked him to, that's how," her voice dripped disdain. "You know Billy supports all my ambitions and aspirations, just as a good brother should."

Was she insane? A *good* brother made damned sure his baby sister didn't get within two hundred yards of anything that went *kaboom*!

"I'm also learning rudimentary field medicine from Steady, and Mac has loaned me all his textbooks from the Academy," she announced with no small measure of pride. "I figure in a few more months I'll have more training than…"

He stopped listening because he was really, *really* busy devising inventive ways to kill the Knights.

Sniping? Explosives? Field medicine? FBI investigative techniques? Next, she was going to tell him she was perfecting her own nuclear weapon.

He couldn't let her continue on this path. It led to nothing but sorrow and death, and he'd sooner gouge out his own eyes with a dull stick than see her put herself at such unnecessary risk.

"Never, Rebecca," he told her, cutting her off from whatever the hell it was she was saying now. "I'll never allow it."

"Allow it?" Her brown eyes widened in astonished disbelief, then narrowed as dark fury contorted her pretty face. "Allow it! Screw you, Frank! You're not my husband, and you're not my father. It's not your place to allow or disallow anything. I'm a grown woman, and I'll do whatever the hell I want!"

He wasn't her husband because he was too old, and he wasn't her father because he was just a smidge too young. But he was her boss, sort of, and he was in a position to make sure she didn't go on with this foolish plan to turn herself into an operator.

Fuck, an *operator*. His heart couldn't even countenance the thought.

"You think anyone will hire you once I advise them against it?" he asked coolly, throwing a couple of pills to back of his throat and swallowing them down. It was a hell of a lot more difficult than usual, considering this conversation turned his mouth into a desert.

Her jaw dropped open. “You…you’d do that? You’d keep me from—”

“In a heartbeat,” he promised gravely. If it meant keeping her safe, he’d do anything.

Her face froze in shock. Then she blinked rapidly as if trying to fight tears, and he dug down deep in order to steel himself against them. Feminine waterworks were usually the kryptonite to his Superman, but he’d be damned if he’d let a few tears sway him this time. What he did was for her own good. He knew it even if she didn’t.

But she didn’t cry, didn’t let a single teardrop fall. Nope. Not Rebecca “The Rebel” Reichert. Instead she drew in a deep, quivering breath. Then she stared at him, wearing an expression he’d never forget even if he lived to be a hundred years old.

It was a look of complete disillusionment.

Yeah, now you’re starting to get the picture, sweetheart.

Seeing that look on her face made his chest tight as a cocked bowstring, but he wasn’t about to take anything back.

This *was* for her own good.

“You’re an uncompromising sonofabitch, you know that, Boss?” she whispered, nostrils flaring. The pulse in her neck beat a rapid tattoo he could see from five feet away.

Boss.

Never in his wildest dreams had he thought hearing that name on her lips would cut him to the fucking bone. He nearly winced as unexpected pain lanced through him like a saber strike, somewhere in the region of his heart.

No matter. If it meant adiosing her plan to become an operator, he could withstand anything. Even her hatred.

"Now you're starting to get the picture, Reichert," he whispered softly.

And just like that, it was game over.

Becky dipped her chin toward Frank, a choppy little motion of defeat, before she turned and marched stiffly from the doorway of his office.

She would not cry. She would *not* cry.

She'd already shed far too many tears over the bastard in the three-plus years they'd worked together. But as of this second, no more. No more pining and self-flagellating. No more waiting for the day when he'd stop thinking of her as an annoying little sister type and start realizing she was a *woman*, a woman with quite a bit to offer a guy like him. A woman with quite a bit to offer an organization like the Black Knights.

But no. He'd just made it abundantly clear that day would never come. He'd *never* see her as anything more than a convenience. A female grease-monkey capable only of ensuring their civilian cover remained steadfastly in place.

Oh, she'd deluded herself into thinking their constant bickering and banter was all in good fun. That maybe, just maybe he felt for her a tiny smidgen of what she felt for him. That perhaps, like her, he was waiting for the day when they could drop all the artifice and bullcrap and finally get around to telling each other how they really felt.

Boy howdy, what a loser she'd turned out to be.

"I'm a frickin' idiot," she whispered miserably to the empty conference room. The quietly humming computers seemed to mockingly agree with her assessment.

Frank didn't harbor any secret pining.

Hell no.

After what just went down, it was readily apparent he didn't even *like* her. Worse than that—oh, yes, there was a worse—he held not the slightest bit of respect for her. And that was just so...so...*awful*.

Damn.

Hot tears burned up the back of her throat until it felt like she'd swallowed battery acid. As she fled up the stairs to her room, her bare feet slapped against the metal risers. The sound was as dreadful and hollow as the gaping hole that'd just been blown through her heart.

"Whoa! Hey, what's wro—"

She gave Patti, who'd been coming down the hall with a set of fresh towels, a frantic *not now* wave and darted into the quiet solace of her bedroom. Slamming the door behind her, she slid down the metal surface and covered her face with shaking hands. Hard sobs wracked her.

"Goddamn him!" she yelled into the silence. The heavy brick walls absorbed the sound, denying her even that small bit of victory. "Goddamn him," her voice broke as waves of defeat washed over her.

She wasn't crying for him, she assured herself as she let the hot tears fall into her palms and drip down her wrists.

Hell no.

She was crying for the loss of her idealism...the loss of her dreams.

"We're not going to visit your parents," Nate said as he cut Phantom's growling engine about a block from the Morgan household.

No use waking up the entire neighborhood.

"That's fine." Ali's voice was strangely intimate through the Bluetooth receiver inside his helmet.

The last six hundred miles had been a test of endurance and willpower, because she'd finally allowed herself to totally relax against him, all soft female curves encased in warm leather along his back and outer thighs. He'd had to listen to her soft breathing in his ear the entire journey...and *goddamn!*

Bright, neon blue.

He was sure that'd be the color of his poor balls if he took the opportunity to give them a peek.

"They're asleep by now anyway. Besides," she sighed and it caused a delicious little chill to snake up his spine despite the warmth of the night, "I don't want to explain to them what's been going on. It'll only cause them to worry."

"Mmm," he murmured, trying to beat down the boner that'd plagued him since...well, since forever, it seemed. Was it unhealthy to have an erection that lasted longer than four hours if it was caused by the nearness of a woman as opposed to tossing back a handful Viagra? Something to ask his doc next time he went in for his yearly physical.

"So," he cleared his throat when it came out all

strangled. Not enough blood reaching his vocal cords, no doubt. "Are ya gonna tell me where the drive is now that we're here?"

"No," she replied, not even trying to hide the smugness of her tone. The zip drive was hidden somewhere in her and Grigg's childhood tree house, that much she'd deigned to reveal. The exact location she was keeping to herself. The confounded woman remained crazily convinced he'd dump her in a safe place quicker than she could say, "double-crossing bastard," if she gave up that last little bit of info.

She was right, of course.

The little run-in with Mystery Man in Kentucky continued to bug the hell out of him, and despite Becky's assurance, with the help of Eyes in the Sky, that Mr. Mystery had taken off down the road, he couldn't shake the feeling that someone was eyeballing them. Right at that very moment.

Unsnapping his chinstrap and hooking his helmet on Phantom's chrome handlebar, he scanned the area.

The neighborhood was filled with Cape Cod style bungalows. Their tiny front lawns all carefully tended, their hedgerows precisely trimmed. Flowers burst forth in colorful profusion from all available spaces, in window boxes, overflowing clay pots, and cheerfully lining flowerbeds.

In short, it was a picture-perfect postcard of the Great American Dream.

And here he was, armed with enough firepower to start a coup and a hard case of paranoia quickly growing to the relative size of Texas.

In his head, he started humming that old song from

Sesame Street that said something about one of these things being not like the others.

Geez. Definitely too much time spent with Ozzie.

A wind chime caught the balmy evening air and tinkled its delight. The tart smell of freshly mowed grass perfumed the quiet night, mixing with the slightly more pungent aroma of newly laid mulch.

A dog barked somewhere down the block. A sound of inquiry. Nothing answered, and silence once more settled over the pristine little neighborhood.

Further inspection revealed no telltale security signs placed strategically in flowerbeds. No ADT or Brinks Security stickers graced the corners of front windows. Hell, he would bet his left nut—his very *blue* left nut—that most of these homes sported either unlocked windows or doors or both. The whole scene screamed safety and security. The kind of place parents still let their kids run around unsupervised.

So why the hell were the hairs on the back of his neck doing that annoying little tango?

"Hey," Ali poked him to get his attention. "What are we waiting on?"

He shook his head by way of answer and reached around to snag his night scope from one of the heavy leather saddlebags. Holding it to his right eye, the world dissolved into a series of greens as he quartered the area, searching for movement, a darker shadow that just didn't belong.

But…nothing. Not one blade of perfectly mowed grass out of place.

Christ, the place could've been the set for *The Stepford Wives*.

Well, wasn't *that* a disconcerting thought?

He scanned the area one more time and was finally forced to shrug away his tension and release his pent-up breath.

Maybe having Ali along had pushed his usual tendency toward paranoia into the realm of straight-up lunacy. And that was never good, especially for an operator whose reflexes were honed to a razor-sharp edge.

He took another deep breath and flexed his shoulders.

"Okay," he told her as he swung from the bike, "we're going in fast and quiet. Understood?"

He watched her remove her helmet and shake her shiny hair loose like some damned *Suave* commercial before she shot him a look clearly stating that she was convinced he suffered from an IQ very close to his shoe size.

"Roger that." She snapped him a surly little salute.

God help him.

He was suffering from a case of blue balls as well as a McDonald's super-sized order of someone's-watching-me phobia, and the minute she got all snarky and sarcastic he forgot everything. All he could think of doing was grabbing her up and kissing her until that sardonic look melted into one of soft passion. That's the way it'd happen, too. That's the way it happened every time he was suddenly struck by chronic stupidity and allowed himself to get his lips on her. She'd tense for a second, just a second, and then she'd dissolve in his arms like a spoonful of sugar in a jug of sun tea. It was the damndest thing, and it made his already throbbing dick play the part of drumstick against his lower belly.

"Now's not the time," he muttered to himself and his little head.

"What did you say?"

"Nothin'."

She eyed him askance.

When he motioned with his chin for her to head down the block, she cast him one last skeptical look, then shrugged, before turning to do as he instructed.

They were only halfway to the Morgans' house when he got that itchy feeling again, like someone had him lined up in the ol' crosshairs. He really wished he'd taken the time to search the area. As Grigg always said, *Time spent on recon is seldom wasted*.

Unfortunately, it was too late for that. They were already in the open or, in grunt vernacular, they were left hanging with their asses in the breeze. Easy targets for whoever might be out there watching.

Easing his .45 from his waistband, he covered Ali's six as she blithely strolled down the quiet street. Keeping his head on swivel and his ears cocked to the slightest sound, he followed her around the side of her parents' house, through the wooden gate and into the cool, quiet backyard.

A mammoth, stainless steel grill took up center stage on the flagstone patio, testament to the many barbecues they'd all shared during those rare times he and Grigg had taken leave. A round patio table and six chairs occupied the remaining patio space and Nate remembered a time, not too many years ago, when he and Grigg had sat right there, after the rest of the Morgan family retired, and talked about quitting the Corps and signing on with the new outfit Frank Knight was trying to put together.

He was suddenly overcome by a terrible case of *what-ifs*.

What if they'd stayed in uniform? Would they be retiring now? Maybe opening up a little pub together, getting fat on beer and steaks and thinking about settling down to start families?

What if he'd missed that last transport back from Colombia? Would they have still been tasked with that goddamned, ill-fated Syrian job?

What if he'd just been able to chew through those ancient ropes a little sooner? Would he have been able to save Grigg's life?

What if—

"Watch that first rung," Ali broke into his uselessly spinning thoughts, "it's pretty frayed."

He glanced up to see her quickly climbing the old rope ladder hanging down the rough trunk of the huge oak tree that regally stood sentry in the Morgan's backyard.

Wow. Her butt was at eye level, causing his neon blue balls to tighten.

So great. His miscreant mind instantly jumped from death to sex. Not for the first time on this mission, he realized there was obviously something wrong with him, and the trip to see that shrink was starting to look more and more unavoidable.

"Say the magic word," she teased after pulling herself up through the dark hole in the bottom of the tree house, grabbing the rope ladder and acting like she was going to reel it up.

"Alliii," he warned and snagged the end of the frayed rope before she could lift it any higher. Not that he couldn't scale the tree sans rope ladder one-legged and blindfolded, but he didn't particularly like the thought of the rough bark tearing into his palms, or the state of Ali's precious neck once he got his hands on it.

"Naaatte," she mimicked his tone, her damn nose doing that irresistible wrinkly thing again when she grinned and peered down at him.

"This is no time for games," he told her, although he was beyond relieved to see her somewhat back to her old, mischievous self.

He worried their little row in his bedroom last night, not to mention the way he'd ended things this morning, had forever wiped that teasing smile from her sweet face—at least as far as he was concerned. And wouldn't that have been a crying shame? Especially considering Ali's smile held an annual spot on his list of Top Ten Great Things to Happen to Me This Year.

"Oh pooh, you're too serious. Besides, there's nothing to fear up here," she sat back as he quickly scaled the ladder and hoisted himself up through the tree house's trap door. "This place has been besieged by dragons, Vikings, bandits, Indians, robbers, and cutthroats. It has yet to be taken."

"Hmm," he pulled the trapdoor shut, effectively shutting out the light from the Morgans' landscaping and closing them into inky blackness.

The interior of the tree house smelled like dry, flaking paint and dusty fabric, like melted wax crayons and old Elmer's glue, like years of gooey s'mores and roasted hotdogs.

It smelled like every kid's wildest dream.

"I bet all those villains had brown hair, mischievous brown eyes, and answered t'the name Grigg," he mused aloud as he fished his penlight from his hip pocket.

A dull *snick* sounded just before diffuse yellow light washed through the interior. Overhead, a single, bare bulb hung from a utilitarian socket.

"Wired for electricity?" he asked, impressed, and re-pocketed his penlight. "You and Grigg weren't playing around when you built this thing, huh?"

"Dad did most of the construction work. Mom's the one who made the curtains and the cushions for the benches," she motioned to the low benches under the four identical windows. "She also painted the faux rug on the floor, *and* she even made sure there was real glass in the windows. Dad was just going to leave them open, but she insisted. I remember her saying, '*Paul,* how are they supposed to keep out the wind and rain and marauders with no glass in the windows?'"

He blinked at her.

"What?" she asked, "Oh don't give me that look. It's not like my parents never spent *any* time with us; it's just that they *preferred* each other. And you're wrong, you know," she quickly added, then smiled when she saw his confusion. "The villains? They were always blond, tawny-eyed, and answered to the name Ali. Did you really think Grigg would deign to be the bad guy? He suffered from save-the-world-syndrome even back then."

Yeah, Nate could see it all very clearly. Grigg guarding the tree fort while a ponytailed Ali stood below, shooting up plastic arrows with suction-cup tips, or brandishing a homemade slingshot armed with rubber balls. "You were never able to vanquish him?"

"Well, once I got old enough to get really crafty, Grigg lost interest in playing Knights and Dragons or Cops and Robbers. About that time he started using the tree house as his personal testing facility for the seduction of Candice Honeypot."

A startled snort erupted before he charged, "C'mon. You're kiddin' me. No sane man names his daughter Candy Honeypot."

She raised a brow that clearly stated, *oh yeah?* "You'd believe me if you ever met *Mr*. Honeypot. Let's just say he could be relied upon to buy us beer while we were underage, not to mention the fact that he smelled like he bathed in his own bong water."

"Jesus."

"Mmm," she shook her head and grinned. "Not even close."

They were silent for a few seconds as they contemplated the great paternal calamity that was Mr. Honeypot. The rhythmic drone of night insects was a distant hum in the background, the biological equivalent of white noise.

"So," she finally said. "You wanna see the memory box?"

"Yeah," he told her, glad for the change of subject because he was seriously considering finding the paragon that was Mr. Honeypot and zealously maiming the guy for encouraging Ali and the neighborhood kids to degenerate behavior.

Man, people should really have to apply for a special license before being allowed to procreate...

With a flourish, Ali pulled a dusty sheet from a large lump in the corner to reveal an old trunk. He raised a brow even as he helped her drag the trunk closer.

"He gave it to me to replace the old toy box we used to use," she said, running a reverent finger over the stenciled letters PFC MORGAN, GRIGG.

"Mmm."

Mmm? Really? That was the best he could do?

He opened his mouth to try to come up with something a little more erudite than *mmm* when she continued. Obviously, she hadn't noticed the inelegance of his answer. No shock there.

After a dozen years, she was no doubt accustomed to his reticence. At least that's likely what she'd call it—reticence. But the truth of the matter was, when she got that soft, vulnerable look in her eyes? He was tongue-tied.

Tongue-frickin'-tied.

"You know, a lot of people thought it was strange that Grigg and I were so close. Brothers and sisters usually aren't, or so I've been told. I think it was because our parents were so lovingly…uh, *inattentive* is the best word to describe it, I guess. Anyway, because of that, Grigg and I had to depend on each other. We'd go together, just the two of us, to Dairy Queen to celebrate our good report cards. I never missed one of Grigg's baseball games, and he never missed any of my piano recitals."

But then Grigg died, and now all she had was a big old chest full of memories.

Nate had never really realized it before, and it broke his friggin' heart to suddenly lightbulb it now, but for all intents and purposes, Ali was alone. And even though he wished it weren't that way for her, he figured there was some comfort to be found in discovering they at least had that in common.

"Grigg," she whispered, still caressing those stenciled letters, "he taught me to tie my shoes, to ride my bike.

He even taught me how to use a condom." Her smile was faint, sweet. "With this giant, garden cucumber as a model, no less. You can imagine my disappointment the first time I actually got the chance to try out my skill on living flesh and blood."

He really didn't want to know but... "How old were you?"

"Nineteen."

"Christ," he growled, hating the guy who'd had the unfathomable honor of being Ali's first and...oh, great. What a wonderful time to have a friggin' epiphany.

As if his day couldn't've gotten any worse.

But hold the phone, it just had. Because he suddenly realized there'd be no more fooling himself. No more pretending this thing he had for her could be explained away as a simple case of unrequited lust.

He loved her.

Bam! as Emeril would say.

He loved her like he'd never loved anyone or anything in his whole sorry life and wasn't that a giant *fuck you* from the universe?

Because it changed nothing.

She could never be his. Not in a million years. Because, and it was as simple and as horrible as this, nothing could change the fact that he'd killed her brother.

Goddamn fucking sucking hell! He wanted to scream at the injustice of it all, give the morbidly unfair universe a double middle-finger salute. Instead, he shook his head and muttered, "I wish...I wish..."

He wished so many things he didn't even know where to start.

"Yeah," she saved him from having to finish, "me too."

And as he stared into her soft, luminous eyes, he thought maybe he believed her. "Let's do this thing, huh?" she murmured, and for a moment he was arrested.

Do what? Finally admit they…

"Let's get the zip drive and get the heck out of here."

Yep. Right. Good idea, lest he break down in tears and declare his love.

And wouldn't that shock the hell out of her? Nate "Ghost" Weller, or as Ozzie liked to call him, Mr. Emotionless, losing it, sobbing like a baby, and professing undying amour?

She'd probably think he'd gone completely crazy, and she wouldn't be far off the mark. That was the really sad thing.

He took a deep, steadying breath as he watched her reverently lift the lid to the trunk.

He just had to keep it together for a few more minutes and then they'd be out and on their way. The sooner the better. Not only was he moments away from blubbering like a baby and pouring his heart out, but his unease was growing with each ticking second.

And then the ticking seconds no longer mattered because time stood still.

Grigg…

The first thing to meet Nate's eyes was the picture taped to the inside lid of the trunk.

"God, I miss him," she breathed, running one slender finger down Grigg's photographed face.

Riiippp. His heart split right down the middle. He was surprised the sound didn't rent the air.

Sweet. Jesus. This was hell. Forget his irradiated blue balls. Forget his unease about this whole goddamned, goatfucked situation. Forget he was in love with the one woman on the entire planet destined to never be his, because…there was Grigg. Looking like Grigg usually looked.

Even pinned down in the middle of a godforsaken jungle, enemy fire shredding the foliage around them, Grigg'd worn that same devil-may-care expression. Face split wide in a silly grin as infectious as the common cold. The stupid sonofabitch had loved life. All aspects of it.

"Do you miss him?" Ali asked, her voice husky. "Sorry that's a stupid question. You were closer to him than any of us. Of course you miss him."

"I knew 'im better than any of you, perhaps," he was quick to correct her. "But he was closest to you, Ali. You were his heart. And I miss him every goddamned day."

"Yeah," she sighed, giving Grigg's photographed face one last caress. "Yeah, me too.

Chapter Thirteen

ALI COULDN'T BREATHE.

It had nothing to do with the heavy Kevlar vest she wore beneath her jacket and everything to do with the air inside the tree house. It was stiflingly close. Filled with too many memories, too much grief and regret.

She had to get out. Now.

Quickly digging to the bottom of the trunk, she pulled out a plastic bag filled with zip drives. Indelible ink listed the dates she'd received them. She found the one dated one week before her life was changed forever and handed it to Nate.

He stared blankly at the thing for a moment, as if he couldn't believe everything they'd been going through could actually come down to this innocuous little piece of plastic. Then he carefully slipped the zip drive inside his deep jacket pocket.

She turned to push the trunk back into place, frantic to get out, but he stopped her, taking her hand and curling his warm fingers over hers.

Whatever differences they had, whatever hurts and humiliations had passed between them, nothing changed the fact that they'd both loved Grigg like crazy. They were both still bleeding out from the deep, ragged wound of Grigg's death.

She glanced up into his handsome face and saw understanding and compassion there…and something more. Something she didn't understand.

Whatever it was, it made her hopeful and scared and…and…

Oh cripes. She had to get out. She couldn't think straight anymore. Maybe it was the exhaustion or the fear, but she thought…just for a second…

She shook her head. She didn't know what she thought.

Giving him a tight smile, she slipped her hand from his, and hastily pushed the trunk back into place. She scrambled toward the trapdoor, but before she got there she stopped and turned.

Here, in this safe place of childhood dreams, she had to know one more thing. "Were you with him? In the end?"

Nate's agonized gaze snapped to her face, and there was such bleakness there it stole away her breath.

Yeah, she may've been Grigg's heart. But Grigg had been *Nate's* heart.

Closer than brothers, her mother once remarked. And now, seeing his tortured expression, she believed it.

"Yes." His voice was gritty as sandpaper, the muscle in his jaw working overtime.

"Was there a lot of pain? Did he suffer?" God, she didn't know why she was asking *that*.

Of course there was pain. *Of course* he suffered. He'd been *tortured*.

"Yes," Nate whispered and the flinch of one eyelid was the only indication of what it cost him to admit as much to her.

It was only one word, harshly spoken, but when she thought about it, she realized that one word revealed a hundred things. A hundred terrible, horrible things.

Good heavens, Grigg, I'm so sorry. So incredibly sorry.

She'd always known her brother wouldn't go easy,

but to hear it confirmed was almost more than she could bear. Dragging in the musty, familiar smell of the tree house, she blew out a shaky breath and nodded. "Okay."

She dipped her head again when Nate hesitated, giving her a hard, searching look. "Let's go. I'm all right."

He ground his jaw, obviously unsure what to do, then he sighed heavily and turned to lift the trapdoor.

She watched him quickly and dexterously clamber down the rope ladder, and furiously dashed away a rebellious tear. She would not saddle him with a blubbering woman when he'd done the one thing she'd asked of him…namely, he'd given her the inexplicably, horrendously, unvarnished truth.

Then his big black biker boots silently hit the soft earth beneath the oak, and she no longer had to dash away tears. They dried quicker than a desert wind when he held up a fisted hand.

Even if she hadn't been trained by Grigg, she'd watched enough movies to know what that particular hand gesture meant. It meant hold still and stay absolutely quiet. It meant something had spooked Nate "Ghost" Weller, and that really scared the crap out of her.

Awful seconds ticked by like hours, and her already frayed nerves wound as tight as a metal spring.

She never thought she'd say it, but right at this moment she actually *missed* the comfort of Nate's reserve weapon in her hands. As soon as they got back on Phantom, she'd ask him to hand over the little Colt.

And wow, would you look at what a turn her life had taken?

Thirty-six hours after running to Nate, and she was downright itchy without the solid weight of a handgun in her waistband. Maybe by tomorrow morning she'd be sporting bandoliers and a red bandana. She could give Ozzie a run for his money in the Rambo impersonation department.

*They drew first blood, not me...*She tried it out in her head and decided Ozzie was probably a lot more convincing.

Finally, after what seemed like an eternity, Nate glanced up, black eyes piercing the darkness like lasers. He nodded his head, never relaxing his steady grip on his matte-black weapon. Despite his reassurance, she gave the surroundings one more solid scan before she scrambled down the rope ladder.

She barely touched good ol' terra firma before he was urging her forward across the lawn.

"What is it?" she whispered, nervously trying to peer into dark corners and through the dense foliage of her parents' hedges.

By way of answer, he merely shook his head, eyes darting around the same corners and bushes.

A chill rushed down her spine like the cold fingers of a wraith. It was the only warning she received before the subtle creaking of the gate's hinges was broken by a strangely harsh spitting sound.

Nate grunted and yelled, "Run!" as he pushed her through the opening.

She didn't need to be told twice.

She bolted across her parents' front yard, her legs doing a fairly good impression of the Roadrunner when the frighteningly loud *boom boom boom* of Nate's .45 split the serene silence of the night and the comfort of the sleepy, middle class neighborhood. Turning just in time to see a large black shadow stumble backward into her parents' side yard—*Hey! That looks a lot like my mugger!*—she was once more propelled forward as Nate grabbed her by the elbow.

"Don't stop," he hissed.

Was he kidding?

Stopping was the dead last thing on her mind.

Porch lights were snapping on, and the neighborhood dogs were barking their canine heads off by the time the two of them skidded to a breathless stop beside Phantom. In one smooth move, Nate swung astride the mean looking motorcycle and started its enormous engine with a grumbling roar.

Ali clambered up behind him and in the next instant they were zooming down the no longer sleepy, suburban street, struggling into their helmets as they headed for the highway and the relative safety of the open road.

Dagan scrambled around the corner of the little clapboard house and stood over the man Nathan Weller had shot mere seconds before.

No mistaking it: the dude was dead.

The two neat holes centered over the guy's heart and the one smack-dab between his eyes—Mozambique style—were evidence enough without the repulsively permeating aroma of shit. As if being dead wasn't humiliating enough, it wasn't unusual for one to suffer a final indignity and fill the ol' drawers.

Mmm, lovely. Just lovely.

Dagan breathed through his mouth as he bent to quickly search the corpse's pockets.

Nothing.

No surprise there. Only a two-bit idiot would bring identification to a hit. And that's certainly what it had been.

Dagan had been sneaking around the corner of the Morgans' house just in time to see a big black shadow pull a Walther P22 with a six-inch silencer from behind his back. The hard spit of the silenced bullet had sounded obscene in the quiet solitude of the quaint little backyard.

Dagan dove for cover and missed Weller's split second reaction, but there was no mistaking the hard bark of an angry .45. Nor was there any mistaking the fact that Weller was a much better shot than ol' No Name here.

Bleck. What a stench.

Breathing through his mouth only made matters worse. He was starting to *taste* the fetid air seeping up from the lifeless body, and what he wouldn't give for a nice shot of Scotch right about now.

He used his penlight to lift Stinky's ski mask and cataloged the Italianesque features it revealed. Tan skin, black hair, brown eyes that'd yet to lose their brilliance in death. A nose that'd been broken a time or two and one front tooth that was pure, fourteen-carat gold.

Stinky looked like a hoodlum, that was for sure. But a well-paid hoodlum if the sparkly two-carat diamond in the guy's ear was anything to go by.

Taking his cell phone from his breast pocket, he snapped the dead man's picture and then quickly slunk back into the shadows.

What the hell is going on?

Flaming hell, he *still* hadn't a clue.

Although there was one thing he was now 100 percent convinced of, if this was an old Western, Aldus would be the one black-hatting it. There was no mistaking this guy was the same man who'd attempted to mug Ms. Morgan—he'd recognize that no-necked sonofabitch anywhere—and he'd take two to one odds that whoever this reeking dead dude was, his paycheck was signed by one Alan Aldus.

Which meant the good senator was now desperate.

And there was nothing scarier than a desperate man with the power and resources of the U.S. government at his disposal.

The sound of one badass Harley firing up down the block had Dagan hurrying to his rented SUV.

"What about my parents? That guy…that guy could go in there and…" She couldn't even finish the thought much less the sentence. They'd been on the highway for five minutes with Ali's stomach firmly lodged in the middle of her throat before continuous swallowing finally got the sucker back down to where it belonged and she was able to ask the question.

"No. He won't," Nate assured her.

"But if he's after the zip drive, he might think Mom and Dad—"

"He's not thinkin' 'bout anything anymore, Ali. I promise y'that."

"Oh," she said, then "*Oh!*" when realization dawned.

Okay, so the man was dead.

Nate had killed a man right in front of her…er, right behind her.

Good heavens, she didn't even know how to feel about that. What in the world was happening? How had her life spun so far out of control?

"Who...who was it? He-he looked a lot like the guy who tried to mug me," she said, refusing to think of the wife or kids who might be waiting at home for the man. If she started down that path, she'd go crazy.

"I don't know who it was. Never seen him before, but I wouldn't doubt he's the same dude who tried to snatch your purse," his voice was even more gravelly than usual. "Only this time, he wasn't after your handbag."

Her stomach began a steady climb back up into her throat, so she swallowed and tried again. "Was he...was he working for the government, do you think? Did we just kill a..." she choked.

"No," he assured her firmly. "I know a trained operative when I see one. This guy was nothin' more'n a two-bit hit man."

"A hit man?" she squeaked. "How do you know?"

"The big gun he pointed at us with its six-inch suppressor was my first clue."

"Suppressor?"

"Silencer."

Good. *Heavens.*

A silencer. People really used silencers.

Well, of course they do, she chided herself. Especially if those people were *hit* men. "Who would send a hit man after us?"

Her question was met with stony, resounding silence. All she could hear was the harsh sound of her too-fast breathing and the rhythmic rush of blood pounding through her ears.

"Nate?" she finally prodded, squeezing her eyes closed as they leaned into a hairpin turn.

"Don't know," he finally replied, shifting gears until Phantom was literally roaring, eating up the asphalt like a two-wheeled demon. And not knowing was obviously causing him some concern if the labored tone of his voice was anything to go by. "But one thing's certain," he added, "someone wants us dead."

"*Dead?*" she screeched.

Of course, she should've made the connection before. Hit men didn't generally pass out snow cones and helium balloons, now did they? But her mind was working a little slowly, and the thought of someone actually trying to kill her was so foreign she was having trouble grasping it.

"But...but..." she was shaking her head and fighting not to panic.

This was not her life. This couldn't be her life.

"How do you know he was trying to kill us?" she beseeched him, willing him to tell her it was all a horrible joke. "Maybe...maybe he was just sent to scare us or something. After all, that CIA guy had a chance to kill us at Delilah's, and he didn't. How do you know this guy wasn't going to do the same? How do you know he wasn't—"

Her stomach was no longer in her throat. Heck no. Now it was spinning around like a whirligig, and... yeah...she was going to hurl. No stopping it this time.

A gurgling sound emanated from the back of her throat.

"Goddamnit!" Nate swore. "Can y'puke while in motion, or do we need t'pull over?"

She couldn't answer him. Not when she was busy

leaning over the side of the speeding bike, lifting her visor, and projectile vomiting.

Well huh, what do you know? It appeared she *could* puke while in motion.

And lucky for her—if anything about this whole disastrous situation could be considered lucky—she managed to miss both her leg and Nate's. She couldn't speak for the fate of the back tire, though.

Saliva pooled thick and hot in her mouth as she watched the guardrail zoom past.

"You okay?" Nate asked, his voice strangely discordant.

Right about now he was probably *really* regretting giving in to her demands to come along on this mission.

Oh, who was she fooling? She herself was regretting it with the burning intensity of a thousand suns.

"Y—" she spit—gross—and tried again. "Yes. I…I think so."

Sucking in a deep breath, she licked her parched lips and straightened.

Okay. Okay, she could do this. She could deal with the fact that not only was the CIA after them, but now a hit man as well. She could deal with the fact that…

"Erp," she ground her jaw when her stomach turned over again.

All right, maybe *deal with* was too strong a phrase.

She wasn't dealing with anything except trying to combat the urge to toss her cookies. Problem there being there weren't any cookies to toss, which meant dry heave time. And she really, *really* hated dry heave time.

"Ali, do y'need me to pull over?"

"No," she assured him. "I'm…I'm fine." She sucked in another cleansing breath and willed herself to be so.

He snorted, the sound loud and particularly disbelieving through the Bluetooth headset.

"Okay, I'm not fine," she admitted shakily. "But I'll live."

His only response was a grunt.

Yeah, she'd live, because Nate was back to his oh-so-verbose self, which meant things must be okay, or as okay as they could be…considering.

She breathed a silent sigh of relief. Her stomach settled…a little. Then something hot and wet slid over her fingers where they wrapped around Nate's waist. Daring to loosen her grip, she held on with one arm as she brought her hand close to her face.

Something oily and black met her eyes.

What in the world?

She couldn't for the life of her figure out what it could be. Then they zoomed beneath a glowing yellow street light, and the black oil turned bright, horrible crimson.

"You're bleeding!" she yelled, fresh panic making her voice break on a hard edge.

"Yep," he grumbled, "that's what happens when y'get shot."

"Shot!" she howled. "He shot you?" So much for the *just sent to scare them* theory.

"Ali, stop screamin'. You're gonna burst my eardrums."

Was he crazy? He was worried about burst eardrums when he was *shot*?

"Where are you going?" She suddenly realized they were flying down the highway, heading away from Jacksonville at a speed that would've scared her to death had she taken the time to think about it. "We have to get you to a hospital!"

"No," he ground out. "It's nothing. Barely a scratch."

"A scratch?" she screeched incredulously, once more glancing down at the sticky blood staining her trembling hand. "A bullet does not leave a scratch, you big dumb idiot. It leaves a *hole*. Where were you hit?"

He didn't answer, just continued to drive Phantom like a bat out of hell.

The cool wind was a hurricane in her face, the dashed lines in the middle of the road whizzed by so fast they almost appeared unbroken. The cars they zoomed past looked like they were standing still.

"Nate," she demanded, "where…were…you…hit?"

"Upper left shoulder. Right above my collarbone. Don't worry, it went in and came out."

Don't worry. Someone was trying to kill them, had actually *shot* him, and he was telling her not to worry.

Was he *crazy*?

He must be since she'd asked herself that same exact question two times in as many minutes.

She looked at his left shoulder and sure enough. His thick, leather jacket was torn, and a frightening river of dark blood oozed down his broad back.

Taking a deep breath, she spoke softly, calmly, lest she start screaming her head off. "Nate, you're losing blood. Now, either you turn this bike around and head to the nearest hospital, or you pull over somewhere where I can examine your wound. If you—"

"We don't have—" he tried to interrupt her, but she just talked right over him.

"—*don't* do one of those two things I swear to God

I'm going to jump off this bike, because I refuse to docilely sit back here while you slowly bleed to death!"

The last three words were screeched even though she'd done her best to remain calm because, really, just how the h-e-double-hockey-sticks was she supposed to remain calm in a situation like this?

When he didn't answer, she clenched her jaw until her teeth ached. "You know I'll do it," she threatened.

No, it wasn't a threat. It was a promise.

"Goddamnit!" he cursed, but she knew she'd won when he took the next exit.

They drove for a little over five miles, although it felt like five hundred to Ali, before coming upon the Happy Acres Hunting Lodge.

Now, the Happy Acres was no more a *lodge* than a motor home was a *mansion*, but at least the vacancy sign was lit up and the place looked like it probably had running water.

Pulling Phantom around back and hiding the motorcycle behind a tall patch of wild hydrangeas, Nate dug his wallet from his back pocket and handed her a couple of crisp, fifty dollar bills.

"Get a room," he instructed, removing his helmet.

Even in the dim glow given off by the flashing Happy Acres sign, she could see his usually swarthy skin was waxy and pale. He was sweating, his black hair damp and curling around his temples.

"Pay with cash and use an alias when signin' the book," he added. "I don't want anyone to track us here."

Yeah, considering someone, or a group of someones, was out to kill them, being tracked here would be bad.

She shook her head, refusing to think about that or

she was going to hurl again. As she strode toward the office, she wiped her bloody hand on the butt of her jeans. *That'd* surely be the way to secure a room. Hand whoever was in charge of running the night shift at Happy Acres a fist full of bloody bills.

Gave a whole new meaning to the phrase, "blood money," now didn't it?

She laughed and then clamped her teeth together when she realized she was inching toward hysteria. She just didn't have time for the total psychological meltdown she so richly deserved.

Dragging in a deep breath—sheesh, the septic was obviously backed up in one of the units and *that* certainly didn't do her sensitive stomach any favors—she pulled open the door to the Happy Acres' office.

Five minutes later, she walked out with the key to room eight, the Big Mouth Bass Room, or so the night-shift guy with the ridiculous comb-over told her while trying to ogle her breasts beneath her biker jacket. When she leaned down to sign the ledger, he tilted his head to get a better look and the thin chunk of hair parted just above his right ear lost its precarious perch and slipped down to dangle onto his scrawny shoulder.

He'd quickly swiped it back into place, but…wow… who was the guy trying to kid with that 'do?

Her night was just getting more and more bizarre. And it was only promising to continue on that path, because…the Big Mouth Bass Room? Really?

She hated to be a broken record, but *whose* life was she living?

~~~
~~~

Nate thumbed off his cell phone when Ali emerged from the Happy Acres office. He'd reported back to Black Knights Inc. on their situation—namely, he had the drive and was mildly wounded by a guy whom Ali claimed bore a suspicious resemblance to her mugger. Their location—namely, they were stopped at some podunk travel lodge in the middle of nowhere. And their agenda—namely, they were going to dress his wound, get some grub, and rest for a few hours until things cooled down.

He only hoped Ozzie could work his magic and keep the local police from coordinating an all out manhunt for the two of them, because there was a very dead guy on the side lawn of Paul and Carla Morgan's house and witnesses had to have heard, if not seen, Phantom leave the scene only moments after the report of those three, unmistakable gunshots.

Ali waved a key with a big, plastic key ring attached. Was that?…Yep, it was shaped like a trout. Oh, the Happy Acres promised to be quite a treat.

"Follow me to our cozy little home away from home," she instructed as she took the duffel he handed her. He shouldered the remaining saddlebags and…

Shit! That hurt!

Yep, he was shot. Best to remember that.

He gritted his teeth as he traipsed behind Ali to a door with chipped and peeling green paint. To add to the air of age and neglect, the poor edifice also sported a dangling plastic number eight. Ali pushed her way inside and…

He blinked.

"Is this a joke?" he asked, stepping over the threshold.

This had to be a joke, because they were greeted upon

entering by a Big Mouth Billy Bass, one of those animatronic singing props. It turned its fishy head outward, wiggled on its trophy plaque, and started singing "Don't Worry, Be Happy."

"I wish," Ali said with disgust, wrinkling her nose at the overpowering smell of Lysol and carpet deodorizer. At least someone had made an attempt to clean the space sometime in the near past. "Unfortunately, due to a septic issue, our choices were this room or the Trophy Buck room. We're going to be treating a gunshot wound, so I didn't fancy the idea of being watched by all those mounted deer heads with their sad, brown eyes. You know, considering they'd fallen prey to a similar fate."

She dropped the duffel bag onto the single queen bed. The damned thing looked ridiculous. The bed, that is. The comforter fabric was a mosaic of fly-fishing lures, and there were four huge, fish-shaped pillows propped against the headboard. Above the bed, two rowboat oars were mounted beside two wicker fishing baskets. He tilted his head to get a better look at the rod-and-reel-shaped bases of the lamps on the nightstands. Even the damned knobs on the drawers of the plywood dresser were little salmons.

Sweet lovin' Lord. The place was like a Cabela's catalog on crack.

Ali quickly toed off her boots, stepping out of her leather chaps and swinging out of her jacket. The Kevlar vest hit the floor with a loud *thump*, and the movement caused the Big Mouth Billy Bass to let loose with the second verse.

"Is there any way to turn that thing off?" she yelled

above the racket, warily eyeing the kitschy eyesore as it sang and wiggled mechanically on its mount beside the front door.

Yep, Nate knew of a way to turn it off. He could stomp it to pieces with the steel toe of his size twelve boot. His patience with tasteless, aquatic décor wasn't copious on a good day. Throw in blood loss, the rather shocking personal epiphany that he was in love with Ali, not to mention the fact that he was going crazy with the thought of some silenced-gun-toting goon having been millimeters away from blowing her pretty head off, and his capacity to endure one more "Don't Worry, Be Happy" refrain was quickly falling into the red.

But instead of giving in to his desire to silence the animatronic fish for the good of mankind and all eternity, he reached up with his left arm—

Shit! Gunshot, he reminded himself.

And though the wound really was superficial—he'd suffered much worse—that didn't mean it didn't hurt like friggin' hell on fire.

He reached for the bass with his right hand—bingo—pulled down the disaster of decorations and, turning it over, popped out the battery. He shook his head and set the newly silent contraption on the small round table placed under the room's front window. The center of the table was a mosaic of fish species. The seats of the two chairs pushed under the table were covered in the same fly-fishing fabric as the bedspread.

Whoever decorated this place should either be shot or placed in the *Guinness Book of World Records* under the title, "Worst Taste Ever."

"Okay," Ali said into the refreshing silence. "Come with me."

He had no choice but to follow her as she sashayed toward the bathroom. Letting his hungry gaze drift down to her pert bottom, he squeezed his eyes shut when his mind automatically pictured the thong she must be wearing beneath those snug-fitting jeans. He'd noticed when he was elbow deep in the pile of her unmentionables, the woman didn't own a pair of underwear with an ass in them.

Sweet Lord, have mercy!

He'd been shot, was losing blood at a fairly steady rate, and the only thing he could think about was the color of Ali's underwear.

Purple. Or more a lavender, really.

When he helped her into the Kevlar vest that morning, the neck of her T-shirt had slipped due to the heavy weight of the vest, revealing her lavender bra strap, and you better believe he took note.

He cracked his peepers when she cleared her throat.

"You're not about to faint on me are you?" she asked, her wide eyes filled with concern.

Only if you decide to shuck out of those jeans and that T-shirt. "Nah," he told her, "just catchin' my breath."

"Well come catch it on the toilet seat. I want to get a look at that wound before I lose my nerve."

"You got nerves of steel, lady. You did me proud back there." And she had. She'd done exactly as he'd told her, no hesitation, no questions.

"I don't know how running for my life could accomplish that."

"You did what you were told. And you held it together."

She shot him a seriously skeptical look and held up one hand, palm down. He could see her thin fingers doing the shimmy-shake even from six feet away. "Is this what you'd call holding it together?"

Geez, he was such an ass. She was scared shitless, and all he could do was stand there flapping his lips. He hastened to remove his own boots, chaps, and ruined, bloodstained jacket, letting them drop carelessly to the floor. Striding toward her, he lifted a palm to the coolness of her cheek and smiled down at her upturned face.

"Yeah, I call it holdin' it together when you're scared t'death, but you continue to function in a reasonable, rational fashion. You're quite a woman, Ali."

Chapter Fourteen

Reasonable and rational?

He must've forgotten the part where she threatened to bail off the back of a speeding motorcycle.

Ali gave him her best *you're certifiably crazy* look and shook her head. "Let's see if you still think I'm 'quite a woman' once I start poking around in that wound."

Sheesh, his undershirt was soaked. If it weren't for the few patches of white left here and there, she might've thought the thing was made of burgundy material, and he was standing there talking to her as if nothing was wrong. As if he wasn't *shot*.

Her stomach lurched.

God, don't puke. Don't puke.

Just thinking the word made her need to puke.

"Y'gonna hurl again?" he asked.

"*No*," she assured him, lifting her chin and motioning him toward the toilet seat. "I'm going to cut away your shirt, clean your wound, and hopefully convince you to take yourself to a hospital." *And try my darndest not to puke my guts up.*

"Negative on the last part."

"Fine," she growled. "But the first two are definitely going to happen. So take a seat, bucko, and let's get started."

He grinned and, like always, the sight left her

breathless. Breathless was good, breathless made her momentarily forget the urge to blow chunks.

With a grace so unusual in a man of his size, he lowered himself to the toilet seat. Facing the tub, he presented her with his back, a move for which she was silently grateful. She may be talking the big talk, but she wasn't sure she was going to be able to walk the big walk once she got going.

She'd never been very good with blood. And there was a *lot* of blood.

Her hands shook as she rifled through her purse and pulled out the little scissors she used to trim loose threads and the occasional wild nose hair.

Nate glanced at her over one large shoulder. "Y'plan to cut my shirt away with those?"

She looked down at the teensy silver scissors and frowned. "Yeah. So?"

"So, I don't wanna be here all night."

With one swift move, he slid the huge knife he kept secured at his waist out of its leather sheath and flipped it in the air, neatly catching it by the wickedly sharp blade to offer her the handle.

"Uh," she gingerly accepted the menacing length of the knife.

"Just make sure the only thing you're cuttin' is my shirt," he said and turned back around. He seemed blithely unconcerned that a woman with shaking hands, who was prone to barf at the slightest provocation, was going to come at him with a seven-inch blade.

She eyed the giant knife for a good long while, silently begging it to do her a huge favor and cut clean and true despite her palsied hands.

"We gonna do this or what?" he asked, still facing the chipped Formica tub.

"*Yes*," she huffed, *don't rush me* implied in her tone. Taking one deep breath and two steps forward, she grabbed the neck of his undershirt. "I'm just going through the steps in my mind." *And trying not to run out the door screaming*.

"It's easy," he told her. "Just pull the shirt out and slice it."

Uh-huh. Easy. She briefly closed her eyes and, before she could change her mind, pulled the material away from his body and sliced.

The blade cut through the cotton like a hot knife through butter. The two halves of his ruined shirt fell away.

And the ragged wound atop his shoulder waved hi-how-are-ya?

Oh cripes.

She dropped the knife and retched into the sink. Twice.

Wow, she was *such* a loser. He was the one shot, and she was the one losing her lunch.

"You must think I'm a real piece of work," she told him as she turned on the tap to wash the foul taste from her mouth and the evidence of her rather humiliating little reaction straight down the drain.

Sweating, trying to breathe through her mouth so the metallic scent of his blood didn't swirl around in her nostrils, she straightened and found him smiling gently.

"Some people'r'cut out for this kinda thing. Some aren't."

"Well, I definitely fall into the *aren't* category, don't I?"

He reached for her hand. "That's not a bad thing."

She grimaced. It was a bad thing when the person who was shot was consoling the person who was perfectly healthy.

She squared her shoulders and said, "Okay, what next?"

"Y'don't have to do this. I can take care of it myself. It's really not that bad."

Not that bad? Not that *bad*?

He had a hole the size of dime through the thick muscle over his collar bone and one the size of a quarter high up on his back shoulder, and it wasn't that bad?

Yeah, she'd speculated about it before, now she was convinced. He was crazy. Certifiable. Had to be. Sane people were *not* so nonchalant about extra holes in their bodies, especially ones that big and bloody.

"It'll be easier if I help you," she told the insane man sitting on the toilet. "So tell me what to do next."

He offered her another grin, and she could only shake her head. Of all the times to break out that elusive smile…

"In the smaller saddlebag there's a first aid kit. Grab the disinfectant, the squeeze bottle, the pack of QuikClot, and the gauze bandages."

She nodded and hurried into the room to do as instructed.

"There's an extra toothbrush in there, too, if y'need it," he called.

Oh perfect. Here he was, bleeding down his back and into the waistband of his jeans, and what was his biggest concern? The state of her vomit breath. The night had careened from simply being frightening and bizarre into downright unbelievable. She felt for sure she must've somehow become a character in an episode of *The Twilight Zone*.

Grabbing the first aid supplies—she snagged a bottle

of ibuprofen for good measure—she turned to head back to the bathroom.

On second thought…she swung around and snatched up the toothbrush and little tube of toothpaste as well.

After she finished helping him clean and bandage his gunshot wound, then and only then she'd attend to her vomit breath.

Crimeny! She'd been mugged, bugged, surveilled, shot at by an assassin, and now she was about to march into that disgusting excuse for a bathroom and clean out a gunshot wound. She glanced over at the silenced Big Mouth Billy Bass and shook her head.

Don't worry, be happy. *Right.*

Trudging back into the bathroom, dreading the next few minutes with every step, she silently coached herself.

You can do this. You can do this. You can—

Oh, boy, there was that wound again. Looking like… well, like a bullet hole.

She quickly averted her eyes and dumped the supplies on the counter. Nate turned and once more presented her with his back.

Ugh, that was worse. The back looked so much worse.

Of course, exit holes usually did—or so she'd been led to believe.

"Pour the disinfectant into the squeeze bottle."

"'Kay," she uncapped the brown bottle of peroxide and emptied it into the white plastic squeeze bottle. It had a long, narrow, painful looking nozzle.

"Now shove the nozzle into the wound and give a good squish."

Ali closed her eyes, silently blew out a breath, shoved the nozzle into his tattered flesh and squeezed. The peroxide spilled from the hole in his back, hissing and bubbling like it was mad at the torn flesh. When she glanced over his shoulder, she could see the same frothing pinkish-red mess fizzing down his chest.

Oh cripes.

"Erp."

"That's fine, sugar. Take a break if'y'need to."

"Nope. I'm good." She thought maybe she'd thrown up a little in her mouth, but...whatever.

"Okay, now grab the pack of QuikClot. Open it up and sprinkle it into the wound, back and front."

Mr. Stoic wasn't fooling her. It had to hurt like crazy when she flushed that ragged hole left by the bullet, but except for the single drop of sweat trickling down his left temple, there was no indication he felt the slightest discomfort.

Swallowing down the burning ball of stomach acid sitting at the back of her throat, she grabbed the pack of QuikClot and ripped it open. His wound, sluggishly oozing before the cleansing, was now bleeding in earnest.

"QuikClot works only if applied directly to the leakin' vessels, so don't be shy. Really get th'stuff in there," he instructed, leaning forward slightly to give her more room to work.

As quickly as she could, she shook some powder from the package and pressed it into the angry wound. Amazingly, the river of blood running down his back dried up in an instant.

Huh, it's miracle powder.

"Good. Now the front."

He swiveled on the toilet seat and leaned back against

the tank. The front of the wound was neater, cleaner, but still oozing blood in a thick line. Straddling his legs, she leaned over him and repeated the process.

Again the bleeding immediately ceased, drying up quicker than a slug hit by salt. And gross. As if the situation wasn't disturbing enough, she had to go and think of that.

"That's good, sugar." His voice was rough.

She looked down, expecting to see him grimacing in pain, but the crazy man was busy eyeballing her cleavage, revealed by the gaping collar of her shirt.

Really? Boobs? That's what he was thinking about?

She was thinking of gunshot wounds and blood and slugs, and he was thinking of *boobs*?

"You men," she grumbled with disgust as she backed away, moving toward the sink and the washcloths stacked there. "You really only have a few brain cells, don't you?"

"Yep," he chuckled, the sound low and intimate and still so totally foreign to her ears. "But they're very committed."

"*Pfft.*"

She wet two washcloths with hot water then twirled her finger, motioning for him to turn back toward the tub. She dropped one of the washcloths over his shoulder and into his lap. "You work on cleaning up your front. I'll do your back."

"Roger that."

As gently as she could, she cleaned the blood from his broad back. Unfortunately, some of it had dried to a sticky paste that required a bit of scrubbing. "Sorry," she said when he grunted.

"Don't be," he hissed, for the first time letting her hear just how bad it really hurt. "It's gotta be done."

Yes it did, and amazingly, she was doing it—without tossing her cookies. It was a day for firsts, that was for sure. Then again, it's not like she had any cookies left to toss.

When they'd washed him clean, she took the bloody washcloths and dumped them in the trash. No amount of laundering would ever make those suckers viable for future use, but she sure as heck didn't trust the housekeeping staff at Happy Acres not to give it the ol' college try.

Peeling open two packages of self-adhesive gauze pads, she applied one to each side of the wound.

"There," she said, dusting off her hands. "All done."

"Y'did good."

She rolled her eyes and stepped to the sink, squeezing toothpaste onto the travel-sized toothbrush she'd taken from the first aid kit. "Yeah, I did just great. I only hurled once…er, twice."

He winked, and she gaped with the toothbrush halfway to her mouth. "Who are you, and what have you done with brooding, morose Nathan Weller?"

He sighed and glanced down at his scarred, callused hands, shaking his head.

It was quite sad, really, that it took the man getting shot before he gave her a true glimpse of who he really was.

"I, uh, checked in with the Knights while you were busy gettin' us these…charmin' accommodations."

She rolled her eyes and started scrubbing the bitter taste of stomach acid from her mouth.

"General Fuller was finally able to speak with the Director of the FBI. It seems he hasn't a clue what

Agent Delaney was investigating. Said the man started actin' strange in the months before his death. *Secretive* is the word the Director used."

She spit. "Well, that's just great."

He made a face and nodded. "Yeah. But there's some good news."

"Oh, yeah?" She wiped her mouth with a hand towel, then wrinkled her nose and tossed it into the sink. The thing smelled like armpits. "Well, what are you waiting for? I could use some good news. Lay it on me."

"I went through Grigg's personal correspondence. It appears this was a one-time thing. I didn't find any other mission requests, so I don't think he was in the habit of goin' off reservation."

"Well," she sighed, "There's that. So he was a rogue agent but at least he was a discerning rogue agent."

"You don't really believe that."

"No," she shook her head, seeing her exasperatingly lovable, but most importantly *loyal* brother in her mind's eye. "I think there has to be a good explanation for his behavior. I can't fathom him doing something to put me or you or any of the other guys at unnecessary risk. Can you?"

"No. I can't."

Good. At least they could agree on that. Grigg may have been a lot of things, but he wasn't a traitor, to his country *or* the men he worked with. There was some comfort there, she supposed.

Nate grabbed the bottle of ibuprofen and twisted off the cap. Throwing four gel caps to the back of his throat, he tilted his head and swallowed.

"Are you in a lot of pain?" she asked as she eyed

the gauze bandages, checking to see if he was bleeding through. He wasn't, thank goodness.

"A bit," he shrugged his good shoulder. "But it's really just a flesh wound."

"'A flesh wound? You're bloody arm's off!'" Okay, so her British accent could use some work.

He lifted a dark brow.

"Oh come on," she raised a hand. "You know, *Monty Python and the Holy Grail*?"

The look he sent her clearly questioned her sanity.

"Sheesh, just when I think you might be normal..." she shook her head and started tidying the mess they'd made.

"We are the knights who say *ni*!" he declared in a pretty convincing accent, and she swung around to face him, her mouth slung open. He grinned. "You really don't know me at all, do you?"

"And whose fault is that?"

"Mine, I guess."

"Yeah, good guess."

"Can't help it," he grumbled. "When you're around, I have difficulty hidin' this," he motioned to the bulge behind his zipper, "so I usually just avoid you."

Now her mouth was hanging open for a completely different reason. "Really? After racing for fifteen hours across the country on the back of a bike that vibrates enough to rattle every single tooth out of your head, after getting shot and having my fingers shoved in your *bullet wound*, you're still able to think about sex? You really must be insane."

"Blame it on the adrenaline rush."

"Fine. So..." she took a step toward him. "Let's do something about it."

"*What?*" He looked like she'd just told him they should shave their heads and join the Hare Krishnas.

"You heard me." And there was nothing to stop them, no one around, and despite his repeated rejection and his assertion he didn't want to physically react to her, it was obvious, really, really obvious—given that substantial bulge—that his mind and his body were on two different pages.

She tended to side with his body because, to put it simply, she wanted him. Like she'd never wanted a man before in her life.

Perhaps it had something to do with the not-so-small fact she might be in love with him. Or perhaps it was simply that it had been a long time coming. Whichever, it didn't really matter, because both reasons only supported her assertion they should give in to their desires.

And if she *did* love him—okay, she did—didn't she deserve at least one night in his arms?

"No." He shook his head, eyeing her approach like a cobra eyes a mongoose.

"Why?"

"Why what?" Oh, Nate knew what she was asking, but he desperately searched for a way to stall, because he just couldn't for the life of him come up with a plausible excuse to—

"Why won't you make love to me?"

Uh, yep. *That* was the question he couldn't bring himself to answer since Ali wasn't the kind of woman to take a night's pleasure and vanish. Hell no. And to offer her anything more was out of the question, given he'd then be compelled to admit he'd killed her brother and *lied* to her about it, which...no, that just wasn't gonna happen.

"Uh..."

"Because it's obvious your body is totally onboard with the idea. And you admitted you like me." She was standing in front of him, so close he could still make out the subtle aroma of her honeysuckle fabric softener even after a day spent on the back of a bike. "I like you—"

He shot her a startled look.

She shook her head and chuckled and all he could think was, *geez, her hair looks good all wild and windblown.*

"Well, I like you *most* of the time, anyway. The other times I usually don't know whether I want to strangle you or kiss you. And that's kinda my whole point, you know? The fact that even when you're making me crazy, I still think maybe I want to kiss you? So..." she made a helpless little gesture with her hands, "why? Why can't we give in and scratch this itch?"

There was a sudden humming in the air. It licked over his skin like an electric tongue, raising goose bumps.

"Uh..."

"And if you're calling a halt because of loyalty to Grigg, because you think you'd owe me, his baby sister, more than a one-night stand, you're wrong."

Whoa. What? Did she just say one-night stand?

"I know your type," she continued with a seductive little grin. "Heck, I grew up with a guy who was exactly you're type. Love 'em and leave 'em, you know?"

"Ali—"

Oh, Lord. She moved to stand between his legs and her pert little breasts were right there. *In his face.*

What was he about to say? Something. Something important, but for the life of him he couldn't remember.

"Nate," she whispered his name and lifted a hand to run her fingers through his hair. Chills raced down his spine.

"Hmm?" he asked, mesmerized by the unsurpassable vista in front of his eyes and the feel of her, *her* touching him…on purpose.

She chuckled again, and it was the sound of a siren. Low and sexy and goddamned irresistible. He wasn't consciously aware of movement, but at some point he lifted his right hand to cup the back of her thigh, urging her forward until he could bury his nose in the sweet smelling valley between her lovely, lovely breasts.

"You said my name," she replied and covered his hand on the back of her thigh with her own, encouraging him upward until he was cupping her full, firm ass.

Lord in heaven.

"I was saying yours in return," she explained in an indulgent tone.

What? What was she chattering about? It was impossible to comprehend anything with her soft breasts cuddling his cheeks and her subtle, honeysuckle scent making his head spin.

This had to stop.

She may talk big about a one-night stand, but she didn't mean it. Did she…?

With the reluctance of a starving man walking away from an all-you-can-eat buffet, he dropped his hand and stood, causing her to step back. She glanced up at him quizzically, then gifted him with a knowing little smile.

The same one women have been smiling for centuries. The one Da Vinci immortalized in the *Mona Lisa*.

He was in trouble.

And, yep, right on cue she stepped forward, went up on tiptoe, and wrapped her arms around his neck.

Oh, man. He should've stayed seated, because now she was pressed all along his length. And it was delicious and distracting and goddamned *dangerous*. He was starting to forget all the reasons he was resisting her. They were important reasons, weren't they?

He was certain they were, even though he couldn't manage to recall them when she grabbed his ears to pull him down for a kiss.

Reasons…important reasons…

Her breath brushed against his lips, and he groaned.

Reasons!

"We have to stop this, Ali. We have to—"

"No," she gave up trying to catch his lips and instead trailed a string of wet kisses across his jaw. "I'm not stopping this time, and you're out of excuses. You say there are things I don't know about you? Well, I don't care about them. You don't want a commitment? Well, I'm not asking for one."

"Grigg," he managed to croak, congratulating himself on finally, *finally* managing to come up with a plausible excuse.

"What about him?" she pulled back and stared into his face, her lips already pink from the abrasion of his beard stubble. He lost a couple of layers of enamel on his back molars when the sight of those plump lips brought to mind another part of her anatomy that would be soft and pink.

"He wouldn't approve." Yes! *That's* where he'd been going.

"Of course he would." The look she gave him was amused and indulgent. "He always told me you were the best man he'd ever known and I could do a whole lot worse than you."

He jerked his head back when she would've resumed her deliciously maddening nibbling. "What? He always told *me* he'd kill me if I laid a finger on you."

The indulgent smile she gave him was the facial equivalent of *well, duh*. "Of course, he did, you big silly. That's what older brothers say to guys who are interested in getting into their little sister's pants. What did you expect?"

What *had* he expected?

"He really told y'that? That you could do a lot worse than me?"

"Yes," she started nipping on his neck again. "But my plan is to do my worst *to* you. How does that sound?"

How did it sound? Like he'd died and gone to heaven.

Sweet Jesus, did he dare?

What was she asking of him really? Nothing more than one night of pleasure and, wonder of wonders, it just so happened indulging a woman's pleasure was one of his specialties, given the tutelage of a nice, widowed Brazilian lady.

Funny, he hadn't thought of Raquel Silva in years, but maybe he shouldn't be surprised she popped into his head now.

On their very first nerve-wracking assignment, he and Grigg had spent a long, hot month doing recon on their target and staying in Raquel's little boathouse. The days had been filled with waiting and watching and copious note taking. The nights, though…oh, the nights had been filled with something totally different.

And despite the fact that randy young men were known to engage in a little locker room talk, neither he nor Grigg had spoken about their experiences with Raquel in all the years to follow that first mission, as if verbalizing the intimacy would taint the spirituality of it somehow.

And it *had* been spiritual. A broadening of mind, body, and soul.

Though they'd been highly trained soldiers, it'd been obvious to both of them they'd arrived at Raquel's boathouse that sweltering South American summer as boys. By the time they'd left, that sweet Brazilian lady had turned them into men.

And oh buddy, how many times had he fantasized about showing Ali everything he'd learned? How many times had he played out each individual caress of his callused fingertips, each laving pass of his tongue, each heavy stroke of his body into hers?

Countless. That's how many. Countless. And he had his chance to make all his fantasies reality.

She was asking him for one night. One night of indulgence, one night of passion and memories. After all the years of denial and sacrifice, didn't he deserve to take this one night and make love to the only woman who'd ever touched his heart?

Probably not. Someone like him, someone who'd seen and done so many dark, vile things, someone who'd crawled around in the rancid sewer of humanity was surely unworthy to lay a hand on someone like her. Someone as clean and pure and radiant as sunshine.

So no. He didn't deserve this one night. But, God help him, he was going to take it.

Chapter Fifteen

SUDDENLY ALI'S BACK WAS SLAMMED UP AGAINST THE bathroom wall, and Nate's tongue was introducing itself to all of her teeth, and…yeah…there went her shirt. He literally ripped it from her shoulders.

Holy crap!

Now she knew what people felt when they talked about the world tilting on its axis. Right at that moment, she didn't know which way was up.

He cupped her breast, lifting it, weighing it. And then her bra was miraculously gone. She didn't know how it happened or precisely when—which just proved this wasn't Nate's first rodeo—but she was suddenly bare, and his mouth was there.

Oh hot.

It was so hot, the hard pull of his lips at her nipple, the gentle scrape of his teeth. That was the deciding moment, right there, right then. The turning point. It could go either way. She could pull back, and he'd slow it down. He'd gentle his hunger and sweetly see to her needs, like he'd done that day on the beach.

But she didn't want sweet. And she certainly didn't want gentle.

All she wanted, all she could think of, was getting him inside her. Having him fill her with his hard length and thrusting until the friction became unbearable and she exploded into a thousand pieces of ecstasy.

They both fought to get her jeans off, hands frantic, bodies wiggling, mouths hungrily devouring heated flesh. When the stained denim pooled at her feet, she impatiently kicked it away.

"Get inside me, Nate," she demanded harshly, tunneling her fingers through the soft curls of his hair and pressing him more tightly against her breast.

She didn't know how he managed it, but somehow he snaked a hand between the frenzied press of their bodies to release those last few buttons of his fly, and... he was there.

He pushed the leg of her panties aside and...oh, *God* he was right there. Hot and throbbing, just brushing against her. Teasing, tormenting.

He groaned against her nipple and then he was pushing, slowly, inexorably, sliding inside her. She momentarily balked at the intrusion, because, *cripes*, he wasn't your average Joe by any stretch of the imagination.

A frustrated rumble sounded deep in his chest, and she knew exactly how he felt. She wanted that final connection, that full penetration. The place where two bodies joined and worked together to fulfill the ultimate goal of release. She took a deep breath, squeezed her eyes closed, and concentrated on relaxing her inner muscles.

Taking immediate advantage, with one final, forceful jab that nearly knocked the breath from her, he was fully seated.

Behind her lids, her eyes crossed in pleasure/pain. He stretched her, filled her to the very brim, stimulating every vibrating, overly excited nerve ending.

And she was there. Impossibly, unexpectedly, she was at that almost frightening precipice where the body took over and rational thought was inconceivable. She was helpless to do anything but squirm, trying to achieve that last bit of stimulation that would send her careening over the edge.

With his big hands holding her hips pinned against the wall, he pulled back, sliding his length outside of her, and she moaned at the loss.

"Condom," he growled, and she shook her head with frustration.

"Pill," she told him breathlessly, aching so badly she thought she'd die if he didn't get back inside her. "Oh, Nate. Please fuck me," she whimpered.

And then he was. His hips pistoning wildly as if they were attached to a motor. And she was flying, flung from the highest cliff of passion until her body was nothing but sensation. Pulsing, liquid pleasure started in her womb and spread through her entire body.

"Sweet Jesus," she vaguely heard him growl before she felt the hot wash of his release as her body continued to rhythmically contract around him, taking everything he had to give her.

Lavender.

He'd been right. Her underwear were lavender with little pink bows. Nate had a pretty good view of the flimsy bra dangling by one strap from Ali's perfect shoulder while his head was pressed against the wall beside hers. He struggled to catch his breath after the most mind-blowing orgasm of his entire life, and his body hadn't even finished convulsing when self-disgust had him pulling back to look at her.

Geez, Raquel would be sorely disappointed in that performance.

Although…Ali didn't seem to notice his total lack of finesse.

Her head was thrown back against the wall, her slim throat arched, her beautiful golden eyes squeezed closed, and a deep crimson blush stained her soft cheeks—the telltale color of a woman coming down from a convulsive release.

Still, that did nothing to appease his regret.

"Shit, Ali," he lifted one hand to smooth damp hair away from the dimpled corner of her kiss-swollen mouth, "I'm sorry."

She didn't even open her eyes when she murmured, "For what?"

"For not makin' it better for you. For…for, *Christ*, for mountin' y'like a ravening bull."

Her lips twisted into a smirk. "I seem to recall requesting exactly that."

"But you deserve—"

"What?" This time her eyes popped open, and he noticed the golden hue had darkened to deep amber in spent passion. "What do I deserve?"

Candlelight, he thought. *Soft music. Slow, thorough seduction that starts with a thousand kisses and ends with a thousand more.* But what he said was simply, "Gentleness."

"Hmm," she leaned forward, nibbling at his lips. "We can do gentle next time. We both needed that first one to take the edge off."

And inexplicably, his unrepentant cock begin to twitch and swell. Was it any wonder considering he was still nestled snuggly inside her?

Her smile was one of feminine triumph when she noticed the added sensation.

Yep, next time. Well, next time was going to be pretty damned soon.

Stepping out of his jeans, he lifted her into his arms, encouraging her to wrap her legs around his hips and palming the firm globes of her perfect ass.

"Nate!" she squeaked. "Your wound!"

"I don't feel nothin' but you, sugar." He told her as he stalked from the bathroom, intent on only one thing, the bed.

And, sweet Lord, he wasn't joking.

The softest, sweetest, most delicious thing he'd ever encountered was Ali, the way she melted against him. And she was his. At least for the night...

Damn. He'd just had her, and he was hard enough to hammer nails at the thought of having her again.

Gently pressing her back against the mattress, he couldn't fathom breaking the connection of their bodies, so he reached down and with a twist of his fists, ripped the side seams of her flimsy panties. He threw the scrap of ruined material over his shoulder.

"Hey!" she protested, but then totally ruined her attempt at ire when she grabbed his ears and ravished his mouth. Obviously the whole barbarian thing worked for her. Which was good, because that's exactly what he was.

"Y'have a hundred more. I've seen 'em," he told her when he could draw breath, right before he started in on those thousand kisses. He chose to plant the first one on the delicate line of her collarbone.

"Hmm," she murmured as she tilted her head back to give him better access, "I suppose that's true."

He didn't quite make the thousand kisses mark. Mainly because at about two hundred she was squirming beneath him and begging. But he did manage slow and gentle, and certainly thorough. After the third orgasm, she went completely boneless. He drifted to sleep with a contented smile on his face and the only woman he'd ever loved softly snoring in his arms.

"Shit!" Dagan swore into his cell phone and slammed his hand against the steering wheel.

"Yup," Chelsea Duvall concurred, her husky voice even huskier over the patchy cell phone connection. Chelsea was the one person inside the CIA who still deigned to speak to Dagan after the *incident*. He was happy to call her friend, though at one point, years ago, he'd been determined to call her so much more. "And it gets worse."

Great. Worse than finding out the photo of the dead guy depicted one Rocco De Lucca, a transplanted New York mafia goon who'd done as Kid Rock instructed and headed out west. Only Dagan was pretty sure ol' Rocco hadn't done so to be a cowboy, baby. Nope. Rocco no doubt found himself in Vegas because there were a lot more legs that needed breaking out that way. Mainly, Dagan suspected, of the gamblers-who-weren't-making-good-on-their-debts variety.

"The guy has two known accomplices," Chelsea went

on to explain. "One Frankie 'The Shark' Costa, and one Johnny Vitiglioni, who happens to be his cousin. Each of them has done hard time, and they all have rap sheets that read like your worst nightmare and that's before you start talking about all the things they're suspected of. Jesus, Z, what've you gotten yourself involved in this time?"

This time. As if he was notorious for finding himself on the wrong side of the equation. He wasn't…except for that one time, but that one time had been enough to ensure his previously sterling reputation was ruined for all eternity. Even Chelsea, whom he thought still believed in him, obviously couldn't completely ignore what had happened.

"Thanks for your help, Chels," he said, ignoring her last question. "I gotta go."

"Z, I didn't mean—"

He hung up the phone before he could hear what she didn't mean, because whatever she was about to say would be a lie. She *did* mean it.

He wanted to scream, "It wasn't my fault! I was duped!" But what good would that do? None. It wouldn't change the past. Nothing could.

And his personal problems just weren't important right now, because Senator Alan Aldus had hired himself a group of thugs to take out Alisa Morgan and Nate Weller, and Dagan was going to do his damndest to make sure that didn't happen.

Was he putting his neck on the line, trying to redeem himself for what happened three years ago?

Yeah, maybe.

But didn't everyone deserve a little redemption?

—

"So, how'd you get this scar?"

Nate groaned and pulled Ali more on top of him, lifting her chin so he could kiss the chatter right out of her mouth.

Two hours.

She'd allowed him two blissful hours of the most glorious, peaceful sleep he'd had in years and then she'd awoken him by peppering his chest with sweetly hot kisses.

He was totally on board with the hot kisses, but engaging in conversation while she was naked—Ali was in his arms, *naked*—rated real low on his Things I'd Like to Do Right Now list.

She kissed him back, full-on tongue action that had all thought draining right out of his head. Then suddenly she pulled back, circling the big, puckered scar high up on his right shoulder with a soft fingertip. "This one. How'd you get it?"

He sighed; obviously she wasn't going to let it go.

"Bad reflexes," he reluctantly admitted, trying to reclaim her mouth, but the exasperating woman eluded him.

"Bad reflexes? What does that mean?"

"It means I zigged when I shoulda zagged."

The look she gave him was so perturbed and so darn cute, he couldn't help but chuckle.

"We got caught in a firefight between two rival drug cartels, and I just happened t'run into a stray bullet."

She pressed herself up on her arms and glanced down his naked torso. "Just how many times have you been shot?"

"Enough t'know one time is too many."

"Are you always this evasive?"

"Yep."

She scowled, and his big stupid heart flipped over because there went her nose again.

"If we start catalogin' all my scars," he told her, "we're gonna be here 'til next week, sugar. Unfortunately, a pretty, scar-free body isn't part of my job description."

"Hmm," she relented and laid her head against his good shoulder. "I think you have a beautiful body, scars and all.

Women, geez, you just gotta love 'em. Somehow they could see beauty in everything. Scars, old dilapidated buildings, newborn babies…

Nate'd seen a few of the latter. They were always wrinkly, tended to be the wrong color, and there was usually something very wrong with the shape of their little heads. He was contemplating this last bit and didn't realize how long she'd been quiet until she said, "Nate?"

"Yep?"

"How do you do it?"

"Do what, sugar?"

"Your job. Do you ever get used to it?"

Geez, this woman…this woman was determined to rip his heart out every which way.

He didn't talk about this stuff…*ever*. Not even with Grigg.

But here was this woman he loved, asking him the tough questions, and for the first time he realized he wanted to talk about it. With her.

"No," he swallowed as a myriad of bloody memories washed over him. So much horror. So much death. He looked at his hands, as he did every so often. They were broad and tough, and he was always surprised to find them unstained by the amount of blood he'd spilled. "You never get used to it."

She shuddered against him, and he pulled her closer, tucking her head more firmly beneath his chin. Rubbing her crown with his beard stubble, he inhaled the earthy scents of sex and dried blood. Overlaying it all was Ali's sweetly clean aroma.

"Grigg would never talk to me about it," she said in a little voice.

"That's because y'don't really wanna hear, sugar. Grigg was just protectin' you."

"But I *do* want to hear about it. Grigg was the one person I had, Nate. The one person who loved me best, loved me more than anyone. And I didn't even *know* him," her voice cracked on the last words.

Rriiippp. Yep, that would be his heart. Again.

He smoothed her silky hair behind her ear, softly caressing the little lobe. Everything about her was small and soft and he loved it, every last feminine inch. "Y'knew the best parts of him. He kept those for you."

She harrumphed. "But it was a lie, can't you see that? *Knowing* a person isn't just knowing their good parts, it's knowing all the dark, scary parts as well."

Okay, but sometimes the dark, scary parts were just *too* dark and *too* scary.

"What'd'ya want me to tell you, Ali?"

"I don't know," she blew out a frustrated breath. "I want you to tell me how my sweet, sunny brother grew up to do what he did. I want you to tell me he did it because someone had to do and it might as well have been him. I want you to tell me that he didn't do it because he was an adrenaline junkie or a sadist. I want you to tell me…*God,* I don't know. Tell me anything. *Something.*"

Damned if he wasn't compelled to do just that, for all the times Grigg had needed to confide in someone but kept his mouth Krazy Glued shut and all the times Nate'd done the exact same thing.

He took a deep, steadying breath. "Grigg wasn't an adrenaline junkie, and he certainly wasn't a sadist," he told her. "He was a soldier and a patriot. A man of honor and integrity. It's true whatcha said. If we hadn't done the job, then someone else would've. Maybe someone who *was* a sadist. It's a very thin line between darkness and true evil. One we tried our damndest t'never cross, although we did once, inadvertently, which is why we got out and went to work with Boss."

She was leaning up on one elbow, watching his face with such sweet acceptance. Like no matter what he had to tell her, she'd never think anything less of him.

Man, if she only knew…

"What happened?" she whispered, searching his eyes.

What happened? They'd killed an innocent man, that's what'd happened.

"When you're doing reconnaissance on a target," he explained, screwing his eyes closed so he wouldn't have to watch her face while recounting the sordid tale. He didn't think after all they just shared he could bear to see disillusionment or censure on her pretty face, "you may watch the guy for days, weeks, sometimes even months. You watch him drink his mornin' coffee, take a piss, make love t'his wife, kiss his kids. He becomes more'n' a target. He becomes a *man.* It's easy to pull the trigger on a target, not so much so on a man."

Yep, even after all the hard, relentless training the Marines had given him, he still cried like a friggin' baby after his first kill. He remembered how Grigg had thrown a steadying arm around his shoulders before quietly and methodically enumerating the man's transgressions. Nate's tears had finally dried, and he'd never shed another for a target…until Moscow.

"So Grigg and I tried t'make sure we did our own research on our targets," he continued, pushing the painful memory of that first time out of his mind. "We wanted t'make certain our kills were just, that the men whose lives we were endin' deserved what they had comin'. That we were doin' the world a favor by wipin' them from the face of the planet."

"You could do that? I mean, didn't you just get orders and have to follow them?"

"If we'd been regular grunts in the Corps, the answer to that would be yes. But we were pulled from our unit right out of Marine Scout Sniper School and recruited into the spec-ops community. That changed things. In spec ops, we were given much more freedom, far more latitude. We were allowed t'work on our own reconnaissance most of the time."

She shook her head, her eyes glistening with unshed tears. "I never knew that. Grigg never told me."

He caught her chin between his thumb and forefinger, forcing her to hold his steady gaze. "He couldn't, Ali." It was as simple as that.

She searched his eyes, reading the truth in them. "So, you and Grigg were the U.S. government's personal two-man execution squad."

"Not just us," he told her, remembering all those men

who'd gone through Marine Scout Sniper School with him and Grigg, the ones who'd been yanked from their units and wrangled into the much more secretive—and much dirtier—work of the spec-ops community. "There are a lot of guys out there doin' the tough jobs, seein' the faces of the men they've killed in their dreams at night, knowin' they'll never be totally free, that they'll always remember the look in their targets' eyes in that last instant."

He felt her breath against his lips and opened his eyes to find her watching him closely. She held his gaze as she kissed him sweetly. A kiss of compassion, of understanding.

God help him. He wanted to cry.

"Tell me what happened to make you guys leave the Corps three years ago."

He still got a sick feeling in his stomach every time he thought of that frigid day in Moscow. The winds had stabbed like ice picks, the moisture from his breath had formed ice crystals in his beard. It'd been nearly impossible to pull the trigger, his fingers almost completely frozen. But he'd managed. And as a result, an innocent man had been left bleeding to death in the icy, Russian snow.

"Intelligence sources indicated a major Russian arms dealer was due t'meet with potential clients. It was our understandin' this one man was almost solely responsible for continuing to supply a certain African faction with weapons that were resultin' in a brutal war and worse…a genocide."

He didn't need to go into detail. She was a smart girl. She could probably put two and two together and figure out just which conflict he was talking about.

Conflict.

That was another one of those ridiculous euphemisms. This one was supposed to describe the rape and mutilation of women, the hacking off of men's hands and arms. The manipulation of children into killing machines.

"Anyway, U.S. forces had been tryin' for months to catch this guy, get hard evidence against him, but he was brilliant and he managed to elude the traps our government, and a lot of others, laid for him. So it was determined to have him deleted. Grigg and I were tasked with the mission."

Geez, he hadn't talked this much in ages. It felt kinda...*good.* A purging of sorts.

"We weren't given any time to prepare. Our target was on the move, and there was only one specific time and location for which Intelligence knew he'd be vulnerable. Sure enough, the guy appeared just where we'd been told he would. Only it wasn't the arms dealer. It was his twin brother. An ethics professor at Moscow State University. A father of three. We didn't find that out until later..."

He shook his head, feeling impotent rage even all these years later. "The Intelligence we received was bad, and we hadn't had time to check it. Because of that, we ended the life of an innocent man. That's when we knew it was time t'get out. Time t'find a job where we could determine, beyond a shadow of a doubt, the culpability of our targets."

It felt like a benediction when she ran one slim hand through his hair, like he'd been touched by an angel and forgiven his past transgressions. He wanted to fall to his knees before her and pledge his soul, but all he could manage to do was stare at her and cling to the understanding in her eyes.

"You're a good man, Nate," she said, her voice low and firm. "You and Grigg, you're both patriots, both honorable. There's no shame."

He swallowed past the ball of cold regret sitting like an iceberg in his throat. "Whatever you may think, Ali, whatever you've seen in the movies…there's never any honor in takin' a life. If you're lucky, very lucky, there's only justice."

She smiled sadly. "And that's what makes you so decent, Nate. So rare and special. You understand the value of life. You took no pleasure in your job, but you did it anyway. Out of duty, for the greater good. You're exceptional."

Right.

"Thank you for telling me," she whispered, kissing him gently and for some reason he wanted to smile. He felt lighter suddenly, almost buoyant. Then she pulled back and grinned.

Uh-oh, he knew that look.

"So, since you're in confession mode. Why don't you tell me what Delilah said to you last night?"

He groaned. Hard to believe he'd just spilled his guts about Moscow, but admitting what Delilah said landed directly on his So Not Gonna Go There list.

"Come on. Spill it," she demanded, swirling her little fingers through his chest hair until he wasn't sure what was making him crazier. Her sweetly mindless ministrations, or the fact that it appeared as if it might be impossible to steer her away from this current course of conversation. "It can't be good to keep so many secrets."

"It's not a secret, it's just none of your business." He tried to catch her mouth to distract her, but she avoided his searching lips.

"I'll get it out of you one of these days," she vowed, gifting him with that impish grin he loved so much.

He growled and decided he'd just satisfy himself with nibbling on her shoulder. "Never gonna happen."

"People always underestimate me," she sighed as she tilted her head to the side, giving him better access to her throat, which he'd quickly learned she loved to have licked. He didn't disappoint. "They think because I'm small I'm a pushover, but I've got something...*Mmm.*"

"Somethin' *mmm*?"

"No," she giggled. It caused her nipples to rasp across his chest, distracting him. He started moving his mouth in their direction. "Just *mmm.* As in, *mmm*, don't stop, *mmm*, keep going."

"Ah," he levered her up until he could pull one sweetly ruched bud between his lips. He tongued it to the top of his mouth and listened to her make that uniquely Ali sound in the back of her throat. That whimper of sweet longing. The one that made him so hard he thought it was a wonder his dick didn't explode.

She did it every time he took her to that invisible line where turning back was no longer an option, and it drained every ounce of blood he had straight into his prick.

"Nate?" she asked as she threaded her fingers through is hair and held him tight against her breast.

"Hmm?"

"Can I be on top this time?"

Her nipple popped free of his mouth. "Sugar," he

told her between nipping kisses trailing toward her other breast, "y'can do anything y'want."

"Even if I want to ride you slow and steady for an hour straight?"

Sweet lovin' Lord. He'd said it before…the woman was going to be the death of him.

"I'll do my best to accommodate you," his voice was harsh, sounding like it'd been run through a blender.

"Mmm, you're such a nice man," she giggled as she sprinkled hot kisses across his jaw and down his neck while her soft hands busied themselves by skating all over his chest.

His snort turned into a groan when her wet mouth landed on his left nipple. She flicked her tongue, back and forth like a wickedly erotic snake.

"I'm about as far away from *nice* as a man can get," he managed, though speech was getting progressively more difficult given her emboldened caresses.

His wildest fantasies hadn't come close to the truth of Ali. The woman liked sex, reveled in it, sought release with a single-minded determination usually only found in the male of the species. But she also gloried in his body, constantly running her hands over him in soft caresses, her mouth always at work, kissing, licking, gently biting, making sure to give as much pleasure as she took.

"Oh, you're nice all right," she raked her teeth across tough skin, causing every cell inside him to begin a slow humming vibration.

"You're nice and muscular." She highlighted her point by gently sinking her teeth into his right pectoral muscle. He groaned and ground his head against the pillow.

"You're nice and sensitive." She blew across his nipple, which snapped to happy attention. She grinned before she sucked it into her mouth.

Snaking one hand between their bodies, she gripped the swollen length of him in one soft palm. "You're nice and big." She chuckled when he drew in a ragged breath.

"But what I like best," she lifted herself from his chest and positioned him against her, "is that you're so very, very nice and hard."

She slid down the length of him in one slow, gloriously sleek glide that had the top of his head lifting away.

Hard didn't begin to describe his level of rigidity. Wood was hard, rock was hard, he, on the other hand, was so stiff a cat couldn't scratch him.

Uncrossing his eyes was a bit of an effort, but totally worth it when he gazed up at her, looking like a naughty, fallen angel. Her golden hair was tousled and messy, her soft cheeks bright with color, her lips rosy and swollen and tilted up at the corners. And that goddamned red belly button jewel was winking in the light spilling from the bedside lamps, making him absolutely crazy.

He thought it couldn't get much better. And then she began to move. A slow, undulating roll of her hips that instantly had his balls tightening, and he realized it got one whole hell of a lot better.

Oh man, he'd never make it. His release was already bubbling at the base of his spine and low in his groin. He'd promised her sixty minutes, but he'd be lucky to last sixty seconds with the way she was moving on him.

In defense, and with the notion that he better bring her up to speed real quick or she was going to be mighty disappointed, he placed his hand against the gentle curve of her lower belly. Working his calloused thumb into the top of her sex, he found the hot knot of nerves guaranteed to rocket her toward the moon.

Slowly he circled, pressed, and circled again. Then watched, mesmerized, as color stained her breasts and spread up her throat. With her head thrown back, her body arched in a delicate, feminine bow as she steadied herself by gripping his legs right above his knees, she abandoned herself to the ride.

And he could only glory in the wonder that was Ali.

Her first release slid through her, slow and warm as summer rain. The sound of his name sighing through her lips was the sweetest music he'd ever heard.

And suddenly, the only thought in his head was to taste her. Now.

Manacling her slender waist, he lifted her from her perch and lowered her against his face, her shaking thighs next to his ears.

"Nate!" she squeaked.

"Shh," he whispered. "Y'said you wanted to ride me for an hour, but y'didn't specify what *kind* of ride that'd be."

"But—"

"No buts," he cut off her protest as his palmed the globes of her ass and tilted her pelvis forward. "Just relax and enjoy."

Soon, she was mewling and swinging her hips helplessly. When he caught the hot knot of her clitoris between his lips and stabbed it repeatedly with the point of his tongue, her buttocks clenched in his palms before she ground down into him and keened, "Nate!"

Yeah, baby, it's Nate, he thought with deep, male

satisfaction. *It's Nate giving you this wild pleasure. It's Nate making you melt.*

And it was a melting, a sweet feminine dissolve.

When the last vestiges of orgasm shivered through her, she pushed up, caught her lower lip between her teeth, and grinned down at him.

Uh-oh. There was that look again.

Before he had time to protest, she scooted down, straddled his hips, and sank onto him in one hard stroke that had his fingers digging into the soft flesh of her hips. She leaned forward to brace her palms on the bed above his shoulders and dipped her tongue between his lips.

"Mmm, I taste good on you," she purred, and he couldn't help but wholeheartedly agree. "And you're going to taste good on me, too." He groaned at the thought of her sucking him into the hot, wet world of her mouth. "But for right now, I have something different in mind."

She gave his lips one final nip before she pushed up from his chest, and he could see the wickedly mischievous light shining in her slumberous eyes. Then she reached back, cupped his heavily aching balls, and swiveled her hips back and forth in a vigorous stroking that brought new meaning to the word *pleasure*.

Groaning and grinding his jaw hard enough to pulverize stone, he simply held on for the ride.

Chapter Sixteen

"General Fuller just got off the horn with the Jacksonville PD. The FBI has taken over the case of the dead guy in the Morgans' yard. The Bureau is spreading around the story it was a mob hit," Ozzie informed Frank while leaning against the same doorjamb Becky had leaned against not six hours earlier.

"Hmph," Frank shook his head, idly spinning his KA-BAR in a circle on his desk. It was a destructive habit, one that'd worn a smooth spot in the varnish beside the coaster he used for his coffee mug—which sort of made the coaster superfluous, given there was really no need to protect the finish on his already wrecked desk. "At least the FBI is proving to be valuable for something. Any idea who the guy was?"

"Not yet. They're running his prints as we speak. As soon as they know something, they'll contact the General, and he'll forward on the Intel." The kid angled his head and took a hesitant step into Frank's office. He shuffled back and forth on the balls of his feet, looking like he was about to burst.

"Spit it out," Frank grumbled, giving the knife another spin and watching the overhead lights glint off the long blade.

"What'd you do to Rebel?"

Well *that* had his eyes pinging up to Ozzie's youthfully obdurate face.

Great. Just...grrrreat. This was exactly what he didn't need tonight. One more person questioning him about what he'd done to Becky. Patti had already nearly flayed him alive with her surprisingly sharp tongue. It was a wonder he had any skin left.

"Who says I did anything to her?"

The kid straightened his lean shoulders and took another step inside the room. If Frank wasn't mistaken, Ozzie looked like he really wanted to offer him an ol' fashioned five-finger sandwich.

He lifted a brow in warning. "You're gonna want to reconsider whatever it is you're thinking about doing, kid."

"You made her cry," Ozzie accused, puffing himself up like a goddamned peacock. Frank suddenly felt every single one of his hard-lived years. "She tried to hide it when she came down to finish up the electrical on the Hawk, but I could tell. She'd been bawling her head off. And this isn't the first time it's happened."

Shit, he didn't want to know that. It only made him feel guilty, which, in turn, pissed him off. He was doing this for Becky's own good. Couldn't anyone but him see that?

"Well, sometimes life's a bitch and then you die," he snarled, mad at himself for feeling guilty, mad at Rebel for putting him in this goddamned situation to begin with, and mad as hell at Ozzie for questioning his decisions. Because that only made *him* start to question his decisions...

No. *No*. In this instance he was right, damnit!

Slapping his palm on his spinning knife, he stopped it mid-twirl and lifted his shirt to slide the wickedly sharp blade into the custom-made sheath attached to his waistband. "She needs to toughen up if she's going to keep working with us. I can't be pussyfooting around her all the time, scared I'm going to hurt her feelings."

"Pussyfooting?" Ozzie raised an incredulous brow and sometimes Frank missed the discipline of military rank. At least in uniform he hadn't had to worry about insubordinate facial expressions, especially ones that really, *really* chapped his ass. "Boss, you don't pussyfoot around anyone, especially Rebel. If anything, you're hard as hell on her. And you don't even begin to give her the credit she deserves. She's good at the techie stuff. Really good. You should give her a chance to—"

"I've made my decision about that," he cut the kid off. "We all have our jobs here. She needs to remember what hers is and stick to it."

"But if you'd just—"

"Enough!" he barked. "This conversation is over, Ozzie. I don't want to hear another word until you have an updated status report."

The kid's jaw worked like a chipper chewing up bark, but the little shit was smart enough to recognize a command when he heard one. Ozzie turned and stiffly marched toward the door. Frank heaved a weary sigh.

"You're wrong about this, Boss," the kid had the audacity to hiss, turning back to cut him a dark look. "Dead wrong."

Okay, so maybe he'd been a little premature about the kid's smarts regarding the situation.

"Well, then, it's my mistake, isn't it?" he asked, unaccountably tired all of a sudden.

Ozzie eyed him long and hard before he shook his head and stepped outside the office, none-too-gently closing the door behind him.

Frank dropped his pounding cranium into his hands. He really didn't need this shit.

He had men in harm's way, what with Rock and Wild Bill still doing duty in the Sandbox, and Christian and Mac in the company of a man whom Frank knew nothing about except for the not-so-reassuring fact that the guy was on a lot of folks' "Most Wanted" lists. Not to mention what'd happened with Ghost.

The ol' plate was full up to the tip-tippity-top, which meant he certainly didn't have room for regrets about Rebecca Reichert, but that's sure as hell what he was having. Regrets.

"Goddamnit!" He jerked his top drawer open, pulled out a root beer Dum Dum, ripped off the wrapper and shoved it in his mouth.

The iron taste of blood filled Nate's mouth as he frantically gnawed through thick ropes caked with sand and God only knew what else. He had to get out of this six-by-ten and find Grigg.

Sweet Jesus, he'd almost gone crazy listening to Grigg's screaming.

Now everything was quiet. Too quiet.

Previously, when their captors left to tie on their daily drunk, he and Grigg whispered through the thick mud walls of the hut, giving each other encouragement, trying to determine why they were here, wracking their brains and their beaten bodies to figure out a way to break free. But he'd bellowed Grigg's name over and over for ten long minutes with no reply before beginning on his ropes in frantic earnest, all gnashing teeth that were no longer careful about what was rope and what was skin.

"Grigg!" he screamed again. "Answer me, goddamn—" He bent over, ravaged by an attack of deep, wet coughing.

Their captors delighted in waterboarding him. "The American Way," or so they laughingly claimed. And yep, Nate was pretty sure he had a corresponding "American" case of pneumonia setting in.

When the coughing finally subsided and he could suck in a tortured breath—goddamn, it felt like he swallowed fire—he spit bright red blood into the powdery sand at his feet.

Shit. He hoped that blood was just from his shredded gums and not coming up from the sickly depths of his lungs.

That would be bad.

Not as bad as, say, being abducted by a group of tangos and tortured for three days for no apparent reason other than the guys were a bunch of sadists bent on taking out their hatred for America on two of its citizens, but it would still be bad. The pickle on top of this shitburger of a situation.

"Grigg!" he yelled again and was wracked by another bout of soggy coughing. More blood ended up in the sand at his feet.

Okay, that'd definitely come up from his lungs.

So...Pneumonia. No doubt about it.

Oh, happy happy, joy joy and a double fuck.

He went back to work with his teeth on the tough ropes securing his hands together in front of him...and Yahtzee! *His left binding unraveled into a frayed mess. Quickly freeing his right hand, he attacked the ropes tied around his ankles. The knots were swollen from his blood seeping into the fibers—the tattered things had soaked up the red stuff like a strand of vampires—and they were so tight he nearly ripped off a fingernail trying to loosen them. After much cursing and praying, they finally came free. Hallelujah.*

He stood...

Whoa.

The world went all weird and wacky.

He screwed the old peepers drum tight and swallowed, forcing himself to breathe deep. It helped, if only a little, considering the room—his lovely prison for the last three days—was pretty ripe with the metallic scent of freshly spilled blood and the far more foul perfume of his own excrement.

Finally, after a few more steadying breaths, he was able to move forward without the walls going all Tilt-a-Whirl. Grabbing his KA-BAR from the rickety wooden table where his captors had left it, he grimaced. Oh, buddy, how they'd exulted in using his own knife to skewer his thigh to the chair. Twice.

He glanced down at his swollen, bloodied leg and felt his stomach heave. If he didn't get some medical attention and a robust infusion of antibiotic on the double, he'd be lucky to keep that leg. It was already oozing smelly, green puss in a slow, thick river down to his knee.

Shit, shit, shit!

He wanted very badly to yell Grigg's name again, but he knew he'd crash headlong into another coughing fit, so he kept his big trap shut, instead using his strength to shuffle over to try the door.

Locked.

Of course. He couldn't be that lucky.

He tried prying the lock open with his knife, but the sucker was made from inch-thick, pre-World War II industrial strength iron and wasn't about to budge.

"Fuck!" he yelled, stabbing his knife into the wooden door and immediately doubling over to hack up more bright blood.

Jesus, Mary, and Joseph, he was in bad shape.

*When he was finally able to stand, he wiped the back of his hand over his mouth, and—*Hello. *What a happy sight to meet his watering, bloodshot eyes. His knife was wedged in the aging wood, the deadly sharp blade protruding all the way to the other side.*

Well, sometimes miracles do happen, *he thought.*

Grabbing the knife's hilt, he pulled the blade free and examined the wood.

Dry rot.

"Okay, Grigg," he whispered, taking a limping step back, "I'm coming, buddy."

He dug his toes into the loose sand, got some good traction, and lurched forward with everything he had, slamming his shoulder into the door.

Sweet lovin' Lord! He felt some ribs give way.

Luckily, that wasn't all that gave way. The wood up by the door's hinges splintered heavily upon impact—giving up the ghost with a satisfying crack.

He held on to his fractured rib cage until he could

breathe without wanting to die, then, grimacing, he stepped back only to run and throw himself against the door again.

Blam! *The whole goddamned dry-rotted thing flew off the hinges, and he and it landed with a hard crash out in the hall.*

He didn't wait to catch his breath—he was a bit afraid to, afraid a deep breath might send one of those loose ribs slam-bam into his lung. Scrambling up, he ignored the pain and dizziness and ran to the room next door, quickly twisting the lock. When he burst in, he stumbled to a shocked, sickened halt.

Oh God. Grigg.

He almost fell to his knees.

Swallowing, shaking his head, refusing to believe what his heart was telling him, refusing to believe the truth of the matter—that he was too late—he dragged himself forward.

Grigg was strapped, spread-eagle, to a rough-hewn table. There was blood everywhere.

Far too much blood and—

Nate turned and wretched into the sand when he got close enough to see the large gash in Grigg's sunken abdomen and the big bundle of bloody bowels looped around a long stick and sitting on the table beside Grigg's waxy body.

"Grigg, my brother," he sobbed as he wiped bloody vomit from his lips and laid a filthy, shaking hand on Grigg's blood-caked hair. "My God, what did they do to you?"

*He didn't expect a reply. Grigg was too white beneath all that blood, too still, too…*disemboweled, *so* *when Grigg coughed weakly, Nate stumbled backward in surprise.*

"Jesus God!" he raced around the table, using his blade to slice through the restraints at Grigg's wrists and ankles. "Hold on, buddy. I'll get you outta here."

"Keh meh," Grigg gurgled, and Nate limped to the head of the table. He cradled Grigg's wonderful face between his dirty palms and stared into his best friend's pain-hazed eyes.

"What, buddy? What'r'ya sayin'?"

"Keh meh," Grigg burbled again, thick blood leaking from one corner of his dry, cracked lips.

Nate smothered a sob and had to hold onto the table lest he curl up in a ball and die right on the spot.

They'd cut out Grigg's tongue.

As punishment for all the filthy names Nate had heard Grigg scream at them while being tortured, they'd cut out his motherfucking tongue.

Nate shook his head, his salty tears dropping onto Grigg's twisted face and turning pink in the caked-on blood. "No, buddy. We're gonna get you outta here. We're gonna make it."

Grigg jerkily shook his head and Nate stopped trying to hold back, he sobbed uncontrollably while leaning down to press his fevered forehead against Grigg's too cool one.

They both knew the score. Tangos one, Grigg zero.

Grigg would never see the outside of this filthy hut. Even if Nate could somehow find the strength in his wounded, sick body to carry Grigg, and even if they could figure out what in the world to do with that big bundle of putrefying bowels, there was no way Grigg would survive the maneuver.

Dear God in heaven.

"Peeh, keh meh."

"God, Grigg," Nate was crying so hard he could barely speak. "I c-can't. I can't d-do it."

"Peeh."

Nate threw his arms around Grigg's neck, wracked by gut-wrenching sobs and wet, sickly coughing. His broken ribs were threatening a revolt, but he couldn't stop the convulsive sorrow ravishing his control.

He couldn't do it. He couldn't kill Grigg. He couldn't live with himself if—

Grigg moaned, a sound of unimaginable pain and Nate suddenly knew…

Pulling back, he sucked in a trembling, tortured breath because Grigg's eyes…Sweet Jesus, they were dulled by piercing agony, but there was no mistaking the dreadful pleading in them. The pleading for Nate to put him out of his misery.

Nate allowed himself one tremendous howl of unspeakable anguish and impotent rage, then he swallowed and wiped the sticky, blood-tinged tears from his face. Looking down on his partner, his best friend, he sniffed and slowly nodded.

Grigg momentarily closed his swollen, bloodshot eyes. When he opened them again, the desperate pleading was replaced with poignant resignation…and gratitude.

Lord, forgive me, *Nate prayed, and moving around to the end of the table, he cradled Grigg's lolling head with one shaking hand and braced the hard, deadly tip of his KA-BAR at the base of Grigg's skull with the other.*

"I love you, you sonofabitch," he whispered, choking on blood and snot and the unspeakable horror of it all.

Grigg smiled.

In that moment, with one last smile gracing Grigg's mouth, Nate shoved the sharp tip of his steel blade between Grigg's skull and first vertebra, instantly severing Grigg's brainstem.

And it was over.

Nate threw his head back and roared.

Good heavens!

"Nate!" Ali grabbed Nate's broad shoulders and shook him, hard. His dark head bounced against the flat pillow. "Nate, for the love of Pete, wake up!"

She'd never in her life heard a more terrible sound than the one tearing up from the back of Nate's straining throat. Even the screams of her mother that horrible day they'd learned of Grigg's death didn't hold a candle to the god-awful noise Nate was making. It was like the furious, helpless call of a dying animal mixed with the roar of an angry dragon swirled together with the convulsive sorrow of a hundred lifetimes.

Then, like someone flipped a switch, the sound ceased.

Thank goodness.

"You're dreaming," she assured him, sucking in one petrified breath after another. She felt dizzy, but it was not the time to hyperventilate.

His black eyes snapped open and lasered in on her face. For a brief moment, he didn't seem to recognize her. "You're just dreaming, Nate," she said again, trying to reassure him and herself simultaneously.

Cripes.

He swallowed, his Adam's apple slowly bobbing in the column of his tanned throat where his pulse pounded so hard she fancied she could actually hear it. His nostrils flared wide, and for a brief moment she saw such utter despair…such gut-wrenching pain in his eyes. Then he turned away, hiding his misery from her as if it was something he should be ashamed of. Lifting the stupid fishing-lure-printed sheet up to his cheeks, he brusquely scrubbed away the wet evidence of his tears with enough force to take the first layer of skin off his face.

The scouring was useless; she'd already seen the tears. Those heartbreaking tears…

She feared she might see them for the rest of her life, them along with the horrible, dark emotion she'd glimpsed in those first few moments of consciousness.

"You, uh…you wanna talk about it?" she asked when he reemerged from under the sheet.

"No," he jerked his head once, refusing to look at her.

"Okay," she blew out a steadying breath and hesitantly wrapped comforting arms around his shoulders—she couldn't quite make the whole circumference, but she wrapped as much of herself around him as she could. Tucking her head up under his stubbled chin, with her cheek against his broad, heaving chest, she could hear the maddening cadence of his heart racing nearly out of control.

Crapola, hers was doing the same. She'd never been so scared in her life as when she'd been yanked from a deliriously peaceful sleep by the sound of Nate's terrible screaming.

Double, triple cripes!

It had to be flashbacks from the torture, right?

Or, on second thought, maybe not. He'd been through so much, seen so many awful things she couldn't possibly comprehend, there was probably no way on earth for her to begin to fathom what hideous demons stalked him while vulnerable and unconscious.

She remained silent for a long time, listening to the second hand on his big, complicated looking wristwatch tick away the seconds, taking the opportunity to catch her breath and letting him do the same.

Finally, when her heart no longer felt like it was going to pull an *Alien* impression and burst through her rib cage, she asked, "Does that, uh, happen to you often?"

She couldn't imagine.

"Often enough," he told her, his voice hard, cold, so much different than the night before, when he'd hotly whispered her name into her ear while emptying himself into her body.

"Is it…is it about the torture?"

He pushed up from the bed; the quick movement nearly had her bouncing right off—which was saying something considering the dang mattress was about as soft and cushiony as a cement block. Then, without a backward glance, he swung his long legs over the side, grabbing his bloodstained jeans. "I said I don't wanna talk about it," he growled, pulling worn denim up and over his bare butt.

Even while being coldly rebuffed, she couldn't help but notice just what a fine specimen of masculinity he represented, which probably meant she was a little loco where he was concerned.

Yeah, well, what else was new?

"Okay," she soothed. "I just..." she shook her head as she pushed into a sitting position. She didn't even begin to know how to handle this situation, where a man sounded like he was dying in his sleep and was obviously embarrassed at having been witnessed at his most vulnerable, but she'd give it her best shot. Or, in this case, fall back on an old cliché. "If you ever *do* want to talk about it, I just want you to know I'm here."

He swung around, his handsome face unusually harsh in the unflattering yellow light of the bedside lamps. "I thought you said this was a one-night stand."

Whoa. What?

"I don't—" She shook her head. "That's not what I mean. I just thought—"

"Well *don't*," he hissed. "Don't think anything."

"Nate," she held out a hand to him as she lifted the ridiculous sheet up over her naked breasts. Suddenly *she* was the one feeling unaccountably vulnerable. "Please stop this. You don't have to tell me what you were dreaming about, but don't...don't use this as an excuse to close yourself off from me. Don't use it as an excuse to push me away. I just want—"

"I'm not usin' anything as an excuse," he cut her off with a scornful snort. "I don't need to. We agreed to one night," he motioned jerkily out the window toward the faint pink light lining the eastern horizon. The new day looked like it was putting on its lipstick. "It's morning, now. So..." he made a rolling motion with his big hand, "the dawnin' of the new day brings this little experiment in lunacy to an end."

His words cut her to the very marrow of her bones.

Experiment in lunacy?

"But I thought—"

"What?" he turned his head slightly, cupping his broad palm around his ear. In that moment, she wanted to hit him. Again. Only this time she wanted it to really, *really* hurt. To hurt him as badly as he was hurting her.

"Look," he said, bending to grab his boots when she just sat there, staring at him in mute horror. "It was really great sex, sugar. Probably the best of my life. But we knew what it was going in. Don't ruin it by tryin' to turn it into somethin' else."

Probably the best of his life? *Probably?*

Now, she didn't just want to hit him, she wanted to chop his frickin' head off.

"I think you are the most—" The shrill *riiinnngg, riiinnngg* of his cell phone interrupted the scathing condemnation bubbling up the back of her throat.

He raised a sardonic brow.

Yeah, saved by the bell. Talk about cliché.

She snapped her mouth closed and angrily watched him pull his iPhone from the hip pocket of his jeans. He cut her a grim look before holding the device to his ear. "Ghost," he barked, giving her his broad back, a back that revealed the garish evidence of her raking nails and the hot ecstasy of the previous night.

A night that was *probably* the best of his life, but one he obviously had no desire to repeat.

She turned away. She wouldn't listen to the rest. She didn't need to. Everything she needed to know had been written all over his dastardly handsome face.

It was over.

He'd agreed to one night, and that night had reached its inevitable conclusion.

So that left her with…what?

Nothing, that's what.

Nothing but the poignant memory of the sweet passion they'd shared. Nothing but the awful knowledge she'd never love a man the way she loved him. Nothing but a heart that'd been burgeoning with hope and was now smashed into a thousand bloody pieces.

She flung the sheets aside and clambered from the bed. Scurrying to the bathroom, she threw on her discarded clothes and refused to give in to the hot tears waiting enthusiastically behind her eyes.

What had she expected?

He was Nathan Weller, Ghost, the Ice Man, Mr. Emotionless—as Ozzie liked to call him. Had she really thought one night with her would suddenly transform him into someone else?

Well, he *had* been transformed, but like Cinderella, his metamorphosis came with a time limit. Not the stroke of midnight like the fairy tale, but the first appearance of the new day.

Only he didn't leave behind a glass slipper.

Oh, no.

He managed to leave behind her stupid, impulsive, shattered heart.

Chapter Seventeen

"I'M GONNA NEED YOU T'HOLD ON TIGHT," NATE instructed Ali as they wove in and out of Chicago traffic, Phantom squeezing between the cars that hadn't already made room for the roaring beast of a bike. "Ozzie just called and told me the river tunnel is inop, so we're goin' in the front door hot and fast."

"River tunnel?" her voice sounded scratchy, unused. Well, no surprise there, considering these were the first words they'd spoken to one another since Nate fucked up royally back in that despicable motel room.

Nearly fifteen solid hours of total, you're-*such*-an-asshole silence where Ali didn't deign to touch him save for the few instances when she'd had to brace herself as they leaned into curves. He'd never thought it possible to crave or…*miss* simple contact from another human being so much in his life.

"Oh, you mean the Bat Cave," she said, answering her own question. "What happened?"

Man, just the sound of her voice made his heart rate kick up a notch. Maybe if he took the next corner real fast, she'd be forced to wrap her arms around him and then…no. Considering she was perched all the way back against the sissy bar, she'd likely choose to go flying off the back of Phantom rather than submit to laying a finger on him.

Damn. For a relatively intelligent guy, he sure could

be a grade-A dumbass on occasion. That morning being a shiningly shitty example.

"Somethin' about a problem with the hydraulics in the motor that runs the door back at Black Knights Inc.," he told her. "We could access the tunnel via the terminating door in the parkin' garage across the way, but then we'd be stuck down there for God only knows how long before Rebel fixes the problem and I don't know about you, but the thought of sittin' in that dank tunnel under however many gallons of fishy Chicago river just doesn't sound like my idea of a good time."

Whoa. He was suddenly all Chatty Cathy? He wasn't sure he'd strung that many words together since… well, since she'd held him safe in her arms and sweetly wheedled the story of Moscow out of him.

Maybe he was trying to make up for all the hours of silence today…or maybe he was just an asshole.

He figured *she'd* bet on the latter.

"Hmm," she grumped, unaware of the turmoil of his thoughts, "I'll agree with that, but I don't understand why we need to go in hot and fa—Hey! You moron!" She shook her fist at a cab driver who'd nearly T-boned them while trying to push a light.

Wow, put the girl through a couple of days of high-level stress, dress her in black leather and give her a gun, and suddenly she went all *Xena: Warrior Princess*.

The cabbie must've read her I-can-castrate-men-with-just-a-thought expression. He lifted his hands, the universal *my-bad* signal, and Ali growled. "Anyway, I don't get why we have to go in the front door hot and fast. Is there something you're not telling me?"

He could hardly believe they were having this semi-rational conversation after the way he'd handled things back at the Happy Acres. He'd behaved like such a douchebag, but dear lovin' Lord, he'd never expected to wake from the reoccurring dream of Grigg's horrendous death to Ali's beautifully concerned face.

Talk about a dagger straight to his already shredded heart.

And because he'd been hurting, humiliated over having her see him when he was crying like a friggin' baby and screaming his idiot head off, because the sight of her there, naked in his arms, looking at him with such compassion and sweet, sweet sympathy when he'd *killed* the one person in the world she loved more than anything only made him feel unimaginably guilty, he'd pulled out the prick card, played his hand like an ace, and said things he didn't mean. Things sure to make her turn away from him so he wouldn't have to deal with the fact that he was dying inside.

Shit.

Just the thought of the look wallpapered all over her face before he'd been forced to turn his back on her—or drop to his knees and confess everything—made him want to curl up in a ball and cry. It'd been a look of such surprise, such disillusionment, such…*hurt*.

Someone should just shoot him and put him out of his misery.

Oh, wait. Someone *had* shot him and that only *added* to his current list of This Is Why My Life Sucks.

"Nate?" she dragged him from his relentless thoughts. "Is there something you're not telling me?"

"Yeah," he flicked a glance into his rearview mirror,

one of the ten thousand or so peeks he'd made at the thing since this morning. "That was Ozzie callin' this morning..." And, oh, great, that's just what they needed, him reminding them both of exactly what Ozzie's call had interrupted. "...Uh," he cleared his throat and doggedly pushed ahead. "Anyway, that guy I shot at your parents' house? The one you think is your mugger? Well, he's known t'work with two accomplices. And if I'm not mistaken, the black SUV back there has been following us since we crossed the city limits. Don't look," he demanded when she began to do just that.

"Do you really think they'd try for us in broad daylight?"

Broad daylight? God love the woman, but she was innocent as a baby. "It's sunset and we're currently headin' west, which puts the sun directly in our eyes, effectively blindin' us. We're at a tactical disadvantage."

He felt her arm move as she reached for his reserve weapon. This morning, she'd asked for the little Colt. He'd lifted a brow but complied with her request, only to watch, quite mesmerized, as she again press-checked the chamber before shoving the piece into the waistband of her jeans.

And why watching her pink-tipped fingers fondle his weapon gave him a hard-on was anyone's guess. It was probably something he should discuss with that psychiatrist whose card was shoved beneath his mattress.

"Don't pull it," he warned her now. "The last thing we need is to get hauled to the clink by the CPD for carryin' an unlicensed, concealed weapon."

"I won't pull unless I need to," she assured him, her voice remarkably steady considering.

"I gotta connect with headquarters," he told her.

"So I'm gonna switch over, and you won't be able to communicate with me through the mic until we're safe inside the compound. Okay?"

"Yeah, okay." He heard her swallow, and the dry, clicking sound was the only indication she gave of her fear. The damned woman looked like a creampuff but was turning out to be tough as nails.

Before he thumbed the speed dial on his phone, he had to get one more thing out there. "Ali?"

"What?"

"I'm sorry."

Silence. He probably shouldn't be too surprised by that.

"I, uh, I just wanted you to know," he finished lamely, then pressed two on his phone, listening to the series of clicks and beeps that established his secure connection once he stated his password.

Dagan ran across the bagel shop's roof and dropped down behind the giant, industrial, air-conditioning unit. The damn thing sounded like a jet-engine, but he wasn't going to need his ears for the next few moments, because he'd heard everything he'd needed to hear just before he'd scrambled up the old iron fire-escape and hoisted himself onto the sticky tar roof across from Black Knights Inc.

Namely, he'd heard the unmistakably throaty grumble of Ghost's monster of a motorcycle.

"Why the hell aren't you using the bolt-hole, you stupid ass?" he growled as he flicked the safety on his Glock.

Fifteen lousy rounds.

That's all he had because he'd left his extra magazines in his go-bag inside the SUV parked down the block.

Stupid, stupid.

But not as stupid as Nathan Weller coming in the front door of Black Knights Inc. when he had a perfectly good, totally anonymous back door he could safely utilize.

Dagan had been reaching for his cell phone, about to make an anonymous phone call to the boys at Black Knights Inc. to inform them of the two shadowy figures lurking around the edges of the Knights' compound, when he'd heard the guttural roar of that badass bike.

So now, instead of one easy-peasy phone call, he was forced to hustle into a covering position with fifteen lousy rounds.

Nate was coming down the street like a bat out of hell. Luckily, there was no traffic on the road or he'd have probably scared the crap out of the other drivers.

He gave Manus in the guardhouse a thumbs-up and the big wrought iron gate was just beginning to swing slowly open when the hairs at his nape snapped to sudden attention. Warning Will Robinson! He barely had time to reach for the handgun in his waistband before utter chaos exploded.

Literally.

The guardhouse nearly disintegrated before his very eyes, riddled with bullets that shattered the glass and shredded the wooden structure.

Sonofabitch! Manus!

He heard Ali's terrified scream even though he was no longer connected to her through the helmet's headset, and—dear God forgive him—but he spared no second thought for Manus Connelly.

His only concern was Ali.

Cutting the front wheel sharply, rubber screamed and foul, acrid smoke billowed up to obscure his vision as he planted his biker boot onto the pavement hard enough to break the bones in his ankle. Luckily, the stiff support of the boot kept that from happening, but…

Shit! The rubber on his sole quickly heated and melted as he did his level best to control the monster bike in its heavy, awkward skid. Every muscle he had strained to the limit as he wrestled with around a quarter ton of custom-made steel.

Control stopped being an issue when a string of hot bullets blasted through his rear fender. The big tire beneath exploded, and he had no choice but to lay down the bike and hope its bulk plus the bulk of his own body would be enough to protect Ali from the hail of gunfire.

She was still screaming when he forced her to the ground beneath him. Trying to use Phantom as meager cover, he used one hand to shield Ali's helmeted head and the other to raise his weapon and…

Where the hell *was* that sawgunner?

He expected to see the black SUV, but it was nowhere in sight. Maybe he'd been wrong. Maybe he'd let his paranoia get the better of—

He ducked when a bullet slammed into the motorcycle's steaming engine, sounding louder than a damned train wreck.

They were sitting ducks out here in the middle of the street, just asking for a terminal case of lead poisoning.

Even the heavy steel of Phantom's chassis provided little cover when going up against a man with an AK-47.

He recognized the *rat-a-tat-tat* of that Russian special. He'd heard it often enough in so many of the shitholes he'd worked all over the world.

Another round glanced off the handlebars with a loud *ping*, and he was able to get a bead on the trajectory. *Finally*.

Lifting his head, he zeroed in on the dark shadow of the guy with the machine gun turkey peeking around the corner of the deli down the block, and just like always, the rest of the world faded away.

He wished he had ol' Sierra and her optics, but that wasn't an option. It wasn't only that he didn't have the time to assemble her, he didn't dare move from his protective position over Ali—who was squirming beneath him, trying to lift her head and his reserve weapon at the same time, the stupid, wonderful woman.

No matter. He was nearly as good with a pistol as he was with a rifle. He slowed his breathing; his heart rate immediately followed.

Calm is king, Grigg had liked to say, and it was certainly true when faced with overwhelming odds and a foolish woman who was *still* trying to wrestle out from under him in order to join in the battle.

Xena: Warrior Princess indeed.

A bullet whizzed by his helmet, so close he felt the heat from the displaced air against his cheek, and then time stopped. The Hogue soft rubber grip of his Para Ordinance CCW .45 melded with his palm as his steady trigger finger slipped away from the trigger guard. A fraction of a second later, perhaps a heartbeat more, he automatically accounted for distance, bullet drop, and Kentucky windage, and then there was nothing left to do but squeeze.

The .45 round left the barrel with a loud bark, and the mad sawing of the machine gun sputtered to a choking stop.

Yep, the guy was likely to have a bit of difficulty continuing to operate that Kalashnikov with a hollow point entering one inch below his right eye and taking out most of his gray matter upon exiting the back of his skull.

In the resounding silence immediately following the sawgunner's death, Nate could hear Ali cursing over the ringing in his ears. "Let me up, damnit! I can help!"

He almost smiled.

"Stay still," he advised her gruffly, not taking any chances as he quartered the area. He must be crushing her, but a few bruises and some road rash were a whole helluva lot better than a bullet...much easier to recover from.

When his eyes fixed on what was left of the guardhouse, he swallowed back the bile that rose to the back of his throat.

It'd be a miracle if Manus were alive.

He didn't want to move from his covering position over Ali, but he had to at least go and check on Manus. The guy was a Knight—by proxy, at least—and Nate couldn't just sit if there was a chance he could help the man.

"I want ya to stay down behind Phantom," he instructed Ali, still searching the surrounding buildings for the sawgunner's partner. "I've gotta go check the guardhouse."

He didn't wait for her reply, just lifted himself from her prone body and—

A bullet plowed into the pavement by his left leg. Hot cement exploded into biting little shards upon impact.

That was no machine gun. Oh, hell no. That was a bolt-action rifle. A pretty good one by the sound of it.

"*Sonofa—*"

He dropped back down on top of Ali, swinging his weapon in the direction of the shot. Then something across the way caught his eye.

There was a man with a handgun held out in front of him running along the roof of the bagel shop. The dude was skylining himself like crazy, and it would've been a piece of cake for Nate to put a bullet in him, but the guy wasn't aiming for them.

Mystery Man?

"What the…?"

He didn't get a chance to finish the question before Mystery Man was discharging his weapon, ducking down behind the building's rooftop air-conditioning unit when he was met with rapid return fire.

Then the bullets suddenly stopped flying. In the aftermath, the silence in the street was thick and heavy as Phantom's chassis. The quiet *tick-tick-tick* of motorcycle's stalled engine almost obscenely loud in comparison.

Nate was scouring the opposite rooftop for another glimpse of Mystery Man when a muffled cry had him turning in time to see the men of Black Knights Inc. barreling toward them, loaded for bear, weapons held at the ready.

And then—

"Oh my God!" Ali whispered, her eyes wide with horror as she glanced through the partially opened wrought-iron gate into the compound beyond. "Is that Patti?"

"No," he groaned, his chest squeezing so tight it was a wonder he was able to draw breath. "Sweet Christ, no!"

But no amount of denial would change the fact that Patti lay sprawled on the pavement not six feet from the gate, the dark pool of blood beneath her slowly spreading out to form a macabre circle. A bunch of...

Lord, it looked like she'd been carrying a tray of chocolate chip cookies when she'd been cut down. They were strewn about her body like some sort of horrific confetti.

One minute Dan was kneeling beside his wife, the next he was barreling toward the barely open gate, screaming like a berserker. He frantically wiggled and squirmed and finally squeezed himself between the two halves, only to break into a madcap dash, muscular arms pumping, big thighs churning and then he—

Holy shit!

He slammed himself into Mystery Man, who was clamoring down the bagel shop's fire escape. The kinetic force of Dan's one hundred ninety-five pound body sent both men flying, rolling, weapons lost and forgotten in the battle for supremacy. And then, in the blink of an eye, Dan was on top, sitting on Mr. Mystery's chest and pummeling the guy's face with both fists.

"Dan!" Nate yelled, scrambling over to the grappling men. "He's not the one!"

But Dan couldn't hear him. In his rage and grief, Dan was deranged and deaf to everything but the awful urge for vengeance.

Nate hooked his arms around Dan's chest, taking a hard elbow to the ear that nearly knocked him senseless, and hauled the screaming, sobbing Dan up and off Mystery Man. No easy task even though Nate outweighed Dan by a good twenty pounds, because Dan had uncontrollable fury racing like fire through his veins, giving him the strength of about ten men.

"He's not the one!" Nate roared straight into Dan's ear, struggling with everything he had to hold on to kicking, hissing sonofabitch. "He's not the one who shot Patti!"

"You stupid fuck!" Mystery Man yelled and oh, great, that's just what Nate *didn't* need as Dan suddenly stilled. He could feel Dan's whole body coil, and he tightened his grip, waiting for Dan to try to explode out of his hold. Only that's not what happened. The stupid fuck—yep, at least Mystery Man had that part right—snapped his head back, slamming Nate's nose so hard bright yellow stars danced cheerfully in front of his vision. He lost his grip as hot blood poured down over his mouth and chin.

Dan took advantage of his momentary shock to ram into Mystery Man just as the guy was pushing himself to his feet. They hit the pavement with a sickening thud, Dan retaining his superior position. Only this time Dan wasn't punching Mr. Mystery. Oh, no. This time he wrapped his hands around guy's throat and squeezed so hard the tendons in his forearms stood out like garden hoses.

"He's…get…ting…a…way," Mystery Man choked, his face turning crimson as his eyes began to bulge out of their sockets.

Dan couldn't hear the guy above his own horrible

choking sobs, nor could he see Mystery Man struggling to speak through the tears and snot running in a terrible mess down his contorted face.

"Dan," Nate ignored the blood flowing into his mouth as he squatted beside the two men. "You've gotta listen to me now, buddy. This guy didn't shoot Patti. He was helpin' us," Nate glanced down at Mystery Man to see the guy's eyes start to roll back in his head. "Let go, now." He placed a heavy hand on Dan's shoulder. The guy was shaking so hard Nate thought he might just rattle his bones to dust.

Then Dan sucked in a tortured breath and met Nate's eyes, clarity slowly returning through the haze of temporary madness.

"Let go," he repeated. "You've got the wrong guy."

Dan glanced down at Mystery Man, whose fingers were clawing at his wrists, leaving deep, bloody furrows.

"You hear me talkin' to you, soldier?" Nate yelled, shaking Dan's shoulder, because he had to get through now, like, *right now* or Mystery Man was toast. "You're killin' an innocent man!"

Dan suddenly unclenched his hands, rolling off Mystery Man to scramble to his feet. He stumbled back over to his dead wife, hoarsely wailing his agony the entire way.

Jesus. *Jesus*.

Nate blew out a ragged breath and wiped the back of his arm over his mouth and chin. Mystery Man was lying in the middle of the street, sucking in great gulping lungfuls of sweet, life-giving O_2.

Well, at least Nate'd been able to save one life today.

He spat bright red blood onto the pavement before he

turned to see Ali take the shirt that Ozzie ripped over his head. She quickly pressed it onto the bleeding wound in Manus's big chest. Manus grimaced and moaned, but his eyes were steady on Ali's face as she leaned down to say something Nate couldn't hear over the sirens wailing in the distance.

Unbelievable.

The guy was still alive.

And he might just stay that way if that was an ambulance headed in their direction which, by the look of Boss's vigorous gesturing and the sound of him barking orders into his cell phone, chances were pretty good it was.

A strangled wail that echoed above the approaching sirens had him glancing back through the gates—which was a mistake. Because the awful sight that met his eyes was one that'd stay with him the rest of his life.

Dan was sitting in that big pool of dark blood, surrounded by that awful arrangement of chocolate chip cookies, his wife's lifeless body cradled in his arms. The guy was rocking and sobbing, his face wet with tears and contorted with grief.

Patti. *God*. Nate didn't want to believe it.

She was the mother of the group. The one who made sure they all ate. The one who made sure they were wearing clean clothes. The one who made sure there was always beer in the fridge and beef jerky in the cabinets. She was the cool voice of rationality when too much testosterone inevitably had heads getting hot and mouths running hotter.

And now she was gone.

In the blink of an eye, and one madman's careless barrage of bullets, her sweet light was extinguished forever.

"Sonofabitch!" he cursed and scrubbed a hand over his moist eyes.

What the hell was she doing by the gatehouse anyway? Everyone was supposed to stay secured inside until he and Ali and the damned zip drive were safely back in the shop and they—

"Where do'y'think you're goin'?" he pointed his .45 at Mystery Man as the guy took a step down the road.

"The second gunman is getting away," Mystery Man rasped as he raised his hands, palm out. Purple bruises were already popping out around the guy's abused throat.

"He's already gone, man," Nate told him, refusing to lower his weapon, still unsure just whose side ol' Mr. Mystery was playing on. In the gun battle, he'd been on the side of the Knights, but that didn't mean the man was gonna stay there. "You know that as well as I do."

"But I might—"

"Nuh-uh. You're not leavin' my sight until we figure out just what the hell is goin' on here, and just who the hell you are."

Mystery Man's split, swollen lips twisted into a dark grimace. "Well, I'm Dagan Zoelner, former CIA. And as for what's going on here? I think I might be able to shed a little light on that."

Chapter Eighteen

Ali sat on a hard folding chair in the conference room at Black Knights Inc., watching dazedly while Ozzie connected the zip drive to one of his computers.

She felt like she was dreaming. She *had* to be dreaming.

The past two hours weren't real, were they?

She hadn't really been in the middle of an all-out gunfight, lovable Patti wasn't really dead, the gatehouse guard wasn't really in the middle of a grueling surgery with very little chance of survival, and the Chicago Police Department wasn't really covering up the whole thing and calling it a "gang-related" incident—via the strict instructions of someone *very* high up in the national government.

As she glanced around at the grim faces of Nate, Frank, Ozzie, and Mystery Man/Dagan Zoelner, she shook her head. She couldn't deny that, *yes*, this *was* reality. She *had* been in a gunfight, Patti *was* dead, the CPD *had* covered it all up, and Manus—she'd learned the guard was Big Red's brother—*was* having the damage to his chest repaired right at this very moment.

This very *real* moment.

To make matters worse, if that was even possible, she was about to find out if her brother really had stolen highly classified files to sell on the black market, as former Agent Zoelner claimed.

"We're in," Ozzie announced, his broad, agile fingers

flying over the keyboard. "Looks like a bunch of Excel spreadsheets and a…wait…there seems to be a video file."

"Play it," Frank grumbled, rotating one heavy shoulder and grimacing. "Maybe it'll tell us just what the fuck this has all been about."

She glanced up at the big man. His rough face was lined with grief and worry, but he seemed to be holding it together. Despite the horrific tragedy of the last few hours, despite the fact that there might be more terrible tragedy to come if Manus died on the operating table and they learned Grigg really *had* turned traitor, he was holding it together remarkably well.

She supposed that's what hard men like him did in tough situations.

They held it all together so folks like her could go on living the American Dream. Free and peaceful and… so oblivious.

For some reason, the thought struck her as particularly awful and that, combined with a horrid flash of Patti lying pale and lifeless in a huge puddle of blood and chocolate chip cookies, had her suddenly fighting the urge to puke.

She'd never eat a chocolate chip cookie ever, *ever* again. Just the thought…

"Erp," she put two fingers to her mouth as she searched the room.

There was a plastic trash can over by the door to Frank's office, wasn't there? So if she had to spew, she thought she could just about make it to…

Oh, crapola.

She wasn't thinking of blood or chocolate chip cookies or plastic trash cans or *anything* any longer, because her lovable brother's face popped up on Ozzie's huge monitor and the breath froze in her lungs like two solid blocks of ice. The blood in her veins ran cold as goose bumps pebbled her skin.

"Hey, Ozzie," Grigg said, the sound of his wonderfully familiar voice choking her.

"Breathe, Ali," Nate's strong fingers squeezed her trembling shoulder. "Just breathe, sugar."

Yeah, breathing was good, especially so that *something* would continue to function while her heart was breaking all over again and bleeding out onto her already unreliable stomach.

"Good job on breaking my code," Grigg continued, his marvelous face looking just as she remembered it. Handsome, dependable, a little bit ornery...Okay, a *lot* ornery. "Not that it was too much of a stretch for you, I'm sure," he chuckled, and the sweet sound was like a sharp arrow to her aching heart and crumbling control.

"So," Grigg's video image leaned closer to the screen and she caught her breath, "if you're watching this, it means Ghost is there with you. Hi, buddy," he waved.

"Jesus," Nate muttered, his voice hoarse with emotion.

"And I'm probably dead." Grigg's image grimaced, his nose doing that wonderful wrinkly thing Ali so loved. "Sorry about that."

"Christ, man," Nate choked and turned away, and that was the last straw for Ali. The tears that'd been hovering spilled over to streak, hot and salty, down her cheeks.

A handkerchief suddenly appeared in her hands. She used it to assert a small measure of control over her leaking face.

"Anyway..." Grigg persisted. "I guess that means the

shit has hit the fan, you've found out about my little off-the-books assignment, and Ali remembered this zip drive that arrived at her house at an unusual time.

"So, let me see if I can clear some things up. I got a call yesterday from Special Agent Delaney of the FBI. I, uh, I met him a while back when Wild Bill and I infiltrated that loony religious sect that was cooking more meth than a thousand-unit trailer park. You remember, Nate? He's the one I told you about. The one who liked to wear Prada sunglasses and Gucci loafers?"

"Shit," Nate spat, and Ozzie hit pause on the video as the group gathered around the monitor turned toward Nate. He raked an agitated hand over his face, the bristles on his chin sounding like sandpaper against his rough palm. "I didn't remember the name Delaney 'cause Grigg always referred t'the guy as GQ."

"What do you remember now?" Frank urged, gray eyes bloodshot but fiercely alert.

"Nothin' much," Nate shook his head regretfully, cursing under his breath. "Just that Grigg was as impressed with the guy's skill as he was with his fashion sense."

"Hmph," Frank grunted, obviously supremely *un*impressed with any man who gave a fig for fashion. As a group, they turned back to the computer screen. Ozzie restarted the video.

"...So Delaney calls me and says he's got a job only I can do since he can't trust anyone in his own office or any of the other alphabet soup outfits. He says it's crucial I don't reveal the mission to anyone, even to you guys. Claims it's highly dangerous and there are elements at play he can't control and he wants to restrict the danger to as few folks as possible. Now," Grigg shook his head and grinned his wonderful, devil-may-care grin, "I know you're all cursing me right now, but Delaney wouldn't have tapped me if he wasn't in a real bind, which," Grigg's grin twisted into another grimace, "turns out he is…uh, *was*. Shit, I'll get to that part later.

"So anyway, I agreed to the job and met Delaney yesterday evening in DC. There he tells me he suspects a certain senator, a Mr. Alan Aldus, has been selling illegal weapons to some pretty extreme Pakistani tribesmen—big no-no in anyone's book. Only up to this point, Delaney hasn't been able to get the evidence he needs to have the good senator arrested. Long story short, Delaney got his hands on Senator Aldus's computer password and the codenames for the files of the weapons sales. He needed me to go in during the senator's shindig last night under the guise of a bullet-catcher and copy the files. And no, Ozzie, the senator's system couldn't be hacked from the outside. I specifically asked Delaney that question. I also asked him why he didn't just do it himself, and he started acting all spooked and shit, said he was convinced the senator was on to him and there were folks within his own agency who knew about the deal and were covering for Aldus. Delaney said he was being watched, followed. You know, your typical government-employee paranoia. Still, I was impressed with the guy's skills in New Mexico, so I agreed to help him and we shook hands and parted ways.

"The job was simple, went off without a hitch. Then, after the party, Delaney failed to show at the drop, and what do you know? Come to find out, the guy's dead. Supposedly fell asleep at the wheel and dunked his car in the river," Grigg rolled his beautiful brown eyes.

"Now here I am stuck with my thumb up my butt. I have no clue who I should send these files to. Obviously this thing goes deep and is dangerous as hell, considering Delaney's convenient sleep apnea episode. I don't know who's involved, but it's gotta be some folks pretty high up. On top of all that, Ghost, you and I are tasked to fly out to Istanbul at oh-three-hundred, which is," Grigg glanced at his watch, "in exactly two flippin' hours.

"So," he puffed out a breath. "Here's the deal. I'm sending this zip drive along with all the information to Ali. She'll think it's just the same-ol'-same-ol'. I'm hoping I come back from this job to nab the zip drive and figure out just what the hell I'm supposed to do with it. But like I said in the beginning, if you're watching this, I'm probably dead, the shit has hit the fan, and I couldn't be more sorry about the whole stinkin' mess.

"That's it," Grigg frowned, his usually grinning face lined with harsh worry, "except for one last thing... Ghost, Nate, brother of my heart, I'm gonna need you to watch over Ali. Just...make sure she's all right, okay?"

They all watched breathlessly as Grigg's video image leaned forward, and then the screen dissolved to blackness.

"Fuck me," Frank cursed as Ali quietly sobbed into the soggy handkerchief.

Oh, Grigg. *My sweet, crazy, dauntless brother*.

"So, I guess that blows your theory of Grigg trying to sell black-market files right out of the water," Ali heard Ozzie say to the CIA guy, Zoelner.

She lifted her head—the thing weighed about a

million pounds—and sniffed back her tears in time to see Zoelner make a face.

"Yeah well, like I said, I'd already determined Aldus was completely full of shit."

"What was in it for you?" Frank asked, his craggy face particularly harsh. "Money?"

"Look," Zoelner spat, wincing when it stretched his split lip. Dan Man had really done a job on the guy's face. One eye was swollen almost completely shut while the other sported a pretty nasty gash right below the eyebrow. The ruined skin was hastily closed with a butterfly bandage but not cleaned. Crusty blood clung to the wound. "I don't have to explain anything to you. Yes, Aldus hired me to track down and secure files for him. Files he told me were highly classified and in danger of being sold to the highest bidder. Yes, I ghosted Miss Morgan here for months, no doubt scaring her to death. Yes, I hung around here, trying to find out just what the hell was going on. But the minute, I mean the very *minute* I became convinced the senator was full of shit, I stopped taking his money. So fuck you and that high horse you're riding on!"

Zoelner jumped from the metal folding chair he was sitting in, sending the thing toppling over with a loud clang. Without another word, he started toward the stairway leading down to the first floor.

"Hold it," Frank barked at the guy's retreating back. Zoelner swung around to face the group, blowing like a winded bull.

"Calm down, for fuck's sake!" Frank bellowed, doing a pretty good raging bull impression himself. "I'm not accusing you of anything, you sensitive prick. I'm just trying to figure out everyone's motives here."

Zoelner pinned his one semi-good eye on Frank's angrily flushed face. "My motives are my own," he growled.

"Fine," Frank threw his wide palms in the air. "Whatever. Keep your damned motives to yourself. But you're not leaving here. You're coming with us."

Zoelner's jaw sawed back and forth, but he managed to ask calmly, "Going with you where?"

"DC," Frank informed him, his tone sufficiently broadcasting there would be no ifs, ands, or buts. "The president and his Joint Chiefs are going to be awfully interested in the information on this zip drive, and they're going want to talk to you about your association with Aldus."

"How do you know the Joint Chiefs aren't part of Aldus's little party?" Zoelner demanded. "You could be leading us all into the lion's den."

"Experience," Frank said, his tone absolute. "And the fact that I personally *know* the Joint Chiefs. They're a bunch of assholes on a good day, but there's not a one of them who'd be involved in this."

"Shit!" Zoelner spat, then winced again and lifted a finger to wipe at the drop of blood that welled on his lower lip.

Oh, crapola, they were leaving. They were going to leave her here as they jetted off to Washington and she…

Well, there was only one thing she was going to do.

"I'm coming with you," she declared, sniffing back her tears and thrusting out her chin as she glanced around at each of their hard, weary faces. Oh yeah, she was daring any of them to tell her otherwise, because if they did…well, she'd just make sure they didn't. "I deserve to see this through to the end."

"Ali—" Nate began but was interrupted by Frank's harsh tone.

"All right, Ali," the big man growled, accurately reading her adamant, no-way-I'm-capitulating expression or, more likely, he was simply unwilling to take the time to argue. "Grab whatever you need. The military transport we're hopping out of Great Lakes Naval Station departs in ninety minutes."

She nodded and slowly stood from the chair, studiously avoiding Nate's worried, belligerent gaze. She knew he wanted to argue, bully her into staying where it was safe. But she wasn't in the mood to be bullied. And right now, she didn't give a darn about safety.

"Their lobbyists say they've only got to swing two more votes and then we'll be on the mark to take—"

Whatever Ron Dunn, the senator from New Jersey, was about to say got cut off when two guys in severe black suits burst into Senator Alan Aldus's office, closely followed by his harried secretary of twenty years.

"I'm so sorry Senator Aldus," she gushed, wringing her veiny hands before pushing her trifocals up the long bridge of her nose. "I told them you were in a meeting, but they just pushed past me."

"It's okay, Janice," Aldus assured her, though by the looks of the men striding toward him it was anything but.

Secret Service?

That's sure as hell what the guys looked like, with their matching dark suits and those clear, plastic wires snaking up from their starched white collars to disappear unobtrusively into the shells of their ears. The Men in Black, up close and in person.

"Senator Aldus," one of the men said in an accent that was no accent at all, "you need to come with us now."

"Ron," Aldus turned toward the blatantly curious man seated across from him. He was very careful to keep his own expression bland. "We'll have to discuss this later."

"Er...sure," the New Jersey senator scrambled to his feet, making no attempt to hide his nosiness as he eyed the two automatons who were moving in to flank Aldus.

He waited patiently until Ron left with Janice close on his heels before standing, and slowly and carefully closing the double buttons on his ultra tailored, Hugo Boss suit. Shooting his gold-linked cuffs, he regarded his stoic companions with all the audacity of a U.S. senator.

"Gentlemen," he said, his tone not-so-slightly condescending, "just what the hell do you think you're doing barging in here and ordering me to—"

He thought the vein in his temple was going to explode when Man in Black I interrupted him. "We've been instructed, senator," was it his imagination or was that a sneer on the guy's face when he used that title? "to escort you to the White House immediately."

He opened his mouth, and it was then that Man in Black II decided to pipe up. "You should know, sir, we've also been instructed to take you forcibly, in handcuffs, if you refuse to come peaceably."

Cold sweat instantly popped out on his forehead and dampened the armpits of his shirt beneath his suit jacket, more slid nauseatingly down the small of his back. Despite that, there was a definite chill spreading through his veins.

"What is this in regard to?" he asked, but could think of only one thing that would bring the Secret Service to his door with orders to escort him, forcibly if need be, to the White House.

Those fucking files.

He hadn't heard from Johnny since they'd learned of Rocco's death, but he hadn't really expected to until tonight. Johnny had promised that Miss Morgan and former sergeant Weller were as good as dead. With the menacing tone of vengeance ringing in Johnny's rough voice, Aldus had believed him.

Now, he felt the weight of the prepaid phone like a lead brick inside his jacket pocket.

Was it possible Johnny had failed? Had the files been found?

It was the only thing that made sense. And for the first time in Alan Aldus's entire gilded life, the threat of personal doom loomed like a poison-fanged monster in front of him.

Frank glanced around the Oval Office and shook his head.

Not only had he never thought to be sitting in this room with its antique furniture, plaster reliefs, and genuine oil painting of, you guessed it, that'd be the original GW, George Washington, he certainly hadn't thought to be sitting in this room with the strange amalgamation of folks surrounding him.

President Thompson was seated at his desk, looking very stern and powerful. His Joint Chiefs, including

General Fuller, were arranged here and there. Some seated on the sofas in the center of the room, some standing along the walls. General Fuller was actually pacing, looking mad enough to take the entire country to DEFCON 1.

Ex-CIA agent Dagan Zoelner was beside the door. He'd unflinchingly answered the questions the president and Joint Chiefs had thrown at him, his personal integrity evident in every well-thought-out word. Now, Zoelner was looking for all the world like he'd rather be any place but there, and his position indicated he'd take the first opportunity to vamoose himself. Frank noticed the man's one good eye never stayed still, constantly darting about. It caught every subtle move, every vague facial expression on everyone in the room. The guy was certainly wound tight, like most spooks, but Frank had to admit to being a little intrigued. Zoelner's file—he'd read it on the flight to DC—was something of a page-turner.

Then there was Ghost, leaning against the back wall, still dressed in his biker leathers with dried blood streaking down his shirt, looking completely out of place. Not that Frank was all that tidy, but, *shit*, the least Ghost could've done before meeting the *president* was change his fucking shirt. Of course, he supposed the guy wasn't all that concerned with his current lack of hygiene.

Ghost had something entirely different plaguing his sleep-deprived brain, and Frank was sure he had a pretty good idea just what that was as he caught the guy sneaking another surreptitious glance at Ali—who was doing her level best not to slide right off the stiff little high-backed chair she was sitting in. The woman had been through hell and back in the last couple of days. She'd been mugged, shot at on two separate occasions, bruised, battered, and all of that was on top of losing her brother.

After learning of her situation, the commander-in-chief demanded to hear the details from the horse's mouth, so to speak, which had earned her a place at this meeting.

Frank was grateful to the president for allowing her to take part, because the poor woman deserved to see Senator Aldus brought to his fucking knees more than any of them.

And speaking of…

A loud knock heralded the senator's much-anticipated arrival.

"Come in," President Thompson commanded, his voice smooth and authoritative. No doubt that tone helped inspire confidence among the people of the nation. Frank had to admit, it even worked for him.

When two Secret Service agents escorted a tall, middle-aged man into the room, he forgot all about Zoelner and Ghost and Ali, because he instantly recognized the senator. He'd seen Alan Aldus on the nightly news a time or two, extolling this or that accomplishment or, more often, ranting about the failings of the opposing party.

He remembered thinking even then that the guy looked just a bit too slick for comfort. Turns out, his instincts were right on the mark. Senator Aldus was nothing more than an arrogant asshole with good diction and a fancy suit.

Frank hated guys like that.

"Senator Aldus," President Thompson said, "we have a few questions to ask you."

"I'm not saying anything!" Aldus barked, jerking his arms free of the agents' grasps. "I want my lawyer!"

"Oh, you'll get your lawyer," General Fuller hissed, his voice as harsh and gravelly as Thompson's was calm and smooth. Right at that moment, Fuller looked very much like the badass commando he'd once been. "In fact, I bet you'll be spending so much time with your lawyer over the next few months you'll get sick and tired of the man's face and beg for one glimpse of our ugly mugs."

Aldus's ugly mug turned a very abrupt shade of crimson, and Frank wondered idly if the man was going to have a coronary right on the spot.

He hoped not. That would be too easy. Aldus deserved to pay for what he'd done.

"It's fine if you don't want to talk," President Thompson soothed, steepling his long fingers under his very presidential looking chin. "We don't really need you to, considering we've got all the evidence we need to bring you up on charges of treason."

"Treason!" Aldus sputtered, white spittle gathered at the corners of his mouth, standing out like two truce flags against his cherry-red face. "How dare you! I *love* my country!"

"You love your country so much you sold illegal weapons to its enemies?" President Thompson looked genuinely perplexed. "I'd hate to see what you would've done had you *hated* your country."

"They weren't our enemies when I sold those weapons," Aldus hotly declared, amazingly unaware that he'd just been maneuvered into a confession.

Frank really had to admire President Thompson's

skill. The man must've been one hell of a lawyer before he decided to throw his hat into the political ring.

"They only turned into our enemies after you stupid, slow-moving politicos failed to sufficiently arm them against the Afghan Taliban. I was doing what needed to be done, goddamnit! What you all," Aldus swung his arm to include the entire array of Joint Chiefs, "were too scared to do."

"Really?" General Fuller demanded, interrupting whatever President Thompson opened his mouth to say. Frank was surprised when President Thompson just folded his hands and leaned back in his chair, apparently willing to pass the interrogatory ball to Fuller. "And how did that work out, senator? Did those weapons you sold the Pakistani tribesmen help eliminate the Taliban?"

"Well..." Senator Aldus hesitated, and General Fuller jumped into the gulf. "No!" he barked, slamming his big fist down on the president's desk. Ali nearly jumped out of her seat at the resounding *boom*, and most of the Joint Chiefs shuffled uncomfortably. Even Frank lifted a brow at the general's audacity. He couldn't help but glance at the president's face to gauge *his* reaction, but Thompson didn't seem to notice the impertinence. His expression remained supremely calm, totally impassive.

Interesting.

"They didn't help eliminate the Taliban, because you'd know if you weren't so goddamned arrogant," continued Fuller, his face contorted with rage, "that what the Pakistani tribesmen care most about is money and land, not peace or religion or any ideology. They don't give a shit about the Taliban, except, oh wait! Because, lo and behold, the Taliban were more than happy to *pay* them to use those weapons you so patriotically supplied them with. Only they paid them to kill our soldiers!"

"But, but…" Senator Aldus sputtered.

"But nothing!" Fuller bellowed, and Frank could only cross his arms and stand in awe of the general's righteous fury.

The man must've been a veritable monster out in the field.

"If you hadn't been busy sitting around fantasizing about yourself as the God of War, you'd have taken more time to read all those shiny dossiers that crossed your desk, and you'd have known what we," General Fuller threw his big arm out to encompass the room, his chest full of medals jangled with the motion, "have known for years. Which is that Pakistan is the epicenter of Islamic terrorism. My God man, the British government has estimated something like eighty percent of the terror threats they receive have Pakistani connections. And what about Bin Laden? I can verify, without a shadow of a doubt, that it was no surprise to any of us military brass that he was found there. So good job, senator. Like the president said at the beginning of your visit, you armed our enemies."

Frank watched, fascinated, as Aldus's eyes darted around the room, searching for some way out of this mess.

Sorry, ol' chap, but you're completely fucked.

"I have contacts," Aldus gushed, all his fight suddenly vanished as he scrambled to find leverage, any leverage. "I'll give you the names of those who helped me if you guarantee to take the death penalty off the block. I have documents to back up my claims. I'll tell you who hacked into the Black Knights' computer system to plant that false assignment to Syria."

False assignment to Syria…

Frank suddenly felt the very real need to plant a nice fat piece of lead in the senator's traitorous heart. Unfortunately, the Secret Service had scowlingly disarmed him before allowing him entry into 1600 Pennsylvania Ave. Touchy sonsofbitches.

President Thompson steepled his fingers, seeming to consider with extreme care the senator's generous offer. They'd been discussing just how to go about getting the names of the senator's cohorts, now the man was offering them up without so much as a fight.

Spineless.

Frank fought the urge to spit on the floor in disgust, but that antique rug probably cost more than his entire life's savings were worth.

"I don't know, Senator Aldus," President Thompson demurred. The man could certainly act, which probably served him very well in his position. "What do you think, Miss Morgan? Your life has been turned upside down by this man's actions. Do you think we should offer him a deal?"

Ali, whose spine snapped ruler straight upon being personally addressed by the leader of the free world, knew the score. She'd been thoroughly educated by the president and the Joint Chiefs on the likely outcomes of the senator's trial before the prodigious man's arrival.

Life in prison was the steepest sentence the senator would receive. Thankfully, Aldus was the only person in the room who didn't already realize that.

"Perhaps, Mr. President," she said, and Frank

watched Aldus almost wilt with gratitude. The guy actually seemed to deflate inside his designer suit. "If he answers some of my questions, honestly, I have no problem with you offering him a deal."

President Thompson regally inclined his salt-and-pepper head.

Frank watched Ali's slim throat work, and he feared she might just puke again—the damn woman had the gastric fortitude of a broken fire hydrant—but then she courageously turned her attention to Aldus.

"Did you have my brother tortured in order to obtain the whereabouts of those missing files?" she asked, her voice firm and true as a struck bell.

Frank would've slapped her on the back for having balls the size of Texas if he wasn't so keenly interested in the senator's answer.

"Yes," Aldus looked ready to faint, his bloodshot eyes glued to Ali's pretty face as if she was his anchor in a storm, his only salvation.

"Bullshit!" Ghost shouted and everyone, including Frank, jumped at the unexpected explosion. "They never questioned us about files. They never questioned us about anything!"

"I swear I'm telling the truth!" Senator Aldus actually put his hands together in front of him, pleading. "I'm not lying. I hired them to get the location of the files from Morgan, but they never did and then you escaped and Morgan was—"

"Looks like you didn't get your money's worth again, senator," Fuller grumbled. "Guess that's what happens when you try to negotiate with terrorists!"

"Pete," President Thompson's voice was remarkably

cool. Frank had never in his life heard anyone use General Fuller's first name. Hell, he wasn't sure he'd even realized the general *had* a first name. He guessed he'd always kind of assumed Fuller came straight from the womb replete with a buzz cut and sidearm. "Please, let Miss Morgan continue."

"I don't have anything more to ask, Mr. President," Ali whispered, her big eyes bright with tears. "I just wanted to know for sure who was responsible for killing my brother."

Oh, *no*.

Frank pushed away from the wall, but he was too late the stop the awful garbage spewing from the senator's traitorous mouth.

"I didn't kill you brother, Miss Morgan." The damned man looked almost gleeful when he swung his beady eyes toward Ghost. He tipped his pointy little chin. "That would be the handy work of one Nathan Weller and his big, sharp knife."

Ghost actually roared, lunging toward the senator.

"Get him out of my sight," President Thompson shouted above the ruckus, and the Secret Service agents dragged a cursing, screaming Aldus from the room, but not before one of them handed General Fuller a cellular phone.

"Found it in his pocket," the guy said and Fuller nodded.

Oh man, Frank didn't want to look, but he couldn't help himself. He swung his gaze in Ali's direction and his stomach instantly curdled. She was furiously blinking back tears as she zeroed in on Ghost's ravaged face. The poor guy was standing in the middle of the room with his eyes screwed shut, as if that could somehow make it all go away.

"Nate?" she whispered. "Is that true?"

When Ghost opened his black eyes, there was enough unspeakable anguish in them to have Frank's own hardened heart threatening to explode into a thousand sympathetic pieces.

"Yes," Ghost whispered, his voice a terrible parody of its usually smooth timbre.

Ali choked, then immediately leaned over and puked all over the Oval Office's fancy antique rug.

Chapter Nineteen

HOLY HELL.

As if Ali hadn't already humiliated herself enough over the past couple of days, now she'd gone and done the unthinkable.

Was it against the law to vomit in the Oval Office?

Sure, it was probably okay for the president. Even the leader of the free world had to succumb to an occasional stomach bug, but for a civilian to blow chunks?

She peeked at the pair of solid doors through which the Secret Service agents had just manhandled the screaming senator and waited for them to burst back inside, handcuff her, and throw her into Gitmo for defacing private property or…or dispersing biohazardous material in a government building or whatever.

But no.

No severe looking men in black came to haul her away.

Thank goodness. She wasn't prison material. Plus, you know, the whole eight-by-ten issue.

She blew out a hard breath and glanced once more in Nate's direction, but he was gone. She rubbed a shaking hand over her trembling lips, swallowing the bitter-tasting bile that stuck to her tonsils.

"Nate?" She turned to Frank. "Where did he—"

"It's best if you let Ghost have a few minutes," he advised gravely.

Choking on tears, she could do nothing but nod.

A few minutes.

She could give him that.

And when he came back, she'd tell him how she couldn't begin to imagine the unfathomable strength it must've taken to mercifully end her brother's life. And it *must* have been mercy. There was just no other explanation.

She'd tell him how she couldn't begin to fathom a world without him. How the thought of going back to her staid, boring old life after what'd happened, after what'd passed between them made her want to curl up and die.

She'd tell him the one thing that mattered most. She'd tell him she loved him…

But the seconds stretched to minutes and the minutes stretched to an hour as the men around her discussed the fate of Senator Aldus.

When Frank finally turned to her, the look on his face told her everything she needed to know.

Nate wasn't coming back.

~

Black Knights Inc. Headquarters
Six weeks later…

"Taking a vacation?" Frank grumbled from the open doorway.

Becky glanced up and quickly back down to the suitcase she was in the process of zipping.

"Yes," she said, spinning the numbers on the lock before setting the bag on the floor and popping up the telescoping handle.

"Had you planned on telling me, *your boss*, anytime soon?"

"Just as soon as I made it down the stairs, Boss," she said, pushing past Frank and heading down those aforementioned stairs. She could hear his big boots pounding down the metal treads behind her. Each percussive step matched the heavy beat of her weary heart.

She hadn't wanted to do it like this. She'd hoped to have a few precious minutes to come up with a little departure speech, something breezy and urbane, but he'd caught her before she had anything prepared.

Wouldn't it figure?

He always seemed one step ahead of her. Possessing some sixth sense when it came to a disturbance inside the realm of his finely tuned little world.

And it was that little world she had to eighty-six herself from immediately or she was going to go *nucking futs*—as Ozzie liked to put it.

"For how long?" he asked, still dogging her heels as she made her way down the long corridor toward the front door.

"A month," she replied, fighting the sudden urge to burst into tears. She'd been doing that a lot since Patti's death. Every time she walked by the little brick house on the north end of the Black Knights' property—the one Dan and Patti had shared. Every time she witnessed the miserable shell of a man that Dan had become. Every time she saw Ghost staring down at his hands as if they were the most obscene instruments he'd ever seen. Every time her big brother cast her a worried look and asked if she was okay. The answer she always gave was yes, but everyone really knew it was a resounding, unspoken hell no. And certainly, every time Frank took another one of his mysterious trips to Lincoln Park—

Yepper. Those had certainly increased over the past six weeks.

And it didn't take a Fulbright Scholar to figure out that he was going up there to get a little comfort.

Heck, they all needed comforting after what happened. So she couldn't really blame him for seeking solace in some woman's arms, but then again, she did. Because it tore her up inside to think of it.

Nucking futs, indeed.

"A *month*," he barked incredulously. "You can't just leave us for a whole goddamned *month*. We've got two theme bikes on order. The first is supposed to be finished in three weeks."

"Ozzie can come up with the designs. He's got a good eye, and I've been working with him on the CAD. As for the fabrication, Dan can handle it. All he does is work and drink himself stupid anyway. It helps keep his mind off…" she swallowed, "you know."

When she went to open the front door, he stopped her with a heavy hand on her shoulder. She took a deep breath before she turned to face him.

"He's not keeping his mind off it," he told her with a look of helpless disgust making the scar at the corner of his lip pull tight. "He's just avoiding the situation entirely."

"We all grieve in our own way, Boss," she replied softly, frowning when he winced. "What?"

"You ever gonna call me by my given name again?"

Ever since the day he'd told her he'd never allow her to achieve her dream of becoming an operator, that he'd go so far as to intentionally sabotage her efforts, she'd stopped thinking of him in such personal terms, instead relegating him to a simple position of authority over her professional life.

At least that's what she'd tried to do.

Some days it worked. Some days it didn't. The days he took himself up to Lincoln Park usually fell directly into the *didn't* category.

"I don't know," she whispered, shaking her head, feeling like someone dropped a bowling ball on her stomach.

She just wanted to get the hell away from Black Knights Inc. Away from the piercing pain and the overwhelming grief. Away from all the terrible reminders of what had happened and all the broken dreams of what never would.

A flicker of frustration crossed his beautifully rugged face. "Fine," he ground out. "Call me whatever the hell you want to call me."

Would he mind if she called him a complete dillhole? Because that's exactly what he was. Two months ago, she would've come back with just that. Now, she no longer had the strength or desire to fight with him.

"The fact remains," he continued, "we can't afford to lose you for a full month."

"I haven't taken a vacation in over two years. I've got four weeks coming to me. Like I said, Dan and the others can handle any orders that come in. Plus, this is a good opportunity for our new recruits to start getting their hands dirty. It'll be good for the Knights to help the new guys come up with some concepts and designs for their own bikes. Maybe it'll create camaraderie, you know?"

He opened his mouth, and she raised a hand to stop

him. "I'm not asking permission. I'm telling you. I'm taking this month. I need a break. There's a black cloud hanging over this entire operation that's absolutely suffocating me. I'll go crazy if I have to spend another hour here, much less another day."

His hard jaw snapped closed with an audible click, and she watched somewhat detachedly as the muscles in his cheek clenched.

It's not like he would fire her. Or maybe he would.

Did she even care?

Wow, she honestly didn't know anymore.

"Where are you going?" he finally asked, eyes sparkling with resigned anger.

"To the Seychelles and then Madagascar," she told him. "I've got a friend who's doing research for her doctoral thesis there."

"That's a long way away."

"Yepper, and that's the *whole* point."

A long, strained silence stretched between them as he searched her face. The molecules in the air separating them began to vibrate.

Where was that frickin' knife to cut the tension when a girl needed it?

"You're not running away from..." he ran a hand over his hair and winced when his injured shoulder popped. She wanted to tell him to get the damned thing fixed already but knew it wouldn't do any good. He didn't want to be out of commission for however long it would take to recover from the procedure.

Stubborn, that's what he was. Stubborn as a mule.

But thankfully, for the next month anyway, that wasn't going to be her problem. "What I mean to say is," he continued somewhat hesitantly, "that *I'm* not the reason you're running halfway around the world… Am I?"

"I'm not *running* away from you or anything else," she assured him, blatantly lying straight to his damnably concerned face. "But I am *getting* away from everything."

"But you're coming back, right?"

She suddenly felt unaccountably exhausted.

"I'm coming back. If I didn't, who'd pay for my weekly mani and pedi? Plus, you know, a girl's gotta eat." She tried to smile but by the look on his face, her effort had fallen flat.

"All right," he jerkily dipped his chin before gallantly opening the front door. The warm September sun spilled in, momentarily blinding them. She used it as an excuse to slide on her sunglasses, hoping it would help hide the fact that for some inexplicable reason there were tears gathering behind her eyes. "Go take your vacation, Rebecca. Relax. Let the sun bake your troubles away."

As if it would ever be that easy. But maybe, just maybe, she'd meet a nice native boy who could help mend her broken heart.

Sure, and maybe there'd be snow in the Sahara.

"Do you need a ride to the airport?" he asked, taking the handle of her suitcase and walking with her toward the front gates. "According to Ozzie, that new transmission you installed on the Hummer is smooth as butter, and I figure I better give it a test drive before Steady gets his hands on the thing and screws it up again."

Becky couldn't help herself, her eyes darted to the spot where Patti had sprawled on the blacktop, breathing her last. Any vestiges of blood had been thoroughly scrubbed away, but she would always know exactly where that spot was.

She couldn't get out of there fast enough.

"Nah, I'm taking the Blue Line in," she told him, referring to the famous Chicago El-track. She inhaled the familiar mix of exhaust from the street traffic and the wet, fishy aroma that wafted up from the Chicago River. The wind was coming in from the direction of the Blommer Chocolate Factory, overlaying everything with the rich scent of cocoa.

She'd grown up close to this neighborhood. These were the smells of home.

But right now she took no comfort in them. She yearned for the sweet scent of suntan lotion and the spicy aroma of thick coconut curry. She yearned for anything to take her mind away from Frank Knight, her broken dreams, and the overbearing despair hanging like a sickness around the compound.

"I'll see you in a month," she assured him, taking the handle of her suitcase, barely wincing when their fingers brushed.

"One month," he echoed, giving her a hard, searching look.

She quickly turned away, unable to stand the worried glint in his eyes.

Without a backward glance, she hurried down Cherry Street. The blocks of gum-pocked sidewalk disappeared under her sneakers, and it wasn't until she turned the corner onto North Avenue that she released a deep, shuddering breath.

She had one month to try to pull herself together,

to try to come up with new dreams to replace the old ones.

But…before she crossed that big blue ocean and started in on her—hopefully—life-altering journey, she had a stop to make on the East Coast.

Bam! Bam! Bam!

"Criminy!" Ali squealed and dropped the fresh baked ladyfinger she was about to shove in her mouth. Someone was trying their level best to knock her front door off its hinges.

"Alisa Morgan!" A familiar voice yelled through the solid wood panel. "Open up! I know you're in there!"

She tripped over her new rug and—"Ow, ow, *ow*!"—stubbed her little toe on the leg of her sofa in her mad dash to wrench open the door.

"What in blue blazes are you doing here, Becky?" she demanded, hopping on one foot while holding her screaming pinkie toe in the palm of her hand.

"I'm here to beat some damned sense into your obstinate, irrational, frickin'…*erroneous* head," Becky hissed, pushing her way into Ali's apartment, dragging a small rolling suitcase behind her.

Good heavens, was the woman planning to stay?

"That's, uh, quite a lot of adjectives," she declared, eyeing that suitcase like a treed bird eyes a grounded cat, with a sort of puzzled apprehension. Her aching pinkie toe was instantly forgotten.

"Oh don't get all teachery on me, and quit looking at my suitcase like it's seconds away from growing fangs and taking a bite out of you. I'm not staying. Consider yourself a minor pit stop on the journey that's going to change my life."

"Where are you—"

Becky waved an impatient hand in the air. "Doesn't matter. What matters is that you've screwed up royally, and you're either going to get your ass to Chicago, double-time, and make things right, or I'm going to have to beat the crap out of you. I wasn't joking about that part."

Good heavens.

"I don't—"

"I *know* you don't," Becky interrupted her, setting aside her suitcase and actually lacing her fingers together to stretch them out in front of her, popping her knuckles, looking like a fighter about to take the ring as she tilted her pretty blond head from side to side to loosen her neck muscles. "You *don't* deserve Ghost's unwavering devotion. You *don't* know the unimaginable guilt he feels about having to, yes, *having to* take his best friend's life. You *don't* have the right to blame him for Grigg's death when what he did was a frickin' heroic act of mercy! You *don't—*"

"You're right," Ali said quietly, grimacing as the ache that'd set up shop inside her chest for the past six weeks expanded until it was hard to draw breath.

God, Nate. Wonderful, loyal, brave Nate. *Why didn't you answer any of my calls?*

"I am?" Becky stopped bouncing from foot to foot and looked momentarily confused. Then she shook her head like a dog shaking off water. "You're damned right I am."

Crapola. Ali was going to start bawling if she didn't

do something to distract herself. Just looking in Becky's familiar brown eyes made her painfully desperate to see Nate again. To watch his resolute face for those oh-so-brief glimpses of sweet emotion, to listen to his deep voice smash up his few taciturn words, to touch him, to feel the vitality of his tough flesh, even if only in passing.

"I was about to have some ladyfingers and a cup of tea," she murmured past the hard lump in her throat. "Care to join me?"

"Uh, sure. I guess." It appeared that Becky didn't know what to do with herself as she twisted her hands together, glancing around uncertainly. She obviously hadn't expected Ali to be so obliging.

Beckoning for the woman to follow her to the kitchen, she took a moment to drag in a burning breath and corral her stupid, stupid tears. If she got started now, she wasn't sure she'd ever stop and wouldn't that endear her to Becky?

Um, no. Most definitely not.

"Have a seat," she motioned to the small, wrought iron bistro table in the corner and busied herself arranging the tea tray.

"Wow. Fancy," Becky murmured as Ali set the antique silver service on the table between them.

She smiled sadly. For such a small, feminine looking woman, Rebecca Reichert was amazingly tough. More times than she could count in the last six weeks, she'd wished for just a drop of Becky's pluck.

As she poured their tea, she wondered how best to pose her next question without sounding pathetic.

Ah, screw it.

"How is he?" she blurted.

"Who?" Becky asked around a ladyfinger. "Ghost? He's horrible. It's bad enough he had to…" she made a rolling motion with what was left of the ladyfinger. "Well, you know what he had to do. But then for you to *blame* him—"

"But I *didn't*," she defended herself. "I didn't blame him or judge him for Grigg's death. Give me a little credit. I know he…" God, it was almost too awful to voice the words, she couldn't imagine the horror of the actual act. Frank had given her the file on the whole, terrible incident, telling her she deserved to *finally* know it all.

She'd read the horrific thing while sitting beside the toilet on the cold tiles of her bathroom floor. Immediately afterward, she'd burned it and then dumped the ashes down the garbage disposal. As if flushing it away could somehow make the abominable words never exist in the first place. But she still saw them occasionally when she closed her eyes…

She choked as one particular sentence flashed through her aching head before she had the opportunity to slam her mental door.

She refused to break down again. It seemed that was all she did lately.

"I know he did it because there was no other way. His courage that day was a gift to my brother," she whispered, swallowing convulsively as she glanced down at the murky liquid of her tea and squeezed her eyes closed.

Oh, Nate.

"I *tried* calling him before leaving Washington," she whispered. "I tried calling him every day for a week afterward. But he wouldn't answer."

"Yeah." Becky nodded. "We all tried calling. I think, being the big, stupid dill-hole that he is, he went into some sort of self-enforced exile. He's back now, though. You should go to him."

If only it were that easy.

"He doesn't want me."

"Say what?" Becky's expression called her an idiot.

"I can't stand his rejection again," she choked. "Not when I need him so much."

"Back up," Becky held up a hand. "You can't stand his rejection *again*? What are you talking about? When did Ghost reject you?"

Ali felt a faint flush warm her cheeks. She *so* didn't want to go there with Becky, but she knew the woman wasn't leaving until she received a satisfactory explanation. "When we were at that motel we…we, uh…we sort of…"

"Made love?" Becky prompted impatiently.

"Yeah." It'd certainly been love, at least on her part. "After we made love, he made it abundantly clear he wasn't interested in anything more than that one night."

Crap. A single tear escaped to trickle down her cheek. She lifted a shaking hand to wipe it away, praying it was an aberration, praying the dam behind which she was holding the overwhelming burden of her heartache wasn't about to break.

"Mind if I ask you a personal question?"

"Oh *now* we're going to get personal?" she almost laughed, glad for the distraction.

Becky rolled her eyes. "Whatever. Look, I only want to know one thing."

Ali swallowed and nodded. "What's that?"

"Do you love him?"

Only with her whole stupid, broken heart. "Yeah," she breathed, admitting it aloud for the very first time.

"Well then, sista, just what the hell are you waiting for?" Becky slapped a palm down on the table and the silver tea service jumped. "Go and get him."

"But…but weren't you listening to a word I just said? He doesn't want me!" she sputtered, baffled the woman would even suggest it. "He made that obvious at the motel and more than obvious when he refused to take my calls!"

"Bah!" Becky waved a dismissive hand through the air. "He was just avoiding you because he thought he couldn't have you. You know," she rolled her eyes in the face of Ali's bewilderment, "because he figured you'd never forgive him for the whole thing with Grigg."

"But in th-the Oval Office he—"

"I know how it all went down," Becky interrupted her. "He ghosted on you. But what did you expect? He didn't want to face your hatred and blame when he already blames and hates himself enough for the both of you."

Was it possible?

"Did he tell you that?" she asked hopefully, her heart lodged in her throat.

"Are you kidding?" Becky's face was plastered with incredulity. "Ghost doesn't talk to anyone, but that's beside the point. I know what I've seen with my own eyes. He wants you, plain and simple, even if he doesn't know it. Men so rarely know what they want…or what's good for them, for that matter. Comes from having their heads shoved so far up their asses," she said in all seriousness. "The real question is do *you* want *him*? And are you ready to make the sacrifices necessary to have him?"

Chapter Twenty

When Nate received word he had a visitor at the front gate, Ali was the dead last person he expected.

He couldn't believe his eyes when he saw her leaning in the window of the new and improved guardhouse, giggling and teasing Manus, who was almost fully recovered from his injury and blushing like a schoolboy with his first crush.

He stumbled, fighting the urge to fall to his knees and beg her forgiveness for…everything. For not getting out of those damned ropes sooner so he could save Grigg's life. For all the years he'd made her uncomfortable by being all Abominable Snowman. For the harsh way he'd treated her the night she came to his bedroom. For the awful, he-needed-a-swift-kick-in-the-ass things he'd said to her that morning at the Happy Acres. For being a coward and avoiding her calls so he wouldn't have to hear the hatred and grief in her sweet, sunny voice.

"What'r' ya doin' here, Ali?" he asked instead, his stupid heart trying to beat right out of his chest.

She turned laughing eyes on him, and all he could think was she was the most beautiful woman in the world.

"Wow," she grinned, and that sweet, mischievous expression nearly felled him. He'd survived hunger and dehydration and broken bones and gunshot wounds and torture, but Ali's smile was enough to have him giving up the ghost. "Why do I feel like we've been here before?"

He couldn't answer her, not when he was in the middle of dying a slow, excruciating death.

Then she was running…toward him.

He braced himself for the blows he so richly deserved but—

Kisses.

Those were hot little kisses falling all over his face and…those were her smooth, slender arms twining around his neck and…*sweet lovin' Lord*, those were her fingers buried in the hair at his nape.

He was dreaming. Had to be.

Ali hated his friggin' guts for killing her brother. She hated him for all the years of dark looks and even darker thoughts. She hated him for his repeated rejections and the unforgivable way he treated her after he'd finally succumbed to his body's demands. She hated him for all the reason she *should* hate him.

So, this was a dream. A sweet, wonderful dream, because there was no way she'd be here now, clinging to him like she never intended to let go, peppering him with soft kisses and murmuring how much she'd missed him.

Funny thing, though…she felt so *real* in his arms, so soft and alive and—

Honeysuckle.

He drew the delicious aroma of honeysuckle deep into his nose.

"Ali?" he pulled back, searching her golden eyes, holding his breath when he saw—

"I love you," she breathed, and the earth came screeching to a halt in its orbit.

He shook his head, unable to comprehend, unable to believe. "But…but…"

"And I don't care if you don't love me, because you *will*. Besides, you *need* me, whether you know it or not."

"But…but…" Uh, broken record anyone?

"And I'm sorry I didn't tell you this before, I *would've* told you this before if you'd just answered your frickin' phone, but…thank you. Thank you for what you did for Grigg that terrible day."

Oh, sweet Jesus!

That was it.

He fell to his knees right there on the pavement, ignoring the hey-what-the-hell! shout his kneecaps sent screaming into his brain. Ali, locked tight in his arms, went with him.

"Shh," she soothed as the warm September sun beamed down on them both, seeming to glow in triumphant welcome of the little spark that flickered to life inside his dark, tortured soul.

And…yep, those were his tears falling hot and wet into her soft hair as he shook so hard he thought he heard her teeth rattle.

"Shh, Nate," she said again, turning her head to softly kiss the side of his convulsing neck.

Warm, her breath was so warm.

"Say it again" he choked, still unable to believe…

"Shh, Nate," she whispered, moving her lips to his jaw.

"Not that part. The other part."

"Thank you for—"

"No," he cut her off, his heart waiting with bated

breath. Had he been hallucinating? Had she said she…? "The *other* part."

Her soft lips curved against his chin. "I love you, Nathan Douglas Weller."

"*Ali*," he crushed her to his chest, seeking and finding her sweetly wonderful mouth with his own as his heart totally Grinched it and grew two sizes in an instant.

He kissed her with everything he had, showed her with his lips and teeth and tongue the limitlessness of his love. She kissed him back with equal fervor and they probably would've started tearing at each other's clothes if Manus hadn't chosen that precise moment to clear his throat.

Ali pulled back, breathlessly laughing. "Let's go—"

"—inside," he finished for her, pulling her to her feet and running with her toward the shop.

"Nate!" she shrieked as he hastily unlocked the big metal door, throwing it open with a loud *bang* before hoofing it down the hall and up the stairs to the conference area, dragging her in his wake. "Slow down. We have all the time in the world to—"

"Good to see you again, Ali," Ozzie said as they darted past his bank of computers.

"You too, Ozzie," she replied, yanking on Nate's hand as if she wanted to stop and actually talk to Ozzie at a time like this.

She was completely crazy if she thought he'd slow down for one nanosecond before getting her alone and, more importantly, naked.

When she planted her feet, he shot Ozzie a murderous scowl before bending to hoist the wonderful, crazy, *slow* woman into his arms.

"Nate!" she squawked indelicately as he pounded up

to the third floor and ran, literally *ran* into his room, slamming the door behind him with an impatient boot. "That was incredibly rude."

"Hmph." He threw her on the bed before launching himself on top of her. The fabulous woman giggled seductively and caught him in the soft cradle of her thighs, grabbing his shoulders and ravaging his mouth.

Savage. She totally dug his savage.

He wasn't sure who took off what, but in an instant they were naked, and he was pushing himself into the hottest, sweetest home he'd ever known.

"Say it again," he breathed.

"I love you," she whispered, arching beneath him, taking everything he could give her, giving everything in return.

Long moments later, they were both sated, gasping as the last vestiges of completion shivered through the sweet, hot place where they remained connected. When he finished blowing like a damned racehorse, he pushed up on one elbow to brush away a damp tendril from the corner of her rosebud mouth.

"So..." he said and, unable to resist it, bent to plant a soft kiss on those plump lips.

"So..." she parroted, opening one sparkling eye and grinning that grin he loved so much.

"I, uh...that is to say, I guess we should talk about... what I mean is...um, do you...would you..." Dear Lord, he was such an asshole. When it really mattered, he couldn't seem to voice the question.

"Would I what, Nate? Do that again? Need you even ask?" She chuckled, hooking an ankle behind his ass and swirling her hips.

"No. I mean, *yes*." He rolled his pelvis forward because the feel of her around him…*Jesus*. It was unlike anything. But that wasn't what he was trying to say. "Ali, would you…"

"Do this?"

She squeezed her inner muscles, and his eyes crossed. Literally. "That works," he managed to pant. Oh, man, did it work. "But Ali, would you…"

"Yes."

A smile tugged at his lips even though he was having a really tough time concentrating on anything but the sheer physical pleasure of having her in his arms. "Ya don't even know what I was gonna ask, woman."

Her sweet, sexy grin brightened his entire world. "It doesn't matter, Nate. The answer is always the same…*yes*."

"Marry me," he blurted, because he was coming up with a big handful of nada when it came to managing some sort of suave, romantic way to ask the question.

"Marry you?" Her beautiful, golden eyes widened and instantly filled with such sweet affection.

He swallowed and nodded, his stupid heart perched dead center in his desert-dry throat.

"Well," she pursed her lips.

His idiotic heart climbed up into his nose, burning like hot coals and making his eyes water.

"It depends," she finished, and he blew out a relieved breath.

He'd do anything. Quit the Knights, become a car salesman, sell Phantom, pick off all the gum stuck beneath her students' desk with his teeth…

She smiled that *Mona Lisa* smile and employed his favorite trick; she simply waited him out.

"What?" he demanded when he couldn't stand it a second longer. "It depends on *what*?"

"On whether or not you think you can grow to love me."

"Grow to—" He shook his head, dumbfounded. "Woman, I've loved you since the first moment I laid eyes on you."

"Mmm," she closed her eyes, "that sounds nice. I might just get used to hearing that."

"I love you," he breathed, holding her beautiful face between his palms so he could drop soft kisses on her eyebrows, cheeks, nose…

"I love you," he whispered against her lips, bending to kiss her and then—

"How?" he asked her, his burgeoning heart freezing solid.

"How what?" she opened her eyes to watch him like a cat watches a thick bowl of cream. When she looked at him like that he wanted to—

No. He shook his head. Before they went any further, he had to know.

"How can you love me after what I did?"

Her cute little nose wrinkled as her eyebrows veed. "What you did? You did the most loyal, courageous, selfless thing I've ever heard of, Nate. How could I not love you?"

"But you…you threw up after you found out—"

"I throw up because I have the world's weakest stomach and that's what I do. It didn't have anything to do with blame, Nate. It had to do with sympathy. When I realized what it must've cost you I…I lost it. Literally. My lunch was all over the Oval Office's fancy rug. And then you ran out and you wouldn't take my calls, so I figured you didn't want me or my sympathy."

And just like that, the sun came out. The weight of his long-held guilt lifted away on the wings of her love, and he could see nothing but magic and…*light* in all the days stretching far out into the future.

"Oh, Ali," he brushed her soft lips with his. "I've always wanted you. I'll always want you. I only acted that way because I couldn't bear to hear you say…" He shook his head and swallowed convulsively. "I thought you'd never be able to forgive me if y'ever found out about—" she placed two fingers over his mouth.

"I know what you thought," she pursed her lips, shaking her head. "You underestimated me again. We'll have to work on that."

"Ali," he buried his nose in her sweet smelling hair, marveling that she was really his. *His*. Was it possible to burst with joy? "I love y'so much," he murmured.

"That's all I need to know," she said, softly kissing his ear, "except…"

He pushed up, and, uh-oh, he knew that look.

Turning his head cautiously to the side, he watched her from the corner of his eyes. He was afraid to ask… "Except what?"

"Except, what did Delilah say to you that night in the bar?"

"Ugh!" he dropped his face to her slender neck, licking at her soft pulse, hoping beyond hope that she would—

"No, you don't," she pushed him back, her expression comically stern. "You're not going to distract me with that. Come on, spill. It's been driving me crazy."

He blew out a defeated breath, then bent his head to whisper Delilah's prophecy into the little shell of her ear. "She said she saw us married within six months."

"And you thought that was funny?"

"It was so absurd I couldn't even fathom it," he admitted, still unable to believe his infinite good fortune.

When he looked at her, her smile was bright enough to light up the room. "Well," she said, "I guess Delilah is smarter than the both of us."

"Guess so."

"Nate?"

"Hmm?" He started kissing her neck in earnest. Enough with the talk, already. He needed to *show* her his love again. Again and again and again.

"I want babies. Lots of babies."

Oh, man, he was instantly filled with gripping fear and unfathomable happiness. Babies.

Ali wanted to have his babies. He leaned up one elbow, looking down at her and imagining little girls with golden curls and little boys with eyes the color of amber. "Define lots."

"I love children, so…at least four." She looped slim, feminine arms around his neck and nipped at his jaw. "How does that sound to you?"

How did it sound? It sounded crazy and wonderful and…and…damned scary. It sounded like his greatest dream come true.

He could barely speak around the hard lump lodged directly behind his Adam's apple. "It sounds…perfect," he whispered.

And that said it all.

His world, once so terribly dark and damaged, was

filled with sweet perfection, because he had the only thing he ever wanted.

He had Ali.

Read on for a sneak peek
at Julie Ann Walker's

In Rides Trouble

Available September 2012
From Sourcebooks Casablanca

Prologue

"We're definitely changing the name." Frank "Boss" Knight pulled the Hummer up in front of the sad little pre-fab building and glanced at the hand-painted wooden sign screwed over the front door: Becky's Badass Bike Builds.

"Too much alliteration for you?" Bill Reichert snickered from the passenger seat while unbuckling his seatbelt and throwing open the door. The frigid winter wind whipped into the interior of the vehicle, prompting Frank to grab his black stocking cap from the dashboard and tug it over his head and ears before zipping his parka up to his chin.

If this thing actually worked out, Chicago winters were definitely going to take some getting used to. Of course, freezing temps were a small price to pay for a good, solid cover for his new defense firm. And joining Bill's kid sister in her custom Harley chopper business, posing as mechanics and motorcycle buffs, promised to be a freakin' phenomenal cover for all the guys he'd recruited away from the various branches of the armed services. Especially considering most of them were bulky, tattooed, and—without regulation military haircuts—just scruffy enough to pass for their own chapter of Hell's Angels.

He pushed out of the Hummer and had to lower his chin against the gust of wind that punched him in the face like an icy fist. Shoving his hands deep in his coat pockets, he trudged up to the front door through the path someone had shoveled in the thick blanket of snow.

Bill applied a gloved thumb to the buzzer, and five seconds later, a familiar noise sounded from the behind the metal door, making the hair on the back of Frank's neck stand up.

How do you know you've been in the business too long? When you recognize the sound of a .45 caliber being chambered from three feet away, that's how.

"Who is it?" a deep, wary voice inquired from within.

"I thought you said she knew we were coming," Frank hissed over Bill's shoulder.

"She does." Bill grinned. "But she also knows she can never be too careful in this neighborhood."

And that was no lie. The graffiti tagging every vertical surface for six blocks in each direction announced that they were smack dab in the middle of some very serious gang territory. The Vice Lords ruled the roost, and they wanted to make damned sure everyone knew it.

Raising his voice above the shrieking wind, Bill yelled, "Open the damned door, you big ape! We're freezing our dicks off out here!"

And that was no lie either. Frank couldn't even begin

to explain to his family jewels why he hadn't jumped into a pair of thermal underwear this morning and instead opted to go commando.

Big mistake. *Huge.*

One he sure as hell wouldn't be making again.

The front door swung open with a resounding clang, and they were met by a giant, red-headed man who looked like he should be wearing a face mask and leotard while smashing a folding chair over some guy's back.

Frank could almost hear Michael Buffer shouting, *Arrrrre you ready to ruuumbllle?*

"Manus," Bill said, stepping over the threshold and motioning Frank through, "this is Boss. Boss, meet Manus. He and his brothers work security for my sister."

Frank waited until Manus tucked the .45 into the waistband of his jeans before cautiously stepping into the small, tiled vestibule. The walls were covered in rusted motorcycle license plates, and as soon as the door closed behind him, the aroma of motor oil and burning metal assaulted his nostrils.

"You the guy who wants to partner with Becky? Invest some money and learn to build bikes?" Manus asked while pumping the hand he offered, a smile splitting the big man's ruddy face and making all his freckles meld together.

Yeah, that was the story they were tossing around until he could get a look at the set-up…

"I haven't decided yet," he answered noncommittally, and Manus's smile only widened.

"That's only because you haven't seen Becky's bikes," he boasted. "Once you do, you're gonna want to give her all your savings and have her teach you everything she knows."

Frank lifted a shoulder as if to say *we'll see* and watched as Bill opened the second set of glass doors.

His ears were instantly assailed by a wall of sound.

The pounding beats of hard-driving rock music competed with the hellacious screech and whine of grinding metal. He resisted the urge to reach up and plug his ears as he followed Bill into the custom motorcycle shop, skirting a few pieces of high-tech machinery.

And then he wasn't thinking about his bleeding eardrums at all.

Beçause his eyes zeroed in on the most beautiful, outlandish motorcycle he'd ever seen.

It was secured on a bike lift. The paint on the gas tank and fenders was bright, neon blue that sparkled iridescently in the harsh overhead lights. It sported a complex-looking dual exhaust, an outrageous stretch, and intricate, nearly whimsical front forks. It also had so much chrome it almost hurt to look at it.

In a word: *art*.

It made the work he'd done restoring his vintage 1952 Harley-Davidson FL look like amateur hour.

And just when he thought he couldn't be any more blown away, the sound of grinding metal slowly died down and a young woman emerged from behind the bike with a grinder in one hand and a metal clamp in the other.

He nearly swallowed his own tongue.

This couldn't be…

But obviously it was. Because the instant the woman caught sight of them she squealed, clicked off the music pouring out of the speakers of an old-fashioned boom box, and dropped both tools on the bike lift before jumping into Bill's arms, hugging him tight and kissing his cheek with a resounding smack that sounded particularly loud in the sudden silence of the shop.

This was Rebecca "Rebel" Reichert, Wild Bill's little sister.

Little being the operative word. If she stood two inches over five feet Frank would eat his biker boots for dinner.

He didn't quite know what he'd expected of a woman who ran her own custom chopper shop, but it wasn't long, blond hair pulled back in a tight ponytail, intense brown eyes surrounded by lush, dark lashes, and a pretty, girl-next-door face that just happened to be his own personal weakness when it came to women.

Something about that wholesome, all-American thing always managed to bring him to his knees.

Well, hell.

Bill finally lowered her to the ground, and she came to stand in front of Frank, small, grease-covered hands on slim, jean-clad hips. For some inexplicable reason, he felt the need to stand up straighter.

It was probably because she had the same unyielding look in her eye that his hard-ass drill sergeant always had back when he'd been in Basic.

"So." She tilted her head until her ponytail hung down over her shoulder in a smooth, golden rope. "You must be the indomitable Frank Knight. Billy has told me so very *little* about you."

And that voice…

It was soft and husky. The type that belonged solely in the bedroom.

"Everyone calls me Boss," he managed to grumble.

"I think I'll stick to Frank," she said with a wink. And for some reason, his eyelid twitched. "After all, there can be only one boss around here, and I'm it. Now, I hear you want to get into the business of building bikes?"

"I'm considering it." He couldn't help but notice the way her nose tilted up at the end or the way her small breasts pressed against the soft fabric of the paint-stained, long-sleeved T-shirt she wore.

Kee-rist, man, get a grip.

"Well, then." She nodded, pushing past him as she made her way toward the front door, "let's go take a look at that bike you brought with you and see if you have any talent at all."

For a split second, he let his eyes travel down to the gentle sway of her hips before forcing himself to focus on a point over her head as he followed her back through the various machinery. Bill was right behind him, which helped to keep his eyes away from the prize... so to speak. Because the last thing he wanted was to get caught ogling the guy's kid sister.

Talk about a no-no of epic proportions. Especially if he didn't fancy the idea of finding one of Bill's size-eleven biker boots shoved up his ass.

Once they reached the first set of glass doors, she pulled a thick pair of pink coveralls off a hook on the wall. Balancing first on one foot then the other, she stepped into the coveralls and zipped them up before snagging a bright purple stocking cap from a second hook and pulling it over her head.

She looked ridiculous. And feminine. And so damned cute.

He gritted his teeth and reminded himself of three things. One, she was way too young for him. Two, if things worked out, then despite what she thought now, *he* was going to be *her* boss. And three, he'd made a promise not to—

"How much money are you thinking of investing?" she interrupted his thoughts as she pushed through the double doors and into the vestibule.

As much as it takes... "We'll talk more about that later." He held his breath, waiting to see how she'd respond to both his authoritative tone and his answer. It was a test of sorts, to determine if they had any hope of working together.

She regarded him for a long second, her brown eyes seeming to peer into his head. Then she shrugged, "Suit yourself."

When she opened the outer door, he once again had to dip his chin against the icy wind. The three of them slogged through the snow to the small, enclosed cargo trailer hitched to the back of his Hummer, and he fished in his pocket for the keys with fingers already numb from the cold. Once he opened the trailer's back door, she didn't wait for an invitation to jump inside.

He and Bill were left to follow her up and watch as she walked around his restored bike before squatting near the exhaust.

"You do all the work yourself?" she asked.

The bike he'd been so proud of thirty minutes before seemed shoddy and unimaginative by comparison.

"Yes," he admitted, amazed he actually felt nervous. Like maybe *she* wouldn't want to work with *him*.

"Your welding is complete crap," she said, running

a finger along a weld he'd thought was actually pretty damned good. "But it's obvious you're a decent mechanic, and that's really what I need right now, more decent mechanics. Plus," she stood and winked, "it might be nice to have a big, strong dreamboat like you around the place day-in and day-out. Something fun to look at when my muse abandons me."

He opened his mouth...but nothing came out. He could only stare and blink like a bewildered owl.

Holy hell, was she *flirting* with him?

He was saved from having to make any sort of answer—*thank you, sweet Jesus*—when Bill grumbled, "Cut it out, Becky. Now's not the time, and Boss is definitely not the guy."

"No?" She lifted her brows, turning toward Frank questioningly.

And now he was able to find his voice. "*No.*" He shook his head emphatically, trying to swallow his lungs that had somehow crawled up into his throat.

"Well," she shrugged, completely unflustered by his overt rejection, "you can't blame a gal for trying." She offered him a hand. "I'm in, partner. That is, once I know exactly how much you're thinking of investing."

"Bill will get back to you with the specifics," he hedged, taking her hand only briefly before releasing it, more eager to get the hell out of there than he'd care to admit.

Again she did that head-tilt thing. The one that caused the end of her ponytail to slide over her shoulder. She regarded him for a long moment during which time he thought his heart might've jumped right out of his mouth had his lungs not been in the way. Then she shrugged and said, "Fine. Go ahead and do that whole mystery-man thing. I don't really give a rat's ass as long as you're good for the green."

And with that, she hopped down from the back of the trailer.

He moved to watch her traipse through the snow to the front door of her shop. Only once she disappeared inside did he turn to Bill. "You sure she's trustworthy enough? She seems a bit impulsive to me."

Impulsive and arrogant and bold and...way too cute for her own good.

Bill smiled, crossing his arms. "Despite all evidence to the contrary, Becky's as steady as they come. We can depend on her to keep our secrets. You have my word."

"And what about the hierarchy? How's she going to react once she realizes I'm the one calling the shots?"

Bill clapped a heavy hand on his shoulder and chuckled. "I have no doubt you can handle her, Boss."

Uh-huh. He wished he shared Bill's certainty. Because there was one thing he could spot from a mile away, and that was trouble.

And Rebecca Reichert?

Well, she had trouble written all over her…

Chapter One

Three and a half years later…

PIRATES…

Wow. Now there's something you don't see every day.

That was Becky's first thought as she ducked under the low cabin door of the thirty-eight foot catamaran named *Serendipity* and stepped into the blazing equatorial sun. Her second thought, more appropriately, was *oh hell.*

Eve—her longtime friend and owner of the *Serendipity*—was swaying unsteadily and staring in wide-eyed horror at the three dirty, barefoot men holding ancient AK-47s like they knew how to use them. Four more equally skinny, disheveled men were standing in a rickety skiff tethered off the *Serendipity's* stern.

Okay, so…*obviously* they'd been playing the oldies a little too loudly considering they'd somehow managed to drown out the rough sound of the pirates' rusty outboard engine motoring up behind them.

"Eve," she murmured around the head of a cherry Dum Dum lollipop as her heart hammered against her ribs and the skin on her scalp began crawling with invisible ants. "Just stay calm, okay?"

Yep. Calm was key. Calm kept a girl from finding

herself fathoms deep beneath the crushing weight of Davy Jones's Locker or under the more horrifying weight of a sweaty man who didn't know the meaning of the word *no*.

When Eve gave no reply, she glanced over at her friend and noticed the poor woman was turning the color of an eggplant.

"*Eve*," she said with as much urgency as she could afford, given the last thing she wanted was to spook an already skittish pirate who very likely suffered from a classic case of itchy-trigger-finger-syndrome, "you need to breathe."

Eve's throat worked over a dry swallow before her chest quickly expanded on a shaky breath.

Okay, good. Problem one: Eve keeling over in a dead faint—solved. Problem two: being taken hostage by pirates—now *that* was going to take a bit more creativity.

She wracked her brain for some way out of their current predicament as Jimmy Buffet crooning, "Yes I am a pirate. Two hundred years too late," wafted up from inside the cabin.

Really, Jimmy? You're singing that now?

Under normal circumstances, she'd be the first to appreciate the irony. Unfortunately, these were anything but normal circumstances.

The youngest and shortest of the pirates—he wore an eye patch...*seriously?*—flicked a tight look in her direction, and she threw her hands in the air, palms out in the universal *I'm unarmed and cooperating* signal. But a quick glance was all he allotted her before he returned the fierce attention of his one good eye to Eve.

She snuck another peek at her friend and…oh no. Oh *crap*.

"Slowly, very slowly, Eve, I want you to lay the knife on the deck and kick it away from you." She was careful to keep her tone cool and unthreatening. Pirates made their money from the ransom of ships and captives. If she could keep Eve from doing something stupid—like, oh, say flying at the heavily armed pirates like a blade-wielding banshee—they'd likely make it out of this thing alive.

Unfortunately, it appeared Eve had stopped listening to her.

"Eve!" she hissed. "Lay down the knife. *Slowly*. And kick it away from you."

This time she got through.

Eve glanced down at the long, thin blade clutched in her fist. From the brief flicker of confusion that flashed through her eyes, it was obvious she'd been unaware she still held the knife she'd been using to fillet the bonito they'd caught for lunch. But realization quickly dawned, and her bewildered expression morphed into something frighteningly desperate.

Becky dropped all pretense of remaining cool and collected. "Don't you even think about it," she barked.

Two of the men on deck jerked their shaggy heads in her direction, the wooden butts of their automatic weapons made contact with their scrawny shoulders as the evil black eyes of the Kalashnikovs' barrels focused on her thundering heart.

"You don't bring a knife to a gun fight," she whispered, lifting her hands higher and gulping past a Sahara-dry knot in her throat. "Everyone knows that."

From the corner of her eye, she watched Eve slowly bend at the waist, and the unmistakable *thunk* of the blade hitting the wooden deck was music to her ears.

"Look, guys," she addressed the group, grateful

beyond belief when the ominous barrels of those old, but still deadly, rifles once more pointed toward the deck. *That's the thing about AKs*, Billy once told her, *they buck like a damned bronco, are simpler than a kindergarten math test, but they'll fire with a barrel full of sand. Those Russians sure know how to make one hell of a reliable weapon*—which, given her current situation, was just frickin' great. *Not*. "These are Seychelles waters. You don't have any authority here."

"No, no, no," the little pirate wearing the eye patch answered in heavily accented English. "We *only* authority on water. We Somali pirate."

"Oh boy," Eve wheezed, putting a trembling hand to her throat as her eyes rolled back in her head.

"Don't you dare pass out on me, Evelyn Edens!" Becky commanded, her brain threatening to explode at the mere thought of what might happen to a beautiful, unconscious woman in the hands of Somali pirates out in the middle of the Indian Ocean.

Eve swayed but managed to remain standing, her legs firmly planted on the softly rolling deck.

Okay, good.

"We have no money. Our families have no money," she declared. Which was true for the most part as far as she was concerned. Eve, however, was as rich as Croesus. Thankfully, there was no way for the pirates to know that. "You'll get no ransom from us. It'll cost you more to feed and shelter us than you'll ever receive from our families. And this boat is twenty years old. She's not worth the fuel it'll cost you to sail her back to Somalia. Just let us go, and we'll forget this ever happened."

"No, no, no," the young pirate shook his head—it appeared the negatives in his vocabulary only came in threes. His one black eye was bright with excitement, and she noticed his eye patch had a tacky little rhinestone glued to the center, shades of One-Eyed Willie from *The Goonies*.

Geez, this just keeps getting better and better.

"You American." He grinned happily, revealing crooked, yellow teeth. Wowza, she would bet her best TIG welder those chompers had never seen a toothbrush or a tube of Colgate. "America pay big money."

She snorted; she couldn't help it. The little man was delusional. "Maybe you haven't heard, but it's the policy of the U.S. government not to negotiate with terrorists."

One-Eyed Willie threw back his head and laughed, his ribs poking painfully through the dark skin of his torso. "We no terrorists. We Somali pirates."

Whatever.

"Same thing," she murmured, glancing around at the other men who wore the alert, but slightly vacant, look of those who don't comprehend a word of what was being said.

Okay, so Willie was the only one who spoke English. She couldn't decide if that was good or bad.

"Not terrorists!" he yelled, spittle flying out of his mouth. "*Pirates!*"

"Okay, okay," she placated, softening her tone and biting on her sarcastic tongue. "You're pirates, not terrorists. I get it. That doesn't change the simple fact that our government will give you nothing but a severe case of lead poisoning. And our families don't have a cent to pay you."

"Oh, they pay," he smiled, once again exposing those urine-colored teeth. "They always pay."

Which, sadly, was probably true. Someone always came up with the coin—bargaining everything they had and usually a lot more they didn't—when the life of a loved one was on the line.

"So," he said as he came to stand beside her, eyeing her up and down until a shiver of revulsion raced down her spine, "we go Somalia now."

And she swore she'd swallow her own tongue before she ever even thought these next words—because for three and a half very long years the big dill-hole had refused to give her the time of day despite the fact that she was just a little in love with him, okay *a lot* in love with him—but it all came down to this...she needed Frank.

Because, just like he always swore would happen, she'd managed to step in a big, stinking pile of trouble from which there was no hope of escape.

She absolutely hated proving that man right.

Author's Note

For those of you familiar with the vibrant city of Chicago, Illinois, you'll notice I changed a few places and names, and embellished on the details of others. I did this to suit the story and to better highlight the diversity and challenges of this dynamic city I call home.

Acknowledgments

First of all, thank you to our fighting men and women, those in uniform and those out of uniform. You protect our freedom and way of life so we all have the chance to live the American Dream.

Major kudos as well to my kick-ass agent, Nicole Resciniti. You go above and beyond, doll. Thank you for taking a chance on a total unknown and championing my work like a veritable lioness. I've said it before, I'll say it again, you rock the frickin' ha-yowse!

And, finally, a shout-out to all the folks at Sourcebooks who've patiently held my hand through this entire publishing process and forgiven me my total and complete ignorance of the industry. I'm a fast learner, guys. I promise!

About the Author

Deep in the heart of the Windy City, three things can be found at Julie Ann Walker's fingertips: a keyboard, a carafe of coffee, and a sleepy yellow Labrador retriever. They, along with her ever-patient husband, keep her grounded as her imagination flies high. Visit her at www.julieannwalker.com.

In Rides Trouble

Black Knights Inc.

by Julie Ann Walker

~

Trouble never looked so good…

Rebel with a cause

Becky "Rebel" Reichert never actually goes looking for trouble. It just has a tendency to find her. Like the day Frank Knight showed up her door, wanting to use her motorcycle shop as a cover for his elite special ops team. But Becky prides herself on being able to hang with the big boys—she can weld, drive, and shoot just as well as any of them.

Man with a mission

Munitions, missiles, and mayhem are Frank's way of life. The last thing the ex-SEAL wants is for one brash blonde to come within fifty feet of anything that goes boom. Yet it's just his rotten luck when she ends up in a hostage situation at sea. Come hell or high water, he will get her back—whether she says she needs him or not.

~

Praise for **Hell on Wheels***:*

"Edgy, alpha, and downright HOT, the Black Knights Inc. will steal your breath…and your heart!"
—Catherine Mann, *USA Today* bestselling author

For more Black Knights Inc., visit:

www.sourcebooks.com

Rev It Up

Black Knights Inc.

by Julie Ann Walker

He's the heartbreaker she left behind…

Jake "the Snake" Sommers earned his SEAL codename by striking quickly and quietly—and with lethal force. That's also how he broke Michelle Carter's heart. It was the only way to keep her safe—from himself. Four long years later, Jake is determined to get a second chance. But to steal back into Michelle's loving arms, Jake is going to have to prove he can take things slow. Real slow…

Michelle Carter has never forgiven Jake for being so cliché as to "love her and leave her." But when her brother, head of the Black Knights elite ops agency, ticks off the wrong mobster, she must do the unimaginable: place her life in Jake's hands. No matter what they call him, this man is far from cold-blooded. And once he's wrapped around her heart, he'll never let her go…

***Praise for* Hell on Wheels:**

"Edgy, alpha, and downright HOT, the Black Knights Inc. will steal your breath…and your heart!"
—Catherine Mann, *USA Today* bestselling author

For more Black Knights Inc., visit:

www.sourcebooks.com

The Night Is Mine

by M.L. Buchman

—∽—

NAME: Emily Beale

RANK: Captain

MISSION: Fly undercover to prevent the assassination of the First Lady, posing as her executive pilot

NAME: Mark Henderson, code name Viper

RANK: Major

MISSION: Undercover role of wealthy, ex-mercenary boyfriend to Emily

Their jobs are high risk, high reward:

Protect the lives of the powerful and the elite at all cost. Neither expected that one kiss could distract them from their mission. But as the passion mounts between them, their lives and their hearts will both be risked… and the reward this time may well be worth it.

—∽—

"An action-packed adventure. With a super-stud hero, a strong heroine, and a backdrop of 1600 Pennsylvania Avenue and the world of the Washington elite, it will grab readers from the first page." —*RT Book Reviews*

For more in The Night Stalkers series, visit:

I Own the Dawn

The Night Stalkers

by M. L. Buchman

NAME: Archibald Jeffrey Stevenson III

RANK: First Lieutenant, DAP Hawk copilot

MISSION: Strategy and execution of special ops maneuvers

NAME: Kee Smith

RANK: Sergeant, Night Stalker gunner and sharpshooter

MISSION: Whatever it takes to get the job done

You wouldn't think it could get worse, until it does… When a special mission slowly unravels, it is up to Kee and Archie to get their team out of an impossible situation with international implications. With her weaponry knowledge and his strategic thinking, plus the explosive attraction that puts them into exact synchrony, together they might just have a fighting chance…

"The first novel in Buchman's new military suspense series is an action-packed adventure. With a super-stud hero, a strong heroine, and a backdrop of 1600 Pennsylvania Avenue and the world of the Washington elite, it will grab readers from the first page." —*RT Book Reviews* (4 stars)

For more in The Night Stalkers series, visit:

www.sourcebooks.com

Cover Me

by Catherine Mann

It should have been a simple mission...

Pararescueman Wade Rocha fast ropes from the back of a helicopter into a blizzard to save a climber stranded on an Aleutian Island, but Sunny Foster insists she can take care of herself just fine...

But when it comes to passion, nothing is ever simple...
With the snowstorm kicking into overdrive, Sunny and Wade hunker down in a cave and barely resist the urge to keep each other warm...until they discover the frozen remains of a horrific crime...

Unable to trust the local police force, Sunny and Wade investigate, while their irresistible passion for each other gets them more and more dangerously entangled...

Praise for Catherine Mann:

"Catherine Mann weaves deep emotion with intense suspense for an all-night read." —#1 *New York Times* bestseller Sherrilyn Kenyon

For more Catherine Mann, visit:

www.sourcebooks.com

Hot Zone

by Catherine Mann

He'll take any mission, the riskier the better...

The haunted eyes of pararescueman Hugh Franco should have been her first clue that deep pain roiled beneath the surface. But if Amelia couldn't see the damage, how could she be expected to know he'd break her heart?

She'll prove to be his biggest risk yet...

Amelia Bailey's not the kind of girl who usually needs rescuing...but these are anything but usual circumstances.

Praise for Catherine Mann:

"Nobody writes military romance like Catherine Mann!"
—Suzanne Brockmann, *New York Times* bestselling author of *Tall, Dark and Deadly*

"A powerful, passionate read not to be missed!"
—Lori Foster, *New York Times* bestselling author of *When You Dare*

For more Catherine Mann, visit:

Under Fire

by Catherine Mann

No holds barred, in love or war…

A decorated hero, pararescueman Liam McCabe lives to serve. Six months ago, he and Rachel Flores met in the horrific aftermath of an earthquake in the Bahamas. They were tempted by an explosive attraction, but then they parted ways. Still, Liam has thought about Rachel every day—and night—since.

Now, after ignoring all his phone calls for six months, Rachel has turned up on base with a wild story about a high-ranking military traitor. She claims no one but Liam can help her—and she won't trust anyone else.

With nothing but her word and the testimony of a discharged military cop to go on, Liam would be insane to risk his career—even his life—to help this woman who left him in the dust.

"Absolutely wonderful, a thrilling ride of ups and downs that will have readers hanging onto the edge of their seats."
—*RT Book Reviews* Top Pick of the Month, 4 1/2 stars

"Wild rides, pulse-pounding danger, gripping suspense, and simmering, sizzling, spiraling passion." —*Long and Short Reviews*